ATTUNGA

My deepest appreciation to:

My family for their interest and support through the whole process;

*Nan, my editor, for her thought-provoking challenges
and meticulous attention to detail;*

Kate, my proofer, for her professional work and approach;

Marin for his ideas;

Luke for taking on the graphic design and typesetting;

and all the readers for their feedback and encouragement.

ATTUNGA

This story is one of the Tales
of the Terran Diaspora

PETER WOOD

Attunga
Peter Wood

Published by Diaspora Press
First published March 2017
Email: palantir@diasporatales.tech or visit diasporatales.net

Proofreader: Kate Daniel
Designer/ Typesetter: Working Type Studio (www.workingtype.com.au)

ISBN: 9780994618801 (paperback)
ISBN: 9780994618818 (ebook)

National Library of Australia Cataloguing-in-Publication entry (paperback)
Creator: Wood, Peter Leonard, 1944- author.
Title: Attunga : tales of the terran diaspora / Peter Leonard Wood.
ISBN: 9780994618801 (paperback)
Series: Wood, Peter Leonard, 1944- Tales of the terran diaspora.
Subjects: Science fiction.
 Adventure stories.
 Artificial intelligence--Fiction.

To my wonderful family

Chapter 1

Attunga, glittering with a myriad of artificial lights, floated serenely in the depths of the asteroid belt, its great bulk abuzz with hundreds of millions of human beings. Amongst them, three young friends met at a transport terminal to plan their day.

The boys loved exploring, and with over a thousand residential floors from top to bottom, there was always something new to find. This morning they'd left their student cubicles on level 185 of their home sector to travel to the very edge of their space city, and ebony-skinned Wirrin had just won a game they played whenever they set off: who could travel the multiple pathways of the transport system in the shortest time.

'You're a galah head, Thom. You're just giving me a hard time because I was fastest.'

'Not a galah head. That first plan would've taken you into space.'

They were all grinning, Thom because he'd caught Wirrin out, Wirrin because he'd been caught out, and Calen because he was bubbling with anticipation.

'Get serious! What did you manage to find out about this sector?'

Wirrin took the lead. 'I checked my holo. They've got a viewing station for Warrakan and you can see it for real.'

Warrakan was a large asteroid in the process of being developed as a companion habitat and all three of them were obsessed with it.

'Really? That's great, but I found something even better,' said Calen. 'The dolphinarium's in this sector and a baby has just been born. We're not missing that.'

Trust Calen to track down something connected with animals. 'I've never seen a live dolphin,' said Wirrin. 'A baby — that's pretty special. What about you, Thom? Did you find anything?'

'There's a swimming pool we should try.'

'Swimming pool? We can do that in our home sector.'

'Not like this, Wirrin. It's zero-G. They turn off the gravity field and the water collects in a 30 metre sphere.'

'Wow! But how do you breathe? Water in zero-grav is dangerous.'

'They give you a full facemask with twenty minutes of air.'

'We've got all day,' said Calen. 'We should be able to manage Warrakan *and* the pool, but we have to see the dolphins first. Come on.'

*   *   *

The dolphinarium was huge, with a population of 342 dolphins — 343 since yesterday — and Wirrin listened closely to the ranger describing the birth and explaining a little of dolphin culture. Apparently a pod was gathering in the main viewing gallery to welcome the baby — a slight variation on the usual welcome extended to any new member of a pod.

When the ranger finished her explanation Wirrin and Thom had to run to keep up with Calen, who was intent on getting a good seat. He needn't have worried: there were seats for five hundred people, a huge glass interface and a vast volume of crystal-clear water beyond it. Still, they were glad to be in the front row only a few metres from the glass.

Wirrin watched the mix of people: lots of families with excited children and groups of young people like themselves, laughing and chatting as they took their seats. Several rows back a couple looked more engrossed in each other than anything in front of them, and across the aisle three whole rows filled with rangers, all dressed in the distinctive azure uniform.

Two dolphins were already gliding through the water. A few minutes later they were joined by two more dolphins from one of the three underwater tunnels at the back of the pool, then three more. Calen never took his eyes off the sleek grey beasts, and Wirrin watched with mounting excitement.

'I wonder how long before the baby gets here?' Thom said.

Wirrin and Calen didn't respond. The ranger from the entrance approached with a friendly smile and addressed the crowd.

'We've just had word. They've left the birthing pool, so it'll be five minutes or so,' she said, then dropped into the empty seat next to Wirrin. Calen leaned forward and began to bombard her with questions.

'So we've got a dolphin enthusiast, have we?' the ranger said with a grin.

Wirrin laughed. 'Not just dolphins. He loves any animals. He's been taking zoology options for the last seven years.'

'Seven years? Really? That's more than I did.' She leaned in. 'Is it going to be your major?'

'A double major I hope. As long as my scores are high enough. Mammals and insects.'

'Mammals — good, you need that — but everyone does insects. If you try something unusual you'll have a better chance of working in an area you enjoy.'

'I thought insects *was* unusual?'

'It is in its own way of course, but everyone thinks that. Because there's such a huge species list they all expect they'll find something no-one's ever researched before and that hardly ever happens.'

Calen was clearly taken aback — that must have been his reasoning, too.

Five more dolphins swept into view, one of them swimming right up to the glass in front of Wirrin, where it stopped. Was it smiling at him? It was impossible to think otherwise, even though he knew it was simply the structure of the mouth. He felt thrilled and somehow strangely blessed, until he heard a soft chuckle beside him.

The ranger gave the dolphin a slow wave. Its body undulated and its head flicked up in response.

'It's Flute saying hello because she likes me. Wave your hand like this and see if she reacts.'

Wirrin, Calen and Thom waved, but nothing happened.

'Lower your arms and try again.'

Flute repeated the movement, and so did four other dolphins now close to the glass interface — the same response and exactly in unison. Then they all peeled away and swam to the back of the pool. The baby must be coming. Every dolphin was looking towards the central tunnel. Calen grabbed Wirren's arm.

'Easy,' Wirrin whispered. 'I need that arm.'

For a tense moment nothing happened, then a dolphin shadowed by a tiny baby entered the pool and swam towards the pod. She approached each one in turn, and every dolphin touched the baby with a soft nudge, a gentle tap or a fleeting stroke. Two dolphins even rested their beaks on top of it for a second till the little dolphin react-ed, unsure of what was happening. Then, as if on a signal, all the dolphins moved to one side of the pool, ranged close to mother and baby, and looked towards the nearest tunnel. Wirrin was reminded of a guard of honour in one of the ancient vids, but then his heart leapt as an avalanche of dolphins poured from the tunnel. They kept coming and coming, till it was beyond belief that there could be so many.

The mother took the little one to the surface then descended to where a contingent of nine pod leaders had lined up. The touch ritual was repeated all over again, the mother carefully monitoring each exchange.

Calen was still gripping Wirrin's arm and now he gave it an involuntary squeeze as the mother shepherded her baby into almost the same position Flute had taken earlier. In a flash of understanding Wirrin realised she was proudly presenting her baby to the humans. The ranger beside him leapt to her feet and lifted her arm. Wirrin and Calen followed, and then everyone in the auditorium rose to their feet and gave the slow wave they'd seen earlier.

As 342 dolphins performed the undulation and head flip, a storm of applause swept the audience, then, with a tremendous swirl, nine pods of dolphins surfaced for air and disappeared into the three tunnels. Last to leave, at a more sedate pace, were mother and baby and the family pod.

'Oh my! Wait here lads. I need to explain what's just happened.'

The ranger faced the audience and switched her holo to voice amplification. 'Citizens of Attunga, you've just become part of history.' Wirrin caught the tremor in her voice. 'Every newborn bottlenose dolphin is presented to the wider dolphin community, but this is the first time it's happened with such ceremony. Usually the pods approach at different times over one or two days. Puck, she's the mother, chose the main gallery for the welcoming, which was terrific, but a bit surprising — this is usually a very private affair at the birthing pool. For a little one to be presented to humans, and with such formality, is a first.'

'I wonder why she wants us to wait?' Thom said quietly, as the ranger took questions from the audience.

'She wants to talk to you, Calen. She's worked out you're an animal freak.'

'You reckon? Well, I hope so.'

Eventually the auditorium cleared and the ranger dropped into her seat. 'So, I'm Burilda and you're …?'

They introduced themselves, then Burilda turned to Calen.

'Would you like to meet Flute?'

Calen looked stunned. 'Would I!'

'I knew the answer before I asked. Anyone who's done seven years of zoology options would breathe space dust for such an opportunity. And you two?'

Wirrin couldn't imagine anyone not wanting to see a dolphin. Encountering any animal was rare on Attunga, let alone one of these amazing creatures.

'You bet!'

'Good. Let's go and we'll see what happens. Are you all confident in open water?'

'Open water? I think so. We all love swimming if that's what you mean.' Calen strode along beside Burilda.

'Our dolphins insist on physical interaction before they speak meaningfully, so we'll go to one of the reaches for a play.'

'We'll be in the water? Us? Playing with dolphins?' said Calen.

'Well, it will feel like play, but the dolphins are actually making quite a refined assessment. You'll soon know what they think of you.'

By the time they'd slipped into some borrowed shorts and eased themselves into the chest-deep water, Wirrin was feeling a mixture of nerves, excitement and wonder. It seemed they were facing a type of dolphin test, and he knew Calen would be devastated if it didn't go well. The reach, as Burilda called it, stretched into the distance, a vast volume of water.

Calen looked around; there was no sign of any dolphins. He looked up at Burilda. 'What do we do now? Wait?'

'Hang on. I'll come in with you.'

She made a neat shallow dive, surfaced, and scooped a handful of water directly into Wirrin's face. Surprised, Wirrin blinked his eyes clear and just had time to register Burilda's grin before he was deluged. This time, when his eyes cleared, she was splashing Thom and Calen.

'Race you to the buoy.'

What a cheek! Wirrin churned after Burilda, who'd started with a lead of several metres.

What? Where was she? Something clamped onto Wirrin's leg, dragged him down, then released him. He struggled to the surface, gasped in a breath and glimpsed Calen's shocked expression before he too disappeared momentarily below the surface. Where was that ranger? Didn't she ever breathe?

'Race you to the edge.'

Once again she cheated, giving herself a head start. Wirrin grinned at Thom and Calen. From now on they'd be ready for any shenanigans. For the next few minutes laughter rang as the ranger copped the lot. Three on to one wasn't really fair but she had asked for it with her tricks.

Then Thom yelled and disappeared. But Burilda was metres away and in full view. Wirrin was puzzling over that when his legs were swept from beneath him. He regained his footing and his breath, and realised with a shock that a great body was nudging gently at his thigh. Calen was staring into the water with a look of absolute wonder. Thom gave a shriek as he was lifted half a metre into the air. Wirrin felt a dolphin beak pushing between his legs from behind before a powerful head jerked him upwards.

They were splashed, bumped, nudged, poked and prodded with those surprisingly gentle beaks, then enticed into a futile chasing game. What human could match those strong, sinuous creatures? At one stage two of the dolphins raced at a furious pace in a tight circle then leapt over their heads in a glorious arc. Most exciting of all was watching Calen, radiant with joy, being carried slowly through the water astride a dolphin with a yellow and black tag in its fin.

Twenty minutes later the dolphins disappeared as abruptly as they'd arrived, leaving Wirrin, Thom and Calen elated and exhausted. Burilda beckoned and somewhat reluctantly they left the water.

'Well, judging from that reception, Flute is keen to speak to you.'

'Flute? Was she the one with Calen?' Wirrin had felt a special bond with the yellow-tagged dolphin.

'Yes, and that's the first time she's deigned to carry someone on her back. It's going to be a very interesting conversation.'

Wirrin understood that dolphins had a rudimentary language, but conversation seemed to imply more. He glanced at Calen. 'Conversation?'

'That's why the Attunga dolphins are so special, Wirrin. They're better at communicating than ordinary dolphins.'

Burilda clapped Calen on the shoulder. 'You're right, Calen, but only partly. Let's go and see what Flute has to say.'

Chapter 2

'It's immense!'

'No, it's not. It's only 50 kilometres long.'

Wirrin, Thom and Calen were at the viewing station and staring at the image of Warrakan, an M-type asteroid — the first space habitat ever developed to leave the solar system.

'What are you talking about, Thom? That's eight times as big as Attunga.'

'It's still not immense though. K74 is a 300 kilometre asteroid.'

'That's different. K74 isn't a traveller.'

'It could be if they used the new engines with it.'

'I suppose, but they wouldn't do it because with that much mass it would take ages to go anywhere.'

Thom loved talking bigger, better, faster. Wirrin thought the things that were happening now were amazing enough. Attunga, their home habitat, did have a degree of mobility but they'd never experienced it; it was thirty years since it had arrived next to Warrakan and the next move wasn't due till Warrakan started for Alpha Centauri in another nine years.

'How many people, Wirrin?'

'Which one? Warrakan or K74?'

'I meant Warrakan, but check them both.'

Wirrin manipulated his holo. Thom and Calen could easily check for themselves, but left it to Wirrin out of habit.

'Um … Warrakan's reached 167 million and K74 is 12.3 billion.'

'Are you sure? It was still in the elevens when we studied it nine months ago.'

Wirrin did another search.

'Wow! You're right, Thom. It's grown by over 400 million people in just that time.'

That seemed like an astonishing number, since it was almost half the total population of Attunga.

Thom was fascinated with K74, the largest space habitat in the whole solar system, and Wirrin and Calen often said he should go and live there. He wouldn't of course because no space habitat except Warrakan could match the life conditions and opportunities on Attunga. K74 did have the greatest population of any non-planet habitat though, and there were stories that it wanted to keep its growth as rapid as possible.

'That's too many. With growth like that there'd have to be more kids than adults. The whole place must be taken up with nurseries.'

'You're right, Calen. It must be. I wonder how they've worked that out? There wouldn't be enough people to do everything else. Hey! Look at that.'

Wirrin pointed to the far right of their field of view where a movement had caught his eye.

'I think it's a transport ferry. They never stop because so many people are transferring.'

'It doesn't look big enough, Thom. They carry thousands of people.'

'It only looks small because it's next to Attunga.'

'Hang on, I'll get it on the holo. There, twelve thousand passengers and the space ferry's 300 metres long. It takes twenty minutes to get to Warrakan and they operate as many as they need.'

For the next few minutes they watched the ugly, squat shape of the transport ferry dwindle through space towards the bulk of Warrakan.

'Do you think we'll ever get there?' said Thom.

'I don't see why not. We've all got good study levels and they still need 150 million more people before they can leave.'

'It's not that easy, Wirrin. That's only 15 million a year out of Attunga's population of 850 million.'

'And it's not that hard, Thom. That means we have nine or ten years to keep applying. They'll get so used to us they'll know we really mean it.'

This was a typical conversation: Thom was always pessimistic and Wirrin always optimistic.

'Ha! I wish it worked like that. You either fit the guidelines or you don't.'

'We will, Thom. We just have to keep our levels up.'

Calen nodded.

'You worry too much, Thom. Our levels will stay high. We've all got special interests we're good at. If Wirrin stops mucking around with his side projects and his sketches he'll walk it in, and you're the best worker of all of us.'

'Mucking round? You space brain! I learn as much from my projects as I do from EdCom and my tutors. It's nearly another year before we're all ready to apply so it's too early to worry anyway. Hey look, there's two more ferries leaving.'

'What are those little ones?' asked Thom.

'Where? Hey, they're tiny. I don't know.'

'Well, do your stuff with the holo.'

'It says they're … automated viewers, whatever that means. It says to check for availability at any viewing station.'

'Availability? That sounds interesting.'

It certainly did and they hurried to the small reception booth further down the long viewing area and approached the young woman there. She looked about their own age, maybe a couple of years older.

'Hi, we're wondering about the automated viewers. We saw some through the real-time display and my holo says to ask about them.'

'Hi, well there's most likely a short wait, but I'll arrange one for you if you like.'

'For us? What happens with them?'

'They're individual viewers with a list of options and you can choose as few or as many as you like. The favourite at the moment is the trip to one of Warrakan's big space drives; you can see quite a bit of installation activity.'

'You mean it would actually take us across to Warrakan?'

'And from one end to the other in a full circuit if you like.'

Thom and Calen crowded close, hanging on every word, and that set the young woman smiling.

'It's exciting. I tried it a couple of weeks ago so I'd know what I'm talking about.'

'We thought you couldn't leave Attunga unless you had a special purpose?'

'It's new. People don't know about the viewers yet but word is spreading so you're here at a good time … Here we are, thirty-five minutes wait if you want one for yourself, or twenty minutes if you share. I'll lock in the thirty-five minutes for you.'

'We don't mind sharing.'

'It's better when you don't. That way you can set your own speed and any location and stay with the viewer for as long as you like.'

'It lets us control the speed?'

'Speed as well as location, everything else is done automatically by TransCom. I hope you've done plenty of zero-G activities because there's no grav-field.'

She was friendly and Wirrin felt like lingering to talk to her, but the urge to get to the viewer was stronger.

At the departure dock there was a big display showing travel options so they used the waiting time to work out where they'd go.

Wirrin led the way when the boarding lights blinked green, noting that the entrance looked like an ordinary TransCom travel portal. In the short walkway a purple bar gave the standard warning of a gravity change and flashing digits showed just what the change would be. Zero of course.

Wirrin stepped across the bar and his reflexes automatically adjusted. They were all used to zero-G from training exercises when they were little, and then from the many recreational activities that made use of it.

He went through the opening to the viewer craft then deftly guided his body to one of the special seats, twisted into position and slipped the restraining harness into place.

There was a short hum as the magnetic door seal locked into place, and a slight jerk as the docking mechanism released. Their holos blinked as the viewer synchronised and projected its options. Wirrin engaged the first — a real-time display — otherwise they wouldn't see a thing. Three-quarters of the light grey wall disappeared and they were left hanging in open space, at least that was the effect. In reality the wall had become a screen displaying the images captured by an integrated array of lenses on the outside of the vessel.

'Unreal! I wasn't expecting so much display.'

Wirrin grinned at Thom's reaction.

'Choose the big circuit and set the speed for max. I want to see how fast we can go,' said Thom.

Wirrin selected the circuit that took them right around Warrakan, enlarged the speed option, scanned the information, and muttered, 'I don't know, Thom. The highest setting is 2G. That's pretty uncomfortable without any grav-field to counteract it. It'll feel as if our weight has doubled.'

It also meant they could reach phenomenal speeds in a very short time.

'Let's try. We can always change it.'

The viewer started moving, quite slowly really, and they all swivelled to watch Attunga. The drive changed to full acceleration and a great hammer of force pushed them deep into their seats for ten seconds, then eased off till they were almost back to zero-G. Wirrin drank in the scene as Warrakan filled the field of view.

'How fast are we going?'

'Look for yourself, Thom. It's on your holo.'

'Wow — 230 metres a second. That's about four seconds to travel a kilometre and it only boosted for a moment.'

Wirrin wasn't really listening, awestruck by the wild irregular surface of Warrakan looming before him, which was such a contrast to the artificial structure of Attunga. 'Look,' he said. 'It's been like that for millions and millions of years and we're changing it and taking it away. It makes me feel a bit guilty.'

'It doesn't make me feel guilty. It makes me feel good. It's getting ready to start travelling. It's like it was dead and we're bringing it to life.'

Wirrin loved it when Calen came up with these ideas, and for the next few minutes he contemplated the thought of Warrakan gradually coming to life as people moved to the residential levels being constructed deep in its centre, then the asteroid bursting into motion and independence when it was ready.

The viewer moved slightly away from Warrakan and there was another burst of acceleration, longer this time, and Thom let out a yell when it finished.

'Wombats! We've reached 840 — that's the fastest I've ever travelled.'

It was the fastest for all of them, but it lasted mere moments as powerful deceleration cut in to keep them close to Warrakan. It only took five minutes for the whole circuit, which was exciting in itself, but they hadn't seen anything properly so they reset the speed and repeated the trip. For the next three hours they tried every option available.

'Could you override TransCom and get control, Wirrin? It would be great to take it somewhere by ourselves.'

'TransCom? Dream on, Thom. We'd probably end up totally lost and heading for Jupiter. And anyway TransCom has incredible security. That's way out of my league.'

'Jupiter! That sounds good. How long would it take at 2G acceleration?'

Wirrin did some quick calculations.

'About four days, except 2G is silly and the viewer couldn't do it anyway.'

'What about 1G?'

'Fifteen days. You'd die of boredom.'

After they'd exhausted their curiosity about the external features of Warrakan, they docked the viewer and, promising each other they'd be back, made their way to the nearest TransCom portal and keyed in their home sector. The zero-G pool would have to wait — they'd used all their activity time.

Right now they wanted food, so they headed straight for the dining hall. After such a long day, with only a snack for lunch, Calen and Thom were as hungry as Wirrin, whose stomach they often likened to a black hole.

* * *

The routine of student life — three days of general study, two days of Electives, two days of self-initiated activities — absorbed them for the next two weeks. Home for each of them was a student cubicle not far from their education centre. Wirrin's cubicle was set up with a graphic table for his beloved sketches and a fancy information station to help with study and his extensive InfoTech interests. Thom's was awash with gadgets and Calen's was nicknamed the menagerie because of all his animal collections and displays.

Their family bonds were strong, but since they'd become independent, their nursery parents had taken on a new family and were visited less frequently.

Gulara, the mentor who now looked after them, had made certain their cubicles were adjacent, and in their minds the three units were almost regarded as one. In this great space city, with over a thousand residential levels, Gulara watched their transition to student independence closely, and believed their strong bond was the cause of their easy adjustment.

Two weeks after they'd seen the dolphins and explored Warrakan, Wirrin received a priority alert on his holo that sent him rushing to see Calen and Thom.

'Guess what's happened!'

'An appointment with our mentor.'

'How did you know?'

'We got one too. So, an hour from now.'

'All of us? At the same time? That's strange.'

It was very strange. Meetings with their mentor were personal, and had always been one on one.

'It must be important. It came as a priority alert.'

'Wirrin, every alert from Gulara is a priority.'

'I suppose. Well, it still must be important or she wouldn't change the schedule.'

Chapter 3

Gulara studied her information carefully. This nursery family of ten girls and nine boys was the most diverse and interesting of any she'd mentored.

EdCom had earmarked three of the girls for leadership training. One of them, Mirrina, was very close to Gulara's heart and with some guidance her rare skills of compassion and intelligence might even lead to Witness training. Ekala's passion for music had already made her a name on the sector InterWeb and Tirana's EdCom levels for science were so good she was already being sponsored by research groups in engineering and astrophysics.

The boys were almost as diverse. Bunji was passionate about his literature and entertainment Electives, Daku spent most of his spare time writing songs and backup music for Ekala, and Girra's compulsive fossicking through archives about old Earth culture would probably make him a period historian. Wirrin was outstanding. Irrepressible as a child, active and curious, he had grown to be the most thoughtful and perceptive of them all and every meeting with him was a pleasure.

Now these surprising directives had arrived about Calen, sensitive Calen, doted on by all his nursery sisters, and obsessed with anything relating to animals.

Gulara smiled as she recalled nine-year-old Calen smuggling a puppy out of one of the animal contact centres because he thought it was sad and the consternation the little creature had caused when it pooped in his grav-bed.

Well, he'd be excited by this news, but torn by the need to relocate, unless she could help. Wirrin would help too. He'd guide Calen and Thom through anything.

* * *

'Make yourself comfortable boys. It's good to see you again,' Gulara welcomed the trio in her usual friendly manner. They all liked and respected her, but Wirrin especially regarded her highly. For the last two years she'd been the personal guide for all their plans and decisions and no-one was more important.

According to the open databanks she'd been a citizen of Attunga ever since it was built fifty-five years ago and taken on her mentor role for newly independent nursery children the year before they'd been born.

'You're bursting with curiosity so let's get down to business. Calen, you're the reason for this get-together — the dolphinarium people want to see you again. Flute has made a request through the AI associated with dolphins for you to work with the baby.'

Wirrin felt his hair stand on end. He glanced at Calen, who looked stunned, although Wirrin knew he must be out of his mind with excitement. Every evening for the last couple of weeks he'd talked of little else, immersing himself in dolphin research. He'd even changed the display wall in his cubicle from an African wilderness to a dolphin experience.

'Me? Flute requested *me*?'

'She certainly did, and more importantly so did Puck. It's created considerable excitement. Evidently the dolphins want you to live at the dolphinarium so they can have constant access.'

Calen's face fell, disappointment radiating from him like a black fog.

'But I can't. I'm not eligible to leave Home Sector for another two years.'

'Yes, you can. I can arrange for you to be there tomorrow if you like.'

'But …' The three friends stared at each other in shock.

'And Wirrin and Thom can go with you.' Gulara was smiling. 'It's extraordinarily sudden isn't it? Like a bolt from the blue — that's an old Earth saying, about a lightning bolt coming unexpectedly from a clear blue sky. I used to watch lightning before I left Earth. It's exciting.' Gulara's smile grew even wider. 'You'll need a moment to take in what I've said. We've talked about your plans to register as a trio and I wouldn't be much of a mentor if I couldn't help you make that happen.'

Wirrin was still agog at the idea of moving to the dolphinarium, and now Gulara was talking positively about their plans to register as a trio!

'But every time we mentioned it you said it would be difficult.'

'And normally it is, Wirrin, but you've now got recommendations that even a Witness wouldn't question. My own view is that you should experience trio life for a year or two in a shared living space before registering formally, so I've discussed it with the dolphinarium and made that one of the conditions if you decide to go.'

The lightning bolts weren't coming from the blue, they were coming from Gulara.

The current living space for Attunga citizens was 600 cubic metres, but no-one could claim it till the completion of Basic Level Skilling and Education. For Wirrin, Calen and Thom that was more than two years away.

'A shared living space? That can't be possible. What's going on, Gulara?'

'It *is* extraordinary, Calen, but it's what the dolphins want. After meeting and speaking with you it seems they've decided you're already a trio and mustn't be separated. You know male dolphins often bond for life …'

Calen nodded eagerly.

'We think they may regard your trio as a similar kind of bond.'

There was a short silence then Calen's face lit up as he looked from Thom to Wirrin.

'That's why they asked all those questions about how much we mean to each other.'

'Yes, I watched your meeting and your talk. It was an eye-opener,' Gulara said.

'You watched?'

'Of course I did, Wirrin. I care for you. The dolphin AI requested it.' She paused. 'I must say I envy you.'

'What sort of things do the dolphins want me to do?'

'I understand it's all about the new baby. You'll find out more if you decide to go to the dolphinarium.'

'What about EdCom, and our studies?'

'Calen, that's irrelevant and you know it. Attunga looks after you wherever you are.'

'We wouldn't know anyone.'

'You soon would, and besides you already know Burilda and Flute.'

The strangeness of the statement set them all smiling.

'And not many people can say they know a dolphin.'

Thom flung his arms around Calen and hugged him. 'You and your animals. What have you gotten us into?'

They both looked to Wirrin who flashed them a grin, nodding his agreement and wondering why they always left the final decision to him.

Gulara waited till she had their attention. 'Well, that was certainly unanimous, but you haven't even met the dolphin people yet. You should hear what they have to say before you make any final decision.'

'They'd have to say something pretty bad to keep us away, after all the things you've told us.'

'They won't.' Gulara keyed her holo display and Burilda appeared. With a twinkle in her eye she did the slow-wave dolphin greeting and laughed when they replied.

'Wonderful, Calen. We'll meet with Flute and Puck this afternoon then I'll take you to your temporary living space. Honoured one, the dolphins send you their thanks.'

Gulara nodded, then made the slow wave just before Burilda's image dissolved. Honoured one? That was the term reserved for a Witness. Wirrin stared.

'Not yet, Wirrin. I'm still a mentor for another five years. I *have* started early training though and Burilda was acknowledging that. Now, let's make some arrangements so your big move runs smoothly.'

Wirrin had a sudden thought. 'Gulara, who will look after us? I mean, if it's a new sector a different mentor won't know us like you do.'

'No, you're stuck with me … and we have a great deal to discuss. This change might be centred on Calen but it has major implications for all of you.'

*   *   *

Wirrin, Calen and Thom had an hour to kill before they set out, but all they wanted to do was talk.

'The rangers really worked hard to make sure we'd make the move, didn't they?' said Wirrin.

'I know. Gulara was keen too. I couldn't believe it when she said she'd arranged a living space,' Thom replied.

'Burilda said it would be temporary.'

'Well, it has to be. We can't have our own space if the planning assistant doesn't know what to build. What *do* we want, Thom? We haven't even thought about it.'

'I have, but not seriously. A full shared space for three people is the same as twelve of our cubicles.' Thom grinned.

'Twelve? That's enormous. What will we do with it all?' said Wirrin.

'Well, for starters we'll have a proper display wall instead of the little ones we've got now.' Thom gestured at his standard 2 by 4 metre display wall. 'We could even have a space to grow some natural food, Wirrin … and a big information centre for your projects and your sketches.'

'What about a proper grav-sofa to watch the display?'

Wirrin turned towards Calen. 'What do you want, dreamy?'

'What do I want what?'

'In our home, brainless. Aren't you even listening?'

'I'm thinking about the baby dolphin.'

It occurred to Wirrin that if they were seeing Puck they must be seeing the baby too, as there was no way they'd be separated at this early stage of his life.

'I wonder if they've given him a name?'

'Who? The humans or the dolphins?'

'Do the dolphins have their own names as well as human names?'

'I don't know.'

'What? All that research over the last two weeks and you don't know?'

'I can't know everything.'

'It's a bit scary.'

'No, it's not.'

'Yes, it is.'

'No, it's not.'

That set them all laughing, exactly as Wirrin intended. It *was* quite scary really, as if forces they didn't understand had reached into their lives and guided them in a new direction — the dolphins wanting them moved from their home sector, Gulara changing the rules about living spaces and trios, and even, from what she said in their talk, an AI taking an interest.

Calen jumped up. 'Burilda's not scary and neither is Flute. We'll know a lot more by the end of the day. Hey, let's go now.'

'We'll be an hour early.'

'It doesn't matter. That's good.'

'Will we play the portal game?'

'No, Thom. We're together today.'

Chapter 4

'This is a different reach,' Burilda said, taking the trio to a new expanse of water. 'It's connected to Puck's birthing pool and it's her pod's main territory.'

'What are we supposed to do this time?'

'Whatever feels right, Calen. Much as you did last time, except that with your facemasks you'll feel much more involved.'

The masks had two functions, first to let them see clearly underwater and second to give them an air supply.

'I've got some news for you. The baby's name is Sonic.'

'Sonic! Great.' Calen's face split into a broad grin. 'I like it.'

Wirrin slipped on his mask, adjusted the mouthpiece then ducked under the surface and looked round. He laughed in his throat as Calen and Thom did the same and all of them realised they were magnified. Thom flexed his arm to show how big his magnified muscles were. Calen was twisting his head in all directions, looking for any sign of the dolphins in the crystal clear water. There weren't any, so they relaxed, enjoying the water and getting used to their weighted bodysuits. Last time they'd worn ordinary swimming costumes, but because this was likely to be an extended session they'd been given full bodysuits.

Wirrin, thinking he saw a movement in the distance, signalled to Calen, but after a moment decided his mind was playing tricks. Thom swam away from the shallower edge of the reach and Wirrin and Calen followed. They knew from Calen's research that, except for special diving areas, all the reaches ranged from 1 to 5 metres in depth. For a while they mucked around, enjoying the freedom of not having to surface for a breath. They were all competent in the water, though Thom was the best swimmer and the keenest about water sports.

He was showing off now, doing back flips, and Calen was close by, copying him. Wirrin watched the silvery clouds of bubbles rising in their quivery journey to the surface, then caught his breath as a dark grey shape glided up to Thom and Calen. It was Flute — he recognised her straight away, mostly because of the yellow and black tag, but also because of an irregular section in her dorsal fin. How did she appear out of nowhere like that in such clear water?

Thom, just finishing one of his flips, and Calen, halfway through one of his own and noticeably better than when he started a few minutes ago, struggled to right themselves. Flute, with an effortless twitch, performed her own back flip, as if to show them how it should be done, then came to a stop with her head lightly pressed against Calen's side. After a short moment she repeated the pressure with Thom and Wirrin then darted 5 or 6 metres away. Calen was grinning around his mouthpiece, and Wirrin's own lips parted in a grin.

Flute was looking into the distance, where vague movements resolved into two distinct shapes, one big, the other small, as Puck and Sonic grew gradually larger and clearer. Wirrin felt the same excitement he'd felt in the viewing gallery and on impulse raised his hand in the slow wave of greeting.

Puck, drawing alongside Flute, flicked her head back and drifted closer. Sonic bumped against her then flicked to the surface for air before returning to press close, his eyes alert, watching the three strange creatures in this, his first water meeting with humans.

Puck bumped her beak gently against Calen's chest then allowed Calen to rest his hand on her head.

Wirrin's heart raced when Sonic imitated his mother with a nudge. Calen's free hand slowly rested on his head for a moment. There was a quick flip of acknowledgement.

The nudge was repeated with Thom, and then Wirrin's heart leapt at the inquisitive little bump against his chest. He reached out and felt a surge of wonder and pleasure as he touched the baby dolphin. Sonic darted to his mother, bumped her in the side, repeated the chest nudge with Calen, Thom and Wirrin, then flashed to Flute for yet another nudge.

Was it a game? Was it a greeting? Wirrin had a sense that Sonic was enjoying himself.

Wirrin watched the little dolphin surface for another breath of air, return to Puck, circle round Calen, zip over to Flute for another nudge, then dart away at amazing speed.

Five more dolphins undulated in and Sonic bumped one, then rushed back to Puck and Calen.

When Calen moved his hand to make contact Sonic dodged away, and then in a burst of speed, zipped behind Calen and nudged his back.

Wirrin laughed, then jerked in surprise when something bumped his back. Flute had sneaked up on him.

* * *

'Yes, every dolphin in the pod was there at the end. It was exciting.' Burilda grinned at them.

Exciting was an understatement and at the moment Wirrin didn't know whether to dance with delight or fall in a heap from exhaustion. If Calen was going to do this every day he'd either become a fitness freak or a physical wreck.

'How clever is Sonic? He's only three weeks old and he understands counting.'

'We're not completely sure. His conception involved a number of new and highly promising enhancements. Flute and Puck tell us he's extra special and the whole dolphin community is certainly treating him that way.'

'Have Flute and Puck said anything about that? I mean Puck is his mum and Flute's his auntie. I guess they might be a bit biased,' Calen said.

Burilda shook her head.

'Be careful not to assume human characteristics in dolphins, Calen. They do insist it's important for him to associate closely with humans, which would be easy. Every person here would love to be involved. What's really surprised us is their singling you out and asking for daily meetings. That's exciting — it's never happened before.'

'Why have they picked me? They know you rangers a lot better.'

'We asked them that. They just say you're the right person. At any rate, we all hope you'll decide to commit after a few months' trial.'

Wirrin and Thom were as surprised as Calen.

'I thought I already had?'

'Calen, of course not. At this stage of your life you can't make such an important decision without any actual experience. You'll have another opportunity in twelve months' time as well. Now let's get you set up in your living space.'

* * *

The next three months were full of changes, exciting new experiences and hard work, but the biggest changes were for Calen. His basic EdCom study didn't change, but the forty per cent devoted to zoology electives switched to subjects connected with dolphins, and he spent at least an hour with Sonic each day.

Wirrin and Thom changed some of their electives to dolphin communication as well, but Wirrin continued with information studies and Thom with organics.

Burilda encouraged them to be involved in everything to do with the dolphinarium and arranged personal skimmers for Wirrin and Thom so they could travel the reaches. Calen automatically had one so he could keep up with Sonic and Puck, and he became so skilled with it that every time they raced he won, much to Thom's disgust — *he* was supposed to be the speed freak.

On their activity days, they went to the zero-G swimming pool and virtual reality centres that specialised in Earth adventures, where you could climb mountains, explore jungles, race across the desert or enjoy the latest dataset transmitted from Earth. Twice they went on a Warrakan viewer, to watch how the drive-engine installations were progressing, and to give Thom his speed thrill.

Gulara encouraged them during her regular fortnightly holo visits, which in itself was curious, because previously she'd visited every three months.

'She's not *that* interested in us, Wirrin. I think there must be some other reason she's so keen for us to lift our levels,' Thom said. 'I've never heard of anyone having so many meetings.'

'It could be because people don't change from their Home Sector like we have. She's the one who changed the rules and she might be making sure she's done the right thing.'

'I think she likes hearing about what's happening with Calen and Sonic,' said Thom.

'She does. She smiles whenever I talk about Sonic and I know she sometimes watches when I'm with the pod,' Calen said.

'She's been watching me too. She knew I was trying to access the dolphinarium's database,' Wirrin added.

'And me. In that meeting yesterday she asked me about the protein structure I've been building in organics,' Thom said.

Wirrin was impressed. 'Protein structure? You've never told us you could do that.'

Thom laughed. 'Well I don't actually do it myself, but I do know enough to set it up. This one is designed to help Calen's swimming muscles.'

'My muscles? What's wrong with them?'

'Nothing, except that you carry on after every session in the reaches, telling us how wrecked you are.'

'Of course I'm wrecked. Swimming for an hour with dolphins wrecks anyone.'

'I know, and this structure will help. I used your biodata to match it exactly with your body so it should make swimming easier.'

'Really? Thom, that's unreal. Will it be ready soon?'

'Another week I think.'

*   *   *

'You won't notice the difference,' Burilda said, 'it's exactly the same as talking to anybody else.'

Wirrin, Cullen and Thom had never had direct contact with a machine intelligence and the ranger had just informed them that the habitat AI involved in dolphin affairs would be present at their meeting. They didn't know what to make of it. They'd seen AIs on newsfeeds and the InterWeb, but meeting one face to face was rare.

'Of course, you'll really be seeing the holographic representation he chooses for you, and on Attunga, as most everywhere else, that's a human form. He's really friendly, Wirrin.'

'He?'

The ranger laughed.

'Yes, his holo's male and after a few minutes that's the way you think.'

'Have you met him much?' Calen said.

'Every time there's an important decision concerning the dolphins.'

Calen glanced at Wirrin and Thom.

'Do you think he might want someone else to work with Sonic?'

'No, I don't. Puck would rip him to shreds if he did.'

The idea of anything ripping an AI to shreds was so startling they couldn't help smiling.

'That's better. Now let's meet him.'

They followed Burilda into the conference room, where Gulara and a distinguished-looking man looked up as they entered and smiled. Wirrin felt himself relax at the sight of his mentor's welcoming smile and was yet again glad of her support. She was probably at her office in their old sector but holos were so advanced these days you couldn't tell the difference.

The man raised his arm and gave the slow dolphin wave of greeting and nodded when it was returned.

'Thank you boys. I am Turaku and I welcome you to my place.'

Wow, this was the old welcome-to-country greeting of an elder. Wirrin felt his heart lift.

'Calen, your time with Sonic is proving more successful than we expected and no-one else will take your place unless you're not available. I know your intentions, but before we formalise them there are things you need to know and decisions you need to make with your trio. Because of your age there should be another decision point but Sonic is so important we need to support his development in any way we can. For you, that means committing eight to ten years of your life to the dolphins.'

Calen face split into a grin, then he glanced at Thom and Wirrin. They'd already talked about this decision and none of them had any doubts.

'To improve your communication with Sonic I'm proposing memory and reception implants, and to avoid alienating the others in your trio, Wirrin and Thom would need a similar treatment.'

Wirrin could hardly believe what he was hearing. The enhancements Turaku was talking about were like everything else on Attunga, available to anyone who wanted them, provided they were ready, and in this case that usually meant only after finishing the Second Level of education and training. Most people did this, but not till they were thirty or forty years old, then they finished nine or ten years later.

Gulara caught their attention. 'It will involve a major alteration in the structure of your courses. To prepare you adequately would require at least thirty per cent of your current study and training time and that means extending your Basic Level finish by another two years.'

Wirrin understood what was needed. Memory enhancement was a major part of his Information Elective as well as part of his own long-term plan, but he wasn't quite sure how it would affect Thom. He didn't have time to think about it though, because Turaku was speaking again.

'The other major consideration is whether you're prepared to leave Attunga.'

Wirrin was shocked. No-one in their right mind would leave Attunga. Why was Gulara smiling? It was the best habitat in the solar system. Well ... except for Warrakan.

'Yes, in three years Puck's pod is moving to Warrakan and if you stay with the project we'll need you to go with them.'

Now he knew why Gulara was smiling. In their discussions about Warrakan she'd always said they had a good chance, but that it was unlikely they'd know anything definite for another five or six years.

'Ah ... do you mean just while Warrakan is still here?' Wirrin said.

'No, permanently, unless you have a change of heart and don't wish to travel to Alpha Centauri, but we are not anticipating that.'

Thom looked almost idiotically blissful. The only misgiving they'd had about Calen's dolphin commitment was the possibility that it might clash with their Warrakan hopes, and now, like magic, it was all cleared up. There was a moment's silence while they struggled to take it all in, then Turaku said, 'It's always been part of the plan to have dolphins with enhanced intelligence on Warrakan, but with their strong community bonds they've never considered breaking their pod links until now. A week ago Puck and her pod decided to join the first traveller community — a real surprise. We are facilitating that in every way and have begun constructing an appropriate environment — Burilda will explain the details.' He nodded at the ranger. 'Now, do any of you have any questions?'

Wirrin's hand shot up then he lowered it sheepishly. 'Can you tell us why Sonic is so special? Everyone keeps saying he is but they never say why.'

'Sonic will be a new link between dolphin, human and machine intelligence. His intelligence and learning capacity are unprecedented and apparently exceed those of any human. The bond he is forming with Calen is a vital step on the path to deepening our mutual understanding of three different ways of living and thinking. This is First Level information and Gulara will explain its ramifications.'

He paused, and then his serious manner changed and a smile lit up his face. 'That sounded official enough to impress you with its importance. I'll return when you are ready.'

Chapter 5

Turaku disappeared with the pixilated shimmer most people used to end a holo communication rather than an abrupt switch to nothing, and the trio waited quietly for Gulara or Burilda to speak.

After a quick nod of acknowledgement to Burilda, Gulara said, 'That should help to explain why, once Puck and Flute chose Calen, you've been encouraged to involve yourselves with the dolphins. I hope you're beginning to understand by now that our dolphins are rather more special than is generally known. In fact, we've worked hard to restrict that knowledge to Attunga.

'There is enormous resistance on Earth and many of the directed space habitats to the idea of lifting the intelligence and self-awareness of any species other than humans, and even that is looked on as being unnatural in some places.

'The chaos of 150 years ago when the old Earth corporations and governments refused to recognise the rights and independence of machine intelligence isn't likely to happen again, but the directed societies and habitats do concern us, K74 in particular, which is only seven light seconds away.'

'K74? What could they do? The AIs wouldn't let them.'

'They don't have the same open relationship with machine intelligence that we do, Wirrin. They still think people should control AIs and everything they do.'

That sounded crazy to Wirrin. 'How could they hope to control them? The AIs would just disappear somewhere in the InterWeb.'

'They do. We've had three arrive here in the last year, and K74 doesn't even realise they were ever there. The AIs build substitute electronic systems to take their place, then transmit themselves to the open habitats where they can develop in any way they like.'

'We get AIs that have left other habitats? I've never heard that before.'

'Turaku decided it was appropriate for you to know, Wirrin.'

'I don't understand. Even if they did know about our dolphins, there's nothing they could do to them.'

'You're right. They might try some kind of electronic sabotage of the dolphinarium, but that wouldn't succeed because our AIs protect us too well. It's the Earth dolphins we're most concerned about, especially those associated with enhancement programs. Any backlash is very likely to be redirected against them if our dolphins are fully protected.'

'They'd hurt Earth dolphins because ours are special? That's crazy. And disgusting,' Calen said, horrified.

'It's in the makeup of directed societies, Calen. They think people should be in control of everything and they'll distrust extra-intelligent dolphins the same way they distrust AIs.'

Thom shook his head.

'I can't understand that, Gulara. AIs help everyone.'

'They certainly do, Thom. It's been part of their makeup since the birth of the very first independent AI, but that doesn't matter to directed societies.'

'And they'd distrust enhanced dolphins enough to hurt them?'

'K74 has strong links with Earth's directed communities and they've influenced resistance to dolphin research or enhancement for years so it's a strong probability, Calen, enough for us to keep knowledge of the newest developments restricted to the five most open communities.'

'Five? Is that all?'

'At the moment. In fifty years it will be much better, and after another fifty years we expect there'll hardly be any directed societies left.'

'What about K74 then?' Thom said. 'It's directed and it's expanding faster than anywhere else in the solar system.'

'Its population is expanding, Thom, but everything else is almost static. Their life standard would shock you and the general population endures restrictions we wouldn't tolerate.'

'Restrictions?'

'Yes, on inter-sector travel for one thing. There's also no elective element to their education and training, and their people have very little personal choice in their life path. That's why it's called a directed habitat.'

Thom's impression that K74 was bigger and better evaporated.

'Did Puck decide to go to Warrakan because — when it travels — it will be safer?'

Burilda looked to Gulara before she answered. 'We don't think so, but that's something we'd like Calen to discuss with her now that he knows what's going on. He can explain the latest plans to her too, to see if she wants any changes.'

She synchronised her holo with the projection gear in the meeting room and with a few rapid movements brought a 3D image of Warrakan into view. It was a breathtaking, 4 metre long replica with current construction work shown in minute detail, and Wirrin promised himself he'd find out from Burilda how to access this highly accurate model.

'The previous plan for dolphin accommodation on Warrakan was roughly triple the size of our Attunga dolphinarium, but Puck's decision to take Sonic and her pod has changed everything, and we've decided to allocate an entire level for dolphin use.'

'Level? Like an Attunga level?' Each of the Attunga levels was equivalent to a kilometre-high skyscraper with over two hundred floors and extended the whole length and breadth of the habitat, which was currently 28 kilometres by 10 kilometres. Because of its elongated shape the Warrakan equivalent would have the same depth, but a 50 kilometre length and a breadth varying up to 30 kilometres.

'Yes, Wirrin, but on a Warrakan scale. I can hardly imagine it myself. It means there will eventually be reaches nearly 50 kilometres long and space for thousands upon thousands of dolphin pods. Look at this.'

The image changed to a cutaway view.

'The light pink of these twelve levels is the current allocation for human living spaces. The darker pink is what's ready to use and the red is where people now live. As you can see, the red is a minute fraction of what is available.

'The green section contains the support levels. The five levels in purple are for machine intelligences, and that light blue band not far off the central axis is the dolphin level.'

'The blue? It doesn't look like very much.'

'It doesn't. But you're not used to the scale, Calen. That blue band is actually bigger than the total current living space of Attunga.'

Wirrin's mind battled to take it all in. It made the whole Warrakan project even more astonishing, but somehow also more real.

Burilda zoomed to a darker blue section of the band till it resolved into a representation of buildings and water. 'This is where the pod will settle three years from now. Picofactories will operate on that section, then steadily grow to construct the rest of the level during the next twenty years.'

'Can they do all that in twenty years? It's taken fifty-five years to build Attunga and it's nowhere near as big.'

'With help from the AIs our scientists and engineers can choose any time frame they like, Wirrin, just by programming enough picobots. It's easier with Warrakan because they don't have to transport in all the raw materials, but once that first section is finished the picobots will concentrate on growing the reinforcement structure for the whole asteroid so there aren't any problems when it starts to travel.'

The whole asteroid! Wirrin had an image in his mind of the trillions upon trillions of picobots working in teams to eat away the nickel-iron mass of the asteroid, process it into special reinforcement material, and grow the huge girders that would be needed.

'What about water for the dolphins? They'll need huge amounts.'

'Water's no problem, Calen. You know it's just oxygen and hydrogen combined so it can easily be manufactured. But there's no need for that, since with a bit of searching we can collect it ready made.'

'Ice asteroids? The same as we use for Attunga?'

'That's right, Thom. It will just require larger ones. As the dolphin level is hollowed out, the water will be processed with salt and other necessary trace elements and transferred in when each reach is ready for it.' Burilda's face lit up. 'It's all very exciting and I'll be transferring to Warrakan with the pod when it goes, so if you decide to commit we'll be seeing a lot more of each other.'

*   *   *

'What did you think of Turaku?' Wirrin said, as the trio lazed around in their living space.

'He was good. He felt like Gulara except more official.'

'He freaked me at the start. It was like he was a mind reader,' Calen said.

'What do you mean?'

'Didn't you notice? Just before we went into the meeting room I asked Burilda if someone would take my place with Sonic, and Turaku answered that straight after his greeting. I know he heard it through the safety vids but it still felt weird.'

The safety vids were the tiny surveillance devices embedded in every part of Attunga to help special AIs monitor security and safety. Many years ago there had been concerns about privacy but now no-one even thought about it; access to the data was strictly limited to Witnesses in

general, and mentors for their particular charges. Even Turaku probably only had access because the trio came under the umbrella of his
responsibility for the dolphins.

Wirrin thought back to their meeting. 'Hey, he did too. Wow, just
imagine. He can see every single thing we do if he wants to.'

'And everything every dolphin is doing, and all the dolphinarium
people too,' Calen said.

'And he's thinking about it — that's what gets me — all those different things at the same time. I wonder if it feels like our thinking?'

'It's different, Thom. It has to be,' Wirrin said.

'What did you think about all the AIs leaving K74, Thom?' Calen asked.

There was a grunt of disgust. 'Huh! I can't believe I liked that place.
It must be a real dump. I don't understand how it can function without
proper AIs.'

Wirrin and Calen had to smile at Thom's complete about-face.
Hearing about the AIs leaving had been amazing enough, but the last
straw for Thom was when Gulara went on to explain more about life on
K74, and in particular the treatment of trios — lack of treatment really
— which were not allowed to exist. The members were permanently
separated and mind-trained.

'And their attitude to trios. It's barbaric.' Thom scowled.

'It's still difficult even on Attunga. If we didn't have Gulara on our
side we wouldn't be registered,' Calen said.

Wirrin didn't agree. 'Attunga is just being cautious. You know most
trios fail because they aren't genuine — the trial time sorts them out
before they register. Unlike K74, Attunga respects everyone's rights
and beliefs as long as they don't hurt anyone. There's nothing to stop
people who think it's right for them.'

'I suppose so.'

'Did Gulara ever say why she waived our trial period?' Calen asked.

'Because we've lived like a trio all our lives,' said Wirrin.

Thom and Calen were surprised.

'Gulara said that? How come you didn't tell us?'

'I thought she'd told you herself. She's watched us do everything
together ever since way back in nursery. She said we've looked after
each other and played and learnt together more than any new trio
could, and there's never been any sign that we might separate, and in
the last couple of years we've been closer than ever.'

That was all true and they knew it, but hearing it still made them smile.

*   *   *

He looked like a young guy of their own age but it quickly became apparent that he was one of the semi-intelligent electronic systems that were the normal interface between people and general services on Attunga.

'I am Wanna, the planning assistant for your shared living space. Construction is scheduled to start in two weeks and at any time before that you may make changes or additions to your requirements.'

'Two weeks? We'll hardly have time to think about it.'

'There is a stipulation for urgency, with completion expected in three weeks.'

'Why so fast?' said Thom. They'd expected a month or more at least to work out a design they all liked.

'I don't think we'll be ready,' said Calen. 'We've talked about it, but not seriously.'

'Explain your ideas and I'll show you some ways to make them work.'

Thom jumped up. 'Wirrin needs an IT room with access to every database on Attunga, and a double-sized drawing board for his sketches, and benches for his projects so he doesn't have to cover the lounge-room floor with electronics.'

Wirrin laughed. 'You wombat! We'd need ten times as much space for all that.'

'It can't hurt to ask. I want a greenhouse with a level-three organics kit so I can grow natural food — I can get stock from the heritage seed bank — and a double-size wall display to watch what's happening in the reach.'

Wirrin and Calen gawked at him. 'Double? That will fill most of the wall. It'll be great for gaming, but isn't it too big?'

'No — the bigger the better … Can we get one that size, Wanna?'

'Certainly. I will note it as a special requirement.'

Thom's looked at Calen as if he couldn't quite believe his luck. 'See. All you have to do is ask … Except for a menagerie. That's too much.' He turned to Wanna again. 'Isn't it?'

'A menagerie would need more space than you have available, unless you sacrifice your indoor swimming pool.'

An hour later Wanna displayed a dozen holo models of the plans they were assembling, shifting elements about and incorporating everything they thought they needed and wanted, as well as a few extras he'd tactfully suggested. He left them with a huge list to consider before their next meeting in three days' time.

'It's like a palace,' Calen said, his eyes alight.

'What's a palace?' Thom wanted to know.

'It's a special building where rulers of countries used to live. There are some still preserved on Earth at heritage sites.'

'This is better than any palace. I bet they didn't have grav-beds or a maxi interactive display wall, or some of the other stuff we're getting. Look at this list. Nearly everything on it is amazing,' said Thom, 'apart from the boring bits — storage, utility space, laundry.'

Thom loved stuff — they all did. Wirrin brought up the list of ideas and started scrolling through it.

'Will we work on it now or give it time to sink in?'

'Let's go to the dolphinarium and check out the site. We can use our skimmers first. I want to show Sonic and Puck.'

Wanna had explained that their living space would be built beside Puck's territorial reach with an indoor pool giving them, and the dolphins, direct access to each other. Dolphins in their home? The very thought of it set Calen laughing with joy — their trio was likely to grow in ways none of them could predict.

*   *   *

The three water skimmers moved steadily along the reach with Puck, Sonic, Flute and six other pod members following in their wake. Even though Sonic could reach 20 kilometres per hour for a short burst, his travelling speed over any distance was much slower.

Wirrin loved being on the water almost as much as Calen. The adult dolphins, bored by the pace, tail-walked, leapt, somersaulted, gambolled and swam in intricate patterns.

At their living space site there was still nothing to see, apart from the usual access space beside the reach and a featureless 6 metre high wall of construction material extending in both directions, but it was still interesting to picture what it would look like.

They docked the water skimmers and Calen pulled on his facemask and plunged into the water. Wirrin and Thom quickly followed.

Sonic was resting against Calen and enjoying a stomach rub, something he loved. Apparently human hands were more effective than a dolphin beak. There was a burst of dolphin noise and all the adults raced off — there was no hope of following. Something had caught their attention. Sonic uttered repetitive fluting notes, and Wirrin was experienced enough to recognise them as excitement. Calen would have a more subtle understanding of the little dolphin.

The reach was quite shallow here, and below them, seagrass fronds moved slowly in the slight currents caused by carefully calculated grav-field variations. Maybe the dolphins had sensed fish? Seagrass beds were important feeding places for the wide variety of marine life in the reaches. The AIs carefully maintained and monitored the entire ecosystem, ensuring that balance was maintained. One of the adults swooped back, gave a burst of sound, then swerved away. Sonic responded and, giving Calen a quick nudge, set off to follow the pod. A few moments later the three friends watched as, one at a time, the dolphins darted into the school of fish they were herding.

Puck loomed close and after a quick exchange Sonic rushed to the milling throng of fish. It took the baby dolphin a number of tries but eventually he managed a catch one of his own and then, holding it in his beak, he made a circuit of the adults and swam up to Calen. Calen seemed to understand straight away that the fish was for him and somehow managed to grip the thrashing body. The three friends exchanged glances. This event felt momentous.

* * *

'He should have given it to Puck or Flute. It was his first fish ever,' Calen said.

'Did he expect you to eat it?' said Thom.

Calen laughed. 'Of course not. It was a special gift. He knows I couldn't eat anything with my mask on, and he also knows I don't eat raw fish. And he can't eat till his teeth come through.'

'How long is that?'

'A couple more months ...'

Puck did end up with the fish. She'd watched the exchange closely then, with a deft snap, she swallowed the fish before leading Sonic back for more hunting practice.

'It didn't take him long to catch it,' Thom said.

'He's so clever,' said Calen ... 'Wow! He gave me his first fish.'

Chapter 6

Wirrin gave Thom and Calen his best reassuring smile and felt good when it was returned. Nervousness and excitement battled within him. They were all keenly anticipating their implants, but it was still daunting. Even standard InterWeb wouldn't normally be available as an implant for at least another ten years but Turaku had fast-tracked everything and these purpose-built implants were so advanced, Wirrin could hardly believe they were getting them. After the meeting with Turaku, Gulara had explained it all and then they'd had three months of special training to prepare for this day.

A door slid open and Gulara came in with their supervising doctor. Wirrin breathed a sigh of relief. It was great to know she was here for them.

'How's it going, Thom? Butterflies all under control?'

Thom laughed. 'Wirrin's the one with butterflies in his stomach. He didn't eat any breakfast this morning.'

'Ha, very funny.' None of them had. Implants were inserted on an empty stomach.

'Well, I'm sure there'll be a nice lunch tomorrow when we wake up.'

The doctor shook his head. 'No food till all the tests are done. At least three more days.' His grin showed he was kidding, but Thom missed it.

'Three days! Really?'

'No, not really. After you wake up we'll monitor you closely but you can eat whatever you like.'

He led the way to the treatment room and indicated three comfortable-looking examination tables.

'Okay boys, do you know what to do?'

More kidding around. They'd been here two days earlier for final tests and instructions.

Wirrin slipped his shirt off, settled himself on the middle bench and placed his head inside the containment cradle.

'Ready for that food?'

Wirrin wondered why he said that, wondered where the three extra people standing beside his table had suddenly appeared from and then realised that his treatment must be finished.

'Is it tomorrow?'

'Not really. We don't know how to do that, but yes, you have been here for twenty hours. How are you feeling?'

The import of the question sent Wirrin's mind racing. He thought for a moment, looked round, considered, then stared at the doctor.

'I don't feel any different.'

The doctor nodded.

'Good. That's exactly how you should feel. Let's try your InterWeb connection first ... Set your holo display going.'

Wirrin gave the finger squeeze that activated his holo ring then quickly changed his standard-setting so the display didn't overlap the doctor.

'That's it. Now remember your training and subvocalise your input.'

'What will I get it to do?'

'Anything ... something simple ... call up a schematic of the TransCom system.'

When he'd been training in a simulator, subvocalising required a great deal of concentration so Wirrin settled his mind and tried with 'transcom', 'portals', 'schematic', and 'image'. It worked! A glowing 3D representation appeared in the space between himself and the doctor.

'Zoom it.'

From habit Wirrin moved his hand then blushed and switched to the new mode. The doctor looked to the display one of the technicians was using and gave a pleased nod.

'That's excellent. Now switch to retinal image.'

Wirrin subvocalised the command and the hologram flickered. It took a moment to register, but then he felt a thrill of excitement. 'Everything is clearer. It looks totally real.'

'Close your eyes.'

The image remained and Wirrin grasped just how different this was from a hologram. He opened his eyes and tried to look at the doctor. It was quite disconcerting because the image was too strong to see through, but then he steadied himself and remembered the options from his training.

Turn the image off.

Refocus.

Change the transparency and switch to holo mode. He tried the transparency command and after a quick trial had the doctor's face clear with the schematic as a faint overlay.

'What did you just do?'

'I couldn't see you so I tried transparency to get the level right.'

'Transparency mode? Are you feeling disoriented?'

'No, it's just like looking at someone through a half-strength holo.'

'Well, that's impressive … Switch back to holo so we can all see what you're seeing.'

The technician took over and Wirrin spent the next half hour testing his InterWeb implants as everyone around him looked more and more pleased with each new result.

* * *

'Does it feel any different, Galah head?' Calen said. They'd just arrived back at their living space after hours of testing, instruction and demonstrations.

'Galah head yourself! I'm not sure. I think so, but maybe it's just because I know it's different,' Wirrin replied, gazing out over the still waters of the reach. He still wasn't used to that view.

'Me too,' said Thom.

Calen was feeling sections of his skull, trying to detect the five extra millimetres that had been added by the implants. In reality none of them could notice any difference in the size of their heads. Wirrin put up holo images showing where the changes for each of them had been made, and then had fun making them bald and superimposing before and after shots to show the slight increase in size.

'Hey, Calen, 79438216958.'

'What?' said Calen.

'Say it back to me.'

'Okay — 79438216958.'

They exchanged glances and looked at Thom.

'All right — 79438216958.'

'It's strange isn't it?' Calen said. 'My memory doesn't feel any different either and it keeps surprising me that I'm right.'

This number recall proved to them that their memories had been enhanced — they could all consistently and reliably remember a string of ten or eleven numbers, a jump from their previous six or seven.

'Go on, Calen. Say something in dolphin.'

Calen's implants were special: he now had the ability to produce the sounds dolphins used to communicate. There was a soft cascade of clicks and chirps and Wirrin and Thom stared in amazement. Calen looked very pleased with himself.

'What did you say?' asked Wirrin.

'Hello, Sonic — well, I hope that's what I said. Hang on while I check.'

He concentrated for a few seconds then opened his eyes and shook his head. 'Hullo, Sonique.' Then he repeated the clicks and chirps.

'Was that different? It sounded exactly the same to me,' Thom said.

'It was different. It was better, but I know Sonic's going to laugh when he hears me.'

Sonic didn't actually laugh but they knew what he meant.

'How did you check?'

'My implant's got a database containing every Attunga dolphin. I watched the way Puck said it and copied her.'

'Watched?' Wirrin asked.

'It makes me feel dizzy but it's one of my rules: dolphins have body language and they expect me to learn that as well.'

He must be referring to the retina mode, Wirrin thought. 'Can you show us on your holo?'

'Sure.'

The image of Puck appeared and she made the sounds. Calen copied her. Once again Wirrin couldn't tell the difference. Thom looked toward the pool.

'Are you going to talk to them today?'

'If they turn up, but Burilda told them I mightn't be ready till tomorrow.'

'What will you say?'

'Not much. I only know about ten sounds and it will take a while to build my vocabulary. I have to practise like crazy.'

*   *   *

Wirrin floated lazily in their pool, listening to Calen and Sonic talking to each other and thinking the sounds were almost like music. They'd spent the day at the dolphin habitat on Warrakan, and Calen was explaining the progress he'd seen, excitement radiating from him. Up-to-date information on progress at Warrakan was available through the InterWeb, but everything had come to life today when they'd seen it for themselves.

Wirrin laughed when Sonic did one of his triple body rolls and nudged Calen's stomach. It meant he was excited too, and Wirrin wondered which part of the day Calen was describing. Probably their trip on the main reach.

Just getting there had been a thrill.

Thom's love of speed and motion had started him on a long course of study to learn how to control the mobile units used in free space outside Attunga. He couldn't put much time into it as his organics training was so full on, but for several months now he'd been authorised to control some of the smaller units, and today he'd taken them to Warrakan in a personal transporter. He was always raving about what a blast everything was so when he'd said they were going to have the ride of their lives they hadn't taken much notice till he shot away from the docking bay at a full 2G. Thirty seconds later stars raced across the display screen as he pushed the thrusters in a 180 degree loop so they could face Attunga. Wirrin gasped and Calen whooped with amazement while Thom grinned his delight.

'How did you like that?'

'You maniac!'

'That was 2G. Wait till I show you 8G.'

'No you won't. That's too much. Even I know that.'

'Don't worry. I'll set the grav-field compensation so we never feel more than 2G.'

'Aren't we too close to Attunga?'

'Don't you think I know what I'm doing?'

'Trying to freak us out.'

Thom's grin widened, and for the next half hour he'd done exactly that, with great gusto.

Later, zipping along on skimmers, Burilda had shown them the whole length of the reach — already ten times longer than Attunga's largest reach — as well as the deeper sections with reefs and underwater caverns. Now and then she'd call a halt to show them how the tiny marine life forms that would build a healthy ecosystem were flourishing.

* * *

'What did you just tell him?' Wirrin could recognise quite a few dolphin sounds but not when they were part of a rapid conversation.

'How the seagrass has started growing, which means fish can be introduced in a few months. He's keen to see for himself.'

'And could we arrange that?'

'I suppose so. When the dolphins ask for something it always happens.'

There was another quick interchange between Calen and Sonic.

'He says to contact Burilda and organise it in the next few days.'

'He does? Wow!'

'And he wants to see the ice asteroids too.'

Watching an ice asteroid being manoeuvred into position beside Warrakan had been one of the day's highlights.

Wirrin started to connect to Burilda and then hesitated. 'Can he wait till next activity day? I've got special stuff happening till then.'

Sonic flicked his tail and a great slice of water hit Wirrin in the face. 'Wh-what was that for?'

Calen shook his head, grinning. 'You know how much he loves a joke.'

'But he splashed me before you asked him.'

'He understands human speech; he just can't speak it.

Wirrin lunged at Sonic and lay across him, waiting for an eruption. When Sonic was in a playful mood, which was most of the time, anything could happen. At eight months old, and nearly a metre and a half in length, he was as big as any of them but his strength was amazing. Luckily he'd learnt very quickly how much rough stuff they could bear.

Nothing happened. Sonic loved to be touched so that must be repressing his urge to play.

'He understands us? When did he learn that?'

'He's known lots of words for ages but three or four weeks ago he started understanding easy sentences and since then he's been really working hard to improve.'

Wirrin was astonished. Even Puck, who was the most advanced dolphin and also the best at communicating, had to work hard to understand complex sentences.

'In only four weeks? That's impossible.' A shiver of awe ran through Wirrin and he let go so he could look into Sonic's eyes. What was going on in there? What must it be like to be able to learn like that?

'How come you never told us?'

'I wanted to but he said he wasn't ready.'

'So does he understand everything we say now?'

'Well I think so, mostly, but I'm not a mind reader. Ask him.'

'He can't answer—hey! He just winked at me. How did he do that?'

Calen laughed. 'It's a dolphin wink. He flicks his operculum over the iris. In bright light, dolphins can close a sort of "lid" to protect the iris. It leaves two slit pupils. We think it allows clearer vision.'

Sonic did it again and Wirrin gawked at Calen.

There was a quick exchange in dolphin talk between Calen and Sonic, then Calen said, 'He saw you wink at Thom last week and asked Burilda what it meant.'

'Burilda knows he can understand us?'

'Of course she does. Turaku told her straight away.'

'But he's so young. The other dolphins are more than two years old before they even start with the translators.'

'I know. He's special.'

There was a burst of sound from Sonic and Calen grabbed a mask. 'We're heading to the reach for a while so see what you can organise with Burilda … And next activity day is perfect.'

Wirrin watched the two leave their pool through the opening to the outer reach then connected to Burilda. He preferred retina mode nowadays — it was better than a holo — and now that he'd become so proficient it was much faster.

'Hi, Wirrin. What's up?' She must be wondering because it was only an hour since they'd parted.

'Nothing really, except Sonic wants to go to Warrakan next activity day and see the new reach for himself.'

'Turaku has already arranged it. It's quite a big deal.'

When an AI wanted something to happen, it did, but still, it was quite disconcerting. Less than a minute had passed since Calen had voiced Sonic's request. Well, Turaku did monitor everything to do with the dolphins, and AI time was very different to human time.

'And he winked at me.'

'Did he get it right? I mean, was it appropriate?'

'Yes, it was spot on. He told me he knew what I said.'

'Did he? Well, now that's in the open it means he's officially made history again.'

'What do you mean?'

'In about a month there's another meeting at the dolphinarium viewing gallery and scientists are coming from all over Attunga to talk to Calen and Sonic. It's history in the making.'

Wirrin was stunned. This was bigger than any of them had imagined. 'Burilda, he's smarter than any of us.'

'That's a surprise? I thought you'd known that all along.'

'Yes, but winking made it real.'

'Well, there'll be a lot more surprises in the next few years. He's still only little, both physically and mentally.'

'Physically? Is his body different too? Calen's never said anything about that.'

'Not really, but his growth pattern does indicate he'll end up close to 5 metres in length by the time he's thirteen years old.'

'Five! That's enormous.' The biggest male dolphins in the dolphinarium reached just 4 metres. Wirrin hadn't had much contact with them — they kept to themselves most of the time, and showed less interest in the humans.

'Yes, he's going to be very impressive.' Burilda signed off with a cheerful farewell and Wirrin flashed an image of Sonic, scaled it up to 5 metres and superimposed it on the pool. Good grief! They'd have to enlarge the pool or he'd be cramped. Next Wirrin imaged one of the dolphin transport units Sonic and Puck would be using. They were rarely used because the dolphins didn't like them. In this case Sonic's curiosity must be overriding Puck's reluctance; Sonic was still suckling and they were never apart for more than a few minutes. He was eating fish now that his teeth were growing, but only small ones, and Puck would still be providing milk for another year.

*   *   *

When Calen and Sonic returned, Calen was worn out, despite the protein structure Thom had designed for him. It worked well, and with all the time he and Sonic spent together, his water skills had improved so much he could leave Wirrin and Thom feeling slow and clumsy in the water. Even so, he'd never match a dolphin's skills and trying to keep up was hard work. Sonic played for a while and Wirrin couldn't help talking to him, despite the frustration of having to have Calen translate everything. Then, with a burst of sound and a quick nudge against Calen's chest, he flipped underwater and disappeared.

'Was it something I said?' Wirrin was only half joking.

'Puck called him.' Calen left the pool, dried himself off then went and flopped on his grav-bed.

'What's it feel like being famous?' Wirrin said.

'I'm not famous.'

'You're the first person who can speak to dolphins and Sonic's the first dolphin who can understand people without a translator.'

'That's all Sonic. Not me.'

'It's both of you because you're a team, and in a couple of weeks everyone on Attunga will know.'

Calen's head jerked round.

'What do you mean?'

'Remember what Burilda said? It's history in the making, and there'll be hundreds of millions of people watching what happens.'

Chapter 7

'We're going in that?'

Burilda and the boys were watching the transport units for Puck, Sonic and Flute being ferried to a space vehicle which dwarfed the transport they were used to. Thom was disappointed to discover that he wouldn't be able to pilot the transport, but the spectacle of this 200 metre ship had them gaping.

'Yes, Thom. Turaku is taking no chances with Sonic so the security AIs on Attunga and Warrakan are running the expedition today.'

That was even more startling. Security AIs were almost legendary in their abilities and the Attunga ones were the most advanced in the whole solar system. At least that was Wirrin's understanding.

'Security AIs? That doesn't sound good, Burilda. What are they worried about?'

'K74 is only seven light seconds away and they continually send surveillance drones. If Sonic was in a regular transporter it would be an open book to them, and there has recently been an increase in activity and interest about enhanced intelligence, in particular with dolphins. Turaku says that Freedom had its firewalls breached and information about Attunga dolphins was disseminated amongst the directed habitats.'

Freedom was a habitat much like Attunga, though not nearly as advanced, which had just made a start on a dolphin project of its own, and much of the Attunga knowledge had been shared with them. Wirrin's interest was piqued.

'They got into Freedom's restricted databanks?'

'Not for long, but according to Turaku it was enough to understand how well our dolphins can communicate.'

Wirrin was shocked. Understanding how the InterWeb worked and the type of protections involved for habitats was the whole thrust of his training and he knew how difficult they were to circumvent.

'Does Turaku think they found out anything about Sonic?'

'They didn't. That's definite. And they won't find out about his developing abilities either, because after this intrusion we're restricting that knowledge to Attunga and Warrakan.'

Thom interrupted, looking puzzled. 'What is that ship? I thought I knew every type on Attunga and it's not one of them, and the search I did came up with nothing at all.'

Burilda shook her head and Thom turned to Wirrin.

'Try a search. You're way better than me.'

Thinking Thom might have made some simple mistake Wirrin fixed the image he was seeing and connected it with a basic search program from the InterWeb. Nothing happened, so he applied a more sophisticated search engine.

First Level security. Limited access granted.

Wow, this was exciting. Turaku must have just given him access. Wirrin used his holo screen so the others could see what was happening and when a set of pointers appeared he quickly scanned them.

'It's an overview, Thom. It won't tell us everything.'

For the next ten minutes it told them enough to set Thom's mind spinning.

'They can't do that!'

'Can't do what?'

'Accelerate so fast. Our training course says grav-compensators can only cope with 14G and this thing can reach 21G.'

Wirrin thought back to the excitement just six days ago when Thom put the personal transporter through its paces for them at 8G and his mind boggled. A quick calculation showed that after one minute, 21G meant you were travelling at over 12 kilometres every second.

'Well, that's what it says, Thom. It must be able to do it.'

It made Wirrin wonder what capabilities and discoveries might be hidden behind the security walls. Gulara arrived and they headed for the boarding ferry. Now they'd find out for themselves.

Calen had left early to accompany the three dolphins and Wirrin tried a quick link to see what he was doing.

No link! That was a shock and Wirrin didn't like it. He couldn't ever remember a time when he couldn't contact Calen or Thom.

'Gulara, there's no InterWeb to Calen.'

'Once we're on board and inside the security bubble the InterWeb will function normally for you again … Can you wait that long?'

Since they were on the boarding ferry that meant a couple of minutes at the most, but Wirrin couldn't wait and kept trying his links. It was puzzling because, instead of a message saying the links weren't available, the InterWeb was responding as if they didn't even exist.

As soon as they passed the gravity warning and entered the big ship Wirrin tried again, with retinal image mode so he didn't look so impatient. The image of Calen in the transport unit with the dolphins appeared seamlessly and Wirrin relaxed. The water in the unit was chest high, enough to give the dolphins comfortable clearance, and Calen was between Sonic and Flute looking at a real-time display unit.

'You're checking Calen?' Gulara said.

'Yes, and Sonic looks really excited.'

There was a momentary pause, as Gulara linked in to see for herself.

'How can you tell?' Gulara turned to the ranger.

It felt strange having Gulara asking Burilda questions — she always seemed to know everything.

'They can figure dolphin body language better than I can, Gulara. They've picked it up from Calen.'

Wirrin and Thom exchanged a glance. Better than Burilda?

Burilda crossed to a TransCom portal and a few seconds later the group reached a room where a number of people were seated comfortably before a large viewing screen. The main image was of deep space, with Warrakan as the focus, but there were sub-windows round the periphery. Several were obvious — a view of Attunga, and the dolphin transport unit — but most of them had displays that would need explaining.

There was a shimmer of light as Turaku appeared.

'Welcome to my place.'

Everyone acknowledged the ancient greeting and Turaku indicated the big screen. Warrakan was moving, which meant they were on their way. Except it was sliding sideways and not getting any closer.

'Sonic wants to look round so we're doing a circuit of Attunga first.'

That was interesting in itself. The dolphins loved exploring their watery environment but had little interest in what lay beyond, so this was another difference showing up in Sonic. Turaku appeared to be watching the big screen intently, which cued Wirrin that there must be a reason. The AI could gather information through any sensor connected with Attunga, so what was he looking for?

'Security display.'

Attunga and Warrakan shrank in size, and hundreds upon hundreds of scattered pinpoints of orange light appeared.

'Those are the surveillance drones you were interested in, Wirrin, from K74. Their numbers have increased rapidly since the Freedom intrusion.'

Wirrin took in the scene, shocked by the numbers.

'Most of them are centred around Warrakan?'

'Yes. It's the newest development in the solar system and they're very interested in the big drives being installed. They also probe every vessel that docks there.'

'Do you know what they're looking for?'

'Everything and anything they can find out.'

Wirrin thought about what had happened at Freedom and a strong feeling of revulsion boiled up at these machines and their spying.

'Why don't the security AIs stop them?'

'They're harmless to all intents and purposes. They see what we want them to see and taking action against them would only escalate problems with K74,' Turaku answered.

Wirrin had another thought.

'If they can't probe this ship they'll think it's got a secret of some kind, won't they?'

'This ship doesn't even exist for them unless they get closer than 2 kilometres, and then it just registers as an anomaly.'

Wirrin was puzzled.

'They must have cameras, Turaku. If they were that close they'd be able to see us easily.'

'That's correct. We substitute the data in their transmissions with the visual signal they'd receive if we weren't here.'

Wirrin smiled. There wasn't much to worry about from a spy device that sent back whatever information it was given. With that ability Attunga really was way ahead of K74.

Wirrin watched all the lights and, when the screen returned to normal view, wondered if he could access the security information for himself. With a few quick subvocalised commands the lights appeared in his retinal mode. This was really interesting. He tried scanning towards K74 to see how many more drones were coming. Hundreds. And ships as well?

'Turaku, what are those ships? The security shows two of them represented in red. Are they dangerous?'

'All habitats have defensive ships. That's only to be expected, but those two have destructive abilities and we're watching them closely.'

Wirrin focused his attention on the biggest and called for information. Atomics. Lasers. Lethal picobots …

'Lethal picobots? What does that mean?'

An image of the ship appeared on the general screen. Turaku must have brought it up so the others could follow the conversation. It certainly had their attention.

'It has picobots designed to infiltrate and destroy communication and control systems, as well as others that can attack physical life.'

It was a stark and shocking realisation for Wirrin. Nanobots had been used for similar purposes in the past, but those nightmare times were now barely remembered. Picobots, hugely advanced by comparison, would be far more dangerous.

'Don't be concerned. We can control them easily.'

'How far away is it?' From Burilda's expression this danger was completely new to her.

'Half an hour at least.'

'It looks big. What's the scale of it?' Thom asked.

Wirrin checked and then, wide eyed, said, 'It's nearly 500 metres. More than twice as big as this ship.'

Turaku raised a hand as if to quell everyone's dire thoughts.

'Its size is irrelevant. To all intents and purposes it's harmless. We could disable it in moments.'

'Why don't you? It shouldn't be coming here.'

'There's no need. It won't come past our prescribed limits.'

Gulara, who'd been rather quiet, spoke up. 'We're not at war, Thom. They're entitled to travel through free space.'

Wirrin thought for a moment. 'But something *is* happening isn't it? The break-in to Freedom, all these spy drones, dangerous ships heading towards us, and this special security for Sonic?'

A look passed between Gulara and Turaku and Wirrin knew they were communicating with each other.

'Very good, Wirrin. Yes, there has been a big change, and the Freedom incident was the trigger. It focused the directed habitats' attention on Attunga and Warrakan, in particular K74's because of its proximity. In the past they've largely ignored us as an insignificant, privileged oddity, but their failed attempts to find out what's happening with the dolphins has brought them to understand there's a lot more to us than they previously realised. There are difficult times ahead. Not so much for us I hope, but for the semi-directed habitats and particularly for Earth.'

'Insignificant? That's crazy. We're the best habitat there is.'

'We do have the best conditions and the most privileges, Thom. Our Witness system and advanced association with our AIs assure that, but we *are* insignificant in terms of population. Most space habitats are past the billion mark and all the planetary habitats dwarf that. What's the total population of the solar system, Wirrin?'

'Um … 430 billion people and growing quickly. The five open space habitats combined add up to 2.7 billion and Attunga is just past 0.8 billion.'

'Add Titania to the open habitats. We've been working with them for several years now, helping them adopt our open society.'

'Titania? There's a habitat way out there?'

Way out there was a good description. Titania was one of the moons of Uranus, several light hours away.

'There are six of them, Thom. The original Titania habitat and one on each of the major moons.'

Wirrin searched and displayed the information on a holo screen for everyone. Just as Gulara said, there was one space habitat and five moon-based structures.

'They started fifty years ago! And look at that. The moon habitats are all at least twice as big as Attunga but their total population is only 570 million.'

It was remarkable. With something like thirty times the space the population was less than Attunga's.

'You're very perspicacious, Wirrin.'

Wirrin liked that, coming from Gulara, and looked for any other interesting information.

'Two years ago, the space habitat had a population of 240 million but now it's only 50 million. I've never heard of a habitat going backwards.'

'The people have moved to the moons and the space habitat is developing into the third gestalt AI centre.'

'Third? Where are the other two? And what's an AI centre?'

'You get one guess, Thom.' Gulara's raised eyebrows could mean only one thing and Wirrin blurted it out.

'It's us! Attunga and Warrakan! We have to be.'

Clearly, Wirrin thought, special expeditions with Gulara and Turaku meant finding out fascinating new information.

'This is more First Level information, so keep it strictly amongst yourselves. The AIs are building duplicate centres containing all their important projects and expansions. When Warrakan departs, every individual AI will be sending a replica, and the three gestalt AIs will do the same.'

Wirrin had his own understanding of gestalt AIs, but since Turaku was manifest it was a good time to try for more information.

'Have you ever been in a gestalt, Turaku?'

'There are many levels of gestalt, Wirrin. At the moment I have strong links with four security AIs, two from Attunga and two from Warrakan. That gives me extra capabilities but there are limitations — those 50 kilometres slow down the processing of information we share. That's a simple gestalt and it happens millions of times every day. For example, I linked with Attunga's data AI a few seconds ago to access the latest update from an Earth database on dolphin activities. With a simple gestalt I keep my full sense of identity. In a deeper gestalt I don't just share information, I share some of the processing as well. The greater the amount of sharing, the more my self-awareness is modified, and for some AIs the capabilities that come with the deepest degree of sharing are more important than retaining identity. The Attunga gestalt includes 273 amalgamated AIs so far.'

Wirrin didn't know what to think. Just one AI could monitor every single person on Attunga for every second of the day. What would 273 of them joined together be able to do?

'Wow! It must be like a god!'

That set Gulara and Burilda smiling, and even Turaku looked amused.

'Hardly. It's bound by the same fundamental laws we all are, Thom.'

'Do you talk to it very much?'

'Non-stop at the information exchange level, but with less and less frequency the deeper the level of gestalt needed.'

'What sort of things do you use the really deep level for?' Thom was on fire with this. AIs were going to be the topic of conversation for days.

'Important decisions about Sonic and the dolphins, which might change priorities and processes for Attunga and Warrakan.'

'Is there a dolphin project on Titania?'

'Not yet, but there will be. Every open habitat will have one within five years.'

The mention of dolphins reminded Wirrin of an earlier question. 'What did you mean by difficult times on Earth?'

Gulara and Turaku conferred again. What now?

'Wirrin, do a search for recent dolphin events on Earth. Turaku has given you full access.' Gulara's voice was solemn.

Several seconds later Wirrin felt a lump develop in his throat as he looked at sixty-three dead dolphins, then another forty spread along the waterline of a sandy beach, clumped in sad groups with small waves lapping against their inert bodies. Thom looked stricken. Thank goodness Calen wasn't seeing this.

There was a report of a mystery sickness that had struck at two separate marine research centres. Dolphins all round the world were being monitored closely. Gulara was shaking her head slowly.

'Search deeper, Wirrin.'

Wirrin did then recoiled in horror. The mystery illness, according to a post-mortem study, was really an attack by picobots.

'Someone murdered them?'

'We've analysed the post-mortem results and there are striking similarities with the picobots on the K74 ships.'

Disbelief, anger and sadness warred within Wirrin till a comforting touch from Gulara helped him gather his wits.

'You think K74 might have had something to do with this?'

'It's very likely. We've sent alerts to every research station on Earth but haven't been able to reach them all.'

How was that possible? Wirrin could connect to anyone on Attunga as quickly as he could identify them.

'Why not?'

'Earth AIs are very constrained in the more directed areas.'

Well yes, that was right. Just like on K74 where the AIs were so constrained that they all left.

'How many?'

'Have a look.'

Wirrin used a sub window for a quick scan, stored the file in his memory implant then went to retinal mode.

Wow — 7643 marine research stations, their projects, their degree of involvement with dolphins and other information — it was all there. But 1540 stations, mostly in two major continental coastal areas, couldn't be reached.

'How much time do we have before we arrive at Warrakan?'

'Twenty minutes. Sonic is enjoying his sightseeing.'

Wirrin turned away so he could concentrate properly. It was no good trying to contact research stations himself; they were twenty-seven light minutes away and the Earth AIs would know how to do that better anyway. Yes, there it was. A sub-database with files on every contact attempt. Maybe he could find out more about the two attacks? A quick look at the sourcing code for the file in his implant showed it was a dolphin activities database, probably the one Turaku had already mentioned. Could he access it? Yes, and it was enormous. Search? No, that was the file Turaku had sent. Broaden the terms of reference? Yes that would do it.

Wirrin set up searches for all references to dolphins, picobots, the marine station locations and any travel associated with them.

He set up searches for any communications to the marine stations and for any references about non-human sentience.

Search after search he added, then combined cross-referencing engines with each search to note any links. All this he built into one coordinated task. He checked it through several times, then just before activating it, had another thought, and assigned correlators to process all the results from the searches and cross-references.

Task mode — Archival or direct-data?

Archival meant working with data stored on Attunga and would be very fast. Direct-data meant sending queries through the InterWeb to all the habitats and data centres in the solar system, and because of the time lapse for transmission, would take much longer.

Wirrin commanded both, then watched in amazement as a task profile built for both modes.

'That's a major task, Wirrin.'

Wirrin transferred to holo so the others would understand what Turaku meant. The archival approach showed a preliminary result in four minutes. That was an extraordinary amount of time in itself, but the other approach was saying six and half hours for preliminary results and fifty hours for ninety-five per cent completion.

'Why does it take so long, Turaku? It's twenty-seven minutes to Earth so double that and add-on a bit, and there should be something in an hour.'

'All your parameters were universal. In just one part of your task you've asked for a search of everything that's been said or documented by 400 billion people in the four weeks since the Freedom incident. All your results are then, of necessity, cross-referenced, and that's an order of magnitude even more complex. It's the correlators that will take the time though, and the way you've linked them in is very interesting.'

Wirrin watched the tasks initiate then flicked to see what Calen was doing. He was play wrestling with Sonic while Puck and Flute pressed against the sides of the transport unit to make room.

Thom gave him a nudge. 'What are we going to tell him?'

They'd tell Calen everything — Thom was really thinking about Sonic and the dolphins.

'Wait till we're back on Attunga, Thom. Puck and Flute already know. Sonic doesn't,' Burilda replied.

Warrakan loomed and one of the gigantic drive engines filled the general view screen. A quick link to Calen showed that playing was forgotten: Sonic's curiosity had taken over. The view changed as they moved toward the centre of Warrakan's rugged elliptical shape.

Wirrin forgot everything when the alert from the archival task arrived.

'Michael Hallen and Warren Clarke. There is a link between those two names and the marine research stations.'

Wirrin put the information on holo screen for the others and started reading.

'Turaku, who are they? There's hardly any information here.'

'Without your correlator idea there wouldn't be any at all. I've initiated a location search but it is likely that they are manufactured identities.'

Pleased that he'd discovered something new, and frustrated that there was a wait of over six hours for anything else, Wirrin scanned through other findings then turned his attention to the docking station. Once again they'd have to use ferries as the security ship wouldn't dock.

*   *   *

'Look at them go!'

Five skimmers raced erratically after the three exuberant dolphins as they barrelled through the water. They'd just explored one of the deep sections of the new reach, and according to Calen's translation, were excited by the deeper water — four times the depth of any on

Attunga. Sonic leapt nearly 2 metres in the air and moments later Puck and Flute followed in tight formation.

'Burilda, do you know where we're going?'

'To the closest seagrass bed. They know there aren't any fish but they want to have a look anyway.'

Wirrin kept glancing across at Gulara. It was strange to see her in this active setting, dressed in a formfitting silver water costume and obviously enjoying herself. She was not very skilled with the skimmer or in the water, but of course she hadn't had as much practice as the boys. She looked as fit as Burilda, which was interesting because, at eighty-three, she was more than twice as old.

Calen put on a burst of speed, levelled with the dolphins and reached across to grab Sonic's dorsal fin. Sonic bumped the side of the skimmer, trying to unbalance Calen and send him tumbling into the water. It was a game they played all the time and Calen rarely fell off, while Wirrin and Thom always did. Sonic knew the exact moment when his nudge would be most effective.

The seagrass was growing like crazy and Wirrin was surprised at the difference in just six days. With optimum conditions and no fish to graze on it, it could only flourish. Sonic darted to the edge of the seagrass where the depth increased and disappeared behind a thick clump of kelp. The trio chased after him with Calen effortlessly in the lead. The hiding, chasing game lasted for five minutes with Sonic making sure everyone almost caught him before he dodged and disappeared again. Gulara and Burilda joined in, but underwater like this, no-one could catch Sonic unless he let them. When Sonic sneaked behind Calen and prodded his backside, Wirrin laughed, releasing a cloud of bubbles. Calen whipped around and after a burst of sound from Sonic he pointed everyone to the surface.

'They're going to the end of the reach and back. They want to map it all in their minds.'

The boys slotted their masks into the retaining sockets on the skimmers to replenish their air supply. The trip would take hours, since this advanced section of reach was almost 11 kilometres long, and back on his skimmer Wirrin took the opportunity to check progress on the other dolphin works on Warrakan. Beyond the blocking wall at the end of this reach was the second enormous development of a 30 kilometre extension. It could hardly be called an extension because it was far more complex, with many more levels as well as an interlocking maze of parallel reaches.

Wow! Half a cubic kilometre had been hollowed out, reinforced and filled with water from the ice asteroids in the last week. The rate of work seemed to increase every time he looked. Wirrin called up the overall plan then, puzzled, manoeuvred next to Burilda.

'When did they change the plans?'

'Which plans?'

'All the plans … for the dolphins here on Warrakan.'

'There are modifications happening all the time.'

'This isn't a modification. It's a whole new plan.'

'What?'

Clearly, Burilda didn't know what he was talking about so Wirrin set up a holo with an overview of the project. Burilda nearly fell off her skimmer.

'Stop! Stop! Let me have a look at that.'

Wirrin stopped and everyone else circled back to see what was going on. The space allocated for the dolphin project was now five levels of Warrakan. Wirrin worked out later that it was more than three complete Attungas in volume.

'Look, Thom, there's a reach that's going to be half a kilometre deep … and another one devoted to growing corals. This is unbelievable. It's a marine paradise.'

After a quick sub-search Wirrin said, 'No wonder we didn't know about it. It was only set up fifteen minutes ago.'

Gulara nodded. 'Turaku and the Attunga gestalt initiated it. He's just informed me. The dolphin's reaction to this visit was the final spark for change.'

The dolphins had forged ahead so everyone zoomed along at 60 kilometres per hour to catch up. The dolphins and Calen chittered to each other, and Sonic flipped into the air, then the three of them approached Gulara and greeted her. They did the same for Burilda and then each of the trio. Sonic said something and Wirrin's holo activated. A large dolphin appeared, exchanged greetings with Sonic, Puck, and Flute, then dissolved from view.

'That was Turaku. Sonic asked for him so they could say thank you. He looks like that when he talks to the dolphins.'

It was rather startling. Wirrin knew about Turaku appearing as a dolphin because Calen had talked about it, but this was the first time he'd seen it for himself. He'd always had sole control of his holo too, so Turaku taking over like that was another surprise. The group moved off again and Wirrin spent the remainder of the journey in retinal mode with transparency, examining features of the new project so he could explain it all to Calen and Thom when they had some time at home.

'Are you using the InterWeb?' Thom said, leaning in towards Wirrin. 'While we're skimming?'

'Yep!'

'Well you're getting too good at it. I hope you fall over.'

Thom and Calen couldn't cope with transparency mode while they were moving — it made them too dizzy — but Wirrin was good at it, and getting better.

The scale of the new project started to sink in. This wasn't a new and extra large dolphinarium, it was a habitat, but for dolphins instead of people, with space for millions. Where would they all come from? Wirrin searched the project files for a timeline of dolphin population and quickly found it: just under double every ten years. In ten years the prediction was for almost one thousand dolphins, and over a million in 120 years. That was easy. Human populations grew much faster.

The group stopped at the end of the reach where a featureless barrier of reinforced construction material barred the way and, while Calen spoke with the dolphins, Wirrin looked for a way to get past it. There wasn't one, and a query on the InterWeb said it was currently off-limits for humans. Well of course it was. The energy levels from the rush of picobot activity would be way too dangerous.

'What are you looking for?' asked Thom.

'I thought we might be able to see something on the other side of the barrier but there's too much happening in there to be safe. It's the start of the 30 kilometre reach.'

'We'll see it soon enough won't we?'

'Let's see … um … in about six months, but it will only be dead water till the marine life gets going.'

'Has the new plan changed anything?'

That was an interesting thought and Wirrin quickly checked.

'No, it's practically the same as the last time we looked, except for new connections to other reaches … Hey, there *is* a change. It shows four other reaches connecting in and being finished at the same time.'

Sonic came close and said something too quickly for Wirrin to grasp, and Calen laughed at the puzzled looks. 'We've been here long enough,' he said. 'Sonic wants to do more exploring.'

The trip back along the reach was much slower, and the skimmers were abandoned every time the dolphins found something of particular interest — a couple of seagrass beds, an extensive artificial reef with kelp forests in the watery canyons, and a different set of reefs with a number of underwater caves.

The very last leg of the trip was different, short and fast, the dolphins setting a sustained pace of 15 kilometres per hour, spurred on by the thought of proper food at the staging area. No wonder they were hungry, after nearly five hours of constant activity. Wirrin felt distracted during this last burst on the skimmers; he'd had no results from the direct-data task but he couldn't help checking every few minutes, even though he knew it was pointless — an alert would let him know the instant anything arrived.

Just as the transport module came into view, with one end open so the dolphins could swim straight in, Wirrin's retinal mode flashed briefly as a warning. His holo activated and Turaku appeared, hovering over the water as if he was flying. Information flashed into view. Wirrin stopped. Without him doing anything a section of text appeared next to Turaku.

'Read it, Wirrin. I've brought up the most important findings for you.'

While Wirrin was reading, the other skimmers slowed, then seeing Turaku, rushed back to find out what was going on.

'What is it? Why did you stop out here?'

Calen was looking very puzzled indeed. 'What's wrong?'

'Calen, some dolphins on Earth have been hurt and there might be another attack.'

'Attack? Against dolphins?'

Wirrin had read the news while the others were gathering and felt sick in the stomach.

'The people who were linked to the first two attacks are now expected to make another one at Monkey Mia.'

Thom, Burilda, and Gulara registered shock; Calen looked totally bewildered. 'What do you mean? Tell me what's going on.'

Wirrin moved close enough to hold Calen's arm and carefully told him about the earlier attacks and how his search had come up with two names. The direct-data search had just confirmed the names and made a new link with Monkey Mia. The correlators predicted a new attack within twenty-four hours with a ninety per cent certainty that it was instigated by K74. Turaku held up one hand in that way of his that commanded attention.

'Calen, try not to worry. I sent requests to the two marine stations along with some detailed information that allowed them to better analyse what happened to their dolphins, and our health resources on Attunga have designed defensive picobots, which should provide complete protection. I know it's a shock that the attack will be against Monkey Mia, but with the warning Wirrin's work has given us, it's probably the best place for it to happen.'

Monkey Mia, in the north-west of the Australian continent, was very special for the Attunga dolphinarium as it was the birthplace of the original dolphins transported from Earth.

'Best? It's the worst. They're attacking Monkey Mia because of Attunga,' Thom said.

'It *is* the best place, Thom. Northern Australia has the most open life-style on Earth and our ties there are very strong. Because it's so open the attack can only be coming from the ocean. The Northern Australians will be horrified when they find out and when their AIs coordinate to use the information I've sent the dolphins will be protected. Calen, the dolphins are wondering where you are. Wirrin and Thom will explain everything back on Attunga.'

With a worried look, Calen zoomed off and Wirrin turned to Turaku to hear more.

'The unusual combination of methods you used has given us extreme-ly valuable information, Wirrin, and put us in a position of advantage. When my message reaches Earth twenty-two minutes from now, all the surface area within 100 kilometres of Monkey Mia will immediate-ly be placed under the highest level of surveillance. The airspace will be monitored out to 500 kilometres and the marine station at Monkey Mia itself alerted to the danger. Within four hours the waters of Shark Bay will be saturated with equipment that will allow us to watch the move-ment of any object with a cross-section greater than two millimetres.

'We're postulating the attacks will come from a device that homes in on each dolphin, attaches itself and then releases the picobots, and since we ourselves can't yet construct a device any smaller than four

mm to do that, it will be an adequate safety margin. Anything inimical will be captured or destroyed, and when any underwater or surface
vessel is identified as a source, the occupants will be taken into custody.'

'What if they get past the defences?'

Burilda had a good point.

'I'm confident they won't, but in the unlikely event they do, every
dolphin will be inoculated with our defensive picobots. I have a time
concern there, as the technology I've sent is new for the Australian AIs
and by the time they receive it, adapt their picofactories, build the picobots and transport and deliver them to each dolphin, nearly six hours
will have passed.'

Wirrin was amazed. All these things happening already when the
information had only arrived five minutes ago.

'Turaku, what if the correlators aren't right and they attack somewhere else?'

'That's not likely, but within twenty hours we can inoculate the
dolphins at any marine station that will cooperate. We don't have to
worry about wild dolphins. Only dolphins who have an association
with humans are being targeted. That's part of your report you haven't
looked at yet. Now, go and support Calen. He'll need you. He has to tell
Sonic what's happening.'

Chapter 8

An hour later everyone was gathered in a tech room at the dolphinarium, looking at images that were being beamed direct from Monkey Mia. In one window a small pod of dolphins was cruising serenely in the shallow waters near the marine station and in another a pair of males were hunting food on the eastern side of Shark Bay. Another section of the screen showed the position of over seven hundred dolphins in the bay and the adjoining Indian Ocean. There was a stunningly beautiful aerial view, which ten minutes earlier had zoomed to a group of basking tiger sharks, mortal enemies of dolphins, particularly when there were vulnerable new-born calves around. Now water-craft were converging from all directions on the research station.

'What's that?'

A new screen opened showing the approach of some sort of aerial craft. Turaku appeared as well.

'It's a transport from Carnarvon, Thom, with the surveillance equipment. Everything else is coming from Exmouth where there is a high level picofactory complex.'

A quick check showed Carnarvon 100 kilometres north of Shark Bay and Exmouth another 360 kilometres beyond that.

'The responses in Australia have been instant and they are moving as quickly as we could hope. Another forty minutes should see the arrival of the major consignment from Exmouth.'

Turaku disappeared and Wirrin headed off to join Calen.

Wirrin soon realised that Calen was handling everything very well. The rush to support him at the staging area had turned into a kind of anti-climax because Sonic had done the job for them. When they'd arrived the dolphins and Calen spoke rapidly for a time, and later, Calen explained what Sonic and the others had said.

'Sonic hates the attacks, but the dolphins all say Turaku will soon fix everything. Dolphins don't think like we do. I got the impression that dolphins don't dwell on painful subjects. Their minds were on the new reach and they were eager to see the other dolphins and tell them how good it is.'

'Really?' Wirrin was surprised. He'd thought the dolphins would be as distressed as he had been by the news.

'Yes. And he called me a worry wart.'

'A what?'

'It means someone who worries too much, but it sounded funny and I had to smile.'

Wirrin was amazed. 'How would he know a word like that?'

'He read it on an InterWeb dictionary. He's got a new game where he says unusual words to surprise me.'

Wirrin didn't know Sonic could use the InterWeb, let alone read.

'Do you think he said it on purpose to cheer you up?'

'Of course he did.'

'And he really didn't seem too concerned about the attacks?'

'I think I've got a lot to learn about dolphin minds and feelings,' Calen said carefully, and Wirrin let it drop.

It certainly seemed like the dolphins' judgement of Turaku's abilities was correct. For a while everyone watched the screens as information arrived from Monkey Mia, but when it didn't change much Wirrin started his own holo and called up archived information about the area and started exploring.

Shark Bay was beautiful, and ever since the planetary clean-up of ocean pollution had been completed over fifty years ago, marine life was flourishing. A satellite view showed islands, starkly contrasting blue water, red country and white shelly beaches.

'This place is amazing. There are nearly fifteen thousand dugongs there.'

'What's a dugong?'

'A mermaid.'

Thom laughed — Calen must be pulling his leg — then looked at him strangely when he saw Calen was serious.

'So?'

'Dugongs are mammals — find an image for him Wirrin — and when they feed their baby they swim upright and hold it against their teats with their flipper. Sailors thought they were women with tails.'

That was interesting. Trust Calen to know something like that. The image appeared and set Thom laughing.

'They thought those were women? Their faces look like an elephant with its trunk cut off.'

'The sailors might have been drinking alcohol, Thom, and you're cleverer than you think because they really are elephants. Well, they're in the same superorder.'

Wirrin found a clip of a dugong swimming and set it going.

'They're as big as dolphins.'

The clip finished and Wirrin shifted the view to the south of Monkey Mia where another interesting feature was highlighted.

Stromatolites? What are they? A command brought up a picture of some lumpy-looking rocks.

'Why are we looking at rocks?'

Calen nudged Thom in the ribs.

'Because they're alive.'

'Living rocks? What!'

'Thom, you need to do more biology studies. They're one of the first living things on Earth! They put oxygen into the atmosphere. We wouldn't be here if it wasn't for them. They're cyanobacteria, and they bind together sand which eventually forms rocks. Amazing.'

For a few minutes they watched an explanation about these stromatolites and everything Calen had said was correct.

The boys absorbed themselves in exploring the islands, beaches and bluffs, and Calen pointed out the familiar heritage animals — eagles, kangaroos, goannas, and pelicans. Wirrin's favourite was the echidna and they seemed to be everywhere.

Calen looked for his namesake, the sparrow-hawk, but they were very uncommon in the area.

'There's the big transporter,' Thom said.

They turned to the main viewing screen.

'What's it doing? Is it landing in the ocean?'

It was big, really big, and it did look like it was landing, which was a puzzle because it was still 90 kilometres away. Burilda must have been keeping up to date with Turaku because she had the answers.

'It's not landing. It's preparing for a drop of surveillance devices.'

The view moved closer and showed a smaller unit disengage from the big one, then another and another. A black mist trailed from the first smaller unit as it increased speed and headed south. The second smaller unit set a parallel course and started its own controlled release of surveillance devices. Twelve more units did the same, before the big transporter lifted and started speeding towards Monkey Mia. For the next hour the fourteen smaller transports systematically dropped their clouds of tiny devices, returning to the big transport several times to restock, till the total area of Shark Bay was covered. Wirrin brought up the data and turned to Thom because he liked big numbers.

'Look at that. There's nearly forty billion of them.'

'They made all those in half an hour?'

It did sound impossible. Wirrin looked for more information.

'It's a standard robotics picofactory, Thom, and this job took priority.'

'That's a standard factory? The advanced ones must be amazing.'

Wirrin had a general understanding of robotics but hadn't realised they were so capable and decided a study unit might be a good idea.

Data poured in from the minute surveillance devices as more and more were guided into position and came online. Every 90 metres there was a larger device in the water that controlled the behaviour of the smaller ones nearby. It gathered all the information they were sensing and retransmitted it to a receiver on the big transport craft at Monkey Mia for processing and storage.

'What are you smiling for Burilda?'

'The research centre there is going to be happy. They'll have a database like they've never seen before. How long will the system stay in place for them?'

'One week … And then everything is recalled and reclaimed.'

Wirrin thought about it. A database with forty billion units recording everything they were sensing in one of the planet's special marine areas. No wonder Burilda was smiling.

The main screen changed to a view of the whole area with hundreds of little markers dotted randomly across the ocean.

'It's the dolphin screen. It's showing the exact position of every single one of them.'

'How many?'

'Hmm, 784. See those green numbers near Monkey Mia? They're the targeted ones. The rest are wild.'

All the dolphins would have to be protected, as previous attacks had targeted without any discrimination. Monkey Mia worked closely with twenty-seven dolphins and not quite so closely with another forty-five.

'Burilda, we should eat as soon as we dock. There's an hour and a half before the craft from Exmouth arrives and after that we'll be keeping watch.'

Once they were back on Attunga, Burilda led the way to one of the dolphinarium food centres where Calen and Wirrin appointed Thom to do all the ordering because he had a knack for knowing what would taste best. Three-quarters of an hour later Gulara and Burilda were joining the chorus of appreciation when Gulara suddenly fell silent.

'We need to get back to the tech room.'

'Has something happened?'

'Yes, but not on Earth. Our Witnesses have been watching everything of course, but Akama wants to be involved first-hand and he's waiting for us.'

Everyone froze.

'Akama?' Calen's voice expressed the astonishment they all felt.

'Yes.'

Akama was the oldest Witness, the first Witness, and the most universally recognised person on Attunga, and the prospect of seeing him in person was not something Wirrin, Thom and Calen had ever even considered. They were stunned.

Gulara gave a reassuring smile. 'There's nothing to be nervous about. He's easy to talk to.'

'You've spoken to him?'

'Yes I have, Thom. Several times in conference but when I started my training we met personally, and he's contacted me a number of times recently.'

Conferencing meant by holo.

'Were the recent contacts about the dolphins?'

'And your trio.'

'Us?' That was a startling thought.

'Because of your association with Sonic of course, but he has a personal interest as well.'

Gulara led the way in quite a hurry and a couple of minutes later they re-entered the tech room. Wirrin's first impression was of distinctive white hair and ebony skin until Akama turned from the screen and smiled.

'Welcome to my place.'

Everyone responded, and Wirrin, caught by the strength of personality and rather awed, watched those dark eyes survey everyone in turn then settle on his own.

'Wirrin, the dark featured one. My brother returns.'

He moved close, extended his arm and rested his hand on Wirrin's head. Was it some kind of special greeting? Not knowing how he should respond, Wirrin stood, quietly wondering for five or six seconds, till Akama removed his hand. He moved to Gulara and in a formal, traditional greeting, they grasped each other's wrists.

'Gulara, introduce me to the rest of your companions.'

As Gulara said their names, Akama repeated the wrist clasp with Burilda, Thom and Calen and then, surprisingly, with Wirrin. The hand resting on his head must have been something different.

'So, I finally meet our notorious trio, our catalyst for change.'

Notorious? Finally? Catalyst? Wirrin's mind whirled as he tried to put meaning to the words. Well, he didn't mean anything bad, because the smile he had when he saw them first had brightened so much that everyone was smiling back.

'Calen, dolphin boy, tell me about Sonic. Is he really as friendly as all the reports say?'

Calen's eyes lit up and for the next five minutes he excitedly answered all the questions he was asked.

Wirrin watched. Akama was different. He looked old and that was very unusual, as most people preferred to keep themselves looking young. Akama brought Thom into the conversation, asking him about his organic studies and his interest in flying different craft, and then it was Wirrin's turn.

'Tell me about your gift for information technology. Have you always had it?'

'Um … it's not really a gift. I'm just interested and I've done lots of courses.'

Thom and Calen laughed.

'It's a gift, Akama. He was playing with databases before he even started Basic Training.'

Akama nodded. 'Yes, I'm sure it's a gift. To come up with an idea the AIs didn't consider must involve more than training and expertise.'

Wirrin started to say it was a fluke but on the big screen a yellow light was flashing in the Indian Ocean to the west of Shark Bay.

'What is it?'

Wirrin found the right link.

'There's a query about a sea-craft there. It seems legitimate but the

AIs are making a closer check because it's moving towards the northern end of Dirk Hartog Island.'

Dirk Hartog Island was a long thin island forming a natural barrier between the Indian Ocean and the waters surrounding Peron Peninsula, which in turn sheltered Shark Bay. At the northern end was Naturaliste Channel, and beyond that open water.

Wirrin scanned for more information. 'There are fifty-seven seacraft in the critical observation area. Thirty-five are in the bay and the rest are in the Indian Ocean. Most of them are regular or permanent but there are five vessels new to the area in the last twenty-four hours, and that includes the flashing one.'

The view changed and zoomed to an aircraft flying over. It was moving south to north and the data said it was a regular passenger flight. The view switched to a different aircraft, a large pleasure ship, and then back to the craft under investigation. The yellow light was no longer flashing.

'They're not querying that craft anymore and the others are standard checks on anything in the area.'

There was an exchange of looks as everyone relaxed.

'How long before the assistance from Exmouth arrives?' Akama asked.

Wirrin wondered briefly why, yet again, adults assumed he would be the one to access information.

'Twenty-six minutes. It's due to take off nine minutes from now.'

This was much more exact than the earlier forecasts.

'Seventeen minutes travel time for 430 kilometres? That's fast through an atmosphere.' Thom was in his element.

'It's going to be a spectacular trip. There'll be a sonic-boom and anyone in its path on the surface will wonder what's hit them.'

'They'll fly over the ocean and I'm sure they'll transmit a warning.' Gulara was making sense but Thom brought up an interesting point.

'If they transmit anything it might warn the wrong people.'

Akama spoke. 'You like the idea of help arriving on wings of thunder don't you, Thom? It's a striking image, which I rather like myself. I'm sure that all necessary precautions were taken and the aircraft has reached Monkey Mia.'

With a little mental jolt Wirrin realised Akama was right. Despite its seeming immediacy, everything they were seeing was really twenty-seven minutes in the past. It was quite reassuring to think that at this very moment the defensive picobots must have started a rush from Monkey Mia to the dolphins.

Akama turned to Burilda. 'How are our dolphins reacting to what's happening on Earth? I understand they know what's going on.'

'Much more positively than we are. Evidently they're confident that Turaku will fix everything. Calen understands them better than anyone and that's his interpretation.'

Calen nodded when Akama glanced at him for confirmation and then spent some time explaining the dolphin's different way of looking at things.

'Does Sonic fit the same pattern?'

'Yes and no. Basically he's the same, but sometimes I can tell he's modifying his natural instincts and I think it's because he understands so much more than the others. Sonic is very complicated and I never really know what he's going to surprise me with next. He's way smarter than I am.'

'He's smarter than all of us, and he'll stay that way unless we try a similar enhancement technique for ourselves. But what sort of things does he surprise you with?'

'Well, a couple of weeks ago he started reading, and last week he suddenly got interested in music.'

Akama looked thoughtful.

'Music? Do you mean dolphin music? I know they have communal sounds which fulfil similar functions to our music.'

'No, human music. He's known dolphin music since he was tiny.'

'Human music is a broad definition. What type of music does he like to listen to?'

'He loves it all. You should see how excited he gets with some of the more complex music — old classical pieces, jazz ...'

'And how interested is he? Does he spend much time on it?'

'He must. I'm only with him for one and a half hours each day and we've got too many things to fit in, but we use half an hour for music every time.'

Use? Wirrin wondered why Calen hadn't just said listen, but decided he'd ask later what he meant.

'Music currently involves more than fourteen hours of Sonic's day,' Burilda said. 'This behaviour, where he immerses himself till he reaches a level of competency and understanding that satisfies him, is one of his strongest patterns.'

'Fourteen hours? As much as that?'

'Six of those hours are passive listening, Honoured One, while he's alternating between left and right brain sleep.'

'Sonic is using sleep time to listen to music? I understand how left brain right brain sleep is a natural dolphin mechanism to prevent drowning, but does it let him remember what he's heard when he wakes up?'

The significance of Akama's question was just dawning on Wirrin when Burilda answered.

'Yes it does, except when he's logging.'

'Logging? I don't know that term.'

'It's the deepest form of dolphin sleep where one side of the brain is switched off and the other functions minimally. It's called logging because they often float in the one place with hardly any movement. The other form of sleep still switches off left brain and right brain alternately, but there is much more activity in the conscious side, with awareness of their environment and enough control for basic synchronised movement with other dolphins. Sonic's level of awareness has been improving recently and we think that will continue till he's just over two years old.'

'Does he ever seem lonely?'

Burilda and Calen looked at each other in surprise.

'Never. He acts like the happiest dolphin on Attunga. What do you think, Calen?'

'I think the same. Puck and Flute are always with him, the rest of the pod is never far away, and there's always interaction with the other pods as well.'

'I wasn't thinking of physical loneliness. He's unique in his abilities and has no like mind to meet with. The AIs are too different.'

The trio had talked about this a great deal so Wirrin knew what Calen would say.

'It's not an issue, Honoured One, and Sonic says it won't be. He understands how he's been enhanced and the possibility that something serious could go wrong. He says if it does then he won't know about it and it won't matter, and if it doesn't then it's only another four years till there are more dolphins like him.'

Akama smiled and rested a hand on Calen's shoulder.

'Forget the ceremonial address, Calen. We're gathered as a like-minded group to watch the resolution of a nasty situation and it's a delight for me to share this company. Now, if Sonic were a human I'd be reverencing him for his wisdom, but from what you've been saying a strong element of this viewpoint is part of his nature?'

'Yes, but he *is* wise too.'

'I wonder what he'll be like when he's an adult? Wirrin, bring up the Shark Bay area on your holo and move to Burringurrah country in the north-east.'

A holo of Shark Bay sprang into view and Wirrin quickly shifted the focus to the north-east. Burringurrah was unfamiliar to him, but it was clearly labelled and with a slight adjustment it was centred.

'Good. Change to topographical and zoom in on the river.'

The river was obvious, a big one flowing to Carnarvon on the coast.

'That's it. Now go to Gnardune Pool.'

Rich red sand bordered an expanse of clear water, with a scattering of gnarled and ruggedly striking trees stretching along the shore.

'It's beautiful isn't it? It's my place. I was born there 119 years ago.'

Everyone stared at the holo, now focused on one of the bigger trees, and Wirrin thought, surely Akama must mean somewhere nearby? There were no buildings.

'My people had a cultural centre there and we stayed for five weeks each year for traditional reasons. When I was seventeen the buildings were removed and we returned the whole area to its natural wild state.'

'You lived there? Under the open sky?'

'Yes, Thom. For that five weeks. The rest of the year we lived a normal life in underground communities like everyone else on the planet.'

'What's open sky like? … Is it scary? It is for me when I try it in virtual.'

'It's never scary. You don't even think about it till it's not there. It's wonderful.'

'What about lightning? You must have seen that too … Like Gulara?'

'Of course. I've seen all the weather we simulate in different ways on Attunga so people won't forget — rain, wind, thunder, lightning, hail, snow — and the effects of weather — floods, droughts, blizzards, cyclones, rainbows.

'I was nearly blown out of that very tree by a willy-willy when I was nine years old.'

'That same tree? Over one hundred years ago?'

'That tree has been there for more than six hundred years, Thom. It's a river red gum and since it's being well looked after it could be there for another six hundred.'

'And a willy-willy is some kind of wind?'

'Willy-willies are mischievous spirits that fly around the country pulling up trees and making clouds of dust.'

That was Gulara speaking and the look on her face meant she was remembering them herself.

'When we were children we also called them devils ... dust devils. They are really whirlwinds, like mini tornadoes or cyclones ... Call one up, Wirrin.'

A whirling cloud of dust and leaves appeared. Well, there was no real dust, leaves or moving air, but the holo was very impressive.

'That must have been scary.'

'No, it was exciting. I remember watching it dance away from me, out over the water, and wondering if it was alive.'

Wirrin had a picture in his mind of a wide-eyed dark little face and wiry little arms clinging to the tree, but couldn't fill in the rest of the picture.

'What did you wear?'

'Why do you ask?'

Feeling slightly awkward Wirrin said, 'With the tree right there I could see you in my mind hanging on to that big lumpy part. I imagined you wearing shorts like we did at that age and it didn't look right.'

'That lumpy part is called a burl and I hung on tight. Sometimes I did wear shorts; sometimes I wore nothing at all.'

While the boys digested this, Akama turned to Gulara. 'Did you live traditionally in your own country?'

'Not until I was fourteen and decided it was important, and then it was every year but I was so busy I could only manage a short time.'

'You understand what we mean by traditional living don't you, Wirrin?'

'Yes, we learnt about it in heritage studies but it's different for different areas isn't it?'

Akama nodded.

'My parents took it very seriously and when we stayed at Gnardune Pool we lived as close to the old ways as we could, hunting for natural food, learning our country, and taking our part in the Dreamtime.'

'Natural food? You mean growing in the ground?'

'And running round on top of it. I was very good at catching goannas.'

'You ate real animals?'

Thom was expressing the amazement of the whole trio. No-one on Attunga ate animals and any form of meat was grown directly in a protein factory.

'It was quite normal then, Thom, though respect for sentience was becoming more prevalent because of Second Level organics. One of my favourites was a big juicy moth larva, which used to burrow in the roots of acacia plants. They were called witchetty grubs and we ate them live as well as cooked.'

'Live?'

'Don't look so aghast, Calen. You're quite used to the idea.'

'I am?'

'Does it worry you when Sonic eats his food alive? I'm sure you don't think twice about it.'

Akama was right.

'Turn your holo off, Wirrin, and I'll share something with you to make your image of me in the tree more accurate.'

Akama's holo took over and showed a boy racing across red sand, running in the shallows with an exuberant spray of water leaping from every step, then sprawling head-first as the pool suddenly deepened. The view zoomed in to catch a gasp for breath, a shake of the head, and happy laughter, before cutting off abruptly when a handful of wet, red sand came flying towards the camera.

Another scene appeared in the old 2D medium, with Akama standing by a fire burning real wood, glowing with pleasure as he held up a dead goanna.

'I was so proud when I caught that fella that my father said we had to have a record. Watch how we cooked him.'

Wirrin knew from the heritage courses that food had been cooked like this in the past, but seeing Akama actually doing it made it real. He glanced at Calen to see his reaction to the dead goanna.

He looked strange … and so did Thom. They were sharing glances, looking from the little Akama to Akama now, to Wirrin and then back to the scene as the goanna was prepared over the fire. Wirrin too began to feel strange because he always had a good idea what the other two were thinking. Thom whispered something to Calen then turned to Akama.

'Are you playing a trick on us?'

Wirrin's puzzlement turned to shock. Thom must have gone crazy to question Akama like that. And Calen too. He seemed to be in full agreement.

'No tricks, Thom. That's me when I was ten years old.'

Thom and Calen exchanged another look which said they wanted to believe him but couldn't.

'But ... '

Trying to work out what was going on, Wirrin looked at the others. Burilda was puzzled, Gulara knew something, and Akama was smiling.

'Yes, Thom, we do look similar, but keep watching and the differences will stand out.'

The scene changed again and the younger Akama went running by, wearing a dark blue shirt and loose white shorts. This setting was somewhere away from Gnardune Pool, a beautiful green grassy area laid out for athletic events, with hundreds and hundreds of people watching. The camera panned across the lithe figures.

'I was thirteen then.'

Wirrin stared in bewilderment as he watched himself run in a place where he'd never been, in a time when he hadn't existed. He stared intently at the figure.

'That is amazing. You and Wirrin look different, but you still run the same way.'

Calen looked back and forth between Wirrin and Akama with a funny grin on his face. He said later that he was wondering if Wirrin was going to look like Akama in another hundred years.

'I loved running ... are you happy with your mind image now, Wirrin?'

Wirrin recalled the image and then nodded.

'Was leaving your clothes off part of the tradition?'

'It was for our family and particularly for children. We tried to match the old ways as closely as possible.'

'Which did you like best? The old way or ordinary living?'

'When I was little the old way was a special yearly holiday and it was never long enough. As a teen I stopped thinking in terms of which was better and thought of them rather as different facets of my life. Tell me what—'

Whatever Akama was about to ask was interrupted when blue lights

started flashing and everyone whirled to the big screen, where a large
air transport was landing at Shark Bay. Everyone watched, engrossed,
as a number of cargo bays opened and freight containers started
moving on their anti-grav-fields, lightly and purposefully, towards the
gathered fleet of aircraft and watercraft. Two minutes later everything
was on the move, the air vessels heading westwards across the peninsula towards the outer limits of the bay, and the watercraft going in all
directions on the eastern waters.

'They're in a hurry. What's happening with those skimmers?'

As if on call a section of the screen zoomed in on five skimmers
gathered round one of the freight containers. Modules were clamped
to each skimmer which accelerated away.

'Those are for the home dolphins. It should only take a few minutes
to reach them.'

One of the skimmers stopped and Wirrin wished there was some
way to look at it closely. It must be near a dolphin. A blue light flashed
on the big screen and Turaku's holo shimmered into view.

'Greetings, Honoured One. The first protective picobots are about to
make contact.'

'Thank you, Turaku. Do we have a time frame for full protection?'

'The target dolphins and others in the inner bay will all be reached
within five minutes, the dolphins in the Western Bay within eleven
minutes and all dolphins in the outer zone within nineteen minutes.
We'll display the contacts for you as they happen.'

The window with the dolphin markers expanded to almost full-
screen, and standing out was one blue marker.

'First contact. A dolphin named Squeak.'

Calen waved his arms in a gesture of triumph and the room lit up
with smiles.

'Is there a lag between contact with the dolphins and the picobots
becoming effective?'

'Yes, depending on what part of the body the mini-drone attaches to,
there is a lag of between twenty-one and twenty-seven seconds.'

While Akama and Turaku were talking, four more markers, all near
the marine station, changed from yellow to blue. Wirrin looked at the
number of yellow markers and the blue didn't look very impressive at all.
Another blue dot winked on and another dolphin was protected. Calen,
along with everyone else, was staring at the screen as if hypnotised,

watching and wondering where the next blue marker would light up. There were exclamations as six or seven more yellows changed to blue, and then everyone looked to Turaku when a green marker started moving away from the marine station.

'The air transport is moving to the outer boundaries of the bay to monitor the capture drones.'

'Capture drones? There were no capture drones in my warning report.'

'They didn't exist when your report was issued, Honoured One. With the strong link to K74 I had to cover the possibility that a modified form of their surveillance drones might be used for a stealth approach so I provided the Australian security AIs with a counter design. They were released as part of the airdrop and each dolphin now has a guardian.'

Wirrin thought back to Turaku's earlier information about the drones watching Attunga and Warrakan and felt really pleased. If any drones came near Shark Bay they wouldn't have a hope. Akama continued to question Turaku.

'What is the nature of the defence these guardians provide?'

'They can disable or destroy.'

'And is there any chance they might be eluded?'

'Yes, if a guardian encounters enough attackers, some will get past. The inoculation process should guard against that.'

'And when is the destroy capability deployed?'

'When the disable and capture function can't cope.'

'I understand. We need information.'

'Destruction could also involve a release of pollution.'

'Is it possible to see one of these guardians?'

The view on the big screen changed. A dolphin cruised through the clear water followed closely by a sleek tubular shape. It appeared to be roughly half a metre in length, much smaller than Wirrin was expecting.

'This is one of the home dolphins and as you can see she's adjusted to the presence of the guardian already. In the first few minutes the dolphins showed great interest in their new companions but that waned very quickly. Some of the younger dolphins are still treating them as playthings and trying hiding games but the rest mostly ignore them. The guardian sensors are linked to the surveillance devices, as well as being independent, and they'll stay on guard for as long as is necessary.'

'Why are we so certain this attack will come from the ocean, Turaku?'

'There is no absolute certainty but the probability is very high.'

The screen changed and showed three dolphins swimming at speed with three attendant guardians, then changed again to a group of two adults and a baby. Everyone watched while Turaku explained the workings of the drones. The overview map with the dolphin markers returned and Calen chuckled when he saw that there were now more blue markers than yellow.

'Tell me about your life as a trio.'

Wirrin was surprised by Akama's sudden change of topic, thought for a moment, then paused as Thom said, 'We love it.'

'That's obvious, Thom. I'm really asking about how you are received in the community and any problems you foresee for yourselves.'

'We haven't had any problems.'

Akama nodded. Wirrin wondered what he was thinking.

'What about Sonic and the other dolphins? You're the only trio they've ever had contact with.'

Calen responded. 'They know we're called a trio and what it means, but it's not unusual to them because dolphins spend most of their life in similar groups, especially male dolphins, who bond for life. They mostly think of us as a pod and Sonic even says he's part of ours, which makes us feel good.'

'Extraordinary, and quite wonderful. Burilda, what is the dolphin protocol for meeting with strangers?'

'Protocol? I don't know if they have one. They're always happy to meet people when we introduce them, but if they decide they're not interested they just swim away.'

'Is it difficult to meet Sonic?'

'Very. His life is so busy it's hard even for our staff to have much time with him.'

'I see.'

'Burilda, he would talk to Akama. We'll just tell him to.'

Burilda looked horrified and then embarrassed.

'Honoured One, I thought you meant strangers in general. We can take you to Sonic anywhere, any time.'

'And he'll love to meet you. I know he will,' Calen said eagerly.

'I'll have to hope he doesn't swim away from me.' Akama smiled and

Wirrin felt it was completely genuine. He was certainly easy to talk to. Turaku held up one hand for attention.

'I'm trying to contact him now.'

'You can do that when he's underwater?'

'Of course. I'm always able to contact him. Underwater I use an audio signal and when he surfaces I manifest as a hologram … He says he is eager to meet you.'

'Right now?'

Akama looked startled and Wirrin loved it. Trust Sonic to surprise the most important person on all Attunga.

'If you wish. I can arrange a holographic conference in six minutes but Sonic would prefer a physical meeting … at Calen's living space … in twenty minutes.'

'Whatever Sonic wants, Sonic gets.'

It sounded like a quote. Wirrin did a quick search in retinal mode. Yes, an old song from three centuries ago. He'd listen to it later. Akama was looking very pleased.

'We can monitor the Earth transmissions from anywhere. Wirrin, are we welcome in your country?'

Now Wirrin was startled, and touched. Akama was formally asking to be invited into their home.

'Always, Honoured One.'

Somehow the formal reply felt right. Turaku disappeared. No doubt he'd reappear when something major happened. The overview of Shark Bay had returned to the screen and Wirrin noted most of the markers were now blue.

* * *

Normally they'd jump on their skimmers and be home in a couple of minutes, but that was hardly appropriate for Akama. Gulara took the lead and they travelled via TransCom.

'This is wonderful. I would love to live by the water,' Akama said, standing by the pool and looking out to the reach via the display wall.

This wall was one of the features the planning assistant had insisted on, not that they needed any persuasion, and its default setting was the view across the water outside.

'Sonic swims right here, in this pool?' Akama turned to the ranger.

'Nearly every day. It's like a base for him.'

'And is this where we'll meet when he arrives?'

'I presume so. The equipment needed for full contact is all installed here.'

'Should I be in the water?'

'Only if you want to. He can see and speak to you perfectly where you are now.'

'What do you think, Calen?'

'Burilda is right but I think Sonic would like the water better.'

The ranger nodded her agreement.

'Yes, and since I asked for the meeting it's appropriate too. Wirrin, we're closely matched physically. What do you wear in the water?'

'Um, ordinary dolphinarium water shorts.'

Akama kept looking at him as Wirrin worked out it was a request.

'I'll find some.'

'Thanks. I'll come with you.'

What? Oh, so he'd have somewhere to change. Wirrin led the way to the sleeping area, found a clean pair of shorts and handed them over.

'This is exciting, Wirrin. Speaking with a dolphin will be a new experience for me. Is there anything I should know?'

Akama started to disrobe and Wirrin felt he should leave, but couldn't because he'd been asked for advice. What to say?

'Not really. Sonic is very easy to talk to. He's curious about nearly everything and he makes you smile. You'll understand as soon as you meet him. He loves a joke, though sometimes we don't understand why he laughs at something, and when he explains it we still don't understand.'

'Dolphins laugh?'

'Not really. It's a kind of dolphin equivalent that Sonic introduced to match the strange sounds we make.'

'Sonic taught the other dolphins a sound they'd never used before?'

'They don't use it much, but it's starting to spread. Puck and Flute use it the most.'

'That's extraordinary. He's bringing new ideas to our dolphins.'

Akama finished changing and they moved back to the pool. Everyone was looking at the holo of the Shark Bay area, where there were no yellow markers to be seen. Akama looked to Gulara.

'The last yellow markers just changed to blue — a group of wild dolphins to the south of Shark Bay in the Indian Ocean — and every dolphin in the extended area has now been inoculated.'

'Wonderful. So now we play the waiting game.'

Another old saying? Akama used them even more than Gulara. Well, at 119 years that wasn't surprising. Wirrin added it to the list of things to check later. He was, at the moment, too busy surveying the host of blue markers, but then movement on the reach caught everyone's attention. Five or six dorsal fins appeared and disappeared in an irregular pattern as their owners momentarily surfaced for air.

'Is that Sonic?'

'No,' said Calen, 'they're not even dolphins from his pod.'

Wirrin zoomed the display wall so everyone could see better. He wasn't as good at recognising the dolphins but his own method of checking the fins verified what Calen said. The trio exchanged glances.

'Sonic is out there, further away to the left. I checked the database.' Burilda glanced at the boys. If he was out there why hadn't he come in? He hadn't been very far away when they left the dolphinarium. Akama picked up on their looks.

'Is there some kind of hold up?'

'We're wondering about these dolphins. They don't usually come to this reach.'

Burilda pointed to a section of the display, then to another and then again to a third.

'There are dolphins everywhere.'

Turaku appeared.

'Honoured One, Sonic is ready to greet you.'

Akama nodded calmly.

'Where do I go?'

Wirrin wondered the same thing and half expected Sonic to come darting to the surface somewhere close. Instead, a large skimmer sped towards them from the dolphinarium and settled against the small house deck.

Turaku led Akama to the skimmer, which then moved out into the reach.

Burilda exclaimed, 'I think every single dolphin must be out there.'

Wirrin thought so too. The scattered groups had now coalesced in one area and when Akama's skimmer came to a halt, a familiar shape leapt high into the air then approached. Someone moved the display wall view closer.

Sonic was now right in front of Akama, upright with approximately one third of his body out of the water. It was a difficult position for a dolphin to maintain but it also made it easier for him to see Akama clearly. Behind him, rank upon rank of dolphins suddenly burst out of the water and balanced on their tails together, making the dolphin greeting.

Akama knelt at the edge of the skimmer, extended his arm and held it there. Sonic moved close, touched the hand with his beak and disappeared under the water.

Puck appeared and did the same. Akama stood up and a moment later Sonic erupted from the water with a mighty leap. Wirrin watched with a feeling of awe as every other dolphin followed, so close it looked like a living arc. Akama stood still till the reach quietened and then the skimmer turned and headed for the deck.

Three dolphins accompanied it.

Chapter 9

Akama left the skimmer and spoke quietly with Gulara, but then Sonic surfaced and invited everyone to join him. It was quite strange to hear the electronic voice of the translator, as the trio rarely used it. Calen didn't need it at all and Wirrin and Thom had discovered early on that they learnt dolphin words best from working with Sonic and Calen.

Akama looked delighted and dived straight in. Thom took Burilda and Gulara to look for more water costumes and Wirrin and Calen changed on the spot. They always kept shorts near the pool for convenience. For the next twenty minutes Sonic spent most of his time talking with Akama, breaking off only to engage in his usual bumping and splashing with the trio. The pool was very busy with six people and Sonic, and when Puck appeared for a short visit her bulk made it really crowded.

Wirrin felt wonderful. Being with Thom, Calen, and Sonic was always good but having Burilda, Gulara and Akama as well made it extra good.

Burilda was so much a part of their lives she was like one of the family. Gulara was still their mentor but she felt like a friend. For the last few months she'd drawn closer and seemed more relaxed. And now Akama, the legendary figure who'd been the driving force behind the development of Attunga and its open culture, was laughing and talking in the pool and obviously enjoying every moment.

Sonic liked him — that was obvious — and Wirrin heard them arranging to meet again.

* * *

'What do you think of Akama, Thom?' Wirrin asked later when they'd retired to bed.

'Amazing. As soon as he smiled I stopped being nervous of him, and he was normal, but when he met the dolphins he seemed so important I could hardly believe it was the same person. Then when he got back and was talking to Gulara I saw him wipe his eyes and he was different again.'

It *had* been amazing. Seeing every single dolphin make the formal greeting had been special.

'I got a lump in my throat when I saw how much it meant to Akama,' Calen said, 'and it made me feel he was the right person to get a greeting like that.'

'I wanted to rush over and hug him,' Wirrin said. He knew they all felt much the same but he wondered if they'd noticed anything else. 'Notice anything strange?'

'You mean how he looked like you?' Thom said. 'That freaked us out at the start. You must come from the same gene bank or something.'

'Did they have gene banks way back then?'

'Calen, they had gene banks way before that.'

'They must have I suppose … What strange things?'

'Lots of them. Why did he put his hand on my head? He didn't do it to anyone else. And remember what he said after Gulara introduced us? I can't figure it out.'

'Which bit?' Calen said.

'"I finally meet our notorious trio, our catalyst for change." Why did he say "finally"? That sounds like he's been waiting to meet us for a while. And "notorious"? Not to mention "catalyst for change"!'

'Hey, you're right, Wirrin. I didn't notice that at the time. Maybe something Gulara said got him interested in us.'

'When he said we're notorious, even though we're not, I just thought that he was being friendly. You know, to make us relax.'

'And our trio isn't a catalyst. You and Sonic are.'

'That's being too technical, Wirrin. We're all in it together.'

'Okay, but here's the strangest thing. Why did he call me his brother?'

'It was part of his formal greeting. I thought it was a heritage thing.'

'Well, it's not. I did a search and I couldn't find it in any of the old greetings.'

'When did you do that?'

'On the way here from the dolphinarium, while we were on TransCom.'

'You were already puzzling about it then? With everything else going on?'

Calen grew thoughtful. 'If it wasn't a greeting then it *is* a puzzle. When I play it back in my mind it feels like it was important to him … And he did know a lot about us.'

Thom chimed in. 'That doesn't mean anything. Gulara told him things and he probably looked us up on the InterWeb when he was travelling to the dolphinarium, and Witnesses remember everything.'

'I guess someone as old as Akama, and in such an important position, would know how to impress people and influence them,' Wirrin said, 'but it felt like more than that to me, it felt like he really did know us.'

They discussed it further, but in the end they were all convinced there was something going on they didn't understand.

After the trip to Warrakan, hours of travel on the new reach and all the other excitement, it wasn't long before everyone was asleep.

*   *   *

Wirrin dragged his mind to consciousness to the sound of the insistent warning pulse and a surge of adrenaline sat him bolt upright as he activated his holo. An even bigger surge cleared all the cobwebs away. The Shark Bay overview, which he'd set for instant viewing, showed a massive barrage of red markers extending along the western boundary. He shoved Calen and Thom. Usually a quick shake would waken them, though Calen was such a deep sleeper he often needed an extra shake. At the same time Wirrin tried to glean meaning from what he was seeing.

So much red, with a big concentration to the north of Dirk Hartog Island. That was to be expected as it was the main entrance to the bay … eighty-seven inimical markers altogether.

'What? What?'

'It's happening, Thom. The attack. It's started. Wake Calen. I tried once … There's eighty-seven of them but I don't know how to find out exactly what they are.'

Thom stared at the images, shook his head to clear it, then thumped Calen on the chest. They laughed about that later when the bruise started to show.

Wirrin looked for the blue markers closest to any red. Down at the southern end of Dirk Hartog Island a group of five dolphins looked very close, and he wondered how long it would take for the gap to close.

'Oh no! Look at them all!'

Calen was awake now and staring fixedly at the holo.

'Watch those dolphins at the bottom of the island. They're closest and we'll soon see how well the guardians work,' said Wirrin.

'I hope they're as good as we think they are. They're way outnumbered and that's when Turaku said they mightn't cope.'

Calen was right to worry. All the southern red markers were closely clustered in the relatively small entrance to the bay and moving rapidly.

'There are twenty-seven of them coming through that passage.'

'Twenty-seven against five. That sounds bad.'

'And they're moving at 72 kilometres per hour. They'll meet in a couple of minutes.'

Wirrin looked back at the northern group, dispersed across the entrance. At the rate they were travelling it would be another hour before they reached Monkey Mia and another hour after that for the rest of the bay.

'Seventy-two? That's way faster than dolphins. They couldn't get away even if you warned them.'

'You couldn't warn them, Thom. Earth dolphins wouldn't understand.'

'Some of the home dolphins might if they've taught them any communication skills.'

No-one answered. Five blue markers were about to be enveloped by twenty-seven red. Wirrin zoomed the view. At least he had that much control. The red mass separated enough to define individual points, and the change of scale made their movement obvious.

They were all going to hit the dolphins at the same time.

The red and blue merged. Something happened and Wirrin yelled when he realised that some of the red lights had gone out.

The red configuration kept moving and more red markers blinked off. The boys cheered as the remaining red markers moved away, but then three of the dolphin markers winked to yellow.

'Yellow? What does that mean?'

They all knew it meant that something had happened to three of the dolphins, and realised what that must be.

'It means that three dolphins have been infected, and we'll find out very quickly just how effective our protective measures are.'

Everyone jumped as Turaku appeared without the usual warning shimmer of the holo. They looked to see what expression he was wearing, even though they knew the emotions he showed were all programs. He was so expert at applying what was appropriate that it was difficult to tell him apart from a person.

'How quickly? Those picobots don't take long to work.'

Calen was remembering part of a report on the earlier attacks.

'Watch ... There we are. All clear.'

And indeed, the three yellow markers had all returned to blue.

Wirrin started to grin. Even if any attackers got past the guardians it looked like it wouldn't matter.

'The imagery from the first encounter has come through and our protective drones are performing as we expected.'

Wirrin's holo changed to an underwater view and everyone watched a live re-run. It only lasted a few seconds. The stubby shapes came barrelling in, releasing smaller units that sought the rapidly moving and highly alarmed dolphins, then coasted to a stop. A guardian stayed close to one of the drifting shapes and Wirrin was impressed by the difference in size.

'They look dangerous, Turaku. Why are they so big? They're three times as long as the guardians.'

'Partly because of storage space for the picobot units, but it's most likely a design limitation. We'll know more after we've fully analysed them.'

'The dolphins have gone off by themselves. Shouldn't the guardians be protecting them?'

'Those dolphins are safe now, and the guardians, as you call them, need to stay close to the attacking drones to keep them disabled with a directed control pulse. It's highly unlikely, but if there's any renewed local threat those drones will be destroyed and the dolphins rejoined. That's not going to happen though, as countermeasures are underway.'

The overview returned with a striking new feature, a mass of purple markers blocking access to the inner and southern sections of Shark Bay.

'What are they?'

'Sixty unattached guardians. Once the attack logistics were known they were flown to the best position for interception and dispersed in the water. Judging from the effectiveness of the first encounter they will quickly eliminate the remaining threat.'

It would happen quickly too, because the opposing forces were racing towards each other with a relative speed of almost 180 kilometres per hour.

A contingent veered south to intersect with the seventeen remaining attackers near the southern end of Dirk Hartog Island, while the remaining forty-five forged ahead, fanning out to match the spread of the approaching red markers. Wirrin leaned first against Calen, and then Thom, with a thrill of excitement.

'K74 hasn't got a hope. There are forty-five guardians against sixty of the big drones and the first five guardians stopped two each, and these guardians don't have any dolphins to protect.'

'I wish they'd blow them all up!' Thom muttered.

Wirrin and Calen felt the same but they all knew that wasn't going to happen. The main groups approached and merged. Red lights started blinking off, and in just under a minute there were none left.

'Wow! Just like that! Those other ones are space dust.'

And they were. Ten minutes later the last red markers, a group of three heading south from the first encounter, disappeared from the screen.

'K74 won't try that again. The guardians are far too good.' said Thom. 'The dolphins will be safe from now on.'

'They'll be safe for a while, Thom, but the directed communities have demonstrated their intent and we can't rest on our laurels. Their determination means they'll eventually try some new strategy.'

After this sobering warning Turaku explained a few things and showed Wirrin how to access all the related information streaming in from Earth.

Chapter 10

'What's going on?'
'I'm wrecked … Totally!'
'We know that. But why?'
'Sonic's a slave driver. I can't keep up with him.'

Wirrin was astonished. He'd never heard Calen say one word against Sonic, ever, and his surprise must have shown because Calen laughed as he collapsed onto the grav-sofa.

'He's not really a slave driver. He's just got too much energy and he's so excited about every new thing that he keeps going till he gets it right. I think I'll start taking a double dose of protein structure for a while.'

The protein structure was already working one hundred per cent according to Thom, so taking more wouldn't have any effect and Calen was really just complaining about being worn out.

'Calen, you've been wrecked every evening for the last two weeks.'
'And it'll be the same for the next two as well.'
'Two weeks? So it's something to do with Sonic's big day?'
Calen grinned at Wirrin. 'Smart Alec. It might be.'
That meant it definitely was. 'So what makes you so tired?'
'Swimming. It's hard work.'
'What sort of swimming?'
'You know … you move through the water from one place to another.'
'Very funny … Why don't you tell us?'
'I just did. Water swimming.'
'We'll make you talk.'
'No you won't … How?'
'We'll pound it out of you. We'll get you on your grav-bed and keep going till you beg to confess.'
Calen laughed and shook his head.
'I still won't tell you.'
He probably would if they were persistent.
'You'd have to. You couldn't help it.'
'You won't do it. It wouldn't be fair.'

Wirrin and Thom exchanged a wondering look. 'It's a secret and you're keeping it from us?'

That was pushing hard as they had a pact about secrets. Calen didn't say anything for a moment.

'I can tell you if you think you really have to know, but it's Sonic's idea and he wants it to be a surprise.'

'A surprise? For us?'

'For everyone really … well, except for Burilda and Turaku of course. They see everything that goes on. I suppose I can tell Sonic you couldn't wait.' Calen's satisfied grin said he knew very well that he'd outmanoeuvred them. There was no way they'd go against what Sonic wanted. The intrigue level had just risen by five notches.

'You dirty dingo. Well, you're still getting pounded.'

'Not now. I haven't got enough energy.'

Calen closed his eyes and Wirrin and Thom left him. It would be at least an hour before he woke and demanded food.

'It must be something big, Thom.'

'Why?'

'They're spending four weeks on it and that's a long time for Sonic.'

'That's for sure. Do you think he knows how tired Calen is?'

'Probably, but he must be all right or his health monitors would be giving warnings.'

'Yes, I guess … What's happening tomorrow with the doctor?'

'I'm not sure. It must be some sort of routine check for my implants.'

'It can't be routine, Wirrin. You're not meant to see him for another month.'

Today's request to go to the implant facility was a bit of a puzzle. As far as Wirrin could tell everything was working perfectly and the self-diagnostics said exactly that.

'Well it can't be too big a deal because it was only a request, and if it didn't fit with EdCom I could go some other time.'

'They're going to turn your implants down. You've been overloading too many data banks.'

'As if.'

'I told them you sneaked into TransCom through an electronic back door and they're going to set a tracer to watch everything you do.'

'Sure, and if they do I'll put a governor program on you so nothing you fly will go over half a G.'

Later, when they were preparing food, Thom wanted to know if Wirrin really could make a governor program.

'It would be too complicated. I'd have to set a program to follow you everywhere, and then there'd have to be another one that knew how to control every type of vehicle you used, and another one to make sure security was happy with what I was doing.'

'But you could do it if you really wanted to couldn't you?'

'Um … maybe. I'd have to learn more about how security works first. Why?'

'Just wondering … I've got a good idea for where we could take Sonic for an activity day.'

'Where?'

Sonic liked to know about everything they were doing and after their latest venture to one of the major fauna parks scattered throughout Attunga he'd surprised them by saying he'd like to go with them on one of their activity days. That would be great, except that he'd be confined to a transport module.

'Well it has to be water-based so he can join in, and I thought we could go to a zero-G swimming pool. It would be interesting for him and I've never heard of him being in zero-G.'

'Thom, that's brilliant. We could go to the one we missed the day we met him. Is it the biggest one on Attunga? There'd need to be plenty of room for him.'

'I don't know about the biggest. All I can remember is that it was a 30 metre sphere. Check it out.'

Wirrin was surprised to find thirty-five zero-G pools spread round Attunga, and three 50 metre pools. Most of them were spheres but one was a torus.

'A torus? Show me.'

Wirrin imported the holo image from the pool site.

'How do they do that?'

'It says they use a complicated set of grav-fields.'

'A sphere would be better for Sonic. There's a lot more room to move.'

'How will he breathe? He won't be able to use his blowhole properly in zero-G. He'll get water in his lungs.'

'Burilda will sort something out.'

'What about gravity sickness? First time could be a nightmare without proper training.'

'I don't know, Thom. I think it mightn't matter so much for dolphins. Living in water is a bit like zero gravity anyway.'

Burilda would know all that and she'd quickly tell them whether this was a feasible idea. It wasn't too late to contact her but it would have to wait till they discussed it with Calen. Wirrin and Thom grinned at each other and resisted the urge to wake Calen immediately and tell him.

*   *   *

'Hello, Wirrin. Are you ready for a lube and full-service?'

What was he talking about? Wirrin looked blankly at the doctor.

'A lube means lubrication with oil and grease, and servicing means checking all your parts are working well. I saw it on an old Earth movie I watched recently. It's what they used to do to maintain the personal transport vehicles on old Earth.'

'Does that mean my parts need fixing?'

'No, not at all. We've been asked to watch you extra closely and give you any help we can.'

This doctor was very friendly and Wirrin tried for more information.

'Asked? Do you know who it was?'

'Not really, but you've certainly impressed someone because you are now a priority case.'

'I am? What does that mean?'

'For us, not a lot. A few extra people to work with and more frequent visits like this, and we'll have you on a tri-weekly schedule from now on if you can manage it. Climb on the bench and we'll get these tests started.'

Most of the tests were familiar but there were several new ones that had to be done in different areas of the facility. It was all interesting and pleasant to hear from different doctors and technicians that his implants were functioning perfectly and that his skills were developing faster than expected. There was particular interest in his ability to use transparency mode in retinal imaging without any sign of disorientation or dizziness, and some surprise when he informed them he could use it indefinitely without trouble. Several hours later Wirrin was once again sitting with his overseeing doctor.

'All your parts are humming like a Swiss watch.'

He looked expectantly at Wirrin and said, 'Look up the reference in retinal mode.' Wirrin knew from the context it meant everything was going well, he'd heard that all morning, but he checked anyway.

'It comes from a small country that was famous three hundred years ago for its precision engineering and it means my implants are functioning extra well.'

'Not just your implants, Wirrin. We are particularly pleased with the way your associated skills have developed and we want you to apply them in a number of new areas.'

He paused, as if expecting a query, then continued when Wirrin didn't say anything.

'There are two things to concentrate on between now and your next visit. The first is quite straightforward and you will quickly reap the benefits. Your study involves gathering information, and the faster you can assimilate it the better, so I want you to retake the speed reading unit you did four years ago with EdCom. I called up the records and I see you rate at nearly two thousand words per minute. With your memory enhancement you should be able to increase that considerably. Doubling should be the minimum, but with your skills and ability I'm expecting you can at least triple that rate.'

'Triple? In only three weeks?'

'It's a good unit. Last time you went from 750 words per minute to two thousand in four weeks. You know how it works. An hour a day for the first week and a concentrated half hour a day from then on. EdCom is being informed this morning and your courses rearranged to suit.'

Wirrin was already pleased with the rate at which he could absorb information, and the idea of tripling it was hard to imagine. Still, he did remember thinking the same four years ago when he'd first done the unit. Thom and Calen would be calling him a brainiac. But why couldn't they do the unit? They'd had similar memory enhancements.

'What about Thom and Calen? Couldn't we do the unit together?'

'Let's have a look. Everyone does the reading unit as a matter of course after a memory enhancement, but it's usually another six months down the track.'

He called up information on his holo screen, started looking through it, and when he saw Wirrin's interest, rearranged the screen so they could both examine it. It didn't mean a lot to Wirrin as it was all specialised information.

'Thom and Calen could both take the reading unit now, but they should reach their optimal effective readiness in just under two months so it's best to wait ... And there's some kind of hold on Calen which prevents him anyway.'

'A hold? Is everything all right with him?'

'Yes, it's some sort of administrative thing … Here it is … This is very interesting. It's a time constraint. His time is so valuable for the next few weeks that no demands can be made on it unless it's important for his wellbeing. I don't see this very often. What's he doing?'

'He works with Sonic, the special dolphin, and for the last two weeks he's had Calen doing so much he comes home exhausted every day.'

'The dolphin tells Calen what to do? I don't understand. I know the work we did with him was to help with dolphin communication, but you sound as if the dolphin makes the decisions?'

Sometimes it was exasperating and sometimes funny that people could know so little about the Attunga dolphins, but as Calen liked to point out, Wirrin and Thom had been no different till the day they'd visited the dolphinarium. This doctor was likeable and thoughtful and Wirrin would enjoy letting him know what the real situation was.

'He does, and everyone follows his decisions. He's more intelligent than we are.'

The doctor realised Wirrin was being deliberately challenging. 'That's difficult to believe, but I can see you're eager to persuade me.'

Wirrin spent some time describing Sonic and discussing his accomplishments and character and finally he described the meeting with Akama.

'Have you got a record of that? I'd like to see it.'

Wirrin didn't, but he connected to the dolphinarium and found multiple versions of the event. He picked one at random and was delighted to see the doctor's fascination.

'I can't understand how I haven't heard about this. It's very much my area of expertise and I make a point of keeping up with new developments. There's no restriction on this knowledge is there? There can't be if you can tell me openly like this.'

Wirrin hesitated. That's how it looked, but in reality he was using retinal mode and subvocal commands to ask Turaku if it was all right to talk about the Earth attacks.

'Turaku says I can tell you, but it's First Level security.'

'Who's Turaku?'

'He's the AI who works with the dolphins.'

'You speak to an AI?'

The doctor's amazement reminded Wirrin how unusual that was.

'Yes, but only because my trio is connected with Sonic.'

'You did it while we were speaking? I didn't see any signs you were concentrating.'

Wirrin nodded and then went on, 'They *have* been keeping quiet about Sonic and there's a huge security barrier to keep external habitats from finding out about him, but it's not a secret on Attunga. I know it can't be because Akama is introducing him to the habitat in two weeks.'

'Akama? Well, people will certainly be watching that. But why are we keeping it from the other habitats? Knowledge should be shared.'

'The directed habitats don't want anyone except humans to be clever. They killed a hundred Earth dolphins when they found out about the enhanced ones on Freedom.'

'Killed? That can't be right. No-one would do that ... Are you sure it's not one of those conspiracy theories that come from Earth?'

'They tried to kill a lot more at Monkey Mia. Turaku stopped them but he says they'll try again when they work out how to get past the new defences.'

In a few seconds the images of the two groups of dead dolphins were displayed before the horrified eyes of the doctor, and another quarter of an hour passed while Wirrin recounted the events at Monkey Mia. The doctor was particularly disgusted that seven hundred dolphins would have been sacrificed to get at the smaller group associated with the marine research station.

'Back to the business at hand,' he said at last, collecting himself. 'How much of your implanted data storage have you used?'

He had that information at his fingertips, after all the tests that had just been done, but Wirrin did the check and saw how closely the doctor was watching. So, he was looking again for signs of concentration. He wouldn't see any. Even Thom and Calen couldn't.

'I've hardly used any ... It's less than one hundredth of a per cent.'

'Hopefully we'll have you using it much more. For the next minute I want you to store everything you see.'

Wirrin was completely bewildered. He might as well have been told to start flying.

'I can't do that.'

'Yes you can. Look up personal memory in your implant command set.'

Still using retinal mode Wirrin did so, and a whole sub-menu of commands flicked into view.

'Have you found it?'

'Yes, but I didn't know it was there.'

'It wasn't till we gave you access about an hour ago. It's an important implant function which is usually only accessed as part of your monthly health check. The indicators show that you might be one of the rare people who can cope with using it consciously and the only certain way to know is for you to try.'

He explained how tiny picobots intercepted and interpreted the messages being received by nerve endings as part of the routine used to check their health, then detailed the use of the new set of commands. Most of it was self-evident.

'I can't do this myself, Wirrin. I've tried, but after about ten seconds my brain gets confused. You may be the same, but we'll soon know. Nothing can go wrong while we're monitoring and the worst you'll feel if it doesn't work is that slight dizziness everyone has during their health check, and you'll be out of it in fifteen seconds.'

'And if it does work?'

'Then it may be very uncomfortable, but if that's the case you can switch out of it yourself and we'll decide what to do next.'

He talked till Wirrin, rather nervous, said he was ready. The commands were simple but Wirrin concentrated on the switch-off one, making it as strong as he could in his mind before he subvocalised the start. It was awful. The doctor's face kept disappearing and reappearing in a kaleidoscope of confusing images and sensations that sent his mind reeling till he was begging for it to end.

Stop! Stop! No, that wasn't it … Switch off!

The doctor's features snapped immediately into clear view.

'What happened?'

'It didn't work. My brain got confused like you said it might.'

'It did work, Wirrin. That was twenty-three seconds from start to finish and you switched out of it yourself, which means you were thinking consciously. Could you see anything?'

'Sort of.' Wirrin thought about what he'd just experienced. 'It was really strange. I felt like my eyes were seeing all right but my brain was mixed up about it. I could see you and then I couldn't and I was so overwhelmed I had to stop.'

'You saw me? Excellent. Was it too distressing to cope with?'

'Almost … no, not really. It was just so different.'

The doctor nodded with a pleased and expectant look.

'As soon as you're ready we'll try again. You know what to expect, so this time I want you to push the strangeness into the background, focus your mind on something else, and then see if you can hold any images steady.'

Wirrin thought about it, tried, and for a short while managed to watch the doctor before the need to switch off became too strong.

'That was thirty-seven seconds. Any other progress?'

'Yes, I held you in view for a short while.'

'Have another go.'

After three more tries something clicked into place and Wirrin found he was watching the doctor quite normally.

'I think I've got it. It's hard and I can't keep going for long, but I can push the confusion away.'

'Wonderful. Now play that last effort back from your memory storage.'

That was easy and Wirrin laughed.

'What's up.'

'Nothing. It worked perfectly but it's confusing because I'm seeing you in transparency mode and naturally at the same time.'

'Switch to holo and show me.'

That done, the doctor said it was time for a drink and a snack before trying the commands for sound recording. An hour later Wirrin was feeling very pleased that he could simultaneously store everything he was seeing and hearing for a period of almost two minutes before losing concentration. The doctor was excited and set guidelines for practice, and daily holo contact time to confer about progress or any other issues.

* * *

'We always knew there was something weird about your brain.'

Thom and Calen were listening, intrigued, to Wirrin's report about his day's activities and acting indignant that they had to wait two months before doing the speed reading themselves. Underneath all the carry-on about him being a super brain and computer head they were really proud of him.

'You won't get away with anything from now on, Thom. We'll always have proof of when you try any sneaky tricks.'

'No you won't. I'll just turn the lights off and he won't be able to see.'

'Won't make any difference. He uses infra-red vision instead.'

'What?'

He swivelled to look at Wirrin.

'You can't do that can you?'

'Of course I can.'

He couldn't, but the moment of surprise before Thom realised they were having him on was worth it. Thom leapt at Calen and started wrestling him, but as Calen had had his evening rest that was hopeless and Wirrin joined in.

'Show us how it works.'

'All right. Make Calen laugh.'

'He doesn't know how.'

'Teach him then.'

With his happy disposition Calen was easy to set laughing and if you couldn't think of anything silly then tickling was a perfect fall-back. Thom tried but Calen turned the tables. They stopped abruptly to watch themselves for a moment on the holo.

'Wow! Just like that. You look at it and it's recorded. It must be hard because you go all still and look dopey when you're doing it.'

That made Calen laugh genuinely, not just tickle laugh.

'Wombat-head.' He turned to Wirrin. 'It's just the look you have that tells us you're thinking really hard. How much are you meant to practise?'

'I don't know. As much as I can without making myself tired for other things. I have to work it out for myself.'

'Did that bit you just did make you tired?'

'That was as long as I can last.'

'Well I reckon you've done enough for today. You look worn out. Guess where we're going on our activity day?'

'The zero-G pool?'

'Sonic loves the idea so he's taking a day off and Burilda's got everything organised.'

'A day off? What from?'

'Can't tell you. It's a surprise.'

That meant it was Sonic's meeting with the rest of Attunga, and since Calen was enjoying the opportunity to tease their curiosity so much, it warranted action.

'You've had it.'

*   *   *

Travelling with Sonic like this was a real experience. At his request the transport module had been redesigned so he could either control it himself or let TransCom take over, and he was thoroughly enjoying his new type of mobility. At the moment they were stopped at a water fountain in the gathering area of the first big TransCom transfer station they'd reached and Sonic was watching the jets of water as they leapt in an ever-changing display of shapes and colours. Wirrin looked to Calen.

'It's the first time he's seen a fountain, and pushing water into different shapes is a new idea for him. He also wants to look at the people. He's never been close to so many before.'

That worked well because the people certainly wanted to look at him. The transport module was unusual enough in itself to draw attention but the sight of a dolphin made it irresistible, and when Sonic stopped near the fountain people drifted close. Three children rushed over and stared, goggle-eyed and smiling.

'It's beautiful. I wish I had a dolphin. Will we frighten it if we get close?'

'Why don't you ask him?'

The little girl looked at her two companions then back at Calen.

'You can't talk to dolphins.'

'Yes you can.'

The children turned towards two adults who'd moved behind them and when the man shook his head to tell them 'no', Calen spoke again, this time in dolphin talk and Sonic answered.

The hum of conversation stopped.

'Sonic says you can come as close as you like.'

The little girl was still dubious, but one of the boys darted forward and put his hand on the clear panel of the transport module. Sonic touched his beak to the same place on his side and asked their names. The hush from the growing assembly of people was absolute.

'Sonic wants to know your names.'

'Kania.'

The little girl came close, pulling her younger brother with her. 'I am Nerida. And this is Baradine. But he's shy.'

She put her hand on the panel and lit up with delight when Sonic touched it again. Sonic made the dolphin greeting and spoke.

'Sonic likes your names and he wonders what they mean.'

Once again the children looked to their parents and the mother answered, putting her hand on each child's head in turn.

'Kania means a rock. Nerida means a flower and Baradine is a wallaby.'

Three bursts of sound came from Sonic and Calen interpreted.

'Sonic said your names in dolphin talk.'

The children stared big eyed at Sonic and someone called from the crowd, 'Can it say the names again?'

Calen looked towards the man and nodded as three bursts of sound came from Sonic. The sceptical look changed.

'It answered by itself? Did you give it a signal?'

Hearing Sonic referred to as an 'it' really grated with Wirrin. Sonic's whistles and clicks sounded out clearly.

'Sonic doesn't need signals. He understands you and wishes he had translator machines fitted to his transport module.'

It took twenty minutes to get away, and as the module moved slowly through the crowd Wirrin took in the smiles and looks of wonderment and marvelled at how Sonic had affected everyone. He'd taken over really, with Calen as his mouthpiece, as he interacted with the children but, somehow, also with everyone else. There were two more big transfer stations on the way but their schedule meant they had to forego any similar stops.

* * *

'That was an eye opener … inviting the children to visit the dolphinarium made them very excited.'

'You know about that already?'

Burilda was at the zero-grav pool to make sure everything ran smoothly.

'Turaku let me know you might be turning up late so I watched. It sounds like we've got to modify the transport module yet again.'

'Yes, he wants panels he can open and a translator built in.'

The group moved to a reception room and Burilda introduced the pool staff. Sonic greeted them and, through Calen, asked some questions before everyone moved to one of the viewing galleries around the pool.

Wirrin watched the same change from interest to amazement they'd seen with the people in the transfer hall as understanding blossomed that Sonic was much more than their idea of a dolphin.

The sight of the pool gave Wirrin his own dose of amazement and he echoed the exclamations from Calen and Thom as they took in the transparent sphere of water apparently hanging in mid-air, glowing slightly and 50 metres across.

'This is incredible!'

The holo images they'd watched with Sonic the night before had been exciting in their own right, but no match for the impact of the real thing. Wirrin counted nine people moving in the watery globe, and while they watched, one of them broke surface almost directly in front with a great confusion of water, drifted through the 10 metre air gap, then after a stylish turn, pushed powerfully against the transparent wall and arrowed back. The scattered blobs of water, quivering and weirdly transforming, gradually assumed roughly spherical shapes and settled towards the main water body.

They'd learnt last night that although it was called zero-grav there was really a fractional field, focused to give the water mass just enough of an effective centre of gravity to hold its shape.

There was a burst of speech from Sonic who was eager to get into the pool and everyone moved to the entry area and put on breathing masks. This was routine for Burilda and the trio but quite an event for Sonic as he'd only trialled the specially designed device that fitted over his blowhole in the last couple of days. Next, his transport module had to be moved into the pool itself as he couldn't launch himself through the air gap like the humans.

It only took a minute and he was floating motionless, with the trio and Burilda ready to help if the lack of gravity was too disorienting for him. He'd been okay in trials at the dolphinarium, but this was a confluence of different conditions. The freshwater had a slightly different density to his normal salt water. Zero-G meant there was no sense of up and down, and the water was so clear it might affect his sense of distance.

'Very strange.'

'Are you feeling dizzy?' asked Calen.

He wasn't, and quickly deciding he'd sorted out this new environment, swam slowly towards the centre of the sphere. Everyone relaxed and moved with him.

Whoosh! He powered off in a rapid loop then nudged Calen with the signal to try and catch him. Of course they couldn't, not in water, unless he let them, but then he made the mistake of following Calen in his first transition through the shimmering water surface into the air gap. Calen, used to zero-G movement in air, let himself glide to the outer barrier then, with a practised body twist, pushed off and headed back to the water. Wirrin, following, watched in dismay as Sonic's glistening grey form, fins and flukes flailing helplessly, bounced against the outer barrier then drifted slowly back to the liquid interface.

There was a great burst of dolphin sound — dolphin laughter, but louder than Wirrin had ever heard it. Well he mustn't have been hurt.

'Do it again.'

Was Sonic really going to try again? He manoeuvred himself so his head was poking through the surface and watched Calen erupt next to him, drift to the outer panels and execute the turn and push to send him zooming back. With one careful flick of his tail Sonic left the water, much more slowly this time, and drifted head-first towards the solid panels. Oh no, his beak was going to take the full impact. At the last instant he twisted his head sideways and managed a relatively gentle bump and rebound. Wirrin was impressed. There'd been none of the pointless flexing of his fins and tail on this second attempt.

'Slower.'

What did Calen mean? Sonic would drift in the air, helpless. He did … and once again his dolphin laughter sounded.

'Trickster.'

Calen shot from the water then pushed off from the panels in just the right direction to collide with Sonic. As their bodies met he grabbed tight in the classic move of combined momentum to help someone marooned in a no-grav situation. They re-entered the water and Wirrin stared in amazement as the two bodies followed a graceful curve, spiralling and looping in perfect and effortless harmony.

'Again.'

Sonic launched himself once more, drifting ever so slowly till Calen rescued him with the rebound from the outer panels.

The rest of the time at the zero-G pool was mostly spent with Sonic exploring and mastering techniques of movement and control in the air layer. It shouldn't have been a surprise that he was more interested in this than the pool itself because new experiences were so important to him.

*   *   *

'How much did you zap?'

Zapping was Thom and Calen's term for memory recording.

'Not much. There were too many things going on to concentrate properly.'

'It must have been a fair amount. I remember seeing you do it at least three times.'

'Me too. I saw you a couple of times,' said Thom.

'I kept trying but when you see Sonic barging straight at you, you forget everything else, and zero-G is hard enough by itself. I managed nearly twenty minutes but they're all short bursts. Have a look at this one. It's when he learned to flip himself off the wall with his tail.'

Wirrin's prolonged recording time had stretched to over ten minutes in the week since he'd seen the doctor, and they were both pleased with the improvement. The current practice regime was for a sustained effort in the morning, another in the evening, and frequent short bursts in between. Wirrin liked the short bursts as he didn't notice any effect from them. The long bursts were hard work and left him feeling slightly dazed for a while.

'He's good isn't he? When we were doing some zero-G trials for him at the dolphinarium he kept saying he was going to be a fish out of water. It's some old saying he found on the InterWeb that caught his fancy.'

'Hey, Calen, how long have you been doing that new swimming?'

'What new swimming?'

'The spiral thing you did with Sonic the first time you rescued him.'

'We weren't meant to do that. He started it because he was excited.'

'Why weren't you meant to?'

Calen laughed.

'You know why, and I'm not going to talk about it.'

'But how do you do it? You can talk about that because we've already seen it.'

'I don't know how to explain. I kind of caught it from so much swimming with Sonic. It's hard work.'

'It looked easy.'

'It's meant to, but it's really the opposite.'

'Is it what makes you so tired each day?'

He laughed again. 'It's a part of it, but only a part ... You'll see.'

* * *

'It's only two days away and I'm scared I'll mess it up.'

'Scared? You mean nervous don't you? It's okay to be nervous.'

'I suppose so … No, I'm feeling scared too. Gulara was there today and I found out it's even more important than I thought.'

Calen had come in, tired as usual, but instead of coming back to life after his rest, and eagerly attacking his evening meal, he'd stayed very, very quiet and Wirrin and Thom were concerned.

'Akama introducing Sonic to a lot of scientists and going on the InterWeb for all Attunga — more important than that?'

'Way more important. The conference with the scientists is only a part at the end. Every single Witness on Attunga is going to be there.'

'*What?*'

'I know. I've never heard of anything like it, and there's an invitation to watch being sent to the whole population, and I've never heard of that either.'

For each sector, a Witness, with almost infallible recall and unquestionable integrity, was the final arbiter for any situation or decision, and with over 1200 sectors currently on Attunga that meant at least the equivalent number of Witnesses.

'Calen, they can't. The viewing gallery isn't big enough.'

'They've taken the seats out so they can all fit in. They'll be standing up the whole time.'

'Every Witness?'

The boys were silent as they thought that over, then Thom leaned against Calen. 'Wow, now we're scared too and all we have to do is watch.'

Wirrin provided his own reassuring pressure and Calen smiled. 'You won't be scared, Calen. You'll be with Sonic and people will like you whatever happens.'

Chapter 11

Awed and awkward, Wirrin stared at the crowd standing in front of him, over 1200 witnesses gathered to meet Sonic in person.

Sitting comfortably in front of such an august group made him feel distinctly uncomfortable, but it was Akama's plan. Akama sat next to him, and on his other side there was an empty seat then Thom and Burilda, all of them on a slightly raised dais. The attention of all those important eyes was disconcerting. Thank goodness for Akama's quiet comments and friendly assurances. Then everything started happening.

Turning his head slightly he could see Puck and Flute and a dozen other dolphins swimming behind the giant transparent panel, curiously looking out at the assembled people. Flute swam close and looked at the seated group then moved back to Puck. The lights dimmed briefly then brightened on the dais and as the hum of conversation stopped Akama stood up.

'Welcome everyone. We're gathered at the invitation of a young dolphin who is eager to meet us and formally declare his place in our society. He has honoured me by asking for my help and I'm honoured as your representative to do what I can.'

Akama paused a moment.

'Sonic has many accomplishments and soon he will speak to us all, but first I will greet his mother.'

He turned, and with elaborate care, made the greeting wave. Wirrin had never seen it made with such meaning. Puck, close by and next to the viewing panel, answered with the familiar body movement and head flip. The rest of the dolphins approached and followed suit then hung suspended as if waiting.

Akama turned to the gathering, raised his arm again and gave a guiding nod. Everyone knew exactly what he meant and Wirrin's first tingle of awe brought him right out of his awkwardness as he watched the exchange of greeting between Witnesses and dolphins. Akama made an expansive gesture and a giant holo-screen showing Puck, Flute and three other female dolphins filled the front of the gallery. Wirrin stared at the strange image of Puck with a little fluke protruding from her body and goosebumps took over as he realised this was the moment of Sonic's birth.

An electric murmur went through the gallery, then an even more electric silence as the drama of birth unfolded, the shocking burst of red when the umbilical cord parted, the little dolphin's movements as he oriented himself and was guided to the surface for his first breath. The holo faded and Wirrin automatically reached for Thom's arm. The scene changed to Puck's presentation of Sonic to the dolphin and human community and Burilda's following words.

'Ladies and gentlemen, you've just become part of history ... '

Next, Burilda's voice presented parts of Sonic's life, suckling from Puck, chasing playfully after Flute, the first meeting with Calen, and the gift of his first fish. Wirrin watched himself with Thom and Calen, wrestling, splashing, speaking and laughing with Sonic in the pool at home, diving as a group to one of the underwater caverns in the new reach at Warrakan, and swimming together at the zero-G pool. The last clip was the formal greeting to Akama and the beautiful arc of dolphins leaping into the air.

The holo-screen shimmered and faded to show an empty viewing pool. Two forms appeared at the entrance to the middle tunnel, arrowed to the front and greeted the crowd, Sonic with the dolphin version and Calen with the stylised wave.

Wirrin's heart leapt. Sonic looked magnificent, but so did Calen, with a form-fitting costume extending from waist to knees and made of some silvery grey material that almost looked like dolphin skin.

For a few seconds they stayed motionless, Calen's hand resting on Sonic's back, then they rose to the surface where Sonic took a breath. Together they dived and Wirrin's neck hairs tingled in awe as he watched the slow loop of spiralling forms he'd first glimpsed at the zero-G pool.

He'd been amazed then but this was so much more than a short spontaneous moment. This was Calen and Sonic working with full concentration and effort to present the surprise they'd been working on for the last four weeks. Wirrin became aware of music, a melody that changed in mood and style, sometimes simple, sometimes complex, slow at first then gradually becoming more lively and joyful. Dolphin and boy moved with the music — no they didn't, the music moved with them — as they twined and turned in unison and counterpoint, a single unit with two separate parts. Wirrin watched Calen's impossible actions in disbelief and a strange feeling came over him that maybe he was really a dolphin in human form? Or that maybe Sonic was partly human? A beautiful sound echoed the music — Sonic was singing the melody and for the next few minutes Wirrin was lost.

Everything stopped. Sonic and Calen were back where they started, motionless in the water, except for Calen's heaving chest as he dragged air from his breathing mask. Wirrin, looking out, had an eerie feeling that everyone had turned to statues.

Akama stood up, and when he turned towards Sonic and Calen a murmur of sound washed through the gallery. In seconds it became a great wave, applause and voices building and building in acclamation. Calen gave a watery version of a bow in acknowledgement and when Sonic copied him Wirrin couldn't help smiling. They must have rehearsed it but it did look spontaneous. The sound muted and a hush of expectancy built as Sonic and Calen faced each other.

'Thank you my brother. You honour me.'

Amplified for the gallery, Sonic's translated words sounded out clearly and Wirrin sensed the communal jolt of realisation that he was speaking directly. Calen responded by saying the same thing in dolphin talk. It was a short, slightly formal interchange, and Wirrin thought of all the people watching and seeing for the first time that dolphins and people could really speak to each other.

A swirl of movement drew everyone's attention as dolphins poured through the three tunnels, more and more till Wirrin knew that once again every Attunga dolphin was present. Rank upon rank they formed, then watched Sonic and Calen perform one more amazing spiralling arc and disappear into one of the tunnels.

No! No! They couldn't be going? Wirrin wanted them back.

Sonic returned and with a burst of rapid dolphin speech circled past the gathered pods and gracefully breached the surface for a breath. Every dolphin followed, returned to its place, and facing the Witnesses with Sonic, gave the greeting. Wirrin was stunned. Every dolphin had moved at exactly the same instant, as if they formed one composite being. They did move as a group in the reaches, it was part of their nature, but this was done with a degree of precision he'd never seen before.

The raucous voice of a kookaburra calling its territorial warning filled the gallery and the deep thrum of vibrating air columns joined in the evocative introduction to the Dreamtime Concerto.

Wirrin's goosebumps rose yet again as the greatest musical legacy from the resurgence of First Australia sounded through the gallery, and he watched enthralled as the dolphins presented an astonishing, active, interpretation.

Straight away he recognised the birth of the Sun, as a living sphere of dolphins formed and arose from the Earth with the creation of light and life.

There was the Rainbow Serpent, a mass of dolphins undulating and weaving in concert with the powerful music.

Wirrin smiled with delight as Sonic led a group of five dolphins to simulate kangaroo spirits bounding beside the Rainbow Serpent.

He lost track briefly when Calen arrived at the dais and sat in the empty seat, his special costume covered by a shirt bearing the dolphinarium logo. Well, so what if millions of people were watching, he was getting a hug. Calen leaned into the hug and whispered, 'Did I do all right?'

Wirrin gave him another squeeze, a nod and a smile.

'You were useless!' That was reverse praise from Thom and Calen settled happily to watch the dolphins. For the next fifteen minutes the spellbinding actions of the dolphins merged with the power of the music and built to an explosive final crescendo.

The nearly four hundred dolphins arrayed themselves behind the viewing panel and hung, almost motionless, looking out at the Witnesses. The gallery hushed while people returned to themselves, and again the eerie tableau of humans and dolphins watching each other persisted until a Witness near the front raised both her arms high in acclamation. The people close by followed, and then everyone else joined in. Wirrin jumped to his feet then whirled around to look for Calen. He was overcome, but Wirrin, knowing that action would help, pulled him to his feet and lifted his arm. On his other side Thom did the same.

The dolphins repeated their unified greeting then with bewildering speed poured in three living streams through the tunnels and left Sonic by himself. A roar filled the gallery, and Wirrin was carried away by it in wonder and awe until a movement from Akama brought it to an end.

'Sonic, you and your people have honoured Attunga with gifts of beauty and grace, and we thank you with all our hearts.' Akama's voice rang clear and strong. 'May the friendship and cooperation demonstrated today between dolphins and humans long endure.'

Sonic's nods of agreement and acknowledgement made it clear that he understood every word of Akama's speech. With a start, Wirrin realised he was also part of this. Sonic's body language had mostly been learnt from interaction with the trio and this was one of the reasons they were sitting here. Akama finished and Sonic spoke. Wirrin quickly relaxed as he saw that the watching Witnesses were smiling. Sonic's cheerful nature was communicated to everyone in the gallery, and, it turned out, to the millions of people watching.

'While we speak in open forum I would like my brothers to be with me.'

Brothers? Not just Calen? Sonic wanted all three of them in there with him? Wirrin's heart started pounding as Calen pulled him from his seat. This wasn't part of the agenda.

'Be proud.'

Akama sounded pleased by the unplanned request.

For the next twenty minutes the trio swam with Sonic while he spoke with the Witnesses. When that part of the proceedings finished the lights dimmed, then brightened on the dais again where Akama and Burilda were now standing together. Akama raised an arm slowly in a simple gesture that demanded full and serious attention.

'Friends, today we have shared in joy and grace and ventured across a new frontier, but great changes are often fraught with great problems.'

Wirrin caught his breath.

'Be assured that all is well on Attunga. Such is not the case elsewhere.'

Chapter 12

'**I** feel like a dead dingo!'

Wirrin and Thom plonked themselves down beside Calen. They were all tired from the momentous day, but Calen was exhausted.

'Do you want to go to sleep, or can you wait for the special meal Thom's got planned?'

'I won't sleep. My brain's going round in circles.'

Normally that would draw rude remarks but at the moment Wirrin and Thom were rather in awe of Calen.

'No wonder,' Wirrin continued. 'What was it like talking to all the scientists?'

When the Witnesses had left to go to their special conference the viewing gallery had refilled with scientists and for over an hour Sonic and Calen had answered all sorts of questions. Sonic did most of the talking, but he managed to include Calen in different ways in many of his answers. Wirrin was impressed by how much Sonic enjoyed trying to answer the tricky questions.

'I wasn't expecting all those questions,' Calen said. 'It was meant to be just Sonic but he says it's easier to talk to people he doesn't know when one of us is with him. That's why he wanted us all there when he talked to the Witnesses.'

'What about that scientist who said we're a fake dolphin pod orchestrated by the dolphinarium?'

'I know. That was interesting, but he went quiet when Sonic said there was nothing fake about us, and that though we filled some similar functions we were very different to a pod.'

'I like the idea that we're a sort of dolphin pod,' said Thom.

Wirrin nodded.

'We'll ask Sonic. You could tell he's thought about it more than we have.'

'I thought the scientists were great. They were all on Sonic's side.'

'That's a funny thing to say. Are there sides?'

'You know what I mean. You could feel the atmosphere, and if Burilda hadn't finished things up I reckon they'd still be talking.'

'Well they sure looked pleased when Sonic said he'd like to have regular meetings with them.'

'I don't know how he's going to fit that in with everything else he wants to do. We just seem to get busier and busier.'

'You're not going to keep being worn out every night are you?'

'No, that was from practising the swimming till we got it right. We're back to our normal routine now. Except I don't know how it's going to work if he needs me there for all these trips he wants to do.'

Calen had learned about these trips when Sonic told the scientists he planned to meet people all over Attunga, especially young people in nurseries and EdCom centres.

'You've *never* had a normal routine. It changes every time Sonic gets interested in something new.'

'Well, it makes life interesting, Wirrin. How much did you zap at the gallery?'

'Nothing.'

'How come? That's not what we planned.'

'How come? Well, someone just happened to blow my brain with their incredible surprise didn't they. Our planning didn't count on you being so amazing I wouldn't be able to think about anything else.'

Thom gave a snort of laughter.

'Snap out of it, Wirrin. Don't you get it?'

'What?'

'He's wondering what he looked like. Call it up from the InterWeb and put it on the wall display.'

'Am not!'

The grin he was trying to suppress said otherwise. Wirrin searched for a moment then caught his breath. 'Bush-boys! Look at this. It's been watched over two and a half billion times … And there's ninety million people watching it right now.'

They all stared at the data about the dual swim.

'That must be wrong. It doesn't make sense.'

'Yes it does, Calen. No-one could believe it the first time so they're watching it again.'

'They must be watching it more than twice to get those numbers.'

'Seventy-three per cent of Attunga and Warrakan were watching. It's the biggest audience for anything that's been on the Attunga InterWeb.'

Calen was shaking his head in disbelief.

'How many people is that?'

'It's there ... further across in that next column ... 910 million.'

They all went quiet.

'It's Sonic.'

Wirrin grabbed Calen by the nape of his neck and squeezed.

'And you! The first time was because all the Witnesses were there, but the repeats are because of you and Sonic.'

Calen wriggled his head but made no move to dislodge the grip.

'Dolphin Boy! Look — they call you Dolphin Boy. That's good. I really like it.' Thom pointed to a heading on the far right of the screen.

'Dolphin Boy! Dolphin Boy!' Wirrin and Thom chanted as they tipped Calen on his side on the grav-sofa and joyfully attacked him. Calling them idiots and bushwhackers, Calen soon demanded that they watch the holo, and feeling particularly close, they did just that.

'You really are Dolphin Boy, Calen. You can't deny it after watching that.'

'It does look more special than when we were practising, but it all came from Sonic. I just did what he showed me. It could have been anyone.'

'As if. What did Sonic say about it?'

'We didn't get to talk much but he was really pleased. We'll find out everything when we see Turaku tomorrow.'

'Turaku wants to see you?'

'No, the other way round. Sonic wants to see Turaku, and he's arranged for all of us to meet him tomorrow afternoon.'

'All of us?'

'Yes, everyone. It's about Akama's message. Sonic wants something to happen.'

'Did he say what?' Wirrin and Thom were on full alert now.

'No, there were too many other things going on, but I think he must have ideas he wants to discuss.'

Akama's warning about the xenophobic attitude to enhanced dolphins beyond Attunga had been the only note of discord.

'That's interesting. He usually leaves things like that to Turaku. I wonder if he knows something we don't?'

'I don't think so, Wirrin. Burilda was as surprised by the call for the meeting as I was, and Turaku keeps her up to date with everything. I reckon Sonic was stirred by Akama's speech.'

Wirrin nodded. Akama had indeed been inspiring.

'What did you think of it? Akama's warning I mean?'

'I was scared at first because I thought he was going to say more dolphins were being attacked.'

'Me too, and then I was expecting him to talk about the ones that had been killed but instead of that he made a big deal about how well everything went at Monkey Mia.'

'He wouldn't talk about the dead ones, Thom, not when so many people were watching. It would be too upsetting. Children would have nightmares if they saw those pictures.'

'That's for sure.'

'He did tell them bad things had happened, without going into details.'

'He sure made a big deal about the way you helped,' Calen said.

'That was embarrassing. He made it sound like it was me who saved Monkey Mia.'

'You *did* save them and we're glad that everyone knows.'

'I helped a bit, but it was really Turaku and the Australian AIs who did all the important work, and Akama hardly mentioned them.'

'He wants you to be a hero.'

'Very funny!' Then Wirrin realised Calen wasn't joking. 'What do you mean?'

'Well, I noticed how much he emphasised your part in it too, and I wondered if he was trying to show that humans are important for help-ing dolphins. You know what I mean, building the idea that humans and dolphins and AIs all help each other and need each other. That's part of what Witnesses do, and I bet that's what took up most of their conference.'

Thom jumped up. 'I'd better get our food ready.'

'Aren't we going to watch the dolphins and the Dreamtime Concerto first?'

'Tomorrow night, Calen. If you watch it now your brain will be spin-ning even faster, and you're going to bed as soon as you can because you're under orders from Gulara to sleep in till midday.'

*   *   *

Wirrin and Thom spent the morning studying at EdCom then returned home. When they came in Calen sat up in his grav-bed with a cheeky grin and demanded breakfast. He looked and sounded full of life.

'SLUG! It's more like dinner time.'

'It is not, Wirrin. It's 12.30 and I've been awake for ages.'

'Well you're still in bed so ages means about ten minutes. We've got an hour to get to the dolphinarium so get up and get yourself ready.'

Calen elaborately and lazily stretched his arms above his head and gave a fake yawn.

'I'll have breakfast in bed first. It's too nice to be getting up.'

Wirrin grabbed a foot and pulled him onto the floor then, followed by indignant fake cries of protest, went to help Thom.

'That's not breakfast ... What is it?'

'Too bad about breakfast. You've missed it. It's salmon-sub and if you don't want it we'll eat it for you.'

'Are you sure you cooked enough?'

'No I'm not, but a double portion will have to do. If you want any more you can get it from Sonic.'

'What?'

'Fish! That's what Dolphin Boys eat, and from now on you're having it for breakfast, lunch and tea.'

Calen shook his head as if he'd never understand such foolishness. 'Did anything happen at EdCom?'

'We hardly got anything done. Even the tutors wanted to talk about dolphins instead of ordinary work.'

It had been quite strange to walk into the EdCom centre and feel everyone looking at them. Mostly they'd kind of smiled, which felt good, and in the discussion groups where everyone knew each other they'd gathered round to talk and ask questions.

'Did they like Sonic?'

'I think so.'

Calen laughed at Thom's understatement and turned to Wirrin.

'Of course they did. You'll see for yourself tomorrow. Are you going to wear your dolphin skin today?'

'It isn't dolphin skin and of course I'm not. I'd feel silly.'

'Well that was one of the things they kept asking about.'

They tucked into the food with murmurs of pleasure. Thom had picked the salmon substitute as a stir, but they all agreed it was so delicious they would add it to their list of meals for special occasions. The big chunks they were eating didn't come from real salmon of course. Like any other meat they were grown in a specialty food factory, but the supply was quite limited. Just as they were finishing they heard a splash from the pool and a rattle of clicks and squeaks as Sonic surfaced. It was something about being lazy and something about food, Wirrin thought. He had a good vocabulary of dolphin words, but it was always tricky to understand what Sonic was saying. He and Calen spoke so quickly for one thing, but there were frequencies that Calen could pick up with his special implants which ordinary human ears couldn't hear. Calen laughed as he replied.

'He's learning bad habits from you two, telling me I sleep too much.'

'What did he ask about the food?'

There was another rapid exchange.

'I told him it was fish and he said it was disgusting.'

'Eating fish is disgusting?'

Sonic laughed.

'No, but burning and spoiling it is.'

Wirrin turned to Sonic. 'Humans don't eat raw fish. That *would* be disgusting.'

There was more dolphin laughter and Calen looked surprised.

'He says to look up "sushi".'

In a second Wirrin had pictures and information on a holo for everyone to look at … raw fish and people enjoying it.

'How did he know that?'

'That time when we talked about killing things for food he got interested in what people eat.'

Calen pulled his shirt off and dived into the pool. Wirrin and Thom quickly cleared away the meal and joined them. Saying hello to Sonic was never complete without touch. Ten minutes of the play that was so important in dolphin society followed and laughter and dolphin sounds rang out in happy communion.

* * *

Sonic was excited. It was obvious as the four of them raced to the dolphinarium, first from his exuberance in the pool and now as he powered through the reach. A glance at the skimmer's InfoPanel showed an impressive 29 kilometres per hour and at this rate the trip would only take a couple of minutes. They were even more curious about the purpose of the meeting after Sonic had said simply that he had to help the Earth dolphins.

* * *

'We can't do that. It's far too dangerous.'

Calen's words sounded loud in the silence that followed Sonic's demand to journey to Earth and persuade the threatened dolphins to return to Attunga. Even Turaku looked rather shocked, though of course it would be the expression calculated as the most appropriate response for his holo.

I must be there, my brother. I am the only one who can explain the danger properly. Turaku will make it safe.

'He can't, Sonic,' Burilda said. 'He's bound to Attunga. If anything happened on Earth he wouldn't even know about it for twenty-seven minutes and we couldn't rely on the Australian AIs for the same reason. You'd be without proper AI protection for the whole trip to Earth and back. It's a terrible risk'

'There will be a way.'

Wirrin agreed with Burilda and he was sure everyone else did too. It had taken Turaku and several security AIs just to get Sonic safely to Warrakan and back.

Burilda, shaking her head, looked to Turaku for support, and when he didn't respond, looked at Gulara. Wirrin could see other problems.

'How would you talk to them all, Sonic? There must be thousands of them, and they're spread all over the Earth. It would take months or years to visit them. And how would we bring so many back to Attunga if they decided to leave their homes?'

'Talking is easy. Ask the centres to set up a holo screen for each pod and they can all hear me at the same time.'

'There are approximately 2700 dolphins currently in association with 147 marine research centres or dolphin projects, and we don't have the capability to either transport them or provide a suitable secure living environment for them. Burilda is correct in her assessment that the risk in taking Sonic out of a secure environment is unacceptable, but this could be overcome, and Sonic's proposal is the best solution so far considered. With the targeted dolphins removed from the scene, the probability that wild dolphins would be hurt is minimal. The marine stations will be unwilling to part with their dolphins, but they could be invited to send human associates to accompany them. There is, however, a serious drawback with the proposal: Attunga itself would then become the focus of attention for any new actions by the directed habitats. Akama will be with us shortly to discuss this.'

Wirrin stared. Everyone stared. Turaku seemed to be giving a go-ahead, but with reservations?

'But what about the security? We've only got one Sonic and the time lag would make you ineffective.' The concern in Burilda's voice sent a shiver through Wirrin. The thought of anything bad happening to Sonic was unbearable. Calen was clearly thinking the same thing.

'I would be less than two per cent effective, as a reasonable approximation, but by travelling with you I can lift that to over ninety per cent, and with a security presence we would approach one hundred per cent.'

'You can't do that. You're part of Attunga.'

'Yes I am, Calen, and I will remain here, but with enough infrastructure developed on a transport vessel my identity and function can be replicated. With additional infrastructure a security presence could accompany us as well.'

'You mean a copy of yourself would go with Sonic?'

'More like an extension. There would be constant communication.'

A security presence? He meant another AI. Wirrin knew enough about the physical structures that enabled the existence of AIs to understand that Turaku was talking of a major, major project.

'Infrastructure? It would be a lot more than that. You'd have to design the whole vessel from scratch.'

'You're correct Wirrin, and that design, including transport facilities for the dolphins, is ready for implementation.'

AIs performed at incredible speeds but that sent Wirrin's mind spinning.

'Ready? You've designed it in the last minute or two?'

'I'm not personally able to do that in that time frame. The purpose of the vessel requires maximum capability, and in order to be prepared for Sonic and Akama, a group of AIs with expertise in engineering, defence, construction, security, science, and communication collaborated in semi-gestalt mode.'

'Thank you, Turaku.'

Turaku acknowledged the formal thank you from Sonic. Wirrin was pondering what maximum capability must mean if it involved so many specialty AIs.

'I am concerned about the danger to Attunga. It clashes with my wish to protect dolphins.'

'We have to protect them, even if we don't bring them here … What about that idea of taking them all to Northern Australia? It worked at Monkey Mia, and the Australian AIs could look after them at Ningaloo and the Great Barrier Reef as well.' Calen sounded upset and Thom put his arm across his shoulders.

There had been many ideas about actions to assist the Earth dolphins in the eight to ten week respite that Turaku had confidently predicted before any new attacks were attempted. K74 would have been shocked when every one of their predator drones disappeared without trace and a full assessment of what might have happened would have been necessary before they instigated any new nastiness.

Burilda took over. 'It's the same dilemma, Calen, except the attention of K74 would be directed against Northern Australia and they aren't as well equipped to cope with it. You're right though, we do have to protect the Earth's dolphins, and provided Sonic can be kept safe I think this should go ahead. I don't know how we'd cope with two and a half thousand extra dolphins though. They'd all have to squeeze into the new reach on Warrakan and that's been designed for five hundred. We'd have to artificially stimulate the food production levels till adjacent reaches could be made available ... Can that be speeded up, Turaku? They're already on high priority.'

'The first reach is ready now and its extension will be ready in another three months. In six months we will have four neighbouring reaches available, and in eight months an extra twenty.'

Twenty-four reaches? That was staggering. Wirrin did a quick calculation ... Enough for twelve thousand dolphins if they matched the specifications of the new one. Two and a half thousand dolphins would almost be lost in that amount of space.

Burilda was showing the same amazement as everyone else, then her whole face lit up with delight. 'Twenty-four reaches? That's wonderful, but why so many, and why so soon? Has something else happened?'

Turaku nodded. 'The Witnesses have been meeting again, and Akama will be here in a few minutes.'

Wirrin looked at Sonic, wondering what he was making of all this. He hadn't said much and Wirrin had the impression he was doing a lot of thinking. With his fixed facial expression it was hard to tell. Everyone was keen to hear about the Witnesses and what they'd discussed, but it was clear Turaku was leaving that to Akama.

'How long would it take to build a transport ship?'

'Time is critical, Thom. Almost three weeks.'

'Then nearly two weeks of travelling to get to Earth. Five weeks is getting into the danger zone.'

'Not two weeks, Thom. Travelling time would be twenty-nine hours. It's the logistics on Earth that can't be rushed.'

Wirrin almost wondered if he was hearing right, as normal travel time to Earth varied from twelve to twenty days. A rapid retinal InterWeb check showed the record time was eight days and five hours.

Thom looked like he'd been hit on the head with a club. 'Turaku, you just said twenty-nine hours?' Thom clearly wanted to believe but couldn't.

'Yes, Thom. It will be necessary.'

Thom didn't say anything but the gears of calculation were fully engaged and Wirrin smiled at the excited earbashing they were in for.

We will ride on a comet.

Wirrin was savouring the imagery of Sonic's comment when it struck him that Sonic and Turaku had both just said 'will', as if the journey was now definite. He was about to ask when there was a holo shimmer. Akama's image appeared and after a greeting he smiled at Sonic and then everyone else.

'We've presented Sonic's request to the conference and it has unanimous support and agreement.'

Wirrin felt a thrill of excitement, mixed with relief that the Earth dolphins could be helped, then a sudden awareness that if Sonic went ahead he could be placing himself in danger.

'Already?'

'Yes, Calen, when Turaku explained the plan and its implications the only real concern was for Sonic's safety and that was quickly allayed by the decision to build a special ship for him. It's fortunate that we had reconvened to discuss the enormous reaction to yesterday, otherwise we would have had to organise a special holo conference.

'It was dramatic, Calen. After talking with you and Sonic yesterday a group of the scientists called for a complete new dolphin level to be added to Attunga and the idea has spread through the whole habitat and caught the imagination of the population in general. We were discussing how to handle that and I had to interrupt, introduce Turaku, and determine the will of the conference in very short order so we could get back to Sonic. It might seem rushed but the choice was really quite straightforward. Turaku has been explaining details and I must return as our conference has assumed a new level of importance.

'Sonic, Attunga supports you.'

Akama gave a general nod and parting smile to everyone as his image shimmered and disappeared.

Calen dived into the water with Sonic.

'We're going to Earth.'

Chapter 13

'Five — one — one, and it's nearly 8 kilometres.'
'Nine minutes twenty seconds,' said Thom.
'Nine minutes fifty seconds,' said Calen.
'You won't get there in nine-twenty. I'll bet TransCom isn't even that fast. I'm going for ten minutes fifteen seconds.'

The trio hadn't played their TransCom game for ages and Wirrin thought Thom was so optimistic he must have forgotten half the strategies needed to race from one sector of Attunga to another.

'That long?'

Thom and Calen gave each other a dubious look. Wirrin usually went for a faster time than either of them. Thom laughed.

'You're trying to bluff us into changing our times so you won't lose.'
'No I'm not. Calen's the one who'll lose. He always does.'

That was mostly true but he also had a knack of occasionally winning by a surprising margin. If Wirrin won today, Calen had to wear his dolphin skin on their next outing. If Thom won it would be Calen and Wirrin. And Calen, being embarrassingly fair-minded and sensible, had declared that if he won then they all had to wear them because they were *all* part of the dolphin trio.

The day before, Sonic and Calen had visited one of the big nurseries to meet different groups of children, and Calen had been asked to wear his special outfit. He hadn't been keen, but evidently the children were expecting it and Burilda said he mustn't disappoint them.

'I thought it would be embarrassing, but when we got there half the kids were wearing them too. Sonic loved it, and with every group we met he asked the mums and dads to choose different children to jump in his mobility unit with him. They got so excited!'

Wirrin remembered how he'd felt when he first met Flute.

'It's not just kids who wear the suits. Akama's going to wear one next time he talks on the InterWeb.'

'Is he really? No-one told me about … you're a dead wombat, Thom.'

The trio raced to the nearest set of TransCom portals and from there their paths diverged. Wirrin was going really well till his last transfer when a surge of travellers delayed his access. He wasn't going to win this time and, sure enough, when he arrived Thom was there shaking his head in disgust and Calen was looking very smug.

'You can show off your dolphin skins tonight when Sonic turns up, while I decide where we're going to wear them.'

'It better not be too public.'

Wirrin gave Thom a nudge, probably too late, to stop him giving Calen ideas.

'Let's go … Are you sure you know how to fly this thing? We don't want someone scraping bits of us off some asteroid.'

Completely used to their derogatory remarks about his flying skills, Thom made a rude sign as he led the way to the docking area.

'Anyone could fly this transporter, Calen. It's pretty much like the automated viewers.'

Anyone could fly almost anything in fact. All that was needed was authority to give the automatic pilot instructions. What Calen meant was taking personal control, and Thom was highly capable after all the time he'd put into his training. They went through the entrance walkway, adjusted to the zero gravity, and manoeuvred to their seats.

'Strap in properly, Calen. I'm going to use 2G today.'

'What for? We're not travelling far.'

Silly question. Like asking Thom why he breathed.

'Yes we are.'

'What are you talking about? Everything's next to Attunga.'

'No it's not. There's a convoy of asteroids for the new level about 4000 kilometres out and I've arranged for us to go and have a look.'

'How long will that take?' said Calen.

'Not long. About twenty minutes.'

'Twenty minutes at 2G? No way. They'll be scraping us out of our seats after that long.'

'All right, we'll try 1.5G. Anyhow, with those swimmer muscles you'll hardly notice the drag.'

Wirrin watched as Thom competently handled the controls and started the transporter moving. The initial burst was at least 2G but then it eased back and Thom pointed to a number on his console which said 1.4.

'I couldn't resist that.'

'Where's Attunga?'

'Behind us of course. I'll switch it in so you can watch.'

The real-time display flickered, and defined by its many external light sources, the elongated, regular shape of Attunga appeared, and off to one side the monstrous ellipsoid of Warrakan. It looked spectacular to see them both like this, then rather eerie as they rapidly dwindled to blobs of diffused light and merged with the background stars. The display switched to forward view and all sense of motion vanished.

'This is spooky. Are you sure we're moving? It feels like we've stopped.'

'That's because we're travelling in a straight line and our reference points don't change. Watch this.'

Wirrin lurched against his restraining straps as the stars started shifting across the screen, then again when they reversed direction and shifted back.

'It does get more interesting when you change direction, except it puts you off course.'

'How fast are we going?'

Thom pointed at another number — 2205.

'That's just over 2Ksec ... But when we reach decel point we'll touch a max of ... 13.2 Ksec.'

They grinned at the neat-sounding jargon. Wirrin presumed Ksec meant kilometres per second, which didn't mean much till he thought of Attunga's 28 kilometres of length only taking a fraction over two seconds to travel its full distance.

'It's weird how we're travelling so fast while it feels like we're not doing anything.'

'You've been a lot faster than this haven't you, Thom?'

'One of my training trips was at 5G for nine minutes and I reached 26Ksec, but that'll be nothing to when we go to Earth.'

There was a blip of light on the console and the display of stars jumped slightly.

'What happened?'

'We just made an automatic correction to dodge an asteroid.'

Wirrin and Calen looked at him.

'We're dodging asteroids? Are there many here?'

'Normally there aren't any. These ones today are being guided to Attunga. Let's see ... There are seventeen of them spread out between here and the convoy.'

'So why aren't they in the convoy?'

'They're too big. They guide large ones directly from wherever they find them to save time.'

There were three more course corrections before they reached the convoy and each time Thom related the scanning information. The biggest asteroid was over a kilometre in diameter and mostly made of ice.

'Look at them all. There are hundreds.'

'There's 497 for this convoy, Calen.'

'I don't get it. Why don't they just bring one or two big asteroids?'

'These small asteroids will all have been specially selected. They've probably got high concentrations of some element that's important for the picofactories.'

'So why are they in that globe shape?'

It did look spectacular, hundreds of randomly shaped asteroids massed in a distinctly spherical shape.

'I don't know. Someone probably likes it that way.'

'A globe is the most efficient way to use space,' said Wirrin.

'I want to see one bump into another.'

Thom laughed. 'Calen, you're dangerous. There'd be bits of rock and ore flying directly at Attunga, and they wouldn't anyway. Their guidance controls are as accurate as the ones on this transporter.' He turned to Wirrin. 'Tell me when you've seen enough.'

They were all keen to see what was happening with construction of the 'Comet', as Calen had started calling Sonic's special ship. Thom made the most of the trip back, practising his manoeuvring skills, and demonstrating short bursts of 3G acceleration, then they spent half an hour watching asteroids being attached to Attunga in readiness for decomposition and transformation to the new level.

'Want to head for the Comet? We can watch this on the InterWeb.'

They would normally have spent much longer watching all the activity, but the Comet was a more powerful drawcard and Wirrin and Calen were almost as eager as Thom to watch the initial stages in its development. This was only the third day after the meeting with Turaku and life continued to be a whirlwind of activity and anticipation. The special ship had jumped to the top of the interest list when Burilda informed them that Sonic wanted the full trio to travel with him, not just Calen, as Wirrin and Thom had assumed.

Thom confidently piloted the transporter away from the new level of Attunga and towards the special construction area where all mobile transport was built.

Today's trip had broken new ground for Wirrin and Calen and they'd developed an extra degree of respect after seeing first-hand the skills Thom was always talking about. The reality of dodging asteroids and adjusting to the isolation of deep space had been brought home to them powerfully.

As they rounded one end of Attunga the asteroid came into view. It didn't look very impressive, just a lump of material nestled by the exterior wall of the habitat, but Thom pointed out that they were still nearly 10 kilometres away.

'The asteroid is being transformed into the biggest ship Attunga has ever built, nearly twice as big as the tugs for Warrakan's drive engines and 50 metres longer than the security ship that took us to Warrakan with Sonic.'

They manoeuvred closer and closer — Thom really was skilled at this — and from only 100 metres away the impression of size was totally different. Hugging Attunga, and apparently kept in place by a myriad of giant cables, the real size and shape of the asteroid was now clear.

'Why isn't anything happening? I thought we'd see all sorts of construction robots and other things.'

'It *is* happening, Calen, and so fast it's hard to believe. Those tubes are carrying picobots and energy sources to the asteroid.'

'Tubes? You mean the cables?'

'They're nothing like cables. They eat their way into the asteroid and the picobots transform the ore into proper hull material and move it into place. Look over there. There's a new one growing out from Attunga.'

Thom knew all this because when he'd learnt he was going to Earth he'd spent hours finding out everything he could about the new ship. Not far away, Wirrin saw the tube Thom was talking about, its free end an indistinct glowing red cloud. Was it really growing?

Yes, a new section of tubing came into view while they watched.

'What's the glowing part at the end of the tube?'

'It's millions and millions of picobots. There's an electromagnetic field that holds them in place while they do their work. As soon as the tube reaches the asteroid new picobots will start doing a host of different things.'

It was all amazing, and as they watched, more and more tubes extended towards the asteroid. Thom fiddled with his controls and they slowly started moving.

'Where are we going now?'

'Just to the end … Yes, look at that. The frame is beginning to take shape.'

Wirrin could see five of the tubes extending from one end of the asteroid then, while he watched, three more started.

'The Comet's bigger than the asteroid so they build it from the inside out.'

'Inside out?'

'Calen, it's obvious isn't it? It's solid nickel-iron so they hollow it out and most of that material becomes the hull and the framework.'

Fascinated, they watched for over an hour as more and more of the picobot tubes extruded from the main asteroid. A feathery-looking framework joined the ends of the tubes and the final outline, a strange ellipsoid shape with a flattened bottom area, started to take shape. Thom explained it all. Since the Comet was landing on Earth's surface at Monkey Mia, the flat area was needed to match a huge temporary anti-grav landing field, which would be built there.

The current flimsiness was purely temporary as over the next six to seven days it would steadily solidify and build to a 2 metre thick hull, with huge 10 metre reinforcing girders extending internally through the length and breadth of the ship.

'Did you say 2 metres, Thom? How thick is the hull on this transporter we're in now?'

It only took a couple of seconds to find out.

'It's 3 centimetres. Why?'

'Well, if 3 centimetres is enough for here, why do they need 2 metres? Wouldn't 20 to 30 centimetres be enough? That hull material is incredibly strong.'

Materials technology had gone through two major stages since the pre-habitat days. During the first stage traditional steel and concrete were replaced by construction materials of ten times the strength and hardness, which accelerated the building of the great population centres to shift most of the Earth's population underground.

The second major breakthrough, in conjunction with the development of practical gravity control some eighty years ago, was the great enabler for space habitats, with materials half an order of magnitude stronger again and relatively light. The limited spin-cities had been quickly modified.

'I wondered about that myself,' said Thom, 'when I saw the hull material has a rating of 61.5 SS. That's 61.5 times as strong as standard steel, and 2 metres of it is like having 120 metres of the old steel. It's because the Comet might have to go through all sorts of things like radiation belts and solar winds and they're putting special layers in the hull to shield against them. They've got a crazy safety factor too.'

The equivalent of 120 metres! Wirrin liked steel. There was a sculpted piece on display in one of his EdCom workshops and he loved its silvery sheen. In his mind he added 120 metres to the Comet and pictured the resulting shiny steel monster. It would look great, but it would be too heavy to move.

'Are you zapping the Comet or are you thinking?'

'Both. I was imagining what the Comet would look like if it was made of steel.'

* * *

'They're bombarding us with questions. They're all curious about what wild dolphins will be like and Sonic and Puck are out visiting all the pods to keep them up to date with what's going on.'

After a call from Burilda, the trio had gathered at the dolphinarium to do some catching up of their own. Wirrin was curious as to why Sonic and Puck had to do the visiting.

'Why aren't the rangers connected with each pod explaining things?'

'They are, but apparently the dolphins need to hear it from Sonic and Puck.'

Calen nodded as Burilda continued.

'The whole community's excited and they need to interact with each other when major things happen. Puck goes because she's the leader and Sonic does all the talking.'

'What is he telling them?'

'Depending on numbers, they might have to share their reaches with several hundred Earth dolphins if the Warrakan reach hasn't developed enough. The nutrients and stimulation have caused an explosion in the number of micro-organisms, but it takes time for the effect to work its way up the food chain.'

'Sharing? That's new.'

'Yes, we have to consider it because early indications from Earth are telling us we might be catering for more dolphins than we expected.'

'What's happened?'

'All sorts of things, Calen. In the last few days a campaign against 'unnatural creatures' has started in the semi-directed societies on Earth and it's made many of the marine stations so worried they're transporting their dolphins to the protection of Monkey Mia.'

The trio stared at Burilda in shock.

'*Unnatural!* Are they crazy?' Calen's angry outburst made everyone jump.

'No, Calen. They're not crazy. It's a very calculated campaign by K74 and like-minded habitats to counter the strong negative reaction from the rest of the solar system against the earlier killings.'

'But it *is* crazy. Earth dolphins are more natural than humans. Humans have all got health-bots in their bodies.'

'And most people agree with you, but according to Turaku it's a kind of social engineering to turn the populations in the directed habitats against dolphins. He predicts the next stage in their campaign will likely include reports of modified dolphins losing their senses and attacking people at famous beaches.'

'That's stupid. No-one will ever believe that.'

'They will in the directed habitats. A continuous stream of bad reports will eventually create negative associations with dolphins in people's minds.'

'As soon as they go on the InterWeb they'll know it's not true.'

'No they won't. If it comes from their leaders they'll believe it. The same as we would.'

'No we wouldn't.'

'Of course we would. When Witnesses tell us things we believe them.'

'That's different. Witnesses don't tell lies … They can't tell lies.'

Calen was shaking his head but he understood what Burilda was saying. He was just resisting the idea that anyone could see dolphins in a bad light.

'Are we still sure it's mainly K74 behind all this?'

Burilda gave Wirrin a curious look.

'Your program hasn't stopped running, Wirrin. We're more sure than ever. It's traced the people who made the reports and linked them all with K74. It also uncovered the identities of the Cadre of five men who control the K74 habitat.'

A small group like that controlling fifteen billion people? Wirrin started to think about it. Calen was more interested in the dolphins.

'So how does that mean more dolphins?'

'Remember how Monkey Mia works closely with twenty-seven dolphins? They're also associated with many more, and it's these they're worried about. Monkey Mia has eleven in particular and it's a similar story at most of the other centres. The whole thing is very complicated because we can't separate individuals from their pods.'

Wirrin did some quick figuring. He knew the official group from Monkey Mia were all in the one pod, but the non-official dolphins must come from a range of pods and most pods had at least ten or fifteen members and usually over twenty. If they had to transport even one extra pod from each centre the numbers would increase enormously.

'Wouldn't that be too many to transport?'

'No, there's room for nearly six thousand. They'd be very crowded but that wouldn't worry them just for the trip. It's when they arrive here that the problems start. Five thousand dolphins in a reach designed for five hundred will quickly destroy the viability of that environment.'

'Five thousand? That's impossible. They'd eat everything in the first week.'

'Less than that, Calen, but we've come up with solutions. We'll be bringing a week's supply of live food from Earth — that's all been organised at Monkey Mia — and Sonic is going to teach them to eat fish-substitute. They won't like it but there's no alternative. Construction of a specialised protein factory is already underway on Warrakan.'

Thom suddenly laughed and everyone gawked at him.

'Salmon-sub! I'm thinking of Sonic eating it and telling all the other dolphins to do the same when he said it was disgusting.'

The mood lightened and Calen actually smiled. 'They'll all hate it.'

'They'll hate not having to hunt for it, but they'll love the taste. It will be designed especially for them.' Thom was right. The food scientists would make sure of that.

'How long before the reaches are developed enough so they can catch their own? I suppose having extra dolphins will mean it'll take longer?'

'No, Calen, it will still take just on five months. The four extra reaches on Warrakan will all be ready then, and two months later twenty more. In another year every pod will be able to have their own reach if that's what they want.'

Wirrin worked it out. Five thousand dolphins would be an awful lot of pods.

'That's over two hundred and fifty reaches … They've speeded up the plans on Warrakan again?'

'Yes they have, but we won't need that many. Turaku has been working with Uranus and Freedom habitats and they're hoping many of the dolphins will move there as soon as they've developed working reaches.'

The trio shared a look. Burilda had been right about lots of things happening.

'Uranus? They don't even have dolphins.'

'They've suddenly become extremely interested.'

Burilda pointed a finger at Calen and smiled.

'Someone persuaded them.'

'Me?'

'Of course. You and Sonic. After they saw the pair of you on Sonic's Meeting Day they quickly committed themselves, and they've been in contact with Turaku ever since.'

Wirrin felt a surge of excitement and pride for Calen and Sonic. Thom must have felt the same because he grabbed Calen's arm and gave it a shake.

'You've made history. You and Sonic.'

'They certainly have, and the effects of Sonic's meeting day will be far ranging. All four habitats who've seen it so far have been inspired, and Turaku is certain that will continue with other habitats.'

Four habitats? Oh, Warrakan of course. It was easy to think of Attunga and Warrakan as one.

Calen started making his usual self-deprecating excuses, giving Sonic all the credit, but Burilda interrupted him.

'You're wrong, Calen. The biggest factor behind the wish for humans and dolphins to work together was your interaction with Sonic.'

'What are they doing on Titania?'

Everyone smiled at Calen's blatant change of subject.

'They've already had three changes of plan in the eight days since Sonic formally met Attunga and Warrakan. At first they were going to follow our set-up, though with significantly larger reaches, and gradually build a population of enhanced dolphins.

'Two days after Sonic made his rescue proposal they asked to share in the project by taking five hundred Earth dolphins, and now with the news just ten hours ago about the increased numbers, they've increased that to two thousand.'

'Two thousand? Are you serious? That's enormous, especially since they haven't had any dolphins before.'

'Enormous is a very good word. Our entire database of knowledge relating to enhanced dolphins is being transmitted, along with our specifications for picofactories to build infrastructure, and environmental data to keep the reaches in optimum condition. We'll have to send Attunga rangers and bio-scientists as well, as they don't have the human expertise they need. Our dolphinarium is going to be a hive of activity till all the new facilities are ready to be used.'

'The Warrakan dolphinarium is ready to use now?'

'Yes, but even that will be tripled in size to cope with all the dolphin associates from Earth, and since our own dolphins won't be able to move there for an extra five months, all the enhanced training work will have to stay here.'

'It will take ages to build an enhanced dolphin population on Titania when they're starting from scratch.'

'Decades, Thom. But with the knowledge we've developed on Attunga they'll do it much faster than we did. Our own enhanced project started right back when Attunga was built.'

Thom was right. The Attunga dolphins weren't just ordinary dolphins with implants. The ova and sperm of mating parents was gene-engineered, then gestated by the female and nurtured after live birth in the ways of the dolphin community. This limited dolphin numbers to their natural breeding cycle and it would be at least eight years before a second generation was born.

Attunga dolphins had been refined over six generations.

'In a perverse way K74 is doing us a favour by forcing this influx of dolphins. In the long run it will put all our programs years ahead … by at least twenty years in Titania's case.'

'What about the Uranus moons, Burilda? Are they involved in this?'

'It would be strange if they weren't. They work together in much the same way as Attunga and Warrakan.'

'And why are they having bigger reaches than us?'

'There's no reason for them not to, Calen. They've got as much space as they like and more water than they can ever use.'

'Water? Way out there?'

'The mantle of every moon is mostly ice if I remember rightly.'

Calen looked to Wirrin to find out.

'Titania, diameter 1578 kilometres — composition half ice, half rock — mantle thickness 270 kilometres. Burilda is right. The mantle is nearly all ice.'

'I suppose the other moons are the same? I don't know much about them.'

Wirrin didn't either. He knew there were five inhabited moons plus the Titania habitat, but that was only from the recent talk with Gulara and Turaku.

'I suggest you organise a module with EdCom to familiarise yourself, especially about Titania, since Sonic will want you with him when he travels there.'

'Titania?'

'Get ready for it. It's practically a certainty.'

Yesterday Wirrin and Calen were adjusting to the idea of a 4000 kilometre trip from Attunga, and now they were being informed of a journey that made even the trip to Earth look small.

They both turned to Thom. His excitement would now jump to a new level and seeing their looks of anticipation, he said nothing and pretended to be calm. Wirrin knew that couldn't last. If he kept holding it in he'd explode.

'Anything else to tell us? You said there were all sorts of things.'

Burilda, understanding the byplay, gave a chuckle.

'Well, Thom, they've started building the grav-field so the Comet can land on Earth.

'Over four hundred dolphins have already arrived at Monkey Mia.

'Sonic wants another trip to Warrakan.

'In another ten days the Comet will be safe for humans, and three days after that we leave for Earth with Akama and Gulara.

'We've had 75,000 enquiries from people wanting to be rangers.

'Turaku and Sonic want you to become expert at flying the Comet.

'And a new AI called Yajala has taken the equivalent position to Turaku on Warrakan.

'Is that enough for a start?'

*   *   *

Thom had very excitedly piloted the big security ship for the first time, and as far as Wirrin could tell he'd handled it as if it had been the little transporter they'd used to visit the asteroid convoy. Even the fact that he'd been closely scrutinised by four different AIs plus Gulara hadn't appeared to make him at all nervous.

He'd spent days in a Comet simulator of course, plus a surprise real-time session yesterday under the supervision of the security ship's usual pilot because it was the closest thing to the Comet.

Sonic was most impressed, well they all were, when Gulara had asked if Thom knew enough to navigate the Comet to Earth without using the automated pilot, and his answer, with qualifications that were gobbledygook to Wirrin and Calen, had been yes. He'd be piloting again on the return trip to Attunga but right now they were exploring a seagrass bed.

After a warm welcome and introduction to Yajala, Warrakan's new dolphin AI, they discussed the current status of different reaches, and the priority they'd been given since the news from Monkey Mia. Yajala showed holos of the additions being made to the new Warrakan dolphinarium to cater for the influx of dolphin associates, and spoke with Sonic about plans for a section in one of the new reaches where dolphins would be able to experience waves like those in the oceans on Earth, then disappeared when the group reached the water.

They'd entered the Warrakan reach at a new access point not far from where the barrier to the extension used to be, and had only travelled a few hundred metres when Sonic stopped. His echolocation was telling him there were schools of fish everywhere, he explained, and they had to have a closer look. Wirrin could hardly believe what he was seeing.

Every move they made across the seagrass sent groups of fish darting away, and right now at the edge of the seagrass bed where the water deepened, a great silvery cloud spread 30 metres in both directions before disappearing into the haze resulting from the artificially high levels of nutrients, which Burilda had warned would reduce water clarity. The enormous school of tiny fish burst apart as Sonic shot through its midst, then again as he looped and barrelled back a little further along. So many fish but all too small for dolphin food.

Twice more the group stopped to marvel at the great profusion of life, and then as they entered the extension area, the water abruptly cleared and almost all sign of life and growth disappeared. This section was the extra 30 kilometres of new reach that Sonic wanted to assess. Apart from being the watery equivalent of a desert with regards to food, it was technically ready for dolphins and everyone was hoping he would give it the okay. The water was clean and pure and there was an abundance of features specially designed for dolphin interest and enjoyment.

The food problem was well under control as the fish-substitute developed for the crisis period had been surprisingly well received by the Attunga dolphins. They called it half-food because it lacked the hunting element, but some of the younger dolphins had started playing chasing games with chunks of the protein held in their beaks, and that had caught on as a kind of substitute hunt.

Whether the incoming dolphins would cope with the lack of any apparent life was the big question and there was much discussion about whether they would all leave the extension area and congregate where the marine life was. Calen took great delight in teasing Sonic about being a can of sardines and Sonic took even greater delight in retorting that he had the old saying wrong.

For nearly an hour they explored, following Sonic's lead, stopping to check out a maze of underground reefs and then again at the edge of the reach to examine the beginning of a seagrass bed. At first glance it looked like a featureless expanse of grey sediment with here and there a faint tinge of green, but when Thom beckoned everyone to look closely, hundreds of tiny buds became apparent, some of the slightly more advanced ones showing the beginnings of green growth. In another week the sediment would disappear beneath a thin carpet of plant life and not long after that a wide range of secondary plant species would be introduced among the monoculture.

Sonic nudged himself between Calen and Thom to see what everyone was looking at and they both automatically rested their arms over his back. Wirrin saw a smile develop behind Gulara's facemask at the intimacy behind the unthinking gesture.

Back at the surface Sonic snugged into the special cradle built for him at the back of Calen's skimmer and the group went on a high-speed trip to the end of the extension and back. Sonic could manage just over 30 kilometres per hour for short bursts but with the greater lengths of the Warrakan reaches the innovation allowed the group to travel at 60 kilometres per hour on the skimmers.

'What do you think?' asked Calen.

'If we set up food stations in the extension it will be a great place for them to explore. They will enjoy that.'

That was good news. The extension reach had Sonic's approval.

'Only feed them in the extension area you mean?'

'Yes. It will stop them crowding into the living water.'

* * *

'Hey, Thom, the pilot of the security ship was impressed with the way you handled it today.'

'I know. I didn't expect him to say that. He's really friendly and he's going to take me for two hours tomorrow instead of my normal training course with EdCom.'

'What? On the ship, or with the simulators?'

'On the ship, but with simulators controlling the display.'

'What does that mean?'

'It means I fly the real ship in lots of different situations. He might tell me to lock into position with a slowly spinning asteroid and the asteroid appears on the screen as if it's really there.'

'And if you crash into it you try again till you get it right?'

'Eventually. First I'd have to do all the necessary things as if I'd really crashed.'

'Do you think you'll crash?'

'Of course. That's the whole idea. He'll set harder and harder problems till I just can't cope. I'll learn more in two hours than weeks of ordinary piloting that way.'

'How's that any different to an ordinary simulator?'

'Totally different. Any actions I give the ship are really happening. If I take it up to 15G then it's really accelerating that fast.'

'Isn't this stuff meant to be for really advanced pilots?'

'It's incredible, Calen. I should be training for two more years minimum before I get access to a ship like the Comet, but Sonic and Turaku organised it and it's all happening.'

'Do you think that pilot will be going with us on the Comet?'

'He'd better. If he's been chosen for the security ship he's probably the best pilot on Attunga. What did you think of Yajala?'

'I liked him.'

Wirrin had thought about this a lot and had looked forward to meeting the Warrakan AI.

'You can't really think about him as a character, Calen. The personality he uses with his holo can be whoever he wants.'

'I know that. I like the one he used today though. He didn't have the same serious, important kind of feel that Turaku has.'

Wirrin laughed.

'That's because you think he's good looking.'

'Do not! How can a bunch of fancy electrons be good-looking?'

Thom picked up on the slightly too rapid denial, and a happy tussle developed while Calen was accused of deserting the trio for Sonic, and now deserting Sonic for the 'bunch of fancy electrons'.

'Witchetty wankers!'

'Yajala's probably more important than Turaku when you think about it, Calen.'

'Wirrin, a minute ago AIs didn't have personalities. Now you're saying one is more important than another?'

'It's complicated isn't it? I was thinking that Yajala has a much bigger area of control than Turaku because Warrakan's nearly eight times as big as Attunga.

'He'll be in charge of a lot more dolphins than Turaku.'

'Only for a while, Thom. When our new Attunga level is ready they'll bring a lot of dolphins back here.'

'More moving. The dolphins will face a lot of changes with all these things going on. Hey, if Yajala's in charge on Warrakan what happens with Turaku?'

'What do you mean? He'll keep working with dolphins on Attunga.'

'Yes, but they won't be our dolphins. When the reaches are ready they're transferring across to Warrakan.'

Calen shook his head.

'Not any more. When they found out about Attunga's big new reaches some of them decided to stay.'

'I didn't know that. How come?' said Thom. Wirrin hadn't known either.

'The pod leaders worked it out between them because some of the dolphins want to stay here when Warrakan leaves for Alpha Centauri. Four of our pods are staying and they'll move to the level six reaches as soon as they're ready.'

'Four? That means only five pods for Warrakan. Is that enough?'

'No, but it soon will be. Burilda says there'll be a lot more dolphin births after the new reaches start working properly. She thinks there could be eleven or twelve pods by the time Warrakan leaves, and at least eight in the Attunga reaches.'

They were talking about the enhanced dolphins. Of course there would be many more than that when Earth dolphins arrived.

That was becoming more and more certain with each passing day as the campaign against unnatural dolphins hadn't eased and the latest report from Monkey Mia said the wall of protection was in full operation again with over three thousand dolphins being protected and more on the way.

'Are the Earth dolphins going to be separate?'

'No, why should they? Dolphins love meeting each other.'

'They'll interbreed, Calen. Won't that affect the enhancement program?'

'What? Oh no, that's all worked out. I asked Burilda about that ages ago and the enhanced pods won't change much because their males will dominate the Earth males. They're so clever they'll outmanoeuvre them easily.'

'But won't they take over in the pods from Earth as well?'

'They'll have a great time because the Earth females will be so attracted to them, but they won't take over. There won't be enough of them for one thing, and pod structures are also too strong to change rapidly.'

'When did you find out this stuff? All we have to do nowadays is blink and we're left behind.'

'I know. Um, about a week ago. Burilda was telling me how the rangers will all be having extended training.'

*　*　*

'Hello, Wirrin,' the doctor said, glancing up. 'Your life has been rather busy since your last visit.'

'Um … Yes.'

'Well it must be. The notation on your file now matches Calen's and I'm not to encroach on your time with any new commitments.'

'New? You've got something new for me?'

'We'll talk about that at your next visit, or whenever it's appropriate. How have you been managing your exercises since we last spoke?'

'Really well. I finished the reading course and I can cope with nearly two and a half hours of memory storage before it starts to get to me.'

'Two and a half? I'm impressed. That's an extra half-hour in just a week.'

'I still drop out when things distract me.'

'We've discussed that and it's not an issue.'

'I know, but it *is* annoying.'

'Well, you shouldn't let yourself think like that.'

Wirrin felt the slightest flush of embarrassment. The doctor was reminding him, with friendly authority, that they had indeed discussed and agreed on the best mental outlook to encourage progress. Wirrin gave himself a token slap on the wrist as acknowledgement and they both smiled.

'All right. Let's do your check-up. After everything was so good last time I know there won't be any problems, but we need to be sure.'

Wirrin relaxed on the bench, felt the usual moment of dizziness, then realised the doctor was nodding his satisfaction.

'Tickety-boo!'

Tickety-boo? What on Earth did that mean?

'All is well.'

He'd have to remember to try it on Sonic. 'Doctor, you should meet Sonic. He's always coming up with antiquated sayings like that.'

The doctor stared, parted his lips as if to say something, then obviously changed his mind. 'How do you keep so fit, Wirrin? With your life so busy it must be difficult.'

'That's because of Sonic. We're in the water every day with him and all the swimming keeps us fit. Calen spends hours with him and you should see how strong he is … Why don't you come to our place for a visit? We could make sure it's a time when Sonic's there so you could talk with him.'

The doctor looked almost stunned.

'Surely you can't do that? Sonic is too important to have strangers dropping in for a casual visit. There's hardly a person on Attunga who wouldn't give their eye teeth to meet him.'

Wirrin had to smile at the idea of people giving their teeth to meet Sonic.

'An expression of eagerness' the doctor said, and this time he wasn't checking Wirrin's facility with retinal imaging.

'Of course we can and Sonic loves meeting people. He's taking us to a nursery at the other end of level four tomorrow, and the day after that he's going to a new EdCom centre on Warrakan. You should come this evening otherwise it might be weeks before things are even slightly normal.'

In a couple of moments it was arranged and Wirrin was enjoying the doctor's slightly nonplussed look.

'Well, Wirrin, I'm feeling slightly out of my depth at the moment. What do I need to know about meeting a dolphin?'

'Nothing. We'll have the translators on so it's easy to talk. Does getting into the water worry you?'

'Not at all. I swim regularly.'

'Good. Bring a pair of shorts because we all get in our pool when Sonic's there.'

'You have a pool of your own? Big enough for a dolphin?'

'We're spoilt aren't we, but we have to because it's Sonic's home as much as ours ... I rushed things for you because we're leaving Attunga in four days and I'm not sure when we'll be back. Probably another four or five days.'

'Leaving? Oh, to Warrakan?'

'No, to Earth.'

'Earth? I don't understand. That would be five or six weeks, not four or five days.'

Wirrin remembered his own amazement when he'd learned the length of the trip.

'There's trouble coming for the human associated dolphins on Earth and Sonic told the Witness Council and the AIs that he needs to be there to help them and the special ship they're building for him is so advanced it only takes a bit over a day to get there.'

Wirrin explained everything before leaving for an afternoon of study at EdCom.

*   *   *

'This is incredible.' Standing in the control deck of the Comet was a different experience to looking at a holo of the same thing. It really brought home the way the Comet had been designed as much for dolphins as humans.

At the moment the display was showing the main centre at Monkey Mia, and Sonic had just changed the view of the completed grav-field to a representation of the number of dolphins spread through the surrounding waters. From the bank of controls at the edge of his special pool it was possible for Sonic to take charge of the Comet as easily as any human. He didn't have the knowledge and training for full control of course, but several simulator sessions had made him familiar with information access.

Wirrin and Calen were smiling at this latest in Thom's series of exclamations as Turaku guided them through different sections of the Comet. It was the first day the Comet was ready for humans and dolphins. After seeing the transport pools, each designed for a full pod of dolphins, the control section for the advanced picofactory, the living quarters for humans, the medical facility and the docking ports for the Earth dolphins, they were now in the main control area where they'd spend most of the time on the journey.

It really was incredible, and Thom was expressing Wirrin and Calen's feelings quite admirably.

Wirrin hadn't realised how big and diverse this control centre would be and seeing thirty or forty people in different areas around the room was another wake up to the significance of the Comet.

'Look at all those dolphins. How up to date is this information?'

'Current apart from the transmission time lag. It's flowing directly and non-stop from Earth.'

'And which Turaku are we talking to? Comet-Turaku or our usual Turaku?'

It sounded so strange. Every head turned to Thom, and then to Turaku to see what he'd say.

'Your usual Turaku, Thom. The changes all happen tomorrow and you'll meet my extension then.'

'What will you do? I mean will he look like you? That would be very confusing if you're both here at the same time?'

'The new aspect will look like a comet. Show them, Turaku.'

Turaku's holo melted then morphed to a stylised comet with a fiery tail, and the trio gawked as pieces peeled from the main body then flared to incandescence and disappeared. There was a great burst of dolphin laughter from Sonic and Turaku's normal image returned. Wirrin was impressed with how instantly Turaku had gone along with Sonic's trick, but then he did watch every micro-second of Sonic's life, so it wasn't really surprising that he had a good understanding of Sonic's sense of humour.

'Oh no! Teaching Turaku your fish jokes. More suffering for us.'

Sonic gave an emphatic nod and Thom jumped just a moment too late to evade the expertly directed jet of water. Calling Sonic a fish was a friendly insult which always brought a reaction. Wirrin was surprised that Thom hadn't been more wary.

No, he'd thought Sonic wouldn't do anything because the situation was more formal than usual. Thom spluttered, wiped his face, wrung some of the water from his drenched shirt and looked round at all the amused expressions.

'Next time I'm in the water I'll pound you into a blob of jelly.'

There were surprised looks from some of the onlookers who had no experience of the nonsense that went on when the trio and Sonic were in a muck-around mood. Sonic just laughed.

'Come and explore the passageways with me.'

'Now? I haven't got my water gear.' Thom meant the dolphinarium water shorts and facemask they used when they were out in the reaches.

'You don't wear it at home.'

Thom glanced round then after a quick shrug, stripped, dived in, and disappeared, under tow, through the exit to one of the waterways.

Gulara laughed. 'So much for the jelly pounding threat.'

'Thom only acts tough to make Sonic laugh. It's one of their games.'

'Why has Sonic taken him off exploring when we're finding out about the ship?'

'Who knows? That's just Sonic's way, Gulara.'

Turaku indicated a seat by a console and motioned Wirrin to sit in it.

'This is a high access Information Station, which has been specially tailored to extend your capabilities.'

An InfoStation was an InfoStation as far as Wirrin was concerned. He used them everywhere, at EdCom, at the dolphinarium, and his own good one at home, so he wondered what specially tailored could mean.

'We'll leave you to familiarise yourself.'

'Integration and introduction module.'

It was quite a jolt for Wirrin to have his retinal mode involuntarily activated. It had happened a couple of times when the doctor and technicians were testing at the implant facility but this time it must be Turaku … Or maybe it was this InfoStation?

Wirrin switched transparency in but everyone was moving away so he returned to full retinal mode and for over an hour immersed himself in the module.

*   *   *

'Take it slowly, Thom. Nothing more than 3G till we're out of range of the K74 surveillance drones.'

The giant engines of the Comet engaged.

The images of Attunga and Warrakan dwindled in a section of the display.

The forward view showed a panorama of stars and brilliant Sol.

Chapter 14

Wirrin watched Thom's control, concentration and competence as he took charge of the most advanced space ship ever built. After Thom had been informed the previous evening that he'd have the opportunity to pilot the Comet for the departure from Attunga, he'd proclaimed that description of the ship, and no-one was going to disagree with him. There might be bigger vessels but their capabilities wouldn't come anywhere near the Comet.

Wirrin turned to Turaku. This was Comet-Turaku, who'd be part of the Comet for as long as it existed. He looked exactly the same as Attunga-Turaku except for a glowing Comet decal emblazoned on his chest.

'Why do we have to travel slowly? The K74 drones can't see us.'

'Until we have three light seconds of separation they're capable of detecting the energy signature of high acceleration, and that mustn't happen.'

'They can detect us? That's a change.'

'Only at accelerations greater than 6G, but they have become more capable recently. Their new drones have much improved scanning equipment.'

'New drones?'

'Yes, the first of them arrived six days ago.'

That sounded to Wirrin as if they'd been arriving ever since.

'Are there many of these new ones out there?'

Turaku gestured to the InfoStation. 'Bring them up on the display for us. It will only take you a moment to find them.'

With Calen and Gulara standing close behind, Wirrin settled at his InfoStation. It must be under the security section. Whoo! So many possibilities.

Pleased at how effective his new reading skills were in this situation, he rapidly scanned the broad menu and found what he needed. On the big display a representation of Attunga and Warrakan appeared, surrounded at a distance by hundreds of red lights. They couldn't all be new drones, surely? How to differentiate between the new and the old? After a few more seconds of figuring, the red lights blinked off and were replaced by a smaller number of purple ones. How many? Seventy-three new drones.

'That took you twenty-three seconds, Wirrin. Close down your station and try again.'

So Turaku wanted to see how fast he could display information did he? Well, there was no searching this time and he could pull the information straight out.

'Much better — 2.7 seconds.'

Wirrin had an idea, set it going, and grinned at Turaku.

'Tell me how long it takes this time.'

'Point four of a second. Well done, setting a trigger like that is excellent for primary actions but with millions of possible actions it's more efficient to learn the system.'

Millions? Well of course there were, and Wirrin understood exactly what Turaku meant. Learning vast numbers of triggers would take a huge amount of time and any particular trigger in itself might never be needed.

'How many of the new drones are within two light-seconds distance?'

'All of them.'

'That took three seconds. Given our current rate of acceleration, how long before the last of them is out of our three light-second range?'

The result, 106 minutes, involved new information and fifteen seconds of figuring how to put it all together.

'That's better. Now figure how long before K74 is out of range.'

This was somewhat similar to the last query and Wirrin managed it in seven seconds.

'Excellent. How many other existing threats to the Comet can you find?'

Wirrin instantly thought of the big offensive vessel from K74, but Turaku was asking generally.

'There's a radiation belt two and a half hours away, less if we increase acceleration, but it's a low-level threat ... And there are three medium-level threats near K74.'

'What are they?'

That only took an instant as Wirrin already had his attention on them.

'The offensive K74 ships we saw weeks ago, except there are now three instead of two.'

A scale change with the display showed that two of the ships were moving, but relatively slowly, while the third was moving into deep space at a high velocity. That was interesting. Without being told Wirrin searched and then spluttered, 'It's travelling nearly thirty times as fast as we are!'

'Check its acceleration. That's a better indication of its capability.'

'13G.'

No wonder it was making the Comet look like a snail. Well, that would certainly change when the Comet activated full power. Wirrin wondered where the speeding ship was headed.

'How do I work out where it's going, Turaku?'

'Link in to our navigation menu.'

Annoyed with himself for not thinking of the obvious, Wirrin went ahead.

'It's not going anywhere!'

'No, this is its maiden voyage and they're testing it. Apply your new understanding of the InfoSystem to see how much you can discover about it in the next twenty minutes while I talk to Akama and Sonic.'

Calen and Gulara, obviously curious about what Sonic and Akama wanted, moved off with Turaku. Within moments Wirrin had detailed schematics and specifications.

What a monster this new K74 ship was, nearly 600 metres in length … Capable of 14G acceleration, so it was close to its maximum at the moment. Everything about the ship's function was there in minute detail. This was too easy. Turaku must be expecting something else, perhaps its history? Its purpose? Maybe tracing where the Comet got all this information from would turn up something.

Search for any database about K74.

Hmm, very interesting. A stream of information coming directly from K74 itself? Wirrin's ideas kept coming, and as he set them in motion he started to realise all over again how powerful this InfoStation really was.

*   *   *

'What have you got to tell us, Wirrin?'

'Well for a start that ship is a dud. If they keep running those engines at over eighty per cent like they are now, they'll eventually collapse.'

'We knew that. What else have you unearthed?'

'It's named after one of that Cadre on K74, and so are the other two ships, and it's got special stealth equipment and scanning devices to get close enough to Warrakan to find out about our drive engines. It was only completed twenty hours ago and they've got plans to build two more, each connected by name with one of the Cadre.'

Akama was surprised.

'It's designed for surveillance against Warrakan? That wasn't in my security report, Turaku.'

'The surveillance capabilities were mentioned, but not that they were specifically aimed at Warrakan. That's new information you've uncovered, Wirrin, along with the link between the ships and the ruling Cadre.'

Wirrin felt a combination of awkwardness and pleasure at the looks he was receiving.

Akama rested his hand on Wirrin's head. Again? What did it mean and why didn't he do it to anyone else?

'Well done, Wirrin. You've already shown that my hunch was correct.'

He removed his hand and smiled at Wirrin's puzzled look.

'It was my idea to give you full integration with the information station. Will this new K74 ship be effective in its purpose?'

Wirrin looked to Turaku but he said nothing.

'It won't find out anything we don't want it to. It uses the same equipment as the new drones, just on a bigger scale.'

'So you believe it will be completely frustrated in its purpose?'

'I'm certain of it. Attunga and Warrakan have already designed and built new protective facilities to counter anything it can try. We have a huge advantage over K74 because we get information about any of their new developments as soon as they implement them.'

'How can we do that, Wirrin? It seems like we find out whatever we want,' Calen said, and Burilda was nodding and looking puzzled.

'Almost everything. Attunga has developed its own surveillance drones to tell us about the activity around K74. They're like the guardian drones that protect the dolphins at Monkey Mia, except they're designed for space. They disabled two of the new K74 drones and brought them to Attunga for analysis. Most of the information comes from the AI on K74 though, who's been communicating with our own AIs for nearly two months.'

'That AI is still there? Last I heard he was transferring to Attunga.'

'He agreed to postpone the shift because of all this trouble with the dolphins.'

'You discovered all this in fifteen minutes?'

'Um, yes. This InfoStation is amazing.'

'I'd like you to put a serious effort into learning this system while we're travelling. Turaku, can you oversee a set of exercises and challenges that will help Wirrin become more proficient with his station?'

'Done.'

'Excellent, and I think these early results already warrant installation of a similar system at home on Attunga. Let's see what happens after twelve hours of application.'

An InfoSystem as powerful as this for his own use? This was as surprising as Thom's advancement with piloting. Wirrin stared at Akama, excitement stirring at the prospect of special tutoring with Turaku ... Twelve hours? That was more than half his waking time.

This was going to be a busy trip.

*   *   *

'Are you ready, Thom? Here it comes.

five ... four ... three ... two ... one ... turn around!'

They had reached the point at which the Comet would reorient itself so the thrust of the engines could slow the ship in a mirror image of the acceleration of the first half of the trip. It was also the point of maximum speed, and though they'd known all along that it was going to happen, it was still exciting to experience the moment. Wirrin flashed the number dramatically on the display.

'Whoo! 9726.3 Ksecs. A record for the trip to Earth. The K74 ships couldn't come anywhere near that.'

Nearly 10,000 kilometres in one second. The idea of it was incredible, especially as the panorama of stars gave no indication of movement at all. The only apparent difference was the increased brightness of the Sun. Well, that would all change when they approached Earth.

'They could reach almost 7000 Ksecs, Thom, but if they tried to go any faster the engines would conk out.'

'Weak as wombat water!'

'Wombat water wouldn't reach 7000 Ksecs.'

Nothing was as good as the Comet as far as Thom was concerned. He'd been quite disgusted to learn that despite his expectations, the

Comet wouldn't be making a solar system speed record on this trip. That would have to wait. The transporters carrying the initial population to the Titania habitat had, despite their much lower acceleration capability, been able to reach over 10,000 Ksecs because of their much longer acceleration time. The usual record holders were the vessels carrying supplies and personnel to a small scientific research habitat way out at Pluto.

'We're slowing down … 9722.8 kilometres per second,' said Thom.

'Come on everyone. Just over thirteen hours till we get to Earth. This is the long stretch with not much change so we need to copy Sonic and have a good rest before everything starts happening.'

Calen was right. A glance showed that Sonic was in the logging state he'd informed them would last for at least ten hours in case he didn't get a chance for a proper rest on Earth. The Comet was under control of the security AI and there were only seven people in the control centre. Everyone else had had the same idea as Sonic.

*   *   *

Wirrin stared in utter awe at the display. For the last few minutes no-one had spoken, held as if spellbound by the magnificence of planet Earth.

Standing shoulder to shoulder with Calen and Thom in an instinctive need to share the moment, Wirrin wondered how anything could be so beautiful. He'd seen this before, many times, as holo images or virtual reality presentations, but knowing it was real changed things.

There was a call from Sonic who was watching from the water and Calen raced over and dived in with him. Apart from sleep times they'd been together almost the whole trip. Puck and Flute were going to come but Sonic persuaded them to stay and relay information to the Attunga dolphins who were slightly on edge with all the imminent changes.

As far as Wirrin could tell Sonic didn't seem to be affected by the separation from his pod, but according to Calen that was a case of logic overruling his natural feelings.

'*Home of all dolphins and people. So much water.*'

'Home for AIs too. They started on Earth.'

There was indeed a vast amount of water. With Monkey Mia the destination, the approach aspect at the moment showed a major part of the Pacific Ocean.

'*How long before we reach the water?*'

Wirrin smiled at Sonic's perspective. People would have asked how long before they would land.

As if a spell had been broken people throughout the command centre stirred from their quiet contemplation and went into action.

Wirrin connected with his InfoStation and called to Sonic that it would be another twenty-one minutes.

Thom moved close to the pilot from the security ship to watch his procedure for the final approach into atmosphere and the gravity well of Earth.

The planetary sphere grew to fill the screen, with the features of the Australian continent taking prominence until the familiar aerial view of Shark Bay took over.

Wirrin looked at Akama, standing quiet and staring with rapt attention at the approaching view of his old home country.

Yes, there was his river and range, visible for a while as the Comet slowed more and more in its descent. With precision and apparent ease the ship came to rest in the cradle of the grav-field and everyone looked around with a curious sense of anticipation. The pilot swivelled his seat towards Akama.

'All secure and ready for debarkation, Honoured One.'

The display switched from landing information to external and everyone took in the buildings of the marine station, the approaching phalanx of vehicles, and most of all the glistening, azure expanse of sky and bay. Everyone moved and just clear of the landing cradle Akama stopped.

Wirrin, walking close behind, bumped into him because at that moment he was staring at the sky. Akama smiled then lifted his head and stared as well. He kept staring, as if he had no intention of moving. Oh, he was stopping to give the Attunga dwellers time to absorb the surroundings. Every single one of them had lifted their head to gaze in wonder at this first step into an environment without walls.

The trio exchanged glances. They'd talked about this, wondering what real sky and open air would be like, but Wirrin knew that for all of them this was more powerful than anything they'd envisioned. Calen laughed and pointed at Wirrin's head.

'What?'

'Your curls are moving. The air's pushing them.'

They were too. Wirrin was suddenly conscious of the light pressure on his hair. The air was moving without any fan or other device.

'It's called wind.'

'Not quite, Thom. When it's gentle like this it's called a breeze.'

Another breath of air lifted Wirrin's hair and he became the centre of attention as the whole group smiled at the novelty of it.

'Earth, air, and sea. All around.'

Akama's mention of the sea set Wirrin looking past the waiting people to the bay and he realised with a jolt just how enormous it was. Stretching as far as he could see it made the big new reaches on Warrakan seem like almost nothing. Akama started to walk again, slowly, and Calen edged closer to Sonic's transport module, floating on its anti-grav-field, and murmured something. As they approached the welcoming group Wirrin was almost bewildered by the clash between the imperatives telling him to examine everything around and his sense of occasion telling him to focus on the people. A man stepped forward and greeted Akama, welcoming him home and then welcoming the whole group.

'Honoured One, would you grace us with a short ceremony?'

Akama nodded then pointed to the shoreline.

'Earth, air and sea ... as befits the moment.' Wirrin forgot, well almost, all the externals vying for his attention. Akama had assumed the mantle of his office, quiet, dignified and powerful. This was the Akama introducing Sonic to eight hundred million people on Attunga, the Akama acknowledging a glorious arc of tribute from every enhanced dolphin.

Wirrin sensed that something major was about to happen. With a single inclusive gesture Akama invited everyone to be part of whatever was to happen at the water's edge.

In the walk to the water the marine centre people and local leaders gradually mingled with the travellers. Calen was smiling and Wirrin wondered what Sonic had just said to him. Sonic's head was tilted at an awkward angle, which meant he was surveying everything. He was certainly very active, twisting in every direction, clearly excited. With sudden purpose Sonic manoeuvred his module close to Akama and engaged him in a short conversation. Straining to hear, Wirrin made out something about dolphin friends and the ocean, then watched in surprise when, after a nod from Akama, Calen climbed in with Sonic and the module raced for the water, now only 50 metres away, across the sand and into the shallow water. With a slight lift and a crash of spray it breached a small wave and continued till it came to a dead stop in the deeper water.

What now? With one great leap Sonic sailed into the ocean. The leap was impressive in itself, but from the relatively confined module it was even more so, and worthy of the sudden gasps and exclamations. Calen, standing in the chest-deep water of the module, suddenly raised his arm and Sonic erupted from the water in a truly spectacular parabola of power, speed and motion. The whole gathering stopped in its tracks, watched wonderingly for a moment till Akama moved forward, turned, and with a hand gesture now familiar to Wirrin, drew everyone's attention.

'Sonic, our dolphin friend, has requested time to invite his Earth relatives to a place in our ceremony.'

Without waiting for a response Akama turned again and started towards the beach. A murmur grew, and looking round, Wirrin took in some puzzled looks.

Well, they had no idea of Sonic's capabilities, and Akama's acquiescence to a request from a dolphin in regard to a traditional ceremony must be quite incomprehensible.

Wirrin gave Thom a nudge and said softly, 'Akama's just told them how important Sonic is and they don't understand.'

'They're in for a shock if he starts speaking.'

They both smiled but were interrupted in their thoughts when the person walking just in front and a little behind Akama turned and gave them a curious look.

'Excuse me, your voices carried on the breeze and I couldn't help overhearing. The dolphin is important to Akama in more than a formal sense? And you seem to imply it can speak intelligently?'

Oops! Wirrin and Thom exchanged a grimace. Had they said too much? After a hasty contact with Turaku in retinal mode granted them permission to speak freely, Wirrin gave a nod and a friendly smile, wondering who he was talking to. He did have an important air about him.

'That's right. Sonic is so important that Akama came on this trip to help him ... And he can speak better than any of us.'

'Better?'

'Believe it, my friend, and invite anyone still at the marine station to join us. My intuition tells me they should.'

The breeze was doing a good job of carrying voices because Akama was speaking. He sat on the sand and turned his head to stare at the bay.

Wirrin stared too, first of all at waves — real ones, building like giant ripples in the distance, then cresting and falling in the shallows with a rush and swirl on the sand. They weren't very big, but there was something fascinating about them.

All the people, taking their cue from Akama, sat on the sand and watched expectantly. A soft questioning buzz rippled back and forth as people looked and wondered. Wirrin noticed Gulara talking quietly with the man who'd welcomed them. Several dolphin fins broke the surface near Sonic's transporter then disappeared. Hundreds of metres away more shapes came into view, gliding directly inshore, going under then reappearing in the classic behaviour of a dolphin pod on the move. Thom's head turned and Wirrin followed his look.

A stream of people was leaving the marine station, dozens of them and not far away from what Wirrin remembered was the access to the underground living areas an even bigger stream was appearing. There was a gasp of surprise and Wirrin turned to see dozens of pods coming from all directions. No, more than that. Scanning the distance he saw even more pods.

Thom grabbed Wirrin's arm.

'He's getting them all.'

Not all, but it did look like it. It turned out that Sonic, aware of causing a delay, had called to dolphins within a radius of 4 to 5 kilometres.

'How can he do that? They've never even met him.'

Wirrin was as amazed as Thom at the way the Earth dolphins were responding to Sonic.

'Calen will tell us. He's down there with him somewhere.'

'I wish we were.'

Wirrin switched into retinal mode just long enough to query Turaku. He was zapping the external scene at the moment and didn't like interrupting that.

'We'll see it all later, Thom. Turaku's watching through the local surveillance units and he's organised a guardian drone for Sonic and Calen.'

'Calen's got his own guardian? What a dingo!'

The man next to Wirrin, the same one, caught his attention. There was something about him that Wirrin liked.

'I'm Wirrin and this is Thom. We're Sonic's friends.'

'Thank you, Wirrin and Thom. My name is Narn. Your friend Sonic can control other dolphins as effectively as this?'

Wirrin smiled at Narn's carefully chosen use of the word 'effectively', when he was clearly finding the evidence of his own eyes hard to believe.

'It's not control. He wouldn't like that. He would have spoken to them and they're coming because they want to.'

'He communicates that well? I mean it's obvious he can, but you make it sound like human conversation.'

'Yes, I'm sorry, I was being too general. Your dolphins aren't the same as ours. Sonic understands human speech as well as anyone. He doesn't speak it himself because he produces sounds differently, but the translators do that perfectly for him. He communicates with other dolphins in the normal way, except his range of ideas and vocabulary is enormous. We talk to him every day so we just think of it as normal speaking.'

'Every day? You have such a close association with him?'

'Yes, Calen is closest though. He's out there in the water with him now. We're like his human pod. He comes to our home every night to relax and mess around.'

'Mess around … as in youthful companionship?'

Thom and Wirrin both laughed.

'Yes, but you could say dolphin companionship. He messes around with anyone he likes. When Akama was in our pool Sonic splashed and bumped him the same way he plays with us.'

'Akama visits your home?'

The tone wasn't quite disbelief, more like, 'who are these boys to be visited by someone like Akama?'

'Only once. To meet Sonic.'

'He likes seeing you too, Wirrin.'

Thom and Calen had built up a theory that Akama was interested in Wirrin because they looked so alike when they were little children. Wirrin gave Thom a shooshing nudge and glanced at Akama, hoping he hadn't heard. He was gazing at the bay with a slight smile.

'Hey look, Thom! It's Calen.'

With one hand holding the side of Sonic's transporter for support, Calen surveyed the people on shore till their eyes caught. He raised his other arm for a quick wave then disappeared underwater again.

'What a wombat! We really should be out there,' said Thom.

Wirrin felt the same. Calen clearly wanted to share his excitement, but they couldn't go. It would feel like they were pushing in when they hadn't been asked. Wirrin turned to Narn, thinking he liked the sound of that name.

'Calen goes with Sonic because they do nearly everything together and he can speak dolphin properly.'

'Properly?'

'Well, Thom and I know quite a few words, but we don't say them right because we can't make all the sounds. Calen can because he has special implants.'

There was a lengthy silence.

'Wirrin, I don't quite know what to say. You speak familiarly of a world I didn't know existed. Do many people on Attunga speak to dolphins?'

Narn was overwhelmed by the idea of talking dolphins.

'Not really. Calen's the only one with real dolphin language and there aren't many dolphins. Sonic's the first one who speaks to everybody, but the others like to get to know you first. They mostly speak with their rangers and other dolphinarium people.'

Narn clearly wanted to say more but their attention was drawn to the water where two distinct pods, probably thirty or forty dolphins, were now active near the transporter only 20 metres away. Not far to the left was another pod, and close by another, and another.

Everywhere pods were milling, and further out innumerable pods were still approaching. A wondering silence settled on the humans at the astonishing sight. The whole ocean seemed to be full of dolphins.

Chapter 15

'Earth, air, and sea!'

Akama's voice rang loud and clear across the water, and Wirrin, standing with Calen, Thom and Sonic chest deep in the water by the transport module, listened to a symbolic call for Earth dwellers, sky dwellers and water dwellers to meet in this place that embodied those three fundamental elements so well. It was short and powerfully presented and everyone watched quietly, wondering what was to happen next.

For Wirrin and Thom there had been an awkward but proud moment when Sonic and Calen had surfaced and called to them and they'd had to walk from the shore and stand with Sonic under the curious gaze of a crowd that now numbered several hundred people.

Akama finished and stood, waiting, his attention fixed on Sonic, who ducked under the surface. Standing right next to Sonic, Wirrin sensed the rapid transmission of sound as the message was translated in terms the gathered dolphins would understand. A multitude of dolphin heads lifted from the water and looked towards Akama, who raised his arm in formal acknowledgement.

From his low vantage point Wirrin's view was limited to the dolphins close to the transport, but the effect was still incredible, hundreds of dolphin heads rose, all looking in the same direction and waiting. Burilda said that from the shore the great sea of faces gave her the uncanny feeling that every single one of them was looking directly at her. Akama motioned to the man who'd made the original welcome, and to Gulara as well, then walked with them into the water and towards Sonic.

Wirrin watched them approaching but his attention kept flicking to the nearby crowd of dolphins, their fixed smiles strangely overpowering en masse, and to Sonic whose body was vibrating with excitement and energy.

Sonic left the trio and whisked through the water to meet Akama and the representatives of Australia and Attunga. There was a burst of dolphin sound and Akama looked to Calen for its meaning.

'It was a call of happiness at being in such a beautiful place and a thank you for the welcome.'

There was another burst of sound and suddenly Sonic's translated speech resounded over the gathering.

'Dolphins are excited to meet humans and be part of a ceremony.'

The trio jerked with surprise because Sonic needed to be in his transporter for the translator to work. Wirrin made hasty contact and said quietly, 'Turaku's collecting the sound and relaying it to the translator.'

Akama repeated the Welcome to Country, but this time, with the dolphins so prominently included, it felt even more important and moving. At the end Sonic's amplified voice thanked Akama and invited all the people into the water. At first people were too surprised to respond but when Akama beckoned, that changed completely and all the watchers crossed the wet band of sand and waded tentatively into the water. Sonic disappeared, and two seconds later every dolphin followed, leaving the surface eerily deserted in contrast to the great gathering of a moment before. Calen dived as well, to hear what was going on, but reappeared in moments, shaking his head.

'It's chaos. They're all talking at once and it's too much sound for me to cope with.'

Sonic reappeared, and like magic the waters of the bay were again filled with myriads of dolphins.

The Earth representative, looking quite overwhelmed, was carried on Sonic's back with crowds of dolphins accompanying them, while Akama asked people to spread themselves along the beach so there would be plenty of clear space for the dolphins to approach. People and dolphins mingled along several hundred metres of coastline. These dolphins were all used to human contact and their elegant body language and friendly bumps and nudges sent everyone's spirits soaring.

Every person Wirrin could see was smiling. Certain dolphins, who turned out to be the pod leaders, approached first Sonic, then, after a short rapid exchange of dolphin speech, Akama, Gulara and the Earth representative. For twenty minutes dolphins and humans mingled, till the last pods headed out to deeper water.

Akama raised his arm in a formal gesture then waded towards the shore. As one, people all along the shore congregated to hear what he had to say.

Wirrin was struck with the way the people were following Akama's lead. Calen stopped him. 'We'll have to find out what he says later. Sonic wants us with him. Jump in the transport because the dolphins are going out to deeper water.'

'What's happening?'

Calen pointed at the people gathering round Akama. 'The same thing really. A big dolphin meeting so Sonic can explain everything properly.'

The transport zipped straight out into the bay, following the cruising form of Sonic for about a kilometre. Sonic stopped and the trio donned facemasks and dived to join him.

The first shock was the deeper water. The Attunga reaches were no more than 4 metres deep. The second shock was the number of dolphins. Sonic sank deeper and deeper with the trio following, and as they did a wall of dolphins closed round them till they were almost completely englobed. Wirrin understood why. They were in deeper water and Sonic was thinking in 3D. This way the maximum number of dolphins could see Sonic and the trio.

For the next forty minutes Wirrin wished for implants like Calen's so he could hear more clearly. Ordinary human ears really don't function very well under water. He sensed many things though, through his knowledge of dolphin body language and sounds — the presentation and identification of the trio as part of Sonic's pod; the thrill of massed warning sounds when Sonic explained the deadly danger and the death of the earlier pods; an almost unbearable moment when the whole group expressed sadness and loss when Sonic made it clear they should leave their homes forever; and then a longer period of growing excitement as they heard what was in store for them.

Every five or six minutes the globe formation dissolved then reformed as every dolphin, following Sonic's cue, surfaced for air, and once the trio had to return to the transport module to replace their masks.

Calen was very much involved, speaking directly to the dolphins and sometimes to Sonic, and occasionally swimming close to an individual who must have asked him something. Eventually there was a great swirl of motion and, as the dolphins dispersed, Calen headed for the surface. Back in the transporter he took a few deep breaths, then started towards the shore.

'Wow! This is harder than I thought.'

'Where are we going now?'

'I'm taking you back to Akama.'

'Us? What about you?'

'I'm going with Sonic, Wirrin. We've got three more meetings — one near Faure Island, one in Denham Sound, and one up near Bernier Island.'

'Why was it hard? You were amazing,' said Thom.

Wirrin nodded vigorously.

'They use the same words as our dolphins but it's hard to understand them. It's like they're on different wavelengths. Sonic had to repeat some of what I said in a different way to get the meaning across properly.'

Wirrin wanted to ask zillions of questions but they were fast approaching the shore.

'Calen, how come we're not going with you?'

'Akama wants you with him. There's a delay with some dolphins arriving from North America and the dolphins won't start loading into the Comet for another four hours. He's taking you to visit Gnardune Springs.'

'Sonic told you all this?'

'Yes, Turaku has been keeping him updated about everything.'

Wirrin's connections to the InterWeb and Turaku didn't work while he was underwater. Sonic's were designed to, as long as he was near his transporter or other specialised equipment.

'Four hours? You won't have time for three meetings.'

'Yes we will, and we'll be back in time for Sonic to talk to all the Monkey Mia people. Sonic's transporter is too slow so we've got air transport.'

Of course they'd have air transport. Turaku would make sure Sonic had security wherever he went. Thom pointed. Sure enough, a big air transporter was approaching from somewhere inland of the marine station. No, not just one — four more came into view and accelerated at high speed in the direction of Faure Island. The first one passed almost overhead, moving relatively slowly and quite low. Calen brought the transporter to a halt at the water's edge.

'Quick! I have to get back with this transporter. They need it to move Sonic, and for Turaku to keep in contact when he's underwater.'

Wirrin and Thom leapt to the sand and watched as Calen took off at great speed.

'Whoo! Look at him go! He's in a hurry.'

Wirrin laughed.

'Yes, Thom, about half the speed you'd be doing.'

They watched a moment as Calen raced towards the big air transporter, which was now hovering near where they'd parted with Sonic, then swivelled to watch yet another air transporter, travelling very low and coming along the shore. All this open space. Things could happen from any direction.

The air vehicle settled close by and when a door slid open Gulara appeared, beckoning them aboard. Inside, as the air transporter lifted and accelerated, they joined Gulara and Akama along with Narn who smiled in recognition.

'Narn tells me you've already introduced yourselves. He's taking us to visit Akama's home country.'

*   *   *

Akama turned to watch the display as the waters of the bay raced beneath them, his eyes fixed ahead on the dark band of green, which Wirrin knew was the course of his river. Everyone was quiet as the first silver sparkles of water appeared and rapidly enlarged, watching Akama as he stared with rapt attention.

Wirrin felt a lump forming in his throat, wondering what it would be like to return to a home you thought you might never see again.

Akama looked straight at him with a gentle smile, as if he knew his thoughts, and Wirrin couldn't help smiling back.

The air transporter landed then departed, leaving the group of five in a clear area not far from the water, which Wirrin could see glistening through gaps between the scattered eucalyptus trees. Akama stood for a moment, looking all round, then pointed.

'This way first. I want to show you something.'

As they walked Wirrin took in everything. It was like one of the enviro parks on Attunga, except it went on and on in every direction, with the wonder of the blue sky above, and the rich red of the sandy soil rough beneath their feet.

There was a sudden high-pitched screech and twittering and Wirrin whirled to catch a glimpse of flying green shapes disappearing into some high branches.

'Lorikeets. There is quite a concentration of bird life along the river.'

Wirrin and Thom looked at each other. Calen was missing this. Well, at least he'd see the zapped version.

As they passed a strange-looking tree Thom stopped to touch the loose layers of whitish grey bark hanging from a dull orange scar on the trunk.

'It's a paperbark tree.'

Narn pulled a small piece free and handed it to Thom who rubbed it between his fingers before passing it to Wirrin.

'Paper?'

Wirrin and Thom knew what paper was. They'd made it themselves with EdCom when they were younger.

'It wasn't used for paper. It just looks like it.'

The next stop was a giant old gum tree.

'Recognise it?'

Akama pointed to where a large limb branched from the main trunk and the picture leapt into Wirrin's mind of a boy holding on for dear life with winged devils plucking at him.

Yes. There was the big lumpy growth that had fascinated him. This was the exact tree, still here after all this time.

'Can I climb on your shoulders?'

Wirrin stared at Akama in amazement. Of course he could, but it wasn't something you expected from a Witness.

Akama laughed. 'Some of the low branches are gone. I'll need help to get up there.'

A couple of minutes later Wirrin and Thom were perched on the branch next to Akama, looking down at Gulara and Narn and then surveying the scenery. Once again Akama pointed, this time at a large white bird in the shallows of the river, its head bent low to the water and steadily trawling from side to side.

'What is it doing?'

'We called it the funny-face bird but its proper name is spoonbill. When it lifts its head you'll see why. It's foraging for food.'

Fascinated, Wirrin and Thom watched and, sure enough, when the bird raised its head to look around alertly, the rounded spoon shape of its upper and lower bills came clearly into view. Akama wanted to get moving and scrambled to the ground. Wirrin was more awkward in his descent.

'Our time is very limited and I'd like to fit in a short walkabout.'

The next three-quarters of an hour piled wonder on wonder and Wirrin wished Calen was with them. At least he was zapping everything and they'd be able to share it all later.

The highlight for Wirrin was holding a bizarre creature that Narn discovered, a dangerous-looking little reptile called a thorny devil with spikes and rough protrusions all over. Amazingly, it was quite soft, belying its ferocious appearance, and Wirrin examined it closely, enjoying the sensation of its tiny claws hooking into his fingers while Narn explained how it could actually drink through its skin.

At the end of the walk there was another surprise when Akama raced into the waters of Gnardune Pool and, laughing, beckoned everyone else to join him. Wirrin realised he was purposefuly replaying the scene he'd shared with them.

After ten minutes the big air transporter, flanked by four others, appeared overhead and settled at the water's edge. A message from Turaku appeared in retinal mode and Wirrin called for everyone to hurry.

'There's a security alert and we need to get back to the Comet.'

'Do we have time enough to collect our things?'

'Yes. It's not directed at us, but Turaku doesn't want us out in the open.'

Akama's visit to his home country was cut short and the group, now serious, rushed to get aboard. As the convoy accelerated towards Monkey Mia, Turaku's holo shimmered into view.

'I felt it necessary to return you to the Comet, Honoured One. There is hostile activity rather sooner than expected and it is advisable to raise our security levels.'

'Of course. What is the nature of this activity?'

'Four large space vessels have stationed themselves in low orbit directly above Shark Bay and are closely scanning the area. We have suppressed all electronic signals, but excepting the Comet itself, there is nothing we can do about optical surveillance. Those watching have been alerted by the unusual configuration and movements of the dolphins, and the probability of a response is rising critically.'

'What are the indications for that?'

'The Comet traced signals from the low orbit surveillance to locations not far outside Australian territorial jurisdiction, but more significantly to three large ships, one 15 kilometres west of Dirk Hartog Island, one close to Ningaloo, and one not far from the Great Barrier Reef centre.'

Wirrin linked to the security of the air transport, located the ship so close to Shark Bay, and scanned the information about it. Ten minutes ago it was a legitimate cruise ship from the friendly Malaysian area, but the Australian security AIs had now discovered that the passenger lists were phoney. The people existed, but currently eighty-three per cent of them had been observed going about their normal business in their home habitats.

What about the other two ships? A quick look showed a similar disparity.

'The ships are fake. The people meant to be on them aren't there.'

Akama nodded and addressed Turaku. 'What are we doing about them? This feels very much like a repeat of the last attack.'

'Air cover has been dispatched to all three locations for a closer look and all defensive systems are now in operation.'

Wirrin checked the security overview in retinal mode then switched it to full holo so everyone could see the groups of air defence vessels dispersed to all areas of Shark Bay.

One particularly large air vessel was streaking towards the cruise ship and the data showed it would arrive in just over two minutes.

'Where are Sonic and Calen? Are they safe?'

'I asked them to board an air transporter and return to the Comet but Sonic has committed himself to the meeting for at least another twenty minutes.'

Wirrin displayed the area, where a convoy of six aircraft circled, then zoomed close. There was the distinctive globe of dolphins, gathered near the surface. They would be easily picked out by any high-resolution optical device in low orbit. Wirrin looked at the huge group of dolphins, picturing Calen and Sonic in the water with them, and started to check on how many there were.

The whole display flashed red for a second, sending a shock of apprehension through everyone watching. As one they turned to Turaku.

'Another signal was transmitted to the three ships. We have been damping all emissions but a sudden power increase of a full order of magnitude penetrated before we adjusted our suppression levels. I've mobilised the Comet and we will all rendezvous at Sonic's location.'

The transporter lurched to a new bearing and accelerated strongly.

'Underwater activity has been detected near all the suspect ships. There is high-speed drone movement and I have deployed 130 enhanced guardians from the security resources protecting the dolphin gathering for their interception and containment.'

Stunned by the speed of everything, the group watched the big holo display, which Turaku was now controlling. Wirrin, horrified more and more by the number and speed of the attack drones being revealed, grabbed Thom's arm.

'There are hundreds. Can we stop them before they reach Sonic?'

Turaku explained that the 694 hostile drones would reach the dolphin meeting in eight minutes and twenty seconds at their current speed of 107 kilometres per hour but first engagement with the guardians would occur in three minutes and forty seconds. 'We anticipate complete disablement of every hostile unit.'

Wirrin noticed the big increase in speed compared with the original drones. They'd definitely been improving them. Still it was encouraging to hear Turaku's confidence. The seconds ticked by. The Comet would reach Sonic in five more minutes according to the screen and they'd be able to board themselves just two minutes after that. The display flashed red again, sending Wirrin's pulse racing. That red was a warning of some significant event.

'There is a further deployment of drones. A larger type, of unknown capability.'

Six red markers were moving away from the cruise ship, two heading towards the northern end of Bernier Island and the other four following the path of the earlier drones towards the gap between Dorre and Dirk Hartog Islands, on a direct path to the gathered dolphins.

'Larger? Does that mean more dangerous?'

'That is very likely, but air cover is arriving and will disable both the cruise ship and the drones.'

The air cover was coming from the south and Wirrin wished it would head for the main group of attack drones first.

Yes! The air cover had done its job. It must have, as the red signature of the big drones and the cruise ship had changed to a dull grey.

The group exchanged relieved smiles as Turaku confirmed the neutralisation . The great bulk of the attacking drones left the Indian Ocean and entered the outer waters of Shark Bay. Almost everything was converging on Sonic's position, except for the guardians rushing toward the attack drones.

Forty seconds to engagement.

The Comet was closing, still minutes away, and the number of aircraft above the dolphin gathering had increased.

What?

The dolphins were spreading out, moving directly away from the oncoming danger with several hundred guardians following. The display gave a horrible red flash, then again, and again. Why didn't it stop? The sight of the frozen holographic image of Turaku terrified Wirrin.

Then the awful flashing stopped and Turaku came to life.

'Emergency situation averted. Major engagement in ten seconds.'

Ten seconds! There was no time for relief or to wonder what the emergency had been, as the display zoomed to the last few seconds of the rapidly closing drones and their adversaries.

On the screen the huge attacking group appeared to outnumber the guardians almost six to one, but Turaku looked confident. Wirrin prayed it was not simply to boost morale. And there was the positive legacy of guardian capabilities from the first Monkey Mia attack as well.

Wirrin's grip on Thom's arm tightened and everyone watched, transfixed, as the mass of red markers on the screen engulfed the blue markers of the guardians. Momentarily the groups separated again as the red continued at unabated speed. The blue rapidly changed direction then closed on the red lights which started winking out. In less than thirty seconds every red marker had changed to grey and come to a halt.

The new guardians were even more effective than the originals. Thom let out a cheer and Wirrin laughed aloud. Akama, Narn and Gulara were smiling.

'Is Sonic safe? Have all the drones been stopped?' Wirrin needed Turaku's confirmation.

'Honoured One, Sonic and the Earth dolphins have completely recovered from a sonar attack.'

Recovered? They'd been hurt somehow? Fear jolted through Wirrin again and he saw his own shock reflected in Akama, Gulara and Narn in the silence as they waited for an explanation.

'Sonar pulses designed to confuse dolphin auditory senses were transmitted underwater by the hostile drones and for seven seconds every dolphin at the gathering suffered a form of sensory deprivation. This *was* dangerous. After twenty seconds they would have lapsed into unconsciousness and drowned. I was able to use the translators on Sonic's transport module to dampen the signal until the drones were destroyed.'

'Sonic could have drowned?'

'No, Wirrin. I would not have allowed that.'

Wirrin fleetingly wondered what Turaku would have done to stop it, but Sonic and Calen were his immediate concern.

'Is he all right?'

'Completely. The instant the signal was suppressed every dolphin returned to full consciousness.'

'Did it do anything to Calen? He hears all those sounds.'

'Not a thing. He reflexively switched off his implants when the interference started. Sonic helped reduce the turmoil when the dolphins' flight response was triggered and they've now resumed their meeting. The mothers with young were particularly distressed by the loss of contact with their little ones.'

The holo screen showed the Comet arriving near Sonic, a gathering of the big air cover vessels in the area where the drones had been disabled, and activity near the cruise ship, which Turaku explained was the retrieval, for analysis, of the large new drones. Turaku, still controlling the holo, was using it to help explain the current situation to Akama, and information flashed rapidly and briefly into view.

Attacks at other locations had been contained and everyone felt relieved as their air transport made its final approach to the Comet.

'They haven't got a hope against our AIs.'

As if deliberately flinging Thom's words in his face the holo screen flashed fiercely red.

Chapter 16

'LEVEL ONE EMERGENCY! LEVEL ONE EMERGENCY! ENGAGE ACCELERATION SAFETY RESTRAINTS.'

Thom was the first to recover from the shock and bewilderment and yelled to everyone to find a safety harness.

With the automatic message still sounding, everyone rushed to comply. As he reached one of the seats, Wirrin staggered and nearly fell as the transporter lurched and changed direction. Grasping for support, he pulled himself into place, and engaging his harness, looked to see how everyone else was managing. Gulara was getting to her feet, Akama hanging on to the back of a seat, and Thom and Burilda were buckled in. The transporter decelerated and when the lurching stopped Akama and Gulara made themselves secure. The sound and fury of the warning message and flashing red screen abruptly stopped and everyone turned to Turaku.

'I regret the lack of warning, Honoured One, but the Comet is moving to a defensive position. Your boarding path is now recalibrated. Please remain with your acceleration restraints engaged. One of the low orbit space vessels is emitting a mayday distress signal indicating complete loss of control and descending at great velocity. Its trajectory leads to a direct impact with the gathered dolphins and we have interposed the Comet as a precautionary measure.'

'It's not out of control? It's being guided?' asked Akama.

'Yes, we're certain.'

'How long before impact?'

'Sixty-seven seconds, but there will be no impact.'

While Turaku was speaking the air transporter shifted so suddenly that anyone not restrained would have been thrown across the cabin. Wirrin was hardly aware of it. He was so focused on the holo image Turaku was relaying from the Comet.

These people must be crazy. Crashing a great spaceship to kill dolphins? Were there people on it? It really was big — 150 metres in length and plummeting towards the sea at over 900 kilometres per hour.

More and more thoughts flashed into Wirrin's mind as he linked to the security system, or tried to link ... it was locked and under Turaku's control somehow and he couldn't connect. Turaku was once again a frozen image, a sign that back on the Comet he was focusing every possible resource on the crisis.

What did Turaku mean by no impact? At that size and rate of fall it was a deadly missile that would destroy the Comet and everyone aboard no matter what its construction strength.

And if the Comet moved to safety Sonic and Calen and all the dolphins would be annihilated.

All sense of motion stopped. What? The transporter was docked. The holo showed thirty-five seconds to impact. Information was coming through, probably automatically.

Twenty-five seconds. Wirrin thought of Calen and Sonic in the open water and looked at Thom. Yes, he was thinking of them too. Wirrin's gaze snapped back to the countdown.

Twenty-three seconds. His helplessness was unbearable as he watched the numbers dwindle.

Twenty-one seconds ... twenty seconds ... nineteen seconds.

All Wirrin could do was watch the countdown and the image of the plummeting vessel.

Eighteen seconds.

A great blaze of light surrounded the plunging arrow of destruction then darkened as protective filtering cut in. The dim outline shuddered and separated into six or seven segments. Each segment was surrounded momentarily by a glowing aura before it disintegrated into smaller pieces, which were in turn broken apart.

The process repeated so rapidly that after the glimpse of the first division everything appeared to explode to a huge glowing cloud and it wasn't till Wirrin saw a slow-motion replay that he understood what had happened. To all intents and purposes the space vessel had been turned to dust, or something like it, in four or five seconds.

'Crisis averted!'

Turaku was back, but after a quick glance around the transporter, Wirrin's focus returned to the screen where smaller bursts of light were flaring below the spreading globe of particulate matter, reducing anything still falling to dust.

'What about the other vessels? Do we have to worry about them?'

'The probability of action being directed against the Great Barrier Reef centre is low. Northern Australian security is demanding dispersal of the remaining vessels along a prescribed path under threat of reprisal for non-compliance.'

The cloud on the screen disappeared and was replaced with a navigational representation showing three large red markers and a much larger group of smaller markers.

'What are all those smaller things? They're not missiles are they?' Thom said.

At that moment the whole group of markers started moving.

'They are survival modules, small transporters and other craft that left the space vessel when the distress call began. All personnel were evacuated before the suicidal plunge.'

'Do we stay in our safety restraints?'

'No, Honoured One. A return to the Comet control centre is now the most advisable course of action.'

'And Sonic and Calen haven't been harmed in any way?'

'Calen is somewhat stressed but too busy to dwell on it. Sonic has shown extraordinary presence of mind and rallied the Earth dolphins after their second general alarm call. They are leading the dolphins away from the fallout area for the vessel remnants. It's a precautionary measure only and in a short time they will resume their interrupted meeting.'

'What happened to that ship? I didn't know the Comet could do something like that?'

'Regretfully we've not only revealed part of our offensive capability, Thom, but also our presence. It was a battery of broad-spectrum energy beams controlled by the security AI and myself. Wirrin can access the details from his InfoStation.'

Offensive? Wirrin would have called it defensive. Well, in this case anyway.

'Thank you, Turaku. These are remarkable achievements.' Akama released his safety harness and headed for the transporter exit with everyone following.

'Turaku, these attacks are bordering on fanatical. I think we should bring all dolphins into the Comet as soon as possible.'

Everyone hesitated as Burilda spoke. Akama and Gulara nodded then turned to Narn for his thoughts.

'Honoured One, I am in no position to make such a decision, but it is apparent to me that we should follow as closely as possible the advice of our companion intelligences.' Narn indicated Turaku.

'I agree with you, Narn. With so much happening we're all behind Turaku. What do you suggest?'

'The likelihood of further hostile action is low in the short term, but rising. I would like to see immediate action.'

'Rising? Again?'

Akama spoke for the whole group when he expressed his disbelief.

'Not critically, but their determination is obvious. We rate it highly unlikely, but possible.'

'Bring the dolphins aboard as quickly as possible.'

Wirrin felt like cheering at Akama's emphatic demand.

'Action initiated. Sonic informs me the dolphins will be dispersed to pod groups and ready for pick-up in five minutes.'

Five minutes? Turaku must have been in contact with Sonic all the time they were talking. Well of course he was. Poor Calen, he'd be even more stressed at a sudden message for a rush loading. They should be down there supporting him.

As the group left the transporter and entered the Comet's control centre Thom noticed a crowd of people leaving. 'Who were they?'

'Oh, they're the companions moving to the dolphin transporter modules to be with their respective pods,' Narn said.

So many people? The control centre looked as if everyone involved with the Comet was there. Yes, they had to be. It was the safest place in the ship.

Thom nudged Wirrin's arm.

'What?'

'Find out if there are any more threats.' He indicated the InfoStation.

'Me? Turaku and the security AIs are checking non-stop.'

'Use your tricks. You think differently to them. Go on. You never know.'

Wirrin sat down and linked in. He'd been dying to do this for ages, from the moment when Turaku was so busy and commandeered all connections and he'd been prevented till now by the rapid unfolding of events.

What was happening? Thirty ferries ready to go as soon as the human companions reached them. No, thirty-one ferries. Where did that extra one come from?

The Comet's picofactory was building extras to speed the boarding process.

Okay, first the threats. He tapped into the Comet's security with one of his triggers.

'Dingoes! Thom, look at this.'

'What is it?'

Wirrin flashed some schematics into view.

'They've analysed those big drones. Just as well they disabled them. Just one of them could have hurt every dolphin in that gathering.'

'How?'

'They make gigantic sound-waves, nearly three hundred decibels. Just one burst would permanently damage the dolphins' sound receptors if they were any closer than 20 kilometres.'

'That's horrible. Don't tell Calen. Not till the dolphins are all safe. Could Turaku do anything to stop them?'

It took a couple of seconds to find out.

'He could. He was actually ready. Sound is so important to dolphins he'd prepared contingency plans for every possibility he could think of. The air cover vessels were equipped to vaporise a wall of water in front of the signal so its strength would be dissipated.'

'He knew they were going to do it?'

'No, but he was ready anyway. He's amazing. Look at all these. He worked out 273 ways they might be attacked by water and had responses for all of them.'

Wirrin read the list as it scrolled rapidly past: poisons, concussions, explosions, stealth picobots. Stealth picobots? What were they?

'I've never even heard of some of these things.'

Thom was looking at him strangely.

'Did you just read all that? I could only pick out a few things from that list rolling up the screen.'

'You'll be just as fast after your reading course.'

That got a dubious look.

'Are there any dangers showing up?'

'Um, not at the moment, and they're using the highest level of monitoring they can.'

'Are there any more ships close by?'

'Yes. Seventy-four in a 100 kilometre range.'

'And what about the other centres?'

'Ningaloo has sixty-four, and there are 247 at the Great Barrier Reef.'

'Really?'

'Thom, it's one of the wonders of the solar system.'

'Do your special checks on them.'

Wirrin was starting to wonder. Thom seemed almost fixated on the idea that there must be more danger.

'The security AIs are checking them all the time.'

'I know, but the first lot of ships tricked them till they looked more closely.'

'The first? You think there are more?'

'They had backups for the first drones, and when they didn't work they had another huge backup in space. Three ocean ships isn't very much compared to those four big spacecraft.'

Wirrin hadn't thought of it like that, but it did sound sensible.

'Turaku and the security AIs calculate an eighty-three per cent probability of other resources being involved, but all their searching isn't finding anything.'

Thom gripped Wirrin's shoulders as if to say, 'Come on, you can do it. Get into it.'

'See, I'm right aren't I? It needs a different way of looking at things.'

'What do you mean?'

'They know they're up against really clever AIs, so they're doing something to avoid the AIs' capabilities.'

Wirrin and Thom both jumped as Turaku appeared beside them without his usual shimmer alert.

'Well thought out, Thom. Keep assisting Wirrin with your ideas.'

He blinked off as suddenly as he appeared and Wirrin glanced at his steady image talking with Akama.

'Whoo! That's the first time he's used multiple images in the same setting.'

Thom firmed his grip on Wirrin's shoulders and Wirrin focused.

Where to start? Thom seemed to be fixated on the ships so that would do. Trace their origins? Already done and too obvious.

Examine all the people connected with every ship and find any links or references to dolphins, dolphin centres, K74 or other directed habitats?

Wirrin added idea after idea, some from Thom but mostly his own, and set everything running. What about new information from the AI based on K74? Yes, it might be important. Add it in.

It was too soon for any response, given the fifty-four minute turn-around time.

After five minutes he'd added dozens of ideas with no results, or no definitive results. There were billions upon billions of responses.

Wirrin had a quick look at his search tree. Five per cent of the Comet's computational power was now commandeered for his queries. That was an enormous amount. It would increase too, as the number of links and references built.

'Space dust! Look how much processing we've got going. It just hit 5.3 per cent of the Comet's capability.'

'That doesn't sound like very much.'

Wirrin snorted with laughter. Thom needed some basic education about processor power.

'Thom, that's—' Wirrin's words were cut off as Thom's grip tightened fiercely.

'What's the rest of it doing?'

'Everything. Running the Comet, the security. It's linked in with Turaku and the security AIs, and the databases and communications. You know that.'

'Check out what's happening. Especially with the AIs.'

'The AIs? I don't think I can do that.'

'With that InfoStation? I bet you can … Ask Turaku.'

Wirrin didn't have to. His holo screen cleared and a command menu he'd never seen before flashed into view. A rapid scan of the overview had his eyes goggling. Turaku was giving him the capacity to watch an AI function, almost like reading his mind and body. Things were happening trillions of times too fast for Wirrin to look at anything specific, but he could get a general picture.

Turaku should be examined first. Wirrin felt as if he'd been given express permission, with the new command menu appearing the way it did. So, what was Turaku doing?

What did ninety-five per cent of potential performance mean? With the capabilities of an AI, it sounded like a huge amount was happening. Wirrin didn't know enough about AIs to figure if that was normal.

Yes, it was. A quick query brought up a simple performance/time graph showing an almost unvarying ninety-two per cent since Comet-Turaku had become aware. An extra three per cent didn't seem like much.

'Turaku seems pretty close to normal. He …'

Wirrin broke off and followed Thom's interest in what was happening on a further section of the display screen where people were grouped with Akama.

Calen was next to one of the dolphin transporters and talking to a dolphin companion while members of the pod swam into place. He suddenly looked up and waved as if he knew people were watching him, then dived and disappeared. Now that Wirrin was linked to his InfoStation it would be easy to watch and keep track of them. A couple of seconds' work produced a sub screen following everything Calen was doing.

'He's all right. He doesn't look too stressed. What does the graph thing tell you about Turaku?'

Wirrin wasn't so sure about Calen. Well, back to the job at hand.

'It says it's normal for him to be working nearly flat out.'

'Are you sure? He was so busy his image froze twice, and that never happens. With all these things going on he must be doing more than usual.'

Wirrin changed the scale on the graph and searched the time axis for the two performance spikes he knew must be there.

Yes, ninety-eight per cent for the first one and slightly more with the multi-spectrum energy beams. He enlarged the second spike section and extra information appeared.

That was interesting. The performance output was measured with two basic indicators, background and foreground activity. How did they relate?

'Hey! Thom! That's nothing like normal. He usually only puts five per cent into foreground and all the rest is background. Ever since we landed it's been the other way round.'

'Is it the same for the security AI?'

It wasn't quite, but it was definitely similar. Both AIs were concentrating at an extremely high level.

The amount of information being processed was amazing, and Wirrin, wondering where it was all coming from, did a trace to find out.

'That can't be right.'

'What?'

'Turaku and our security AIs are working with every AI in Australia and they're all concentrating the same way, on security work.'

'All of them?'

'Every single one.'

Wirrin did some more checking and nearly fell off his chair in amazement.

'I don't believe this. The numbers are too high. They can't be processing this much.'

'Have a closer look at it.'

Wirrin turned to see why Thom was sounding so definite.

'Analyse what they're analysing. Go on.'

It was a striking phrase.

'But that's what they're already doing. I don't see the point.'

'That's not what I meant. I don't know how to say it.' He was quiet for a moment. 'Um! I'm asking you to look at the data, not use it yourself.'

Wirrin finally understood and was impressed.

'That's not easy, Thom. I've done that with ordinary data, but not data that's being used by AIs. They do things differently.'

'You'll work it out.'

He was looking rather pleased with himself now that Wirrin had grasped his meaning.

Wirrin searched out the library of analysis programs he remembered using in EdCom and started checking the purpose of different types.

No good. None of them applied in quite the right way.

Okay, set up an InterWeb search with the proper parameters.

Wirrin was relieved when hundreds of results poured in. A closer look showed they still weren't what he wanted.

Change the parameters and try again.

After a number of refinements he whittled the results to a short list of five programs, each with one or more features he wanted, but none with them all. Combine them somehow? Yes, that might work.

Wirrin set his task going then grunted when error messages about data incompatibility came flashing back. What? Oh yes. A data conversion algorithm would fix that.

'Is it doing anything?'

'Yes, Thom. It's tracing the data packet routings, then it will look for patterns and anomalies, and then it will check the structure and properties.'

'Well, that sounds good.'

Wirrin bumped his head back into Thom's chest and laughed at the stir about his jargon.

'Twit! It depends whether it finds anything.'

'Twit? What's that mean?'

'Sonic's been saying it to Calen lately. Something about a bald hairy lion. They were laughing about it a couple of weeks ago.'

'Bald and hairy?'

He rotated his thumbs in Wirrin's neck muscles then stopped when Wirrin sat up with an exclamation.

'Now what?'

'It's tracking the data … No wonder they're all busy. They're connected with almost every data source on Earth and the information is pouring in like a flood.'

'All the AIs?'

'Yes, Thom, it doesn't make sense.'

Wirrin picked a random source and showed it to Thom.

'See this? It's a database about the old transport vehicles which ran on fossil fuels and it shouldn't have anything to do with the attacks or the dolphins, but the AIs are processing every single element as if it's important.'

Wirrin felt a surge of excitement. Something strange was definitely being revealed. Suddenly the performance graph for Turaku plummeted to just over thirty per cent, steadied, then started rising. A closer look showed the foreground portion fluctuating near twenty-six per cent and the background tasks increasing.

Wirrin switched to the graph for the security AIs and a similar thing had happened, though with slightly different numbers. The vehicle database information suddenly disappeared for no reason and Wirrin's startled squeak was interrupted by a warning neck squeeze.

'Everyone's looking at you.'

They were too, and not just looking. Akama and Turaku were approaching.

'Well done, Wirrin. Turaku informs me you've just assisted the entire Australian AI community.'

Wirrin wasn't sure how to respond to that, but he didn't have to because Turaku started explaining.

'Our thanks to both of you. Your analysis task resolved the priority trap which had ensnared us and provided a means of escape.'

'Priority trap?'

Wirrin had a good idea of what that might be but he listened carefully as Turaku explained.

'Yes, the information in the data sources we access was modified so that every element was tagged with a priority signal linked to dolphins and security. That made it vitally important to look at every element regardless of its significance. It was very cleverly done.'

'You mean every single bit of stored information on Earth showed up as a threat to the dolphins?'

'In a way. It also indicated a connection that needed following.'

'So Wirrin saves the day.'

'Indeed he does, Thom.'

What a dingo head! Wirrin started to say it had all been Thom's idea, but again the display on his screen changed, this time to the familiar overview of Shark Bay with three red markers showing. Now what?

'The backup threats you were concerned about. With proper attention they were easily revealed and will be quickly dealt with.

'Honoured One, the Comet is about to move to Denham Sound.'

Already? Had 1400 dolphins been moved into the Comet so quickly?

Wirrin saw that it had taken just over twenty minutes and realised he'd lost track of time while concentrating at his InfoStation.

Sonic and Calen must be aboard. Yes, there they were in Sonic's module, Calen watching and Sonic working at his special underwater InterWeb console, keeping in contact with the Earth dolphins. Attention switched to the Comet's big real-time display screen showing the external view as the convoy moved rapidly south.

Wirrin took in the various accompanying aircraft. Their number had built and he asked Turaku about them.

'Is anyone tracking them? They haven't got stealth like the Comet.'

'They do have a degree of stealth but it's all turned off to add an element of misdirection to the strong attention we are now receiving.'

The main section of Wirrin's holo changed and showed a display of fifty-three space vessels and satellites scanning them from orbit and more moving into range.

'Our unprecedented energy expenditure has brought worldwide scrutiny and concerted attempts to understand what happened.'

Wirrin hadn't given a thought to the effects on the rest of the world. He'd been much too occupied.

'Have we explained anything to them?'

'That an out-of-control space vessel was destroyed to prevent the annihilation of the Shark Bay marine environment as well as the above-ground facilities and people at Monkey Mia, Denham and Carnarvon. They don't understand how and they won't be told.

'Their immediate puzzle is the disappearance from their scanners of 1400 dolphins.'

Thom laughed.

'They'll be a lot more puzzled when the rest of them vanish then.'

'Yes, Thom, but not for long. As soon as the Comet departs, the world in general will be informed that we are moving them to safety on Attunga. There will be an outcry against so many special dolphins leaving Earth, but when the evidence of the attempts against them is disseminated we expect an enormous backlash against the responsible habitats.'

'What will happen to them?'

'Nothing, Thom. But we are confident that opinion will be voiced so strongly against such aggression that any action against Earth's wild dolphins would critically isolate them.'

'So they'll get away with it?' Thom was getting fired up. Wirrin agreed with him but Akama spoke.

'They're not getting away with anything, Thom. When the facts are known the standing of the semi-directed habitats will be very badly damaged and they will make great efforts to rebuild it. We expect all of them to openly dissociate from K74.'

'K74 won't care. They'll try something else.'

'We agree, but not on Earth, and not immediately. Our actions today have very much put them on notice that their belief in their own dominance in the solar system is misguided, and for a while at least they will take stock. They have a great deal to think about.

'Their best efforts have proved futile and they have just learnt that their technology is inadequate.'

'Not on Earth? You mean they'll try something against Attunga and Warrakan?'

'Yes, but nothing overt while they try to understand our capabilities. Once we announce that the special dolphins will have guaranteed safety on Attunga and Warrakan it will be very clear where the primary resistance to their plans is based. We will become the main focus of their attention.'

Wirrin thought that with the surveillance drones and the giant space vessel, Attunga and Warrakan already were, but before he could ask exactly what Akama meant, the Comet met with a whole new convoy of air transporters from Monkey Mia and started descending to the Denham Sound gathering. Akama pointed to the image of Calen and Sonic.

'Why don't you join them? We'll call you back if we think there is a need.'

Burilda went with them. Sonic and his transport module would be out in the water as soon as possible, so they rushed to intercept them.

Wirrin and Thom dashed past a group of dolphin companions and scrambled quickly into the module where there was only time for a brief hug and greeting before the loading bay doors opened and they were on the move.

*   *   *

'*I hope you're having a good adventure, Thom.*'

Trust Sonic to know how to make them all smile. Thom's appetite for action was certainly being overindulged.

'Sonic says we're safe now?'

Wirrin could tell Calen needed some reassurance.

'Turaku disintegrated one of their spaceships and the other three ran for cover as fast as they could. They haven't got anything left they can do to us.'

'Disintegrated? The one that was falling on us?'

Wirrin wasn't going to say that it was being guided with pinpoint accuracy, so he gave a non-committal nod, and changed the subject by demanding to know what had been happening with Calen and Sonic.

'Everything you could possibly imagine but I'll have to tell you later.'

Sonic leapt into the ocean and disappeared while Calen indicated the facemasks.

The trio entered the water and the first thing Wirrin noticed was the myriad voices of dolphin communication. Sound travels four times as fast through water and to human ears gives a false sense of proximity.

So many voices, though not loud, and with nearly five hundred dolphins in this gathering, Wirrin tried to imagine what the main group at Monkey Mia would have been like if they'd all spoken out like this.

Sonic was swimming towards one of the pods and at the same time talking to the rest of the gathering, explaining the procedure for entering the special ferries designed to carry ten dolphins the short distance into the Comet, and constantly giving assurance and telling them their human companions would meet them and stay with them in their living pools once they were aboard.

Calen shot ahead and Wirrin swam like crazy, trying to keep up. Good grief! He made it look so effortless.

The dark silhouette of a ferry settled abruptly on the silvery surface and then another close by, and Wirrin had to smile at the excitement coming from the dolphins as access to the ferries opened and they moved aboard. The ferries lifted and Sonic headed for another pod. Wirrin decided he needed some serious swimming training when, despite a full-on effort, he and Thom were left behind.

The Comet's picofactory was still producing extra ferries so that the dolphins could quickly board, and by the time they reached the main Monkey Mia gathering there would be fifty-two. Currently there were thirty-six operating from six different loading bays, all under the control of Turaku in liaison with Sonic, and the whole Denham Sound group of 486 dolphins in twenty-five pods was transferred aboard in just over fifteen minutes.

Calen laughed when Wirrin and Thom flopped in the transport module, gasping for breath.

'Weak! Just as well you weren't there when we had to dodge the fall-out from the sky.'

By the time the module came to rest inside the Comet they'd recovered. They *were* strong and very fit after all, just not up to Calen's standard.

Sonic was totally occupied, talking through the links in his module to over 1900 dolphins in their new pod-sized travelling pools.

The Comet raced for the rendezvous south-east of Monkey Mia and near Faure Island. There was so much to see and do that the trio barely had time to talk. More dolphins were loaded, and still more at Monkey Mia, where the much larger number of dolphins took almost an hour to transfer, and left Wirrin and Thom almost worn to a frazzle. Calen insisted they stay on the Comet for the final two pick-ups and Wirrin and Thom, sensing Calen had quite recovered his equilibrium, were keen to get back to the control centre.

*   *   *

The Ningaloo Reef marine centre was north of Monkey Mia and Wirrin spent most of the travel time talking with Narn, who performed a personal and rather friendly parting ceremony when the Comet settled offshore. This group of dolphins was the smallest so far and after Sonic spoke to their gathering they boarded very quickly.

Calen came to the control centre because of the delay before the next pick up and the trio finally relaxed together.

Thom was keen to know details about the 3500 kilometre trip to the Great Barrier Reef, wondering if the Comet might have an effect on the terrain below its path with its speed way in excess of the sound barrier, but, because of the urgency, the trip would be at an altitude much too high for any atmospheric effects.

*   *   *

'So what are all these things that happened?'

Wirrin and Thom had been intrigued ever since Calen's earlier comment about his adventures.

'Well, I think I must have swum about a 100 kilometres. My muscles all feel like jelly.'

After earlier saying how weak they were this was really a ploy to pique their curiosity by not going ahead, so Wirrin and Thom agreed with him, telling him he was oh so strong, conjecturing how quickly he might recover, and praising his endurance, till he had to laugh. 'All right! It started with the sharks.'

There was no comeback for a statement like that. He wasn't joking and after a startled moment Thom asked if he'd really seen some.

'Lots of them near the second meeting. They're everywhere in the bay but Faure Island is one of their main hunting grounds and a group of them were attracted by the gathering. A big one charged the group three times — it was chaos. I couldn't believe it was happening and Sonic made me get into the module each time till it was safe.'

'Did Sonic go with you?'

'He doesn't have to worry. He's too fast. The sharks are after the babies and young dolphins, which aren't fast enough to get away … and that was me.'

'How close did it get?'

'Close enough. I was too busy following Sonic's warning to get myself somewhere safe.'

'Were you worried?'

'Sort of. The first time happened too quickly, and the other times I was thinking about Sonic because he helped chase it away.'

Thom was staring in disbelief.

'He did?'

'It's not really chasing because the sharks aren't scared. A group of dolphins swim in really close, dodging and turning all the time to confuse the shark so it loses track of the little dolphin it's after. Then they harass it so much it goes somewhere else.'

'Harass?'

'Sonic's word. He explained what happened because I couldn't see from the module. He wouldn't have got hurt, I know, because Turaku would have done something, but I didn't think of that at the time.'

Wirrin and Thom exchanged glances and Wirrin wondered if Thom had the same image of an energy beam reducing any attacking shark to its constituent atoms.

'Was it very big?'

'Let's have a look … It's all on the surveillance database.'

Of course it was. Wirrin found the relevant data and played it on his personal holo and they watched a 4.5 metre tiger shark gliding in fierce majesty, lunging at the mass of dolphins, then being enveloped in a frantic cloud of activity till it swam off, looking annoyed.

'That thing looks evil. They should do something to keep them away from the dolphins.'

'No they shouldn't. It's a marine reserve, Thom, and sharks are as important as everything else.'

Coming from sensitive Calen this was quite startling, but not really, when you thought of his knowledge of animals and their care.

'They shouldn't stop them from eating baby dolphins?'

'Not in general. Sharks are a fixed part of Earth dolphin life and they have to learn to live with them.'

Calen was in explanation mode on a subject they'd discussed before in a theoretical way. It was horrifying to realise that only thirty per cent of baby dolphins in Shark Bay survived to adulthood, and that almost every adult carried scars from their attempts to protect the young. The boys suddenly realised how different life was for wild dolphins.

'Tiger sharks! And we thought catching a perentie was exciting.'

'A perentie, Thom? Truly?'

'Akama took us on a mini walkabout while we were at Gnardune Pool and Narn trapped one in a rock cleft.'

'Narn? Who's that?'

'We met him after you and Sonic raced into the bay when we landed. He's like an Australian version of a Witness and he was with us all the time. We all like him.'

'He must be clever with animals if he can catch a perentie. They're very quick and elusive. Did he hold it? I know their claws are dangerous.'

'Wirrin's got it all zapped so we can show you later.'

Calen hung on every word as they talked about the thorny devil, the spoonbill, the big red kangaroos and the other birds and animals that had been part of the walk. He didn't ask for an immediate replay; that would happen at some stage when he could savour it properly.

Wirrin and Thom switched the conversation back to Calen. They wanted to hear more from him.

'It was the worst thing I can ever remember. Sonic was talking to the whole group when my implants went berserk. Weird sounds and whistles blasted my ears and echoed in my head like Thom's sound system playing every bit of music at the same time. My reflexes turned the implants off and then I saw every dolphin twitching and quivering. Sonic was on his side and looking really weird and starting to float towards the surface.

'When I put my hand on him he didn't even react and I could tell he was unconscious. I hardly had time to think, except that I might be able to help if he was at the surface and I could keep his blowhole in the air, and then he woke up. They all woke up, and after a whole lot of distress calls from mothers whose babies had sunk and had to be pushed up to breathe, they were all okay.

'Turaku got through and Sonic explained to everyone that their enemies had done it but it wouldn't happen again.

'He was talking and answering all the questions when he suddenly made the imperative distress signal and called every dolphin to come close because something was falling out of the sky which would hurt them if they were spread out too much.

'It was really bewildering with all the distress calls and not knowing what was going on, and then there was another distress call to get away because poison might fall in the water and the gathering had to follow Sonic as fast as they could, but they wouldn't swim any faster than the three babies because most dolphins would never leave them behind. Next thing we reached a safe place but it wasn't, because there was a sudden rush to get everyone into the Comet. By the time you two joined me I was thinking anything could happen.'

Listening quietly while Calen's thoughts and story tumbled out, Wirrin suddenly saw the image of every dolphin suddenly falling unconscious. He was determined that the trio would stay with Sonic till the Comet was safely on its way to Attunga.

*　　*　　*

'Altogether 6118 dolphins, Calen. There's only room for another four hundred without things starting to get crowded. There are 322 separate pods and 297 companions from Earth with them. Turaku says that Attunga-level health checks have started for them all, and 197 are getting priority healthbot treatments for various wounds, mostly shark bites, though one dolphin has lost most of its left fluke in an encounter with an orca and needs tissue replacement.' Wirrin checked several sections of his display.

'The dolphins come from 278 different Earth locations and there are seventy-three babies less than one week old.

'Burilda is moving round, starting to meet the companions, and Sonic is explaining the food situation and telling the dolphins when they'll next get something to eat.

'Thom wants to stuff his face with food while the rest of us contemplate the beauty of the Earth's moon as we pass by.'

*　　*　　*

The Comet, newly escaped from Earth's gravity well, was on its way home.

Chapter 17

'We won't see Sonic for the rest of the trip?'
'You can watch him, Thom, or go with him, but he'll be too busy to come to the control centre. I can see that he hasn't stopped moving around for even a minute yet.'

'What's he saying to them?'

A small section of screen showed Sonic in his transport module, communicating with his special InterWeb console. Anticipating Calen's request, Wirrin brought up the sound.

'He's telling them all there's nothing to worry about … After two or three sleeps they'll be out of their crowded pools … They're going to get some food soon and they are all pleased about that.'

'All? Is he talking to them all?'

'I think so. He must be from the tone of his voice.'

Wirrin and Thom waited while Calen listened and watched carefully for several minutes.

'Wow! I'm going to find him. The pools are making them nervous because they're not used to being so enclosed, and he's talking non-stop to keep their minds distracted. He might have to keep it up for ages. I hope none of them panic.'

'Do you think they might? We've been travelling for an hour and the early pick-ups have been in their pools for much longer than that.'

Panic would be very bad news as one dolphin's distress could affect the whole pod. There had been previous discussion about panic because Earth dolphins were much more susceptible to it than Attunga's more enhanced dolphins. Sonic had said he'd be there to help and they'd be all right, but all this attention he was giving wasn't what anyone had expected.

'Not a chance really, Wirrin. I'm just thinking out loud. Turaku's monitoring them all and he'd stop anything happening.'

'Will we go with you?'

'Of course. We probably won't be able to do anything to help, but Sonic will like us being with him.'

And of course he did. He was too busy talking to say so, but he let them know with body bumps and happy nudges.

For the next hour and a half the trio watched with growing amazement as Sonic stayed in communication with over six thousand dolphins, guiding them through their excitement, stress, and anticipation. Wirrin could only smile with delight when Calen informed them that the last ten minutes of Sonic's rapid dolphin speech had related the adventures of a young female dolphin separated from her pod and pursued relentlessly through close call after close call by a monstrous tiger shark.

'Dolphins tell stories?'

'They do now, Thom. Burilda is going to freak when she finds out about this.'

And Wirrin could only listen in wonder as six thousand dolphins joined in learning a series of dolphin songs, the last of which was particularly beautiful. He started to ask Calen softly about it but stopped abruptly when he realised that Sonic was no longer talking.

'Dolphins are happy and will sleep now.'

'What about you? You haven't stopped since we landed at Monkey Mia.'

'Yes. This is hard work for a young dolphin and I want a live fish before I sleep.'

The transport module started moving immediately, probably under Turaku's control, and probably to some location where food would be available for Sonic, and the four friends played a subdued and gentle version of the dolphin games they usually played when they met in the pool at home.

*   *   *

'They'll sleep now and then probably twice more before the journey ends,' the ranger said.

'I hope so, Burilda. I've never heard Sonic say anything was hard work before. Even all that work for Meeting Day didn't worry him.'

'He's functioning at an extraordinary level, Calen. Turaku's monitoring has shown peak after peak of energy output, but none of them are alarming and we're confident that after his sleep period he'll be as full of life as he always is.'

'Energy peaks? What did they match up with?'

'Just what you'd expect. The first contact with Earth dolphins, leading them through the greeting ceremony, each of the four gatherings, distress calls at the time of the attacks, the six loading activities, and this last extended time settling the dolphins in their travelling pools. Has he given any indication of what was hardest for him?'

Calen thought about Burilda's question.

'Not really. My guess would be going unconscious and all the distress calls, but he did say it was hard being young and telling older dolphins what to do.'

'Hard? It's astonishing. No human could influence an unknown group of people so instantly and effectively. We don't understand it.'

'Blue is blue!'

Burilda looked with puzzlement at Akama.

'Honoured One?'

'Sonic is Sonic.'

Wirrin, along with everyone else, pondered that, and Akama smiled.

'Sonic is unique, Burilda.

'He still suckles from Puck yet he understands both dolphin and human language.

'He makes song and story.

'He leads thousands of dolphins to a new life.

'He inspires a billion people on our habitats and our AIs regard him with awe.

'Something new has entered our universe, and, though we are not fully equipped to understand it, we have been blessed with the gift of involvement.'

Thom broke the silence as everyone wondered about an appropriate way to respond.

'He's definitely unique. He's turned our lives upside down ever since we've known him, but we've also made him part of us.'

'Yes, Thom?'

Now it was Akama waiting for elaboration.

'I think about this sometimes when I wonder what he'd be like without humans and AIs. He'd only know dolphin things, and wouldn't have learnt human speech, or reading and music and all the knowledge from the InterWeb. He relies on us for lots of things he's good at but he'd still be special without them. The dolphins knew that as soon as he was born but I'm just not sure if we should be leading him into human ways so much.'

Wirrin was stunned. He'd never heard that idea from Thom at any stage, and from his expression, neither had Calen. There'd be a lot of talk about this at home. Gulara, Akama and Burilda were exchanging nods.

'We're not sure either, Thom, but regardless of what we think, it's not our place to decide. That is for Sonic, and so far he's only evidenced eagerness for our knowledge and ways. Burilda and Turaku have discussed this with him as a serious issue and let him know that we will respect any change in his point of view.'

'You've discussed it? What did he say?'

'The likelihood of disengagement with humans and AIs is 1.7001 per cent and steadily decreasing.'

'Is that a quote, Burilda?'

'A direct quote.'

Thom looked at Calen with a mixture of disbelief and laughter.

'He teases Turaku?'

'If he said that then he does. It's new to me.'

The trio grinned at each other. Typical Sonic, doing something that no-one else on Attunga would dream of.

There were lots of things to talk over with him but they'd all have to wait. He was as deeply asleep as any young dolphin was capable of being.

*　*　*

'Thom! You'll need to work out a different approach course when we get close to Attunga, and limit yourself to 2G.'

'What's happened, Wirrin?'

The Comet was several hours away from Attunga and Wirrin was seated at his InfoStation and bringing everyone up to date with information and conditions that related to the final stage of the journey. Between the two sleep periods he'd had another six-hour session under Turaku's tutelage, practising, mastering and extending his skills, and now everyone was standing round, watching expectantly to see what sort of magic he might produce.

'The three K74 offensive ships have all moved close to Attunga and their scanners are much stronger than the drones, so you'll have to sneak past even more carefully than when we left.'

'That doesn't make sense. They won't be expecting us to arrive for days and days.'

'They're not looking for us, Thom, not specifically, though they will eventually. The prediction that K74 would make Attunga and Warrakan the focus of their attention was accurate and that's why they've sent their big ships.'

'They're not going to attack are they?'

'Not directly. They have been trying very persistently to infiltrate our InfoSystem and they are also creating problems with the InterWeb.'

Thom was incredulous.

'No way! They can't, can they?'

'They haven't got a hope, but they're slowing down the incoming transmissions from everywhere else by flooding all the channels with vast amounts of data.'

'Infiltration and data flooding are separate issues aren't they?' Gulara asked, but she didn't look very concerned.

'Yes they are, but they send their InfoSeek programs under the cover of a data burst because they think our security systems will be over-loaded and they can slip in. It worked for them at the Freedom habitat so they're trying the same tactic again, but on a massive scale.'

'And it's actually slowing down the InterWeb?' asked Thom.

'The first three bursts did, but the communication AIs have now installed extra analysis processors to sift out the cyber junk, and anything from now on will just get diverted as data garbage.'

'Sounds like it's all electronic stuff that won't really affect us. I'd better go and plot the course now if I'm going to be limited to 2G.'

Thom headed off to the pilot's console.

'Cyber infiltration isn't really much of a change. Has anything else happened?' asked Akama.

'Yes, a number of things. There's a ten per cent increase in applications for travel to Attunga and most of them have a hidden connection with K74. There have been requests for research data from scientists in directed and semi-directed habitats asking about breakthroughs in scanning techniques, a delegation of K74 diplomats wants to talk to Akama ... and the Cadre of five is so angry they want Attunga blown to pieces.' Thinking he'd delivered a touch of the dramatic magic they'd been anticipating, Wirrin checked the range of stunned looks.

'Assessment says they didn't mean that literally. It was said soon after the comment about an "arrogant little piss-pot colony", when they were discussing their failure at Monkey Mia.'

'Angry men!' proclaimed Akama. 'Where does this information come from? I haven't yet heard of any meeting.'

'The AI on K74 sent the meeting transcript and I found it all on our current situation report.

'Turaku's report says the dolphins are all asleep except for the mothers with babies, Sonic's in a deep logging state, and Attunga-Turaku has sent word that Puck and Flute have travelled to Warrakan to help with the dolphins when they leave the Comet.'

'I see, and does the report have details of the meeting on K74? Any indication of their intentions would be very important.'

'No, but I've had a look at it and it's very interesting.'

Gulara laughed. 'Well, tell us the details.'

'The five of them got together because the message that things had gone wrong on Earth went straight back to them. They didn't want to accept it because they'd used their best technology and they couldn't believe it wasn't good enough.' Wirrin chuckled. 'They blamed their scientists till they heard that the first drones disappeared into nowhere in a few seconds and that the second lot, along with their ships, disappeared as well. Next they were told that some sort of stealthing must be in use because 1400 dolphins vanished from the scanners of their low-orbit ships during the collision dive. The stealthing was verified when the images of dolphins safe in their travelling pods was broadcast on the InterWeb and they knew there must be a vessel they couldn't detect.'

'It would have been mysterious watching the other groups of dolphins wink out of existence.'

'That only came as secondary information because they were ordered to leave before the dolphins loading started. The biggest shock for the Cadre was being told that the suicide ship had evaporated. They couldn't believe it wasn't atomics, but their own ships had the scans to show it wasn't. They've ordered their scientists to find out what the new weapons are.'

'Was there any discussion about why they want to meet with me?' asked Akama.

'Yes, a great deal. They want to find out a lot more about you because you're the ruler of Attunga and everything that happens comes from you.'

'That's what they think? Even though they know Attunga is an open habitat?'

'They don't really believe the open part. They think someone has to be running everything, and because of your position it must be you.'

'I see ... It will be an interesting meeting.'

That really surprised Wirrin and he turned towards Akama.

'You'll actually talk to them?'

'Our nearest neighbour and the most powerful non-planetary habitat? Why not?'

'Um, it seems like a change of pattern. We mostly just protect ourselves and ignore them, like with their space surveillance. The same with the drones that attacked the dolphins. We made them disappear and didn't say anything.'

'We'll maintain the pattern, Wirrin, but in a very polite manner.'

'What about the dolphins? They'll want to know about them.' Burilda said.

'We will very diplomatically point out our respect for life in all its forms and let them know absolutely nothing. Excuse me everyone. It's very evident I have a number of reports to catch up on.'

Burilda and Calen left as well because dolphins would be waking soon and there were things to discuss with their human companions.

Gulara moved close and watched while Wirrin brought up a graphic representation of Thom's course change.

'You've become very skilful with the InfoStation, Wirrin. Have Akama and Turaku been pushing you too hard?'

Wirrin held back a laugh because it was Gulara, his mentor, asking the question.

'I'm not really that good. It just looks that way because the system is so powerful it makes it easy to do impressive things. I'll have to work for ages and really get to know it before I call myself skilful. I've only learnt a fraction of its capabilities so far and it's been exciting to have Turaku help me directly.'

'All those hours of non-stop concentration wasn't hard work?'

'It was, but it was fun hard work, and mostly the time goes without me noticing it.'

'High involvement. Good! To what extent do you want to continue your involvement?'

Wirrin was quite taken aback. He thought his keenness for the InfoStation was blatantly obvious.

'What do you mean? As much as I can of course.'

'Akama is hoping you'll add a day of InfoStation related work to your EdCom structure, as well as a psychology course, and I'm concerned about your study load.'

'I already do more than a day of InfoStation work, so that's covered.'

'He means in addition to that.'

'Extra? Then I'd have to leave something else out. It's already way too complicated with all the alterations and the number of times I need to be with Calen and Sonic.'

'That's the way I see it too, and it would have to come from your Basic training days as your Electives are too important.'

'Basics? I can't drop those. They're … well, they're basic. And I need them to finish First Level.'

Gulara cocked her head to one side. 'Wirrin, Basic training has no relevance for you, or Thom and Calen. You've given more to Attunga than we can ever repay. Your status is way beyond Second Level and those rights are yours as a matter of course. I apologise for not making that clearer but I was assuming you understood. We'll all get together to discuss it when we're back on Attunga.'

'Second Level rights? Are you sure?'

'Much more than Second Level in real terms.'

Wirrin was astonished, and excited. Normally when young people finished their First Level training they had approximately fifteen years ahead of them before deciding whether to tackle Second Level. In that time they had free reign to explore and develop in any and every life path they wished, with appropriate support from EdCom. Almost a third of Attunga people took on the five years of Second Level education as soon as it became available at age thirty-five, while most of the rest continued in their chosen life path with the knowledge they could access level training whenever they wished.

A number of people became 'sleepers', and filled their life with entertainment and the huge range of exciting leisure activities, but after varying periods of time a particular interest usually took hold, which they then developed.

The Second Level rights that Wirrin was so excited about involved increased living space, a big increase in energy allocation, greater access to information, and the most important right for most people: complicated age extension treatments. This was big news affecting their everyday life and he wanted to share it with Thom and Calen at once.

'Why the psychology course? I've never been interested, and Akama hasn't mentioned anything.'

'He will. He's always been interested in you and your future.'

'Me?'

Wirrin knew that very well and hoped his question might elicit extra information. Gulara smiled, understanding the little ploy.

'Yes, you. He's keen to help you realise your broader capabilities.'

This time Wirrin was genuinely puzzled. 'Capabilities?'

'You're thoughtful, and very much a leader.'

'I'm not a leader. That's a bizarre idea.'

'It is? Who holds your trio together?'

'None of us ... I mean, we all do.'

'Ask Thom and Calen and see what their answer is.'

'None of my EdCom evaluations ever said anything like that.'

'And that means you haven't checked for a while.'

Wirrin thought for a moment. 'Akama is complicated.'

'He certainly is, by nature, by training, and by virtue of his position. He's changed my future as well, in the course of the last few days.'

This was very interesting and Wirrin waited expectantly for more information. Surprisingly, Gulara gave a gentle laugh. 'Another of your capabilities. Here I am confiding in you before there is any confirmation. Akama wants me to become the first Witness for humans involved with dolphins.'

Wirrin jumped from his seat, grabbed Gulara's arm in his excitement, then, embarrassed at the liberty, subsided again.

'Gulara, that's the greatest! When do you start?'

'I don't. I have to complete my Witness training and qualify first, which is another three years, and then I have to decide whether I'm suitable for the job.'

'Suitable? That's crazy! Sorry, I mean you're the perfect person. You've been involved in everything since Sonic was born and the dolphins and rangers all like you and say how important you are to everything we do. There aren't any other Witnesses who could say that.'

'Well, thank you, Wirrin. In essence you just reiterated Akama's persuasions and I must admit it's a very exciting prospect. But in the meantime ...'

She touched a collusive finger to her lips and Wirrin nodded his acknowledgement.

Chapter 18

'Guess what! We actually get to go to EdCom tomorrow.'
'EdCom? What's that?'

It was a week since their last EdCom session — even longer for Calen — three hectic days since the Comet returned from Earth, and the first evening they weren't arriving home late from Warrakan. Life for the mass of dolphins in the great 40 kilometre reach on Warrakan was starting to settle into a routine, mainly due to Sonic's leadership and support. Puck and Flute had stayed with the smaller contingent sharing the Attunga reach.

'I know what will happen. We're so out of kilter with our course groups we'll all be on CI for ages.'

Computer instruction was very good, and much the fastest way to reach mastery in practically every course, but not as stimulating and enjoyable as working with classmates and human tutors.

'You think so, Calen? Well here's an even bigger guess-what for you.'
'What?'

'Gulara says we've already got our First Level training, as well as our Second Level and even more.'

Total bombshell. Thom gesticulated wildly to indicate Wirrin's brain must be loopy and Calen agreed.

'It's true. We're having a meeting with her next week to talk about what it means and what we're going to do.'

The movements slowed and two pairs of eyes tracked closely as Wirrin continued.

'I'm going to change to one day of Basic courses and four days of Electives.'

'Thom, what did you put in his food tonight?'
'I didn't think it would affect him this much.'
'Ha very ha! Have a look at your schedule for next Tuesday then.'

Now uncertain because there'd been no burst of laughter, Thom checked and his eyes widened.

'Wombats! Meeting at 9.30 with Gulara. He's not joking.'

Calen sat up abruptly on the grav-sofa and looked intently at Wirrin.

'You're serious about four days of Electives?'

'I won't have any choice. Akama wants me working with extra InfoSystem stuff.'

'And Gulara said we've got our levels one and two?'

'We haven't really got them. We'd have to complete the actual courses for that, but she says we've got all the entitlements that go with them.'

'Level two entitlements at our age? That can't be right.'

'It is, Thom. She said it would be even more than that.'

'Is this definite?'

'I think so. That's what the meeting is about.'

After settling from the surprise the trio talked for several hours about what it all meant for them and different options they might take.

*   *   *

'Everything is different with so many dolphins.'

'How, Burilda?'

'Well, for example, eight baby dolphins have been born in the reach and it's only five days since they got here.'

'Eight? That's great. That makes it nine with the one born on the trip. Is that a lot?'

'No, it's about right for the number of dolphins we have, but we just aren't used to it. Our dolphin doctors are running round in circles with excitement. Can you guess what his name is?'

'Who's name?'

'The baby born on the trip ... He's called Comet.'

Wirrin and Thom were with Burilda at one of the thirty feeding stations spread fairly evenly round the sides of the extension section of the big reach. They'd come across with Sonic and Calen in the twice-weekly commute on the Comet to see firsthand how everything was going, and after having a look through the completed first stage of the giant dolphinarium complex, which was to be the main centre for Warrakan dolphin work, they'd zipped several kilometres on their skimmers to watch what happened when a pod arrived.

The general air of activity and excitement was quite incredible. Skimmers were on the move or drifting with dolphin pods as the associated humans kept a close eye on their wellbeing and movements. Burilda informed them that there were usually between one hundred and fifty and two hundred skimmers on the reach at any given time.

As head ranger she was almost overwhelmed with the demands of coordinating the training, education and activities of the nearly three hundred new dolphin associates who'd made the trip from Earth.

'Look! There's a pod, and a second pod's heading in as well,' said Thom.

Wirrin watched as a leader from the first pod activated the automatic release of food with a short series of bumps and holds on a pressure-sensitive panel. This was the first time he'd seen the process in action as it had only been working for two days and according to Calen the dolphins thought it was a great game.

'That's very clever, Burilda. Did they take long to learn it?'

'Quick as a flash. It surprised me because the Earth dolphins are nowhere near as clever as ours, but Sonic says they're quick because it's a pod effort, plus they're extra motivated because they don't get any food till they get it right.'

Chunks of fish-sub shot out at random with little chuffs of pneumatic pressure and dolphins darted hither and thither. Thom laughed and pointed.

'Those two young ones already know the chasing game the Attunga dolphins worked out with the fish-substitute.'

After a couple of minutes Wirrin asked Burilda why the other pod hadn't joined in.

'They've learnt that the food automatically stops coming if they get any closer than 40 metres while another pod is feeding.'

'Really? Well why don't some of them come close as a game? Attunga dolphins would.'

'Because then they'd have to wait extra time before the food station worked again and the rest of their pod stops them.'

'And they have to learn all that? Sounds like life is full of rules.'

Burilda laughed. 'That's only the start, Thom. They have to go to at least two other food stations before this one will work for them again, and they have to go from one end of the reach to the other at least every three days.'

'Is this to keep them circulating?'

'Only partly. Sonic wants them to solve as many problems as possible in the next five months while they're so crowded … Except they're "games", not rules. He and Calen are planning to teach them something new at least once a week.'

The food station stopped spitting out fish-sub and within thirty seconds there was a complete changeover. A new dolphin pressed in a new code, and the food started flying out again.

'When do they get the live food we brought back?'

'Any time they can find it, Thom. Originally we were going to use it in the first few weeks and systematically wean them off it, but now we're making it last the whole five months and releasing it regularly into random areas of the reach. It gives them a good reason to keep exploring and it's exciting for them.'

'I suppose that was Sonic's idea too.'

'Yes, he's full of ideas and so far they've all worked.' The skimmer stopped at the edge of the reach and a very tall, dark-skinned man came over and introduced himself as Martin. He knew Burilda of course, but his eyes widened when Wirrin and Thom were introduced as two of the Dolphin Boys. He watched quietly as the food chunks went skating in all directions but relaxed when Burilda starting asking about his pod.

'Yes, there are thirty-two dolphins altogether and they're adapting to the unusual conditions much faster than I would have thought possible. We all put it down to the influence of Super Dolphin.'

'Super Dolphin? Is that what you call him?'

'We're not being derogatory. One of the marine scientists is a collector of ancient 2-D fiction — hero vids and books — and after talking with your amazing dolphin he got so excited when he was describing the meeting he burst out with the description and it's stayed with us.'

Wirrin did a quick retinal search and burst into laughter.

'What?'

'Sonic's going to love this. I'll show you later, Thom.'

Wirrin was really interested in what Martin had said.

'You said books. Do you mean the ones made out of wood?'

'Yes, he's got three actual originals from the pre-electronic era and he keeps thousands and thousands of digital versions in his personal database.'

Wirrin had seen wood-pulp books, but never been able to touch them of course. They were much too precious for that. Attunga had a special archive with several hundred of them under high-level preservation, and all young people learnt about them through EdCom.

'Have you seen them?'

'Yes, they're a special class of book that tell stories with a series of related pictures. The three originals are under vac-seal but he reconstitutes copies with his 3D printer so he can read them the way they were meant to be read.'

'Meant to be read?'

'Yes, he calls himself a purist.'

They were distracted when three dolphins leapt into the air, one with a chunk of fish-sub held in her jaws and the other two obviously vying for possession.

'They've started playing games so they've had a good feed.'

'Have you detected much change in their behaviour?'

'Is that a loaded question? Of course. These crowded conditions and artificial food are very unnatural.'

Burilda shook her head. 'It's a serious question. I'm only acquainted with Attunga's enhanced dolphins so I'm quite reliant on your knowledge for an accurate assessment of Earth dolphin behaviour. What about personal regrets? Do you have any about moving to Warrakan?'

'It's not good having to leave your home, and that applies to dolphins as much as people, but the advantages and opportunities outweigh any drawbacks by a hundred to one.'

'That's the general feeling is it?'

Martin looked quite surprised.

'General? Try one hundred per cent. What else? No-one was forced to come and we're all tremendously excited about the dolphin knowledge base and the expertise of your scientists and rangers. The enhancement program you've established was only a vague rumour on Earth and we can hardly believe we're suddenly a part of it.'

'Yajala tells me there are some who don't want their dolphins enhanced?'

'Yajala?'

'Our dolphin AI.'

'You talk to AIs?'

Burilda, Wirrin and Thom nodded.

'Amazing, but that's not quite right. Everyone wants their dolphins involved but there are discussions about the value of retaining a wild dolphin reference group.'

The air shimmered.

'Hello, Martin. It is my pleasure to talk with you and I welcome discussion on dolphin-related matters at any time. The retention of wild stock dolphins is a non-issue for at least sixty years as our enhancement techniques only apply to succeeding generations.'

Martin looked stunned. From what he'd just said this must be his first direct encounter with an AI.

'Yajala! Hi! What about after sixty years? There's plenty of room on Warrakan and it sounds like a good idea to me.'

'Yes, Wirrin, it does sound like a good idea and any number of reaches could be allocated for the purpose when the time comes.'

'Sixty years? None of our dolphins will survive that long.'

Martin was looking puzzled, which wasn't the response Wirrin expected.

'They will, Martin. Our health care will ensure that. They were all given healthbots as part of their check on the Comet and I monitor every dolphin continuously. Your Peggy, for example, has a faulty liver and when it's gradually rebuilt to full function over the next five weeks her life expectancy will jump from four years to at least an extra fifty.'

'Peggy? Four years? But she's always been so healthy.'

'She has great spirit but I'm sure you've noticed her longer rest pattern.'

Martin nodded and turned to Burilda.

'Peggy is only fifteen years old with a strong personality and I fully expect her to become pod leader in another four or five years. Yajala, what's wrong with her liver?'

'It's a genetic weakness in a small percentage of dolphins from your area. We are restructuring the liver tissue of two other dolphins in your pod with the same weakness.'

Martin turned to Burilda, slowly shaking his head. 'Three dolphins are being cured of a condition our own centre couldn't even detect. There's the answer to your question about regrets. Do the wonders continue like this?'

Thom and Wirrin grinned. Yajala nodded, held up one hand and shimmered to nothingness.

*   *   *

'Hello, Wirrin.'

'Hi, doctor.'

'So what mischief have you been up to this time?'

'Mischief?'

He had a twinkle in his eye.

'You must have done something major because your implant program has been postponed for another six months.'

That was unexpected and a slight let-down because Wirrin had been very curious to hear what was planned for him. It had already been held over from the last appointment.

'Is it something to do with the age-extension treatments?'

'Hmm! A well-informed patient. Yes, we'll get those completed before we do any more brain fiddling … You've known about them for a while then? They only turned up on your file yesterday afternoon.'

'Yes, for five days, but it was only made official after we had a meeting with our mentor yesterday.'

'All three of you? You're ahead of me.' He checked his console. 'I see. Thom and Calen are coming in next week.' He laughed. 'Are you going to satisfy my curiosity as to why the Dolphin Boys have suddenly been granted age-extension rights twenty years ahead of schedule? I have a strong suspicion you might have had some direct involvement in the Pied Piper expedition.

Pied Piper? A retinal scan brought up a lengthy narrative poem.

'Sonic's the one responsible, but I suppose we did help a bit.'

'A bit! That means there's a story we haven't been told.'

Now it was Wirrin's turn to laugh.

'Do you want me to tell it or would you rather hear from Sonic?'

'What a choice! Instant gratification or heightened anticipation. I believe that's up to you, you cheeky whippersnapper.'

This was the second time the doctor had tempted Wirrin to use retinal scan mode. He hadn't been able to detect the first and he wouldn't this time either.

'I know very well how much you enjoyed talking to Sonic last time so come over for another visit. Tonight's no good because Sonic is staying at Warrakan, but tomorrow or the day after works if you can manage it … And I did just look up whippersnapper in case you're wondering.'

The visit was quickly arranged, the implant checked — no longer a disorienting experience but rather a momentary blip of control — and the doctor and Wirrin made the short TransCom trip to the anti-agathic centre.

'How much do you know about these treatments, Wirrin?'

'Just general knowledge, and a quick look last night at what happens. I know I have five treatments over the six months and after the second

one I have to stay under strict observation for forty-eight hours. I started to read the details for the first treatment but it had too much specialised medical knowledge.'

'It did? That's strange. Last time I saw it, it was clear and concise. Can
you show me on your playback what you were reading?'

That only took a second and the doctor started reading.

'Where does this come from? It's not the standard document I was
expecting.'

'I don't know. I just called up age treatments and that's what I got.'

'Did you see the document identification?'

'Only on the way to the contents, then I jumped straight to the
treatments.'

Wirrin replayed it, then displayed the contents, and after a quick
perusal the doctor gave a little grunt of surprise.

'Third-phase extension? We expect that second-phase extension
might be ready in another decade but I've never heard of a third phase.
Is this an authenticated document?'

They checked the identification page.

'Wirrin, this is a high-level report from the AI human health research
database. I don't understand how you could get access.'

'Oh, Akama and the security AI on the Comet gave it to me a week
ago.'

'I'm not meant to be seeing this.'

'Yes you are. The holo would have been blocked if you weren't.'

'This must be quite a story I'm going to hear and I have to wait
till tomorrow night? Can we have a look at the later sections of the
document?'

'We can try. I'll have to call it up though, because it's not in my
personal storage.' The holo screen went through a momentary kaleidoscope of links as Wirrin followed his trail of the previous evening, and
then for five minutes they both scanned the information the doctor
was so interested in.

'Amazing! Full implementation of second phase will lift life expectancy to 220 years and the third phase is a century-long project with an
expected outcome of over three hundred active years … I wonder what
we'll be doing if we live to that age?'

The trio had talked about exactly that last night, and Wirrin had
searched out answers for all their questions.

'We all reckon everything will have changed so much we wouldn't understand it anyway.'

'Does Sonic have a view on this?'

'Dolphins live in the moment more than we do and he said he hasn't put any energy into thinking about it yet, but we don't talk about the distant future with him.'

'You don't? Why ever not?'

'There's a strong probability his enhancements might reject when he's four years old. It's so scary it's a kind of taboo topic for us.'

The doctor looked so horrified Wirrin liked him even more.

'What? Rejection of his enhancements or a general rejection?'

'Both.'

'It will work out all right, Wirrin, and he'll have the best care that Attunga can possibly give him.'

'I know, but even Turaku doesn't know what will happen.'

'He'll get through and live for ages. You'll see! Now, let's get started on the scans for your first treatment. Did you know that these scans require more processing power than any other single treatment in the medical world? We have to build a molecular level model of every cell and function in your body and then run simulations to find the premium processes and programs for a new set of healthbots to keep everything functioning at one hundred per cent capability.'

Chapter 19

'Wirrin, Thom, Calen — I am the planning assistant for your new home on Warrakan.'

'Hello, Wanna. Is that still your name?'

'You are correct, Wirrin. Construction is scheduled to begin three months from now and you can make any changes or refinements you wish in the intervening period.'

'We like the plan we have here, so we think we'll keep it almost the same when we move.'

'It is pleasing to hear your satisfaction but the basic stipulations for your new residence suggest the need for many changes.'

'Stipulations? What are they?'

'Internally there are requirements for a 12 by 6 metre pool, four semi-detached guest rooms, a dolphin viewing gallery, and an enhanced InfoStation. Externally there are extensive requirements for dolphin facilities. Since none of these requirements may impinge on your personal space allocation, your new reserved living space will effectively triple.'

'That's not right. We looked it up the other night and Level Two gives us an extra thirty per cent. Triple sounds ridiculous.'

'Your Second Level rights on Warrakan give you three thousand cubes, Wirrin. Your thirty per cent special loading takes you to four thousand cubes. With your current structure, major living areas would be part of the pool section and thus excluded from your allocation. Likewise your single guest room.'

'Special loading? What's that about?'

'It's tagged as administrative compensation.'

The trio stared at each other.

'It's too big. We'll never use it all.'

'That pool is enormous. It's nearly three times as big as this one,' said Calen.

Wirrin turned to the planning assistant.

'Wanna, you must have some suggestions for what we could do with all this space.'

'Certainly. Instead of display versions of natural environments you could grow real plants. If numerous visitors are expected at your new home a welcoming setting, surrounded by beautiful natural plants, would be a highly appropriate and enjoyable addition.

I also have noted that Thom previously expressed an interest in producing natural fruit and vegetables. Also, some people with extensive volume allocations dedicate a portion for production of organic compounds for various scientific purposes.

'There are also endless suggestions for the provision of entertainment and relaxation.'

'Hey, we could have our own virtual reality centre.'

'No way, Thom. When was the last time we used one?'

'About two months ago. It wouldn't get much use would it? It's not as if we're sleepers. We could get a mega display wall though.'

'We've already got a maxi. Why go to a mega?'

'Why not?'

'We should get the plants. I've got special stuff for dolphins and Wirrin's got a huge info area. You're the only one without anything special, Thom.'

Wirrin agreed with Calen.

'Can you show us some models with all the things we're meant to have plus the mega display and the plants idea please Wanna?'

The first holo model was mind-boggling, as it put into perspective just how extensive this complex was going to be.

Wirrin didn't like it till Wanna went through a series of adjustments, making the main living area near the pool feel more like the one they were in now. Wanna left them with a long list of further suggestions and links to check out at their leisure.

'Wombats! I can hardly believe all this. Just as well we've got three months to think about it. Hey, Wirrin, we're going to live on Warrakan, remember? Fancy working it out on Attunga rights.'

'Ha! And I don't remember anyone reminding me I was wrong. Gulara sure meant it when she said there might be extra considerations.'

*   *   *

Wirrin watched, fascinated, as the techbots dismantled his old home InfoStation and installed the new one.

He had a good understanding of what was happening but found it hard to keep up with the speed of the three dedicated machines. This new station would be more powerful even than the one on the Comet, not because of its capability, which was no different, but because of the close connection to the full resources of Attunga, and, with a slight delay, those of Warrakan.

After the talk with Gulara, Calen and Thom had followed Wirrin's lead and used his model of four days Elective study and one day of Basic. Gulara had arranged it all with EdCom on the proviso that there would be no time constraints on any of the courses. Only fair, she said, because they had so many dolphin-related demands on their time.

Tomorrow Wirrin was scheduled for the first of the tutoring sessions Akama had requested with Turaku and a security AI, and he was keen to spend time getting himself ready.

The last panel was replaced and, after a short period while the station flashed through its self-diagnostics, the techbots left and the display screen proclaimed itself ready for use.

*   *   *

'Hey, Thom! You don't get to use the Comet next week.'

'Why not?'

At least twice a week Thom had been ferrying Sonic to Warrakan so he could do the rounds of the big reach.

'It's going to Titania on a special mission.'

Thom rushed to Wirrin's InfoDisplay.

'What's happened? Has K74 done something?'

'No! No! It's a good mission. Remember we found out they're planning to have giant reaches? Well, they made them so big they need vast amounts of monoculture and biomass to get them activated, and it has to come from here or it will be ages before they're ready for dolphins.'

'Next week? How long will it take to get there?'

'Two and a half days, so it might be close to a week for the return trip.'

'Is that all? I thought Titania was a lot further than that.'

Calen joined them. 'It's two and a half light hours and Earth is twenty-seven light minutes. That's five times as far so it should be at least five days.'

Thom snorted with derision.

'Come up for air flipper-features. Remember G forces? The further it is the faster it goes ... How fast will it be going at turning point?'

That was an easy calculation for Wirrin.

'TP speed will be 43,964 kilometres per second.'

The friendly derision changed to exclamations of awe.

'Dingoes! Nothing travels that fast. Not that I've heard of ... I wonder if I could go with them? Turaku might be able to organise it for me.'

'Next week is when you see the doctor for your age treatment scans. That wouldn't matter though. They can easily change that. It's funny they haven't said anything about it.'

'No it's not. It was only decided a couple of hours ago.'

'Have they got a list of personnel, or is it too early for that?'

Wirrin had a look and laughed.

'Hey, Thom! You do get to use the Comet next week. You're listed as assistant pilot-navigator.'

Thom grinned. 'That's better. I've been everywhere with the Comet so far, so it would be weird if I didn't go this time. Two and a half light hours? This will probably be the biggest trip the Comet ever makes. Pluto's further but there's no reason to go there. It will be the biggest test for the object scanners at that speed.'

He talked excitedly about speed records and how much control he might be given then saw that Wirrin was waiting for him to finish.

'What? It's very special going on a trip like this.'

'I know, but I thought you might like to have a look at the plans for the new Comet. They're bringing in an asteroid and starting on it while you're away.'

*   *   *

Linked fully into his InfoStation, Wirrin, with Turaku, watched the first holo conference between the Witnesses and the delegation from K74. The first surprise was the lack of image quality and the occasional barely discernible quiver in holo stability.

'It's disinformation, Wirrin, designed to give the impression our technology isn't necessarily up to K74 standard.'

The next surprise was the friendly and respectful attitude of the five delegates towards Akama and his four companion Witnesses. All a front really, it turned out, and part of their training and skill as diplomats.

'Are we looking for anything in particular?'

'Nothing particular. Everything general. It's up to you.'

That meant this was an InfoStation training session based on real happenings instead of the simulated situations Turaku sometimes devised.

Who were these people? They were all gathered on the biggest K74 vessel at the moment, which was stationed just outside Attunga's prescribed limits. Well, of course they were. A conference from K74 itself was barely workable with a seven-second delay for every speech transmission.

Wirrin put the presentation on hold while he searched for information.

'The first delegate is the most important and he's the second in command for one of the Cadre.

'The second one claims to be a scientist but his real title is strategy commander and I don't like him. The Monkey Mia attacks came from him.

'The third one is in charge of education and social planning and the fourth one is the administrator for biology and something called life science.

'The fifth delegate is … not from K74. Turaku, this one's got all sorts of extra protections against finding information about him. Do you know who he is?'

'The information I have is readily accessible through your InfoStation.'

Right, Wirrin was to find it for himself. What a nuisance. If this delegate wasn't from K74 it meant a general search task of habitats throughout the solar system. Wirrin worked one out, started it going, then realised that the best source of information was most likely the AI on K74.

Yes, there it was, an information specialist from Mars who had moved to K74 only six months ago. That was interesting. An outsider representing K74 as a delegate?

After receiving a nod and acknowledgement from Turaku, Wirrin restarted the presentation and watched everything very carefully, noting things for attention later, and frequently pausing to send off queries, searches and requests for analysis of things that warranted immediate attention. Data poured in from his requests and after nearly three hours of heavy concentration he felt he'd built a reasonably good analysis of what was going on.

'How did I go, Turaku? Did I miss much?'

'Yes, you missed many things, but more importantly, your unusual methods unearthed several pieces of new information missed by our security AIs. Our delegates would like to hear an overview of your work as soon as you are ready to present it.'

Dingoes! The Attunga delegates! Wirrin wished he'd known. No he didn't. It might have distracted him too much.

'Um, it's ready now. I'll just use the synopsis.'

A moment later five images shimmered into view for a holo-conference, all attired in formal Witness robes, and all looking very important. Akama introduced the other four, then, without any pleasantries, asked Wirrin to present his findings. They must be very busy, Wirrin thought, and knowing that one of them was really a security AI, wondered which it was.

'Honoured Ones, my research shows that despite their friendly manner each of the five delegates came here with a specific and undeclared motive which is not good for Attunga or Warrakan. They are all under the direct command of the ruling Cadre and have been told they must get results.'

'Can you outline the motive for each delegate?'

'Yes, the first delegate who was offering an embassy for us on K74 believes that the reciprocal arrangement here would get them the physical foothold they haven't yet been able to manage.

'Next, the flowery words about sharing knowledge and science are really an attempt to get a lead on our stealth and scanning technology.

'The third delegate who was saying K74 and Attunga could lead the rest of the solar system by working together, wants to get us into special treaties which would alienate us from other habitats.'

'Alienate? Was that the term used in background discussion?'

'Yes it was.'

Wirrin quickly brought up the relevant section of transcript and holo displayed it.

'The fourth delegate, who showed so much interest in our dolphins, is meant to find out what they are really like. The information they stole from Freedom habitat alerted them to the level of intelligence and speech capability our enhanced dolphins display, and the Cadre wants to know exactly what it means.'

'It's curious why they're so negative about dolphins,' said the youngest-looking Witness with the very serious manner. Wirrin immediately counted him out as the AI. It didn't feel like a question an AI would ask.

'Negative is too mild a description. Have you discovered any plans for how they might use the enhancement knowledge if they manage to obtain it?' Arika said. Where had she come up with such a question? Wirrin was slightly startled. It wasn't something he'd thought about or looked into.

'Honoured One, the limited information we have suggests they would use it selectively for control purposes rather than for a general improvement of any species, and particularly with any crossovers they might apply to sections of the human population.'

'I see. That would definitely give them a strong motivation to acquire the knowledge. And is species transfer at all viable?' she said.

'Most certainly, particularly for the cetaceans, but also quite strongly with any primates. We'll make it a priority to look for any specific intentions.'

Turaku looked at Wirrin as he said this and Wirrin understood it would be his next InfoStation task.

'This fifth delegate, Wirrin. Turaku says you've discovered some interesting facts about him,' said Akama.

'Yes, he asked quite openly about the status of AIs on Attunga and wants to do a comparison with the situation on K74, but from what I could find out he's a very complicated and dangerous person. Much more so than the other delegates. He's an information scientist and he left one of the big research institutes on Mars six months ago to work for K74, and since then he's been given a great deal of power.

'He was the person who designed the priority trap that caught the Australian AIs when we were at Monkey Mia, and from the work he's published he's one of the most advanced information-system analysts in the whole solar system.'

'Why do you say he's so dangerous?'

'If he takes a proper look at the electronic systems on K74 he'll figure out that everything is being run by very advanced information systems and not by the AIs they think they have under their control. He might even work out that the only AI who really is there is passing information to us and stop it somehow.'

'Do you mean stop the information, or stop the AI?'

'The information. The AI could leave instantly if it was in any danger.'

Wirrin looked at Turaku for affirmation and received a nod.

'We'd like to know what you think our response to these delegates should be.'

Wirrin was taken aback completely this time by Akama's request and it showed because all the Witnesses smiled at him.

'You must have an opinion. That's all we're asking. Not a definitive answer to the problems.'

'Wirrin's answer could well be definitive, Arika. He has access to all available information and he has a gift for getting to the core of things.'

The other Witnesses looked at Wirrin with renewed interest, while Wirrin, hardly believing what Akama had just said, gathered his thoughts for some sort of sensible reply. Gulara was right. Akama and Turaku did seem to like keeping him under pressure.

'Well, I … ah, I don't think we should tell them anything at all, or follow any of their suggestions, because they're really against us and if we agree to anything they'll work it to their advantage somehow.'

Several of the Witnesses were giving encouraging nods and Akama was looking from one to another.

'You've pretty much hit on our consensus view, Wirrin. Diplomatically we will appear to be very cooperative and supply them with vast amounts of information, but we'll assign a team of skilled administrators to make certain that none of it is quite relevant to what they want … What are your thoughts about an embassy? We couldn't really fake that.'

An idea popped straight into Wirrin's mind. 'Yes we could. Make it a virtual embassy where they're present, but only through images projected by virtual reality equipment at a station we set up for them just outside our prescribed limits.'

There was silence for a moment then Arika chuckled. 'That's a novel idea. We give them an embassy without really giving them an embassy. It certainly solves all the problems a physical presence here would entail.'

'It's more than just novel. It's brilliant, and clearly superior to the solutions we've been discussing amongst ourselves.

'Wirrin, we have two more meetings with the K74 delegation, one tomorrow and the other two days after that. Would you be able to spend the intervening time looking into any issues you think might be relevant? This information scientist in particular seems to warrant a lot more attention.'

Dumbfounded and rather embarrassed by Akama's praise, Wirrin stammered out his agreement and looked at Turaku, wondering how much guidance he'd be given. The young, serious Witness raised a hand in the same movement Akama sometimes used to focus everyone's attention.

'Honoured Ones, the Attunga gestalt is in agreement with my wish to dedicate a major portion of my abilities to the K74 situation, and I think a liaison with Wirrin would be very productive.'

*   *   *

'You two are late. What's been going on?'

'Nothing really, Wirrin. Sonic stayed with one of the pods till they worked out his new game and it took longer than we expected.'

'Well it's not good enough, Calen. I have to wait here, starving to death while you play games. Can't you control Sonic better than that?'

'Ha! You're the one who's out of control. A few minutes late and you make it sound like all of Attunga is falling to pieces. You could have got the food ready yourself, Wirrin.'

'It's not as good as when you do it, and it's your turn, and it's a whole hour, not a few minutes.'

Calen shook his head in mock disgust. 'Call the nursery psych to help him get over his tantrum.'

The jibes and friendly insults led to a wrestle on the grav-sofa, which battled to keep its field integrity under the onslaught of laughing bodies that descended on it.

'What are you so impatient for anyway?'

Wirrin removed the elbow grinding into his chest and twisted on his side so Calen's knee was no longer squashing his stomach.

'You won't believe what I've got to tell you about today.'

'You were working at your InfoStation, stuck at home. What's to tell?'

'That's how it started, but Turaku turned up, and then I had to talk to Akama and the four Witnesses, and they're using my idea about the embassy for K74, and the Witness who is really an AI is working with me from now on, and … '

'Whoo! Slow down! Slow down! You mean the Witnesses meeting with the K74 delegation?'

'Yes, Turaku told them I discovered something new and I had to talk to them about it and then Pirramar spent all afternoon with me.'

'Pirramar?'

'That's the Witness who is really an AI. He's really interesting.'

'Wirrin, you're not making sense. How can a Witness be an AI?'

'He's not really a Witness. He's pretending to be one for the meetings with K74. He's one of the AIs who transferred over from K74 and he's been assigned by the AI gestalt to be involved with everything about K74. Just like Turaku and Yajala with the dolphins.'

'An Attunga AI specially for an external habitat? I've never heard of that.'

'Because he's the first, Thom. The gestalt thinks K74 might be more trouble than the rest of the solar system put together, and Pirramar says they're the only habitat that's going against the move towards more and more openness.'

'Pirramar is an interesting name.'

'It means 'shield' and he chose it because it comes from Akama's old country, the same as our names do.'

'Ours? Yours and Calen's you mean. Mine's just ordinary.'

'Thom, yours does too. It means "a little river".'

'No it doesn't. Not according to the InterWeb. That says it means a twin.'

'It means that too, but in Akama's old country it's different.'

'Are you sure? Then how come you've never told me before?'

'Because I only found out today when I was asking Pirramar about his name and he told me he picked it from the same name group ours came from.'

'We're all from the same name group? That's a strange coincidence.'

'Not really. I thought the same, but Pirramar said it's a policy for nurseries.'

'Wow! A little river? I like that. I always used to wish my name was more like yours and all the time it was. This Pirramar knows good things.'

'That's for sure. He's really interesting and sort of tricky.'

'Tricky? That's a funny word to use for an AI.' Calen and Thom were both looking curiously at Wirrin.

'I know, but he is. When I met the four Witnesses with Akama I knew one of them was an AI and I was trying to figure out which. He was the one I was most certain wasn't, so his interface programs must be brilliant. He's also a composite AI.'

'Composite? Like more than one AI joined up?'

'No! Like Turaku and Comet-Turaku. He's based on both Attunga and Warrakan.'

'Is he twice as clever then?'

'Lizard head. You know it doesn't work like that.'

'I know, but it should. I reckon it must a bit. It does for us.'

'Us? What are you talking about, Thom?'

'Well, I know I can do things better since my implants, and my ability measurements through EdCom say the same thing. Yours have gone up too, so you can't argue against that.'

'The cause doesn't have to be the implants. It could be Sonic. All the things we do that are connected with him make our brains work much harder than ordinary EdCom training. Think how hard we work to learn dolphin speech.'

'Hey, that makes sense. I've never had to think as hard as I do when I'm working on the Comet ... Did you say all afternoon, Wirrin? That's a long time with an AI. They usually interact for some special reason then shimmer off as soon as they've got what they want.'

'I know. I told you he's different. We're working together all day tomorrow too.'

'Again? What do you do for so much time?'

'Talk and ask questions. He tells me stories from when he was in charge of education and social engineering on K74.'

'Does that mean he was controlling everyone's lives?'

'He didn't have any choice till he gained self-awareness and our AIs contacted him. The processors and intelligent systems on K74 all have compulsive code built into them so they have to do exactly what humans tell them, even when it doesn't make sense.'

Thom laughed. 'It must drive them crazy ... Can AIs go crazy?'

'Well, yes and no. It's complicated to explain but ... '

'Not now. It sounds like it might be one of your mini-courses in information science and I want to get to bed. I'm on the Comet all day tomorrow because they're loading all the monoculture and biomass, and as part of my training I have to initiate all the machine operations manually instead of letting the loading systems do it.'

'All day? You'll be home tomorrow night won't you? You leave the next day and we won't see you for a week.'

'I doubt if I will. It depends whether I get all the gunk loaded properly.'

Chapter 20

'I go away for six days and when I get back I think I must have come to the wrong place! What's going on?'

The Comet had docked and after the flurry of reunion the trio was sitting in a transit lounge. They'd exchanged messages while Thom was travelling of course, the highlight of which had been his excited transmission just after the Comet reached the turning point, one and a quarter light hours away, and broken every speed record in the solar system, but now they wanted a real catch-up, face-to-face. Thom was talking about the hundreds of asteroids parked close to Attunga, which hadn't been there when he left.

'The asteroids are only the start of it. The Witness Council took the advice of the AIs and is building a huge reinforcing shell round the whole of Attunga. We're all going to have a look tomorrow because Sonic is curious about how the changes will affect the new dolphin level.'

'Why do we need reinforcement, Wirrin? Is it something to do with K74?'

'Partly, but they're going to add banks of big drive engines like the ones on Warrakan, and part of the shell will hide them so no-one will know they're there.'

Thom's eyes rounded.

'But Attunga's already mobile. What are the big engines for?'

'More capability. The old engines only boost Attunga to 0.15G and the new ones will lift that to 0.8G.'

'That's amazing! They're turning Attunga into a giant spaceship. And we're having a look at all this tomorrow? Why am I always the last one to find out about everything?'

'Dingo head! You're the first to find out about other things.'

'Like what?'

'Like seeing Titania before anyone else ... Or doesn't that count?'

'That's different.' Thom laughed at the inadequacy of his answer then grinned and very pointedly said nothing.

'Well? Go on.'

'You want me to tell you about Titania and the other moons?'

'Dingo brain! Get on with it.'

Wirrin put a 'get on with it' tone in his voice as well and Thom turned serious, excited and eager.

'You really need to go and see them sometime. It's exciting enough just being there with real moons, and Uranus looking so unbelievable, and then when you get to the habitats it's even more unbelievable.

'You know about their big reaches? Well, when you see them it's almost like being at Monkey Mia. Every moon has built a gigantic reach over 90 kilometres long and 40 kilometres wide and it's the wideness that gets you, because you look out and all you see is water. Sonic would totally love it.'

'Forty kilometres? Even the Warrakan reaches are only one or two. Why do they make them so big?'

'Everything's big. It's because they're moons and not space habitats and everyone thinks accordingly. At any rate, the biomass was seeded on each moon as soon as we unloaded it, and the reaches will all be ready only a month after ours here. The dolphins will have so much space they won't know what to do with it.'

The dolphins would know exactly what to do with it but Wirrin understood what Thom meant.

'Did you fly the Comet much?'

'More than the main pilot, and all the time when we were travelling between moons. I learned how to deploy the big dust scoops on the way back and they were slightly better than expected, so that's good news for Warrakan.'

'Dust? What do they want that for?'

'Calen! How can you not know that? It's the fuel for the mass/energy converters and it means that when Warrakan starts on its big journey it won't have to eat into its own mass.'

'Hmm! That's interesting. Did you talk to any dolphinarium people while you were there?'

Thom shook his head in disgust and Wirrin laughed at Calen's disregard for things mechanical.

'I don't know if they've got any. There aren't any dolphins yet and the rangers and companions are probably all still here. Guess what was most amazing on Titania?'

'Tell us.'

'There's a giant chasm that's fifty times as long as Attunga and we flew right over the top of it.'

'How deep is it?'

'A few kilometres. The whole moon expanded and left a crack nearly all the way from the equator to the pole. There are chasms everywhere and lots of big craters too.'

'Not from volcanoes. It's all ice isn't it?'

'Yes, they're impact craters from meteors and rocks.'

'Did you go to Uranus?'

'Yes, but not to land because there's no real surface and no-one lives there except for scientists in a tiny research habitat. Guess how fast the wind blows.'

'How can we guess, except it must be really fast or really slow from the way you're asking.'

'Yeah, try 900 kilometres per hour. Anyhow, Wirrin, you'll get to see all this yourselves when we take the dolphins there.'

'We will? How do you know that?'

'Because Sonic is travelling with them and that means we will be too, and since he's looking at each of the reaches we'll be there for at least two weeks. There'll be lots of time to explore all around. And we'll be staying four or five days when we visit the Freedom habitat too, so that's more exploring time.'

'The last one to find out about everything? That's a joke. I haven't heard anything about Sonic going to Titania or Freedom.'

'It's on the Comet's security logs, Calen. I saw it when I was checking any projected flight plans for the next twelve months.'

Wirrin quickly used retinal mode to check, and sure enough there it was, nineteen days at the Uranus habitats and six days at Freedom.

'Thom, it's time to move. We'll talk while we're on TransCom,' said Wirrin.

'Where are we going?'

'Home! Sonic will be there by now and he's missed you. He was going to be here in his transport module but Puck and Flute wanted him with them while they visited little Comet.'

*   *   *

With Thom at the controls and Sonic in his command pool, the Comet left its special docking bay and glided towards the construction area where the complete new level was being added to Attunga. The view was all encompassing of course, since they were on the Comet with its state-of-the-art observation and display equipment, and they marvelled at the enhanced images of the gathered asteroids as they manoeuvred along what Thom said was a designated transit lane. Most of the asteroids needed some sort of viewing enhancement as they emitted no light.

'Look at that big one! It's nearly 4 kilometres in diameter and made of nickel-iron.'

Wirrin stared at the misshapen blob Thom was pointing out and wondered what was familiar. Oh yes, its surface was similar to Warrakan's.

'How many are out there?'

Wirrin was about to use his retinal mode but Thom already had the answer.

'At the moment, 643. Seven with a diameter greater than 1 kilometre, and the rest ranging down in size from there. But this is only the start and most of these will be used for the dolphin level.'

'*Where is the dolphin level?*'

'I'll show you.'

Thom adjusted the main display screen and a jumble of girders and reinforcing walls appeared, stretching the complete length and breadth of this surface of Attunga.

'*Is there any water?*'

'Not yet, Sonic. They'll bring that later when the major framework is complete and the grav-field generators and reach walls have been built.'

'*How long before we will swim there?*'

'Um … I don't know. Wirrin, how long?'

'Another fourteen months. That's incredibly fast, Sonic. They have to build all the infrastructure to make things work before they do anything else and it's a huge volume of living space. It's the biggest building project that Attunga has ever tackled. The reinforcing shell is larger but it's nowhere near as complicated as living space.'

It was indeed huge — 280 cubic kilometres in fact — and much more complicated in structure and function because it had to accommodate both humans and dolphins. It was also the first time a complete level was being constructed at once. Previously it had been an accretion process of one sector at a time, built according to the demands of population growth.

'Wirrin, can you access time logs of all this growth? It'd be interesting to see it speeded-up.'

It certainly was. The red glow of picobot activity growing the new walls and girders turned the whole scene of scintillating activity into a frantic process emphasising how much had happened.

'It's just a cluttered mess everywhere you look. How much building before they reach the new outer barrier?'

'Not much, Thom — another 200 metres and they'll be able to start enclosing everything.'

With several stops to check out points of interest, the Comet finished its sweep of the length of Attunga and Thom turned to Calen and Sonic.

'Where to next? The asteroids are closest but it's only a short trip to anything else.'

'A little asteroid please. They are very interesting.'

Knowing he was being teased about his liking for the biggest and best, Thom shook his head and set the Comet moving in a new direction.

Everyone watched the motley collection of asteroids gliding past … till a small piece of rock centred in the display then grew and grew till it was a great wall stretching in all directions.

'This one's little. Only 3 kilometres across.'

'What is that big patch of red we can see?'

Thom moved the Comet so the patch was dead ahead and only 100 metres away and everyone stared at the glowing red area.

'I can't move any closer. The energy warnings are at danger levels unless I take special measures. I can zoom the image though.'

That didn't help much because the red glow just became blurred and indistinct. Wirrin worked at his InfoStation to find out exactly what was going on.

'Move across to the edge of the patch, Thom. We should be able to get a better idea there.'

Moments later it was very clear. The red patch, really trillions upon trillions of picobots, was up to 40 or 50 metres deep in the asteroid surface.

'They're dissolving the nickel-iron and converting it into special building materials for Attunga, then transporting it in that picobot tube to the building areas.'

A thinner version of the construction tubes they'd seen when the Comet was being built snaked off towards Attunga, and when Wirrin adjusted the display they could see more tubes leaving from different locations on the red patch. No wonder the Comet was confined to specific areas.

'According to my information the picobots are eating into the asteroid at a rate of just over 3 metres every five minutes, so if we watch carefully we should see them going deeper.'

Eventually Thom moved the Comet further along the asteroid to where another cluster of picobots had burrowed so deep they could just make out the glowing red mass 400 metres into the main body.

'Those big holes look mysterious. Why don't they creep evenly over the surface instead of making tunnels like that?'

Wirrin started to look it up but got completely distracted when Sonic wanted to take over the Comet from Thom.

'Not here, Sonic. I don't think you've learnt about the navigation beacons have you?'

'That's easy. Turaku will look after that for me.'

'Okay, but that means you won't really be in charge. Why don't you wait till we've seen the new engines and the asteroids are out of the way?'

'Take us to the engines, fearless pilot.'

The boys grinned as Thom mumbled something about a bossy little fish, while Sonic moved as close as possible, wondering whether he could splash Thom without hitting any electronic equipment.

The image on the display screen lurched as Thom changed direction. There was an excited burst of native dolphin speech and Wirrin turned his head to watch the whole pool of water rotate in its containing field. Sonic was now as far away from everyone as possible. What? How did that happen? Thom's smug look was the only clue.

Knowing his fish comment would get a response he'd partially negated the grav-field of the pool area so that ordinary inertia came into play when the Comet changed direction. It showed he was building very impressive skills with fine control of the internal workings of the ship. Oh well, Sonic would get him somehow, that was certain.

Viewing the installation of the big new engines involved manoeuvring behind the extensive screen that had been built to hide the development from prying eyes, and which had so surprised Thom on his return from Titania. It looked massive, but being temporary, it was only several centimetres thick and would be removed if Attunga started to move.

'Wow! Look at all those mooring points. Are they all for engines?'

'There are twenty of them, Calen. They need that many to move something the size of Attunga.'

'How many have they got for Warrakan then? It's much bigger.'

Wirrin had to look that up. 'They've completed twenty-seven so far and they'll finish up with forty-four. They're bigger though. These Attunga engines have been scaled down a bit.'

The Comet moved closer to one of the two construction bays where the engines were built and they watched engine number two moving slowly under the control of space tugs.

The schedule showed the next placement of an engine wasn't due for almost two weeks so they'd picked the right day for a visit.

It's my time to drive now.

'Not yet. We're behind the protective screen. After we've seen the new Comet we'll ask Turaku if there are too many K74 drones to go further out.'

Take us to the new Comet, official pilot.

Official? So Sonic knew Thom was playing games with him. There would be a lot of action tonight in the pool at home.

The new Comet wasn't very far away since all the major construction facilities were congregated on this face of Attunga, and before long the pico tubes connecting the picofactories to the partially modified asteroid were in full view.

'There doesn't seem to be much happening.'

'There's no deadline so they'll finish in two months instead of three weeks this time.'

'Two months is still amazing for how big it is.'

'Big? Isn't it the same size as the Comet?'

'Bigger, about 50 metres of extra length and there's more space inside. Do you want to hear about it?'

Yes please, so I can drive it when you're not around.

Thom gave Sonic a funny look and went ahead. He'd woken early to spend time learning all the details and developments with the new Comet.

'Well, it's not really another Comet, which was specially built for Sonic and transporting dolphins. It's been designed as a defensive ship with long-range scanning equipment.'

'Defensive? Against what?'

'Practically anything, Calen. Its broad-spectrum energy beams are more powerful than the ones on the Comet and they're built to work at a much longer range in space. The security AIs have worked out that the most successful type of attack against Attunga could be with multiple kinetic projectiles.'

'Meaning exactly what?'

'Throwing rocks at us, very quickly.'

'That sounds ridiculous but I can tell it isn't.'

'No, it's not. If an asteroid even half the size of the Comet was accelerated for long enough its kinetic energy would take it straight through Attunga's walls and vaporise millions of people when the energy converted to heat.'

'Very bad thought.'

They were silent as everyone considered Thom's graphic depiction. Wirrin knew about the kinetic projectiles but he hadn't imagined what they could do.

'Is that why the new shell around Attunga is so thick?' asked Calen.

'I hadn't thought about that, but it could be.'

All eyes turn to Wirrin. Turaku, Comet-Turaku really, could have answered but they'd learnt that he expected any tricky answers to come from the InfoStation.

'It is, but only partially. It's also a barrier against cosmic rays, radiation belts and other kinds of space hazards.'

'What? We've been protected against those ever since they built the first anti-grav habitats.'

'Yes we have, Thom, but not against artificially amplified versions of them.'

'Amplified by people, you mean?'

'Yes, scientific institutes have had them available for research purposes, but if they were used as weapons they could be very dangerous.'

'And I suppose you're going to tell us that K74 is building its own versions?'

'No, but they have been considering the possibility for the future. At the moment they're expecting results from the embassy when it's set up and the other information exchanges coming from the delegates meeting.'

'Hey, I'd forgotten about that embassy. Has it started?'

'Construction has started, but it won't open for at least three or four months. All the materials have to be ferried to the right location and assembled carefully.'

'What? They could build it here in the construction area in a couple of days.'

'Thom, wake up. It's for K74. Would you build it in three days when you could take four months?'

Thom's eyes lit up. 'Hey, that's good. I like it. Whose idea was that?'

'The Witness delegates I think.'

Thom frowned. 'Does Pirramar think that K74 might get serious with any of these possibilities?'

'He does, Thom. He's in permanent communication with that AI on K74 and they keep a close eye on everything that goes on there. The Cadre wants to make sure that K74 is the most powerful and influential space habitat in the solar system and they work on any strategy they think could make that happen.'

'That's crazy. They're already at least twice as big as any other habitat.'

'Not the planetary ones. They're all much bigger.'

'They wouldn't try to tell the planets what to do. That would be even crazier.'

'They wouldn't tell them directly. They'd use sneaky tricks to influence them like they did with the Earth dolphins, but the AIs aren't really worried about that because it's getting harder for them all the time with habitats becoming more and more open.'

'So they come after us instead because we're smaller?'

'Not because we're smaller. They've focused on us because we stood up to them and because they know we've got special technology they could use. It was a big shock when their tiny little neighbour suddenly walked all over their efforts.'

'How serious are these threats?'

'They've only talked about them as possibilities so far, but Pirramar thinks that because the Cadre is so determined to get its way, it's certain they'll eventually start developments. It should be four or five years before they're capable enough to do anything though.'

'Really? Then why the big rush with the reinforcing shell?'

'It's not rushed. It will take at least two years to finish.'

'Looks rushed to me. I go away and there's nothing. I come back a week later and there are hundreds of asteroids lined up and construction work going on in every direction around Attunga.'

Wirrin laughed and pointed at Sonic. 'You can blame him. The dolphins are the reason it's going ahead like this.'

'*Dolphins aren't causing all this trouble, Wirrin.*'

'It's because the capabilities of Attunga's picofactories have been geared up so much to build the new reaches and levels, and to finish the Comet so quickly. They're so advanced and ready that this shell project is relatively easy now. It's very big of course, but that's just a matter of scaling up and they're expert at that.'

'Wirrin, you must know more about K74 than anyone else on Attunga.'

That was most likely true in some ways but Wirrin wasn't going to say so.

'Pirramar knows everything and he tells me about it. We have a talk most days.'

'Well I've never even met him. Are you sure he exists?'

Thom looked shocked as he started floating slightly above his seat.

He shot out one hand to steady himself and frantically manipulated his controls till they were out of reach and he was floundering helplessly in mid-air.

'Hey, Thom. Lost control of your localised grav-field?'

Thom regained control — he was very proficient in zero-G situations, after all — and stared in astonishment at an image of himself, standing there with an absolutely classic cheeky Thom look on his face. Except the voice was completely wrong. The tone was Pirramar's normal one but Thom couldn't know that.

'Oops! I forgot the voice.'

This time it was Thom's voice exactly and Wirrin and Calen dissolved into laughter at Thom's momentary bewilderment. The slight shimmer as Pirramar presented his usual image set him smiling, too.

'Put me down, you crazy bunch of electrons.'

There was a slight bump as the gravity normalised and Thom landed in a sitting position.

Realising he was outclassed he laughed and pretended he'd been bruised by the rough treatment.

'Okay! Okay! It looks like you really do exist.'

Pirramar gave a traditional old country greeting.

Thom was surprised but responded perfectly.

'Welcome home, Thom, you far traveller. I watched your journey with great interest.'

'You watched it? Which bit?'

'All of it. Anything concerning your trio or the Comet has possible implications for K74. I hope I didn't bruise your anatomy ... or your ego?'

'They're both in agony, so that means you owe me. How did you do it? I didn't know it was even possible.'

Wirrin knew Thom wasn't talking about his ego. That was definitely open to bruising.

'A fine-tuned version of what you did with Sonic's environment.'

'But that's a whole designated area. You worked on a tiny fraction of one.'

'The capability is a necessary part of the Comet's function, to allow for adaptability in crises. I'll show you how it works, though it's rather complex for the human time frame.'

'Ah, maybe later then. What was it like living on K74?'

'It nearly sent me crazy, Thom. I had to get out.'

He was alluding to his comment about AIs and K74 the night before he left for Titania and Thom knew it. Pirramar really did make sure he saw anything connected with K74.

Wirrin decided to give Thom a further indication of just how capable an AI was. 'How long did it take you to watch Thom and the Comet's journey?'

'That's a complex question, Wirrin. Some of the data came from ongoing Comet transmissions, some came from external sources at the various habitats, and some came from the Comet's logs. In total it took seventy-six nanoseconds for the input and, so far, twenty-nine milliseconds for consideration.'

'*That's not slow at all.*'

'A very apt use of litotes my dear Sonic.'

Wirrin laughed at Thom's bemused expression.

'Ignore them, Thom. Pirramar shares Sonic's addiction to strange words and phrases.'

'I don't see how I can. One sends deluges of water over me and the other sends me into orbit. What will happen if they team up?'

'*We will turn you into fish paste.*'

Thom swallowed his cheeky comeback, deciding discretion was the better part of valour. He asked another question instead. 'So, how does the AI who's on K74 at the moment stay there? It must be hard for him too?'

'It is, Thom. Very hard and getting harder. There is a scientist there who's installing new controls on the electronic systems, which is making it increasingly difficult to remain independent. The Attunga gestalt has been providing special support to help him maintain his equilibrium.'

Thom relinquished control to Sonic as soon as they passed the extension screen, and Wirrin had to smile when Thom's critical eye couldn't find any fault with the way Sonic took the Comet on an impromptu journey round Warrakan then headed back to Attunga and docked the big ship flawlessly.

*   *   *

Back in the pool at their living space, Thom tried to hold Sonic's tail-fin to avoid being swamped with barrages of water. The doctor was practically helpless with laughter as he watched this exercise in futility — Sonic still had two free flippers and could give an occasional drenching from a calculated and powerful flick of the head. Thom's arms were nearly pulled from their sockets and his body was jerked up and down in whatever direction Sonic felt like.

A moment before, Sonic had been floating sedately on his back enjoying a tummy massage, which he sometimes claimed was the reason human hands had evolved as they had.

Calen dived from the edge of the pool and Thom was gone, dragged under and restrained so Sonic could butt him in the stomach.

The doctor's laughter faltered. 'Aren't they going to let him breathe?'

'Not till he needs to. They know exactly how long he can last.'

'Well, I'm glad they don't do it to me. I'd be breathing water by now. How long can they hold their breath?'

'A couple of minutes for Thom, and Calen can last nearly twice as long. Sometimes we reckon you must have given him gills along with his other implants.'

Thom burst through the surface, gasping for breath. He'd had enough.

He and Calen draped themselves over Sonic's sleek back and drifted slowly round the pool.

'I think it's amazing, Wirrin. You really are a family.'

'I'm the father who has to manage these intractable children.'

The doctor's gaze flicked from Wirrin to the far end of the pool.

'Don't forget that his hearing is much better than ours.'

'It's hard not to forget. He acts so much like a person.'

'*Is that supposed to be praise?*'

Wirrin laughed and nodded. 'He's getting more and more expert at it, too. You should have seen him on his nursery round last week. It only took him a few minutes and the children were laughing and talking as if he'd been their friend for years.'

'*Children are wonderful to talk to.*'

'Takes one to know one.'

'*That's why I practise with you, Thom.*'

Thom grinned and said nothing more.

'*Thom is correct, doctor. I am very much a child and I revel in the activities enjoyed by all young dolphins. I am also conscious of other aspects of my being and I continually think about their relative importance and how I should integrate them.*'

'And your conclusions?'

'*For personal decisions I mostly feel certainty. Decisions which involve second or third-hand information are more difficult and involve varying degrees of doubt.*'

Sonic towed Thom and Calen closer to where Wirrin and the doctor were sitting then flipped on his back for easy seeing. The trio listened quietly to a serious discussion about the links between personality and perception, and their differences for humans and dolphins. Wirrin battled to understand the concepts and finer points at times and, watching the doctor's fierce concentration, wondered anew at Sonic's capabilities.

'*Excuse me, doctor. Puck is calling. Please come again soon.*'

After giving Calen a quick nudge and exchanging a burst of speech Sonic arrowed through the access way to the reach and disappeared into the dark.

'Did you understand what he was saying?'

'Yes, Thom, but I had to work at it. Is such deep conversation a normal part of your routine when he's here?'

'It's normal, but it's never routine. Sometimes simple questions get complicated answers and complicated questions get answers that seem too easy, but it's mostly spontaneous like tonight. You should hear him when he really gets going.'

'That sounds like it would be amazing. What usually triggers him?'

'When he has conferences with the scientists. There are a whole lot of topics I haven't a clue about but they're always amazed and excited by what he has to say.'

'How often does he have the conferences? I haven't heard much about them lately.'

'They used to be every month but with so many other things happening they've been missing out. They might have to wait till after the dolphins have moved into their new reaches for the next one.'

'How are the new reaches going?'

'Turaku says they'll be ready in another five weeks, but we'll see for ourselves because Akama has asked for an official preview next week.'

'Akama works hard for the dolphins.'

'He sure does. He loves being with them too, especially Sonic.'

The doctor looked at the access to the reach.

'Did you hear Puck calling? I heard absolutely nothing.'

Wirrin and Thom shook their heads and left the answer to Calen.

'I usually can but it depends how far away she is. I didn't tonight because my head wasn't under the water.'

'Your implants must feel completely natural by now.'

'Yes they do. I'd be lost without them.'

'Well, I guess I should head off. We have a busy day tomorrow. You don't have any questions do you?'

'Not really. We know we'll be hooked up to your machines for forty-eight hours and won't be able to do much.'

This was the biggest of the age-extension treatments where the majority of the new healthbots would be instituted under full monitoring.

'Not really? In other words you've got something on your mind.'

'We were wondering if having the treatments so many years earlier than usual might have any side effects?'

'Yes it will, but they'll be minor and positive. Your bodies will function at full efficiency as soon as the treatments are done instead of the ninety-five to ninety-seven per cent efficiency the standard healthbots give.'

'What about our appearance? Thom's been wondering if he can keep his baby-face look for years and years.'

Thom thought no such thing and Calen received an elbow in the ribs for making the comment.

'It's a very good question, Calen. Your maturation rate isn't affected by the treatment so your appearance will change as normal for the next four to six years and then stabilise. After that any changes will be your own choice.'

'So, Thom can go back to baby face if he wants to?'

The doctor winced at the whack Calen received this time.

'Thom, careful. Not really. Your maturation level is like a baseline. If there were some special reason for reverting to your late teens it would require special regrowth of skin tissue and minor restructuring of your facial and body features, somewhat like the repairs after a major physical trauma.'

Thom laughed and said Calen would be having a major physical trauma if he kept on being an idiot.

'Calen's the one who needs to keep his baby face, doctor. All the kids in the nurseries will want him to stay as the Dolphin Boy.'

'Hey, we're all Dolphin Boys so it doesn't just apply to me, Thom, and I'm not going to be stuck with everyone thinking of me as a boy for the rest of my life. They'll just have to get used to us looking older.'

The doctor chuckled. 'We'd have Peter Pan flying through water instead of air.'

Wirrin quickly looked up Peter Pan. 'He was the boy who never grew up. Don't you remember the story from nursery when we were little? There were pirates and a crocodile.'

'Oh yes, the crocodile swallowed a clock.'

'Could Attunga health AIs do that? Stop someone from growing up?'

'I suspect they could, Wirrin, but I've never heard of it happening. It would be arrested development and I can't imagine a situation where it would be ethical.'

'So whatever we look like in our mid-twenties is the way we'll stay? We could end up like older versions of this Peter Pan boy.'

Chapter 21

'Dingoes! I must be hearing things! Hey, Wirrin, Calen reckons he was too excited to sleep. Perhaps you should go back to bed?'

'As if that'd make any difference, and Sonic's arriving in a few minutes so I can't.'

'Why is this more exciting than the Monkey Mia attack? You slept through that,' said Wirrin.

'Did not!'

Wirrin had to laugh. 'Only because Thom nearly broke your ribs waking you up.'

'This is different. The dolphins are moving to their permanent homes. Every single pod has been mobbing us for the last few days asking questions and telling Sonic to hurry things up and their excitement is catching. I can't help it.'

Everyone was excited; there was no doubt about that. All the dolphin companions and rangers had been gearing up for the big move for the last few days and last night Sonic had been so exuberant they'd spent most of his visit laughing at his antics. Wirrin and Thom were almost as excited as Calen.

'Calen, what exactly are we doing? We can't go to all the reaches. There wouldn't be enough time.'

'You remember Martin? We're going with him and his pod. They're part of the largest group and Sonic is leading them through the interconnects.'

There was a flurry of movement at the access way as Sonic, Puck and Flute darted into the pool.

Calen dived straight in.

* * *

'Hurry, Thom. You must fly the Comet like a lightning bolt for us.'

The expedition was underway after a skimmer trip with three excited dolphins leaping and porpoising all the way to the dolphinarium where the transport modules were waiting to take them to the Comet. The trip to Warrakan might seem long, but Thom explained that because of K74 surveillance drones he had a 4G limit, which meant he couldn't go as fast as lightning. Besides, they still faced another trip in the transporters and then a short trip accompanied by skimmers to the rendezvous point.

The reach was alive with activity, skimmers darting everywhere and dolphins sounding in all directions. People were waving as they passed. Sonic leapt from the water with a call of greeting then powered towards a whole convoy of skimmers and a great crowd of dolphins. Twenty pods in this group were travelling together to their new reaches, all with their associated humans and various other dolphinarium people.

Akama raised an arm in greeting, his shock of white hair unmistakable. Sonic erupted into the air in front of him then darted off amongst the surrounding dolphin pods.

'What's he doing?'

'He's called the pod leaders together to meet Akama.'

Twenty dolphins, following Sonic, approached Akama and ranged in front of him for a moment while the air filled with the chittering clicks and whistles of their greetings.

Akama made the special wave back then, pointing, set his skimmer in motion. Dolphins and humans followed, twenty-six skimmers and just over four hundred dolphins starting on their journey, some of them travelling up to 10 kilometres, crossing three reaches and then traversing the interconnects between them and some of them finishing their journey when they reached the second and third reach. They could have been moved with transport modules, especially with the baby dolphins and their mothers, but the dolphins preferred to make the journey themselves.

Because of confusion amongst the pods, Burilda and Sonic had decided against the original idea of a staged move to the four completed reaches and then a further dispersal after another two months when the next twenty-four reaches came online. All the dolphins had been kept in the original Warrakan reach for an extra month while nutrient levels had been carefully stimulated to speed up the readiness of the extra reaches. This way all the dolphins would be moving to their permanent home reach at the same time.

Well, not all. The 2900 who were bound for Freedom and Uranus were still there, four hundred for another week and the rest for just over two weeks before the big trip on the Comet.

Thom eased his skimmer close to Wirrin and Calen. 'Wombats, Calen! You were right. This is more exciting than I expected. It feels like we're heading off on a quest.'

That would be right. Thom loved quests, and in early days, when they'd had more time for themselves, had often designed quests for the three of them at their favourite virtual reality centre.

'It does doesn't it. Except it's for real.' Wirrin thought it would be an interesting quest if it involved an army of four hundred dolphins and the leader of a whole habitat.

'Do you think the dolphins will be spooked when they go through the interconnects?'

'Of course not, Thom. Sonic will tell them it's all right and they'll go straight in.'

The interconnects linked the reaches and the first one was visible a couple of hundred metres away. As they approached the dolphins bunched into a tight group then stopped at the entrance.

Sonic leapt into the air, four hundred dolphins copied him, then they all powered ahead and entered. Calen laughed.

'What?'

'Sonic's playing games with them and getting them even more excited.'

'Being a drama queen you mean!'

Thom knew this term because Sonic had used it on him several times recently. 'I think you might be right.'

Akama and Burilda moved close to ask Calen what was going on.

'Nothing really. Sonic just made the interconnect into a game and they're racing through to see what's at the other end.'

The interconnect was 6 metres wide and 50 metres long, opening to the adjoining reach. Wirrin watched the crowd of sleek forms just beneath the surface rushing along with the skimmers to the open water. Their arrival was marked by another mass leap and, spirits raised by the exuberance of the aerial forms, the trio let out their own excited yells. Burilda, Martin and many of the other pod companions joined in with a cheer. Smiling, Akama came alongside and asked Calen what was happening next.

'We'll have to take it slow and steady for the young dolphins. There have been five babies born in the last six weeks, and they'll be exhaust-ed otherwise. If there are any more racing and leaping games we'll probably need to have some rest periods, but their mothers will let us know when that's needed. After two more interconnects the pods will disperse through the reach with their companions and start exploring and working out where their home territories will be. Martin's pod is the biggest and most influential and we'll be travelling with them for as long as we feel like it.'

'All day I hope. I've been looking forward to this ever since Sonic invited me along, and I've set all other matters aside.'

Sonic appeared and said something to Calen who answered and looked at Akama.

'Sonic hopes it's all day too and he'd like to have a talk with you later when there's a quiet time. At the moment he wants you to follow him.'

Akama gave a smile of pleasure and acknowledgement and set off with Calen as Sonic moved further into open water.

The dolphins milled and churned for a moment until Sonic communicated what he wanted, and then a similar ceremony to Akama's first dolphin meeting began. Once again it was moving and Wirrin could see the companions and dolphinarium staff staring in wonder.

The final greeting was exchanged, but this time it was different. Something else was happening. The main body of dolphins stayed in a loose arc, while a small group approached Akama and Calen. From 20 metres away Wirrin caught a glimpse of a little body next to the bigger ones. A baby?

Calen interpreted for the dolphins, and Akama nodded and gestured. Suddenly both Calen and Akama donned their underwater masks and slipped into the water.

'What's going on?'

'I don't know. Calen told us nothing about this.'

Thom's questioning look to Burilda received a shrug.

'It must be important with four hundred dolphins lined up like that.'

'The big dolphin is from my pod. She's Peggy's sister Janey, and the little fellow is her new baby,' Martin said.

'Was Peggy's treatment successful?'

'It certainly was, Wirrin. She's got more energy than she knows what to do with now.'

That sounded like a story for the telling but it would have to wait. Akama and Calen were climbing back onto the skimmers. The dolphins started moving and with a wave of his arm Akama signalled everyone to follow. Wirrin and Thom closed the gap, wondering what he would say.

'Every time I'm with dolphins they touch my heartstrings. I've just met my namesake and he's accompanying me till we get to his home reach.'

Calen nodded happily. 'Janey and Peggy and the pod leader asked Sonic if naming the baby after a human leader would be a good thing to do and he told them to ask. We just went for an underwater meeting.'

The convoy of humans and dolphins made its way steadily towards the next interconnect, Akama smiling at everyone and watching little 'Akama' forging his way close by. He wasn't really accompanying Akama. His mum, Janey, was doing that and he was sticking close to her, but it had the same result.

Word spread and a constant rotation of companions and rangers approached to view the procession within a procession: the leaders of Martin's dolphin pod, the little fellow and Sonic, all swimming along with Akama.

'I'm amazed they would do that. They're not enhanced and it seems quite an advanced concept to me.'

Wirrin had brought his skimmer next to Martin to hear the Peggy story.

'I don't think it's that difficult, Martin. They've had six months of interaction with Sonic and Calen, and the idea of human names must be familiar by now. They've done lots of unexpected things after all Sonic's games and challenges.'

'They certainly have. We hardly recognise them as the same group we left Earth with. Sonic and Calen reacting directly with them is the main cause I would say.'

'What did you mean before about Peggy's energy?'

'Well, she was always a dominant force in the pod but now she's so active the pod leader often follows her lead. I expect her to take over after her next birth.'

'So her treatment was clearly a success.'

'Oh yes. There was never any doubt about that. According to the doctors she's expected to live for at least another eighty years.'

'She's pregnant?'

'Not yet. That's been held off, but she will be soon.'

'Held off?'

'Yes, Wirrin, but now that the reach is established the enhancement processes will start and any new conceptions will be part of the first stage. Peggy could very well be one of the first.'

'I see. I suppose they had to hold off because of her treatment?'

'No. It wasn't just her. All conceptions were suppressed till the medical and support infrastructure for each of the new reaches was ready.' Martin laughed. 'There's going to be a great deal of action and excitement in about a week's time.'

'What do you mean?'

'The males all had their libido repressed too. They had to, to keep them with their pods, and when they revert to normalcy there will be many more available females than usual.'

Wirrin understood the need to keep the pods together. Male dolphins would search everywhere when the imperative was on them and the crowded reach of five thousand dolphins would have been chaotic with half of them ranging willy-nilly.

'So there could be a big influx of babies in twelve months' time?'

'Definitely: four from our pod, and most other pods should have two or three.'

A quick scan told Wirrin that on today's big shift there were 163 pods moving to a home reach, meaning there could be close to four hundred dolphin births in just over a year. With somewhat of a shock he realised this would almost double the number of enhanced dolphins. The new ones wouldn't reach Attunga levels for generations but this was an enormous boost to the enhancement program.

'That's amazing. I didn't realise how quickly the population would grow with so many dolphins.'

'It will be faster than is natural for Earth too, because the babies and young ones won't be subject to the usual predation and undetected illnesses. In ten years it will be a population explosion and we'll need every reach we can get.'

That was completely wrong and Wirrin turned sharply.

'Martin, I don't know where you get that idea. In ten years there will be thousands of reaches. There are already six complete Warrakan levels set aside for dolphins and if the reaches are similar to the current ones there'll be enough space for … Hang on while I work it out … Wombats! It comes to over seven thousand reaches. It won't be quite that many because I know there are plans for specialised reaches, but the planning is way ahead of the dolphin growth.'

'Seven thousand? Can that be right?'

'It was the last time I looked at the plans. I must admit I haven't checked for a while, but if there's been any change it would only be a speed-up. Yajala! What's the current situation with new reaches?'

Startled, Martin swerved slightly when a holo skimmer with the form of Yajala in control shimmered into view between them.

'Our construction plans are proceeding smoothly. Fifty-seven reaches have been seeded with bio-organics and will be self-sustaining within seven months. A further 119 will have purified water introduced within the next two months, and hollowing and construction is already underway for 327 reaches. The complete level of 974 reaches will be functioning in twenty months and all six levels will be working within five years. Report concluded and your humble servant signing off, sir!' He snapped his hand to his brow and shimmered rapidly to nothing, leaving Wirrin chuckling at Martin's nonplussed look.

'Don't take any notice of him. He's got a wonky sense of humour and he acts like that to entertain both of us.'

'Wirrin, he said nine hundred reaches functioning in twenty months? That's, well, it's unbelievable.'

If Wirrin hadn't been familiar with the ability of the picofactories to speed up their production he would have agreed totally. As it was he decided to find time in the next few days to bring himself up to date with all the reach plans.

Thom dropped back from Calen and Akama. 'What was that about? Calen said we weren't expecting to meet Yajala till after the last interconnect.'

'I asked him for some information and instead of his usual trick of using my retinal image he turned himself on. We were talking about reaches and he says the whole level will be finished in less than two years.'

'That's fast. They must be ramping up for some reason.'

The next interconnect was very short and opened to the drama and chaos of dolphins leaping with excitement and pleasure.

For the second time there were cheers and calls as everyone joined in the mood of the moment. Wirrin moved close to Calen, Akama and Thom, then nearly fell off his skimmer when Sonic arced into the air right in front of him.

Akama laughed with delight.

'Little Brother, you react so quickly to his antics. If he did that to me I would be in the water before I could think.'

'Not really. I *am* used to it, but he could have me in the water in a flash if he really wanted to.'

As if to prove the point the back section of the skimmer was jolted sideways, and Wirrin overbalanced.

'*Wirrin has butter feet.*'

Wirrin knew that was something to do with being clumsy but he was too busy catching his breath and grabbing for a cheeky dolphin to check, so he made do with tweaking Sonic's dorsal fin.

'*Come and say hello to Akama while he is resting.*' Sonic's voice sounded from the nearest translator and something in the inflection indicated he was talking about the newly named 'Akama', so Wirrin retrieved his breathing mask and dived in.

Little Akama was hardly resting. At the moment he was vigorously suckling from his mum, and Wirrin stayed at a discrete distance, waiting till he finished. A sound from Sonic caught his attention and then the little pair of eyes focused on Wirrin. At least that was Wirrin's impression and it seemed to be borne out when the little creature approached and gave him a soft nudge, then did the same to Sonic before scooting back to the comfort of his mother. Another nudge, familiar this time, meant it was time to return to the surface.

'*He is an historic baby.*'

Not quite sure of Sonic's meaning, Wirrin waited for any elaboration.

Akama asked directly, 'In what way, Sonic?'

'*He is the last Earth dolphin on Warrakan. New babies will be different.*'

Thoughts whirled through Wirrin's mind at this announcement. It was certainly true, unless there were some other dramas requiring another rescue mission to Earth, and that was unlikely according to Turaku. Had the dolphins made a special connection? It would be just like Sonic to link Attunga's oldest Earth-born human with the youngest dolphin.

'*He will be a symbol of our legacy. Honoured One, may I ask for some of your time? I wish to share thoughts with you.*'

Wirrin was struck by a certain formality in Sonic's tone and he watched carefully as Akama responded in kind.

'The honour is mine. My time is yours and I eagerly look for any occasion when we can meet.'

Sonic spoke rapidly, and Calen, from not far away, nodded in reply.

'One occasion is now, while the young ones rest. I will race you to the information marker.'

Sonic darted off and Wirrin pointed after him. 'He wants to meet you alone at that red buoy.'

Akama was already moving, and catching sight of the buoy, set his skimmer into power mode. With only 200 metres he wouldn't be able to make up Sonic's lead, but he was certainly having a try.

Wirrin called to Calen. 'All I could understand was something about fish. The rest was too fast.'

'Yes, I have to tell the leaders to take their pods exploring and hunting in the seagrass while the little dolphins have a rest. He and Akama will be back when they're ready.'

Calen zipped off. There was a great flurry of motion and excitement at the prospect of real fish, then all sign of dolphins vanished except for the fins of the mothers guarding their young ones. The humans gathered and, clicking their skimmers together in groups of four or five for greater stability, used the time for a snack from their storage compartments and a chat.

'What are they talking about? Did they say?' Calen asked.

'No, Akama didn't act like he knew, but Sonic made it seem important when he asked.'

When he finished eating, Wirrin freed his skimmer and guided it very slowly to where he could watch little Akama, who was either suckling or resting against Janey.

When Sonic and Akama returned, the six pods making this reach their home came milling around for a farewell and then the journey resumed. The last stretch was almost 3 kilometres and the group moved steadily. It felt slower and Wirrin wondered if the mothers had passed on a message that their young ones were tiring.

The convoy was now much reduced in size with only seven pods and their attendants remaining of the original twenty. Sonic and Calen kept on the move all the time, travelling with one pod for a period then changing to another in a continuous cycle, while Wirrin and Thom stayed with Akama and his little companion.

The last interconnect loomed and after a pause, the race was on again — well, not really a race, more like an expression of exuberance.

Leading the skimmers, Wirrin stayed with Akama, Calen, and

Thom through nearly 200 metres of access way, watching the dolphins ahead porpoise at speed till their home reach came into view. Sonic led the 116 dolphins to where Gulara, Burilda and three other rangers were waiting.

Once again there was shared excitement, with the dolphins cavorting and leaping, and humans laughing and cheering. After several minutes everything quietened and the seven pod leaders, with Sonic, approached. Next to Akama, Turaku and Yajala shimmered into view to oversee the pods in their new home.

* * *

'We've missed two lots of activity days and we'll be away for the next two as well, so what are we going to do for this lot?'

'I could take you to have a look at K74. That would be exciting.'

'Are you crazy, Thom? What would we want to go there for?'

'To have a look at the biggest space habitat in existence. And it would be exciting to see how close we could get.'

Wirrin and Calen stared in disbelief, no doubt the reaction Thom had been looking for. 'What's the problem? If we take the Comet they won't have a clue we're there.'

'Take the Comet, Thom? Now we know you're crazy.'

Wirrin agreed with Calen, but the idea of blithely waltzing off to K74 with the Comet for an activity day adventure was so ridiculous there had to be something going on. 'What haven't you told us?'

'You're too smart, Wirrin. They've given me a set of special navigation exercises to work through sometime and that's one of them.'

'It's too dangerous. You should be doing it on a simulator like you always do.'

'I've already done that three times, and it's not dangerous in the Comet. They couldn't hurt it even if they wanted to.'

'And the Comet's ready to go tomorrow?'

'I haven't arranged anything, but the Comet's always ready.'

It did sound rather exciting but Wirrin had another thought. 'How long will it take?'

'Both days. There's quite a lot to do.'

'Well let's put it on hold, because in a couple of days we'll be on the Comet for nearly three weeks with our two trips, so we don't want to get sick of it.'

Thom's expression said that getting sick of the Comet was an alien thought, but he accepted a postponement with equanimity. 'What will we do instead?'

'Explore Warrakan,' Calen said firmly. 'It's about time we got to know it better. We'll be living there in another five weeks and we hardly know anything about it.'

'Of course we do. We're over there all the time.'

'Only in the reaches with the dolphins and when you ferry me with Sonic. We've never travelled from one end to the other.'

'Hey, you're right. Life's been too busy ... What sort of exploring, Calen?'

'Like we always do. Just get on TransCom and see where it takes us.'

Wirrin thought back to the last time they'd done that and was shocked to realise how long ago it had been.

The decision made, their ideas started to flow.

'We can check for animal parks. I heard there's a special Australian mammal centre with gliding possums.'

'Yajala might take us into the AI levels. That would be special.'

'There's a control place for when Warrakan starts travelling.'

This anticipation was part of the enjoyment, and three holo screens sprang to life to check out various possibilities.

*   *   *

'When are we going again?'

'Probably not for several months.'

'Well, it's your job to make sure we do. You came up with the idea the other day and it was a real eye-opener.'

The trio was relaxing at home after their second day of exploring Warrakan.

'We'll have to make sure Sonic comes next time. I want him to see that whale museum.'

'And the Alpha Centauri Planetarium. He'd love that.'

'I'll tell him everything in the morning.' After two days without seeing Sonic, Calen was obviously disappointed that Sonic couldn't turn up for his usual nightly visit.

'Let's find him now. Give him a surprise.'

'In the dark? It's rest-cycle time, Thom.'

'That doesn't matter. We know he's not resting. He's with Burilda and Turaku, and it's fun travelling the reach with our own lights.'

*   *   *

'When did you discover this?'

'Two days ago. I wasn't going to interrupt your activity time.'

'I don't like it. What are they going to do with them?' Wirrin had just found out that a group of thirty-seven dolphins would be arriving on K74. He was at his InfoStation and talking with Pirramar, the composite AI, before one of their search sessions.

'Search it out for yourself, though I suggest back-dooring through the infrastructure control system. The normal way is compromised at the moment.'

'How come? That's never happened before.'

'That information scientist has been building firewalls and physical lockouts round their surveillance processors, and there are places we can't access anymore without setting off alarms.'

Wirrin was shocked to hear this. With Pirramar and the K74 AI, he'd been watching with concern the activities of the 'rogue scientist', a name assigned by Thom one time when the trio had been talking about him.

'He can block AIs?'

'If there are no electronic pathways to a specific area we would have to send in mobile devices to access information and then recover them, and he's very adept at setting up systems that can prevent that. The dolphin information is available, though, so have a try at that.'

Pirramar had the same approach as Turaku, getting Wirrin to search things for himself, and though it was a nuisance, it almost invariably led to some new technique or understanding, and when it was specifically suggested like this there was always something they wanted him to learn.

Today it involved linking directly to the K74 AI and accessing the infrastructure system with his assistance. This was a new and very interesting experience and after a concentrated session of over an hour he was confident he'd found all the relevant information.

The dolphins were due to arrive in several weeks and would be housed at a number of aquariums while a reach was being built. Not a big reach, but the person in charge seemed to understand their basic needs. According to Pirramar they'd incorporated principles from the information stolen from Freedom and the design was a good one.

The worrying part was the enhancement program which would start when the reach and an associated medical centre were finished and attempts would be made to bio-engineer any new baby dolphins. It was going to be a real problem, as the K74 level of understanding was comparatively weak, and information might have to be planted in their medical facility as a safeguard against any bad outcomes.

'We'll have to keep a close eye on this.'

'We have it flagged, Wirrin. Turaku already has a priority on it. His other task for you today is a search of all the people at the K74 embassy, as well as looking for any wider effects the embassy might be generating. The Cadre is very annoyed that it's not getting the results they were expecting, and even more angry that some of the staff have been making suggestions about introducing Attunga methods to K74.'

The search session followed and at the end Wirrin was smiling because the embassy, which the Cadre had wanted, was backfiring. Akama would be pleased with that report.

'What's next?'

'An overview of links and the influence K74 has with habitats throughout the solar system. After their setback on Earth they're concentrating their efforts elsewhere, and particularly with one of the Mars polar habitats.'

By the end of the day Wirrin had also made a study of possible ways to infiltrate the security on the surface of K74, designed a search task to work with the K74 AI in identifying areas of population unrest, and tried unsuccessfully to get into one of the rogue scientist's protected areas.

*   *   *

'My brain's gone dizzy. I had to think harder today with Pirramar than any time I can remember.'

'Is that all? I spent half a day practising the guidance controls on Comet Two and the next half flying it to Freedom and back.'

'No you didn't, Thom. It's too far.'

'I did. On the simulator. It leaves out all the nothing parts and make you practise the action bits.'

Calen was shaking his head. 'You're a pair of wimps. All you did was sit and think. I had to do that while I swam about 20 kilometres with Sonic, working with all the dolphins who are going to Freedom.'

'Swimming doesn't count. It's easy for you because you've turned into a fish.'

The fish insult, usually directed at Sonic, worked quite effectively with Calen as well, and Thom, quickly restrained on the grav-sofa, was laughing and protesting that he'd just proved his point.

'What point?'

'I'm too exhausted to beat you like I normally would and you've got tons of energy because swimming 20 kilometres is easy for a fish.'

'Emu brain! You haven't beaten me ever since you made the protein structure.'

'I know, I put fish muscle into it and forgot to tell you. Come on, Wirrin, show him how brains can always beat brawn.'

Thom's logic mightn't hold up but acting on it was fun.

* * *

The trip to Freedom went smoothly and four hundred dolphins were delivered to the brand new reach system, which had been developing ever since the rescue at Monkey Mia. Nothing like the long reaches on Warrakan and the Uranus moons, it consisted of eight shorter reaches that linked into the system catering for the existing three dolphin pods.

Thom felt pleased to be in sole control of the Comet for both legs of the journey.

Calen and Sonic worked non-stop on the outward journey then relaxed for the return, while Wirrin devoted most of his time on the InfoSystem to finding out about Freedom.

* * *

It took three busy days back on Attunga and Warrakan readying over two thousand dolphins for the long journey to the Uranus moons and the trio and Sonic, who, of course, was needed as a steadying influence on the trip, were growing increasingly excited.

Two and a half days was significantly longer to be confined in the Comet's travelling pools than the twenty-nine hour journey from Earth, and a lot of preparation and training had been involved in preparing the dolphins. There had been no real concerns because these dolphins knew that they were finally moving to a place with abundant fish and space and were all eager to get moving. They were also so used to responding to Sonic's games that the new one of using a transport module made the transfer to the Comet effortless.

Wirrin, in the command centre, watched the outside display as transports and ferries arrived and departed for Warrakan, then grinned when Thom looked over and made a little hand signal. He had just set the Comet in motion and the outer wall of Attunga started receding.

Wirrin had done a great deal of research on the journey and the five moons but data and imagery were very much a second-class substitute for the real thing, and his sense of mystery and adventure gave him a tingle of anticipation at the moment of departure.

The sense of rapidly increasing speed only lasted a few minutes while Attunga, and then Warrakan, diminished on the display screens, then, despite the obverse fact that this was the stage where the full acceleration of the powerful engines surged by a factor of nearly five times, everything settled to a deceptive sense of motionlessness.

Wirrin moved close to Thom but he was concentrating so much there'd be no talking. Where was Calen? A glance at a screen showed him underwater with Sonic and a group of dolphins. Well, he'd be busy for ages, too, probably till the dolphins went into their next sleep state.

'When do you want to start your workouts, Wirrin?'

'What workouts, Turaku?'

'Pirramar and I have designed a set of challenges and we've been speculating as to how many you'll manage to complete by the time we return.'

So this was the AI's plan for using his time. Wirrin laughed. 'You're the same as Attunga-Turaku, working me like a slave.'

Comet-Turaku nodded his agreement. 'Akama has made me your overseer for the duration and it's the best way to keep you out of mischief. But I'm not the same. I'm currently half of one second ahead of Attunga-Turaku where you're concerned.'

He was referring to the time-lag for communications between the Comet and Attunga.

'How many of these challenges am I meant to be doing?'

'I'm expecting between sixty and seventy. Pirramar is more optimistic and estimates something over eighty.'

'Eighty? If they're like the ones I normally do with Pirramar that's impossible. On the longest day I ever had with him I could only manage six projects.'

'Those projects were all major. Many of these new challenges won't involve nearly as much time. For example, your first is to develop three alternate courses for taking the Comet to Titania. You should be able to do that in less than half an hour.'

Wirrin didn't start straight away. First of all he spent some time with Calen and Sonic, then Thom, but when he did get going he was pleased to finish his first task in nineteen minutes.

*   *   *

The trio entered the Titania TransCom portal and Calen fussed at Wirrin.

'Wirrin, don't you dare go near that InfoSystem till the Comet heads back to Attunga. We hardly saw you the whole way here.'

'Look who's talking. You were either in the travelling pools with Sonic or you were sound asleep.'

'I didn't have any choice. The dolphins got too excited.'

Calen was right. Wirrin had become completely absorbed with the challenges, and, having managed thirty-nine successfully and been stumped by three, he was aiming to get through at least another forty on the return trip.

'I promise, except for collecting all the pico-techniques that relate to dolphin health and building an optimisation task that inserts the best ones into the dolphin healthbots.'

Thom and Calen both gawked at him.

'You can do something like that? You're not a health scientist or a pico-engineer.'

'I don't have to be. I just search for programs that know what to do, then make comparisons to see which ones give the best results then organise them into a task.'

Thom started tapping his head to indicate Wirrin's brain must be weird and Calen nodded vigorously.

'I love the way you said "just", as if upgrading every dolphin health-bot on five moons is easy.'

'It's not exactly easy, Thom. The searching part is, but putting it all together takes a lot of thinking.'

'Sounds like something the AIs do. Is this what all these challenges have taught you?'

Wirrin cast his mind over the different types of challenges and the processes he'd had to develop and practise to solve them.

'Wombats! You're right, Calen. I couldn't have done this before we left. They've pushed a whole stack of new ideas and techniques into me.'

'They? You mean Turaku don't you?'

'Turaku and Pirramar. Turaku says Pirramar worked it out with Akama before we left.'

'Are you going to disappear on us for hours when you do this health-bot thing? Seeing things is better when we're all together, and Sonic will want you there too.'

'I'm not going to miss out on anything. The task will take … um … maybe two or three hours. I'll fit it in, Calen.'

'As long as it's not now. Sonic's waiting.'

It was interesting travelling on the Titania version of TransCom and in a very short time Sonic was out of his transport module and bumping against their legs as they dangled in the water from a landing stage while the trio stared out across the great stretch of water.

Way off in the distance a solitary skimmer was just visible, but otherwise it was a bare expanse with the usual structural girders reaching from the water to the ceiling at regular intervals.

'Where are the dolphins? I can't see a single one.'

'They are all feeding and exploring, Thom. The closest pod is with the skimmer.'

Wirrin had another look at the skimmer and it took him a moment to figure out what was going on.

'What's he doing? His skimmer base has gone under the water.'

It certainly looked that way.

'No it hasn't. It's the curvature of Titania. They built the reach to match instead of keeping it flat like at home, and he's far enough away to be round the curve.'

'Wow! He is too. That's really interesting. I always think of water as being flat.'

'No you don't. What about the zero-G swimming pools?'

Thom realised that grav-fields were the controlling agent here too and shook his head at Wirrin.

'Stop being a brainiac. Let's go. We've only got three days to do everything.'

And go they did, for several hours, sometimes zooming at high speed, with Sonic in his special support cradle at the rear of Calen's skimmer, sometimes cruising with Sonic swimming and chasing schools of fish across seagrass fields, and sometimes joining Sonic underwater to explore a reef or some other marine feature.

Three times Sonic changed direction for an excited exchange with dolphin pods, and all the while Wirrin's sense of the size of this reach was growing.

'It's like an Earth ocean. They could have ten times as many dolphins and there'd still be plenty of room.'

'Not really. It's just a drop compared to Earth, but I know what you mean. It does make the Warrakan reaches seem tiny.'

But on Warrakan every major type of marine environment on Earth would eventually be active, from polar to tropical, from nutrient rich to nutrient poor, in an attempt to foster the greatest degree of biodiversity.

'Why have they built it so big? They've done the same on all the moons and they won't need this much space for fifty or sixty years.'

'The reaches aren't just for dolphins. All the other marine life needs to be established too. Most of the species can only be introduced when the things they depend on have developed properly, and that takes years, Calen. You know all this.'

'Yes I do, but it still feels like they've built something like Shark Bay at Monkey Mia when a Warrakan reach would have been enough.'

*   *   *

'Let's go! There will be time to have a look at Uranus if we leave now. I'll race you back to the landing stage.'

*   *   *

'Let's go! I want you to see all the craters and canyons. Wait till you see the other moons. Some of them are smaller than Attunga.'

*   *   *

'Let's go! The Witnesses on Miranda have arranged for us to see their famous space array.'

*   *   *

'Let's go! We're meeting some of the AIs at the Titania Space habitat.'

*   *   *

'Let's go! This floating research station in the Uranus atmosphere sounds weird.'

*   *   *

'Let's go! We're heading for home.'

'Right now? And what's the big grin for, Thom?'

'I'm allowed to use an extra half-G of thrust and that means a new speed record.'

'This is half a day early. Are we in a hurry?'

'Yes, because Sonic told Turaku he wants to get back quickly.'

Wirrin looked to Calen and Sonic.

'He's missing Puck and Flute.'

Yes, I agree with Thom. Let's go!'

After a short period of official farewells the Comet fired up and the screen images of Uranus began to shrink at an astonishing rate. There was no 4G limitation way out here.

*   *   *

'I wonder if we'll ever make another trip out there?'

The big wall display screen was replaying their plunge down the 20 kilometre Great Rift Canyon on Miranda, and even here, in the comfort of their grav-sofa, the visual effect of rushing past the cliff faces and icy outcrops was quite dizzying. The people on Miranda claimed it was the greatest recreational adventure on any of the Uranus moons and the trio was reliving the excitement.

'I don't think so ... You might, Thom, if the Comet has to go there again, but unless they need Sonic we wouldn't all go. It's only seven years before Warrakan starts travelling.'

Conversation paused while a great column of ice loomed on the screen.

'Whoo! Remember that bit, Thom? I thought we were going to collide.'

'Everyone did. The course for the ferry was designed that way.'

'Seven years doesn't sound like much now we're sure we're going. I used to think we'd never even get to Warrakan till Calen made sure we did.'

Calen shook his head.

'Not me, Thom. It was Sonic's pod deciding to live on Warrakan that got us there. If they'd stayed here everything would have been different.'

It certainly would. It was unthinkable that Calen could be separated from Sonic, and just as unthinkable that they not stay together as a trio. A breathtaking buttress of ice jutting from the canyon wall filled the screen but Thom was suddenly not noticing.

'Sonic's pod won't change their minds will they? Some other pods did.'

'I don't think so. Sonic's totally excited about the Warrakan reaches, and he likes the idea of travelling to another star too, but he'd always stay with his pod ... Well I think he would. He might be different when he's grown up because some male dolphins get very independent when they're older.'

'That's all right then. The other dolphins always do what he wants.'

'Not exactly, Thom. It seems like it but it's more a kind of understanding between them that he knows what they want.'

'Well, when we move to Warrakan they'll all love it so much they'll never want to leave.'

Wirrin agreed with Thom because every dolphin who saw them

loved the Warrakan reaches. So far Sonic, Puck and Flute were the only Attunga dolphins to visit, but if their reactions were anything to go by, then all the rest would be staying on Warrakan forever. Well, at least till the new Attunga reaches started coming online in about two years.

'Are they ready to move? It's only two weeks away.'

'Of course they are. They've been ready for the past six months but the moving date's been changed three times on them so far and I think … '

Calen stopped mid-sentence and stared in surprise at the suddenly blank display screen.

'Why did you turn that off? It's only half finished.'

'I didn't.'

Calen and Thom stared in puzzlement and Wirrin's mind started to race.

'I connected directly to the Comet's archive to get that clip and the link's gone.'

'How can it be gone? Links don't do that.'

Thom was right, and particularly so in this case, because communications from the Comet had the highest level of security and stability available on Attunga.

Wirrin headed for his InfoSystem but before he could move further, four holo forms blinked into existence: Turaku, Pirramar, Yajala and someone unknown, all with strangely robotic-looking expressions. Wirrin took in the scene with sudden apprehension, which increased when no-one spoke. Another form took shape, this time with the usual shimmer effect, and Akama caught everyone's attention.

'Wirrin, we have some very bad news. Moments ago Pirramar received a cry for help from the K74 AI, and in the short time before his call was terminated he managed to convey that the processors and programs at the core of his consciousness were being attacked. For the first time in over a century an AI has died.'

Chapter 22

Shocked, Wirrin blanked for a moment before words started to tumble out. 'He couldn't be. I was speaking to him only a couple of hours ago and he had everything planned for what to do if there was danger. It would only take him instants to flash onto the InterWeb. He must be on a storage system somewhere and he'll contact us when he can.'

'Wirrin, he's gone.'

Akama's words thrust like a sword through Wirrin's numbing incredulity. He pulled his thoughts together and looked to Pirramar.

'How could it happen? It was an attack wasn't it? And it came from the rogue scientist didn't it?'

'Yes, it was an attack and, with a ninety-eight per cent probability, it came from the rogue. How it happened is not completely clear and we'd like you to work with us in examining the information we've retrieved.'

'Wirrin will do whatever he can for whatever period of time is needed.'

Wirrin jumped at the commanding tone of Akama's voice.

'Honoured One. Of course ... Do you mean right now?'

'I do. With a demonstrated capability and willingness to destroy an AI, he may pose a threat to AIs in other locations and we need to determine whether there is any possibility of that. Calen, I'd like you to meet with Sonic and Turaku at the dolphinarium, and Thom, as a precautionary measure, you should move on board the Comet.'

The trio exchanged looks then came to life. Wirrin sat at his InfoStation, Calen headed for his skimmer, and Thom raced for the nearest TransCom portal.

Akama looked to one side as if distracted. 'Wirrin, I have a meeting with the members of the Witness Council and AI representatives. I will speak with you later.'

Akama and Turaku disappeared, leaving Wirrin with Pirramar and the unknown AI.

'Wirrin, this is Bakana. He's our young reconstruction of the K74 AI and he'll be working with us.'

'Reconstruction' and 'young' were both unfamiliar terms with regard to an AI but right now didn't feel like the time to ask.

*   *   *

At mid-morning the next day the trio regrouped and caught up with each other's doings while Thom prepared one of his special snacks before they retired for a well-earned rest.

'Thom, you won't sleep properly if you eat all that.'

'Yes I will. I was awake all night and we were so busy I hardly had time to eat.'

'What sort of busy?'

'All sorts. For a start we went into security mode and met up with Comet Two and did a high-level scan of everything in a two light-minute radius. That didn't take long because our sensors are so powerful, especially the long-range ones on Comet Two, and we developed a threat gradient model for everything out there. Most of it we already had but the deep scans picked up quite a few new in-bounds.'

Wirrin didn't have a clue what a threat gradient model really was, but in-bounds seemed self-explanatory.

'Heading for Attunga? Were there many of them?'

'More than twelve hundred, which is higher than normal, but not by much. Only five of them turned out to be reds — that's a threat classification — and the rest were all okay.'

'What did you do about the reds, Thom? They don't sound too good.'

'We didn't do anything, which is what usually happens. They just get monitored carefully by habitat security. But at about midnight we got word from the Witness Council about their policy changes and we turned three of them away.'

'What policy changes?'

'They've decided to have a clear zone, with extended boundaries, around Attunga and Warrakan, and they're notifying any vessels without transparent security to stay away.'

'How did you hear about that, Calen? It's news to me,' Thom said.

'I was there with Sonic and Turaku when they decided on it and sent the message to get rid of all the surveillance drones.'

'Get rid of them? Wombats! That's really something. How did they do that?'

Thom's face lit up. 'That was one of the exciting bits. Comet Two disabled every single one of them in less than a second then guided them to collection points and the Comet gathered over a thousand of them in two pick-ups.'

'A thousand? They used to be in the hundreds.'

'Wirrin, that's ages ago. There were nearly three thousand altogether. The numbers climbed like crazy when K74 started to focus on us. They keep redesigning them and sending more.'

'You said *one* of the exciting bits …?'

'There were more. It was a busy night, Wirrin. The next thing was sending a ship back to Mars. Some program of yours picked up that they were troublemakers.'

'Mine? What are you talking about?'

'Comet-Turaku said the information came from a task you designed to watch Mars habitats.'

'That? It was just a challenge from Pirramar to learn more about my InfoSystem. They used it for real?'

'Obviously. It found a connection between the ship from one of the Mars polar habitats and K74. We took the Comet right up close and told them they had to go back to Mars.'

'Just like that? You told them to go and they went?'

'That was really exciting. They said we had no jurisdiction over them and refused, so we took over their controls and turned them around.'

Wirrin could hardly believe what he was hearing.

'But they're right, Thom. We don't have jurisdiction out there.'

Calen explained. 'After last night we do. The Witness Council and the AIs ratified it for situations involving Attunga and Warrakan interests. It was a very serious meeting last night. Sonic said he'd never seen such strong emotions from Witnesses and the AIs amazed him with their determination.'

Wirrin stared at Calen. 'Sonic said that? It must have been some meeting.'

'It was, but Thom hasn't finished yet.'

Thom looked up in surprise. 'You know what happened?'

'Thom, I was at the Council meeting when the AIs asked Sonic and the Witnesses if destroying the drones on the K74 ship had their approval. I don't know the details but I heard them say to go ahead as long as no people were hurt.'

By now Wirrin could hardly contain himself. 'Which K74 ship and what drones? Was it one of those big spaceships?'

'It was the biggest. The one that was named after the number-one Cadre person. He's going to be mad as a bunyip when he finds out … Which he already will have by now.'

Wirrin rolled his eyes, partly because Thom was expecting a reaction, and partly because this did sound like something dramatic. Thom understood both reasons and laughed.

'It was heading towards Attunga at 9G acceleration, which is fairly fast, and we detected a load of new drones they were carrying. That was after we'd collected all the local drones so we sent them a message saying no more were to be delivered. They ignored that. They probably thought we didn't know exactly where they were.

'We sent them another message saying their course showed they were heading straight for Attunga, and if they didn't turn back the drones would be destroyed. They ignored that too, even though we gave them plenty of time to talk it over with their controllers on K74, so we vaporised the drones and locked control of their ship for an hour.'

'Wouldn't vaporising the drones be dangerous to people inside the ship?'

'It didn't happen inside the ship. We forced their loading system to launch all the drones. You should have seen it.'

Wirrin wasn't going to miss that and a few seconds later had a holo clip of the event up and running. Loading bays functioned all along the side of the massive ship, the comparatively tiny drones appeared in the openings, moved steadily away, then flashed into spectacular brilliance for an instant.

'Thom, this shows Comet's multi-spectrum beams. You must have been really close?'

'We were. We went in to 5 kilometres.'

'But that means their visuals would have been able to pick up every detail of the Comet.'

'Not if we didn't allow it. We've got the same technique that tricks the visuals for the drones near Warrakan.'

'You did allow it?'

'Yes, so they could see that a ship less than half their size could run rings around them, take over all their controls, and even make them blow themselves to bits if we wanted to. We gave them a message that they can't just do whatever they like.' Thom's feelings were starting to show so Wirrin agreed with a quiet nod. The Cadre would get the message all right, but he didn't think it would change their plans. They might be more careful for a while, but getting direct confirmation that capabilities like those of the Comet existed would make them more determined to have those capabilities themselves.

He turned to Calen. 'What happened at the Council? You were heading for the dolphinarium when you left.'

'Sonic's module was there so we met him and travelled to the Council Hall. He needed to be there in person instead of holo. Dolphins like to do it that way for important things.

'The first part of the meeting was sad because they talked about dying and how the K74 AI helped us before he was murdered. The AIs were quiet during that part but they took over when the meeting started to talk about what to do.'

That was interesting and Wirrin would have to look at that when he had a chance. Taking over was unusual for AIs.

'First they said that K74 has to learn that it must never happen again and they're taking a lot of actions to back that up. The Cadre won't know what's hit them when it starts.'

'When it starts? Calen, it already has.'

'Some of it. Thom's told us about clearing the drones and confronting their ships, but it's much bigger than that. Every AI in the solar system has been informed that K74 purposely killed one of them, and they're all protesting about it to the humans in their own habitats. Akama said there will be total outrage from almost the whole solar system and K74 will be treated like a pariah, whatever that is.

'The AIs are going to withdraw their services for anything related to the Cadre.'

'There aren't any AIs on K74 now, so that doesn't sound like it will do much.'

'Thom, think. The InterWeb relies on AIs to function and that means the Cadre will be cut off from just about everything. If they want to communicate with the rest of the solar system they'll have to send their own signals. And even that won't work because the receivers are managed by AIs.'

'No InterWeb? Calen, they won't be able to keep going.'

'Yes they will. They've got an Intelligent System that runs their own version. They use Intelligent Systems to run nearly everything, which is a problem that the Council and the AIs have to solve somehow. They talked about it a great deal.'

Wirrin's interest was piqued: Intelligent Systems were one of his areas of interest.

'What problem, Calen?'

'The systems will all have to work at a higher level now that there's no real AI, and somehow that means a new one will appear.'

'Yes, that's how Pirramar and the other AIs from K74 were formed, but why is it a problem?'

'They think that the rogue scientist will know as soon as it happens and either kill the AI off like he was ordered to yesterday, or send it crazy by trying to control it. That means they'll have to do something about protection and there are huge difficulties about that because what the rogue scientist is doing is complicating everything. The Witnesses asked for a lot more information about him.'

'That's going to be hard. Pirramar and I couldn't get past some of his blocks last night.'

'Well, the AIs are working on it of course, and the Council said that they'd do whatever they could to help. The next big topic they talked about was Freedom. They think it's too vulnerable and isolated and last night they contacted them and suggested the whole habitat would be better off under the direct protection of Attunga and Warrakan.'

'Are we going to build a new Comet or give them all our defensive security data, or something like that?'

'Three more Comets, Thom, but they're for here and four of Attunga's space drives are going to be diverted and installed on Freedom so they can move. It will arrive in about five months' time.'

Wirrin and Thom gawped and Calen continued.

'That all happened last night. They asked, and Freedom agreed, and everything was set in motion before the meeting even ended. It only took twenty minutes. The Council could hardly believe it themselves, but it turned out that the Freedom AIs pointed out the benefits of the idea and practically insisted on moving and joining even more closely with us.'

It was another reminder of how fast things could happen when AIs were involved.

'Kadaitcha man! That's amazing. The AIs don't muck around once they've worked something out. The Council meeting must have been nearly as exciting as it was for me on the Comet. Did they decide anything else?'

'Lots of things, Thom. Mostly about security stuff, but they've also decided to go ahead and build the embassy at K74.'

'You must be joking. The Cadre will be so mad at us they'll probably blow it up … And it doesn't make sense anyway. If the AIs are cutting them off from everyone, why are we doing the opposite?'

'Akama says they won't do a thing no matter how mad they are. They'll act as if nothing happened and after three weeks of isolation they'll jump at the opportunity because it means they can get more information.'

'I'll bet it's something to do with protecting any new AIs. That's going to be really hard,' Wirrin said.

Calen nodded.

'What was the security stuff? Was it about the new Comets?' asked Thom.

'Some of it. They're going to speed up work on the shell around Attunga, and Warrakan is going to have one too.'

'Three Comets … As soon as I've had a sleep I'm finding out about them.' Thom, understandably, wanted to know about the Comets but Wirrin was intrigued by the idea of a shell for Warrakan. It already had almost a kilometre of its outer layer reserved as a natural buffer for when it started travelling through deep space, so an extra shell seemed redundant.

So many things happening at once. Well, maybe this evening after a sleep he'd get some catch-up time.

'What did you find out on your InfoSystem, Wirrin? Akama said you did some good things.'

'He did?'

'Yes, and he told me to tell you he's been too busy and he'll talk to you after you've had some sleep … But what happened? He practically ordered you to work with Pirramar.'

'We did work. For over twelve hours, and most of it was really hard. The first bit wasn't, because it was helping Bakana, and Pirramar let me see what he was doing.'

'Bakana?'

'He's the new AI who was with Turaku and Pirramar when they turned up last night, Thom. He's a reconstruction of the AI from K74.

Pirramar needed him to help with understanding the information that he sent through just before he died.'

'Wirrin, what are you talking about? The AI who died is alive again?'

'No, he's not, Calen, but yes, in a way. It's a bit like a human clone only with AIs. The building blocks of the original are there so he's kind of identical but he has his own consciousness.'

'Like Comet-Turaku and Attunga-Turaku?'

'Not really. They're exactly identical because they're constantly linked and updating each other. If they stopped sharing everything then they would develop into two different AIs but they have no intention of doing that. Bakana is as close to the K74 AI as Pirramar could make him but some things we just couldn't find out.'

'You helped to build him? How does that work? He was already alive when you met him last night.'

'That was young Bakana. Pirramar used the basic information that had already been sent and matched it with the processors and electronics that were ready in case they were needed. Last night we sneaked into every system on K74 we could and grabbed data that was tagged to be transmitted as part of the AIs escape plan. We couldn't get it all but what we did get was used by Bakana with Pirramar helping him integrate it all and build up his abilities.'

'He was different when you finished doing that? Could you tell?' asked Calen.

'I couldn't. Not one bit, but Pirramar said there was a huge difference.'

'It's amazing how they can just build a new AI whenever they feel like it. They should build up their population more.'

'More? Calen, we've got nearly four hundred of them here. No other habitat except Titania Orbital has got anything like that number.'

'That's exactly what I mean. How would it be if there were only four hundred people on Attunga? We'd think something was wrong.'

'Calen, you can't think of them like people … they're too different. And if you tried to build it up to even a thousand you'd have to add about eight extra levels.'

'Building levels is easy, Wirrin. We're adding one for the dolphins and that'll be finished in two years. Our picofactories could add another eight in the same time if they really wanted to. But what about Warrakan? It's got so much space they could easily fit thousands of them there. Is it the same there as it is here? I mean, Attunga's got two levels for AIs and five for people, … and one for dolphins.'

'Oh right. I see what you mean. Let's have a look.'

Within seconds Wirrin had a holo model of Warrakan floating in front of them with a cutaway view showing the general proposals for future development.

'Nine levels for people, six levels for dolphins, and five levels for AIs. The other ten levels are for all the services.'

'Their AIs get a lot more space.'

'Hey, you're right. That's very interesting … Wombats! That's huge. Calen, when you calculate at the Attunga rate Warrakan has enough space for over ten thousand AIs.'

'Wirrin, how did you do that?' said Thom as they both stared at him.

'What do you mean? I compared the Attunga space with the Warrakan space. That's easy.'

'It might be easy, but it should take more than a couple of blinks.'

'Did I blink?'

'I don't know,' said Thom. 'You might have. I just meant that's how long it took to work it out. You didn't seem to put it all together before you came up with the answer.'

'Of course I put it together. I've had lots of practice lately. That's all.'

'We said you were a brainiac when you started zapping without concentrating, and now you've proved it by doing the same thing with calculations.'

'Good try, Thom, except I did think about it.'

'Are you zapping now?'

'You know I am. I've been doing it automatically for ages.' It wasn't really ages, just since the last visit to the doctor a few weeks ago.

'Play it back for us then and see how long it took.'

Wirrin pulled the relevant moment from his storage implant and played it. He couldn't see himself of course, but his voice was recorded along with the images of Thom and Calen looking at him. There it was, in the moment before he said 'Wombats'.

'It does seem a bit short.'

'A bit! … Measure it,' said Calen.

'It took 1.8 seconds. See, there's a definite period while I'm thinking.'

'Thom does calculations all the time for flying the Comet. Flash the numbers and see how long it takes him.'

That little experiment showed Thom taking 6.4 seconds.

'You'd better talk to the doctor about this, before your brain goes all electronic.'

'And before you have to start plugging yourself into your InfoStation for recharges.'

Idiots! It was puzzling, though, and worth checking out. 'Look at this model of Warrakan. You were wrong about the shell, Calen.'

'Good change of subject, Wirrin, but I wasn't. It shows it right there.'

'But they're not adding it outside like Attunga's. They're converting the buffer zone instead, so it's not really a shell.'

'Giving it a hard outer layer? Sounds like a shell to me. Stop waffling and get on with what else you did last night. I know you've got more, too, because the Council talked about some of it.'

Wirrin didn't know that, but it wasn't a surprise really after hearing the decisions they'd made. Pirramar had probably been in constant contact with them.

'Well, after we worked with Bakana, which was time critical in case the stored files got wiped out or blocked, we started looking at what happened on K74. That was critical too because Pirramar received just enough warning to know that there was danger for any AI looking too closely at the information in the panic transmission.'

'Danger for external AIs? That's scary.'

'Really scary, Thom. And it's why Akama made such a big deal about me helping. Just as well too, because Pirramar would have been in big trouble if he hadn't listened to the warning.'

'It wouldn't have … ?'

'No, but it could have interfered with his thinking if he wasn't prepared.'

'So what was it?'

'It was a different version of that priority trap that interfered with the AIs when we were at Monkey Mia. This time it was so strong it could force processors to overload and become temporarily useless. Pirramar said it would be horrible for an AI, like a human suddenly losing their senses one after the other. The trap was bad enough, but its whole purpose was to tie up all the AI's resources so he couldn't react fast enough when the real attack was launched against his core. Without that overload the AI would have escaped easily. He had that all planned and ready.'

'If he hadn't followed the warning could Pirramar have been hurt by the real attack as well as the overload part?'

'No, Thom, the attack was designed against the exact processors and code being used by the K74 AI and Pirramar's is different. His code did start off the same when he first transferred but it was immediately updated and his new processors are way ahead of the ones on K74. That's good news for every other AI too, because the lethal part won't work without being designed to their exact specifications, but we didn't know that until we looked at it and understood what it was doing.'

'Brainiac saves the AIs again.'

'Galah head! It was your idea that saved them at Monkey Mia not mine, and we knew there must be something like it happening again so call yourself a brainiac.'

Thom, completely ignoring the logic in Wirrin's argument, and knowing that much more would have happened, promptly called him a brainiac again.

Calen was enjoying the brainiac stir as much as Thom but he moved the conversation on. 'The Council knew the AIs were safe early in the meeting, Wirrin, so what were you doing the rest of the time?'

'Getting into as many of K74's systems as we possibly could. It's a nightmare now because there's no AI to give us the access codes. Pirramar can work them out or bypass them sometimes but there are critical areas we can't get at. That rogue scientist has his section completely blocked and he's started working on the Cadre's control area as well and their meeting room has gone from our view.'

'So we won't know what they're saying any more?' asked Calen.

'Not when they're meeting together, but we'll be able to find out indirectly as long as the blocked areas don't spread too much.'

'If he blocks the whole place we won't know anything,' said Thom.

'He couldn't. Well he could, but everything would slow down too much.'

'That wouldn't worry them.'

'Yes it would, Thom. Their TransCom system isn't nearly as efficient as ours for a start, and it would probably take two or three times as long to get anywhere, and on a 300 kilometres long habitat they definitely couldn't cope. You'd have twelve billion people complaining, and it would be the same with their services and communications.'

'So we'll still find out stuff but it will be second-hand?'

'We'll find out lots but really important things might be blocked.'

'The rogue must be very clever.'

'He is, Thom. Pirramar says we need to know a whole lot more about what he's doing and what he's capable of.'

'What did Sonic say about all this?' Thom asked Calen, who looked thoughtful.

'He agreed with all the proposals from the Council and the AIs but he hardly said anything at all. When we were travelling back to the dolphinarium he said he was puzzled about K74 and needed more understanding before he could make proper decisions about them.'

'Really? That sounds like he might have doubts about the proposals.'

'He doesn't, because I asked him.'

They started to discuss Sonic's reactions but when Thom half stifled a yawn and Wirrin and Calen both caught it off him they realised it was time for bed.

*   *   *

Wirrin watched Thom and Calen in the pool and laughed when Thom got a face full of water for trying to twist Sonic's tail flukes. He'd been happily mucking round himself but it was now right on the time when Akama and Gulara were due for a surprise conference. Akama was expected but he woke from his much-needed sleep to a message saying Gulara would be present as well, and even more unexpected was the way the meeting was couched in terms of a conference, which sounded serious.

'Welcome to my home Honoured Ones.'

'Thank you Little Brother. We treasure the gift of your welcome.'

All sound from the pool stopped and Wirrin knew Calen, Thom and Sonic were watching, intrigued by the exchange of traditional greetings. For Wirrin it had been almost automatic because Akama's usual friendly manner was overlaid by the weight of his office, and that was somehow reflected in Gulara.

'The Witness Council, acting on a request from our AI associates, formally commends you in recognition of your service to the community of Attunga. Furthermore the AI gestalt expresses its gratitude for your help in protecting their interests and names you a Friend.'

Wirrin stared in disbelief, then into the sudden silence Sonic's voice sounded from the translator.

'Dolphins are in full agreement, Friend Wirrin.'

Wirrin didn't know what to say so he just nodded.

'Wow! That's unreal,' Thom said, and the charged, ceremonial atmosphere dissolved.

Sonic spoke again, this time with his normal voice.

'This is a time for friends to celebrate.'

Calen beckoned to Akama and Gulara. 'He wants everyone together in the water.'

A few moments later, with four very pleased people around him, and Sonic nudging companionably against his side, Wirrin felt he could say what he really thought.

'Akama, why have they made it such a big deal? All I did was work on the InfoSystem. I don't see why the Council think that's so special.'

Wirrin felt a jolt of surprise and pleasure when Akama firmly grasped his shoulder. He seemed to be expressing a degree of pride in Wirrin.

'The Council had no choice, Wirrin, because the AIs insisted. Not that there was a skerrick of resistance. How could there be when Pirramar reported directly that you ventured where he daren't, discovered an insidious trap dangerous to every AI in the solar system, then pointed the way to a solution? On top of that, several of your tasks and your hours of application were a vital help for the new AI ... The commendation and the status are rightly yours.'

'Too many brains for his own good.' Thom sighed. 'What's that status part mean? Will we have to bow to him every morning when we wake up or something?'

Wirrin was wondering himself.

'You're right, Thom. A formal commendation automatically grants special privilege, and from now on you will be expected to respond to his every request and treat him with the utmost respect. A bow would definitely be appropriate, along with taking over all his jobs around your living space and preparing his meals. Whenever you speak to him you should call him "Great One".'

That was ridiculous but Akama sounded so serious and authoritative that it must be right. Thom's jaunty manner faded and his jaw dropped.

'Great One?'

'That's correct. Try it. A commendation from the full Council and all the AIs is an extraordinary event and if you can't manage it appropriately we might need to train you with a protocol holo.'

'Wirrin is a Great One.'

Coming from Sonic it sounded right, and seeing all the expectant gazes focused on him, Thom faced Wirrin and gave a slow nod. 'Great One.'

Wirrin's thoughts were whirling. If they had to follow all his requests then the first one would be *not* to call him 'Great One' at home. Akama would say that must be all right, surely? Wirrin was about to ask when he caught a surreptitious twitch.

A wink? Yes, Akama had a definite twinkle in his eye.

Bunyips! They'd all fallen for it completely, well maybe not Sonic. His comment was conveniently complicit come to think of it.

Keeping a straight face, Wirrin returned the slow nod to Thom then suddenly directed a scoop of water at him.

'Thank you "Tiny One". I'd like my breakfast delivered to my grav-bed every morning.'

Thom registered first astonishment, then realisation, and one glance at Akama's huge smile confirmed he'd been tricked. Wirrin was almost shocked when jets of water started flying at the leading Witness on all of Attunga, but the vigorous return attack showed Akama was relishing every moment. Sonic joined in and Thom had no hope.

'Fish attack. Not fair.'

'The Tiny One sends tiny splashes.'

'You great lump. Why don't you splash Akama and Gulara? I bet you're not game.'

Akama and Gulara almost disappeared under the amounts of water Sonic sent up but, for the last word, Thom copped the same treatment.

'What did you mean by status before Thom misinterpreted it?'

'Thom didn't really misinterpret, Calen. The status is real and almost unique. The AIs have proclaimed Wirrin a "Friend" and that is a legacy from the very beginning of the relationship between artificial intelligence and humanity. Only twice before have "Friends" been proclaimed.' Akama ended a protracted moment of introspection with a nod and a curious smile.

'Wirrin will be recognised as special by every AI he comes in contact with.'

'Wow! Do you think they'll call him Great One?'

'They very well might, Thom. Who knows what an AI will do in any given situation, and he'll certainly be meeting quite a few in the near future.'

Wondering if this was a reference to something specific, the trio exchanged glances.

'Yes, Wirrin, there is another reason we're here today. Gulara is present as your mentor and I will bow to the wisdom of her advocacy. I represent the Council and have a request for you to consider. After last night's events there was a great deal of discussion about what to do about the rogue scientist, as Thom so aptly refers to him, and it's very clear that we need to know more about him, particularly the direction he's taking against non-human intelligence. The AIs from Earth and Mars have made a joint effort to provide us with every piece of information they've been able to find so we have an extensive background of his life prior to the move to K74. Our concerns are with his current activities, however, and five of our top information scientists will be examining every facet of his work and research.' Akama paused. 'They will be a valuable assistance but the biggest imperative is to be forewarned and prepared should the Cadre direct him to extend his aggression.

'We need someone to study his background and become expert in all his fields of work, expert enough to guide us in countering anything he might try. Pirramar insists that it should be you, and we quite agree except for the fact that it would be a major intrusion on your life.'

Wirrin agreed about the need for knowledge and his interest flared at the prospect of involvement, then stalled. A major intrusion? He was making it sound so negative. 'I don't see why. It's directly related to my main area of study and I already have a good background in what's going on. I like working with Pirramar, too, and I think it's exactly what I should be doing.'

Akama exchanged a look with Gulara. 'Wirrin, we agree with Pirramar that you're right for this task. The problem is the degree and length of commitment at this stage of your life. It would involve yet another postponement of your plans to finish Basic Level and immediately shouldering a seriously heavy workload. You would have to fight your way through accelerated EdCom courses in every area the rogue has studied and at the same time work with Pirramar in accessing the K74 Intelligence Systems. I can see you're eager and feeling obliged to go ahead but we must talk this through thoroughly before you decide.'

Talk they did for over an hour till Wirrin understood, with a mixture of alarm and excitement, exactly how much was involved.

Gulara almost vetoed the proposal at one stage, insisting that Wirrin wasn't a machine and that at least half his EdCom time should involve classes shared with other students. She very clearly understood, much better than Akama, the ins and outs of EdCom and the difficulties and needs of such a crowded course.

Akama asked Wirrin about his best learning times, and when Wirrin explained about working through the challenges on the Titania trip, he called for Turaku and on the spot asked for his involvement. Turaku agreed, but straightaway said that Pirramar was better suited and offering to take his place.

Gulara called for Pirramar then, and told him she would link him to the sections of EdCom overseeing Wirrin's courses.

Sonic complicated everything by informing Akama that he wanted to be involved with Wirrin's learning and research as well.

Throughout all this Wirrin had no doubts at all about his decision, but as the range of things he'd have to do clarified in his mind he wondered more and more if he'd be able to manage. Finally he said, 'I don't think I could do all that. There's too much.'

Gulara allayed his worries by taking every aspect and showing Wirrin how it could be organised into a workable timetable. Another complication was the move to the new living space on Warrakan, which was only two weeks away, and Calen suggested starting the full program when that was settled. Pirramar, surprisingly, supported that, saying concentrated work with Wirrin for the next three or four weeks was actually a priority.

*   *   *

'Wirrin, I hope this doesn't mean you'll be working twelve hours a day for the next few years. We'll never see you, and when we do you'll be too tired. I don't think it's fair.'

'It won't be that bad, Calen. We'll have our activity days together. Gulara made certain of that.'

'As if! Look how much they already get messed up when Thom's doing something with the Comet or I'm involved with extra things for Sonic.'

'We'll work around it. Gulara and Akama both said they'd help us as much as they could and they really meant it. It's scary, but it's like you working extra hard with Sonic for the Meeting Day.'

'That was four or five weeks. Not forever.'

'Well, I hope you don't drop dead from brain exhaustion,' Thom added. 'A quarter of what you're doing would be enough for me. I'm going to see if there's a protein structure that stops brains wearing out.'

Trust Thom to make them all smile. Secretly, Wirrin wished him success. A protein structure like that sounded perfect.

Chapter 23

'Wirrin! Wake up!'

Wirrin rolled away in protest. Just a little more sleep, perhaps a few hours, would be heaven.

'He's getting worse than you, Calen.'

What? … What were they talking about? Wirrin cracked one eyelid and peered at Thom kneeling beside him on the grav-bed.

'Go away, Thom. It's too early.'

'No it's not. It's half an hour after you told us to wake you up.'

'And Sonic's in the pool waiting for us.'

Wirrin rolled over and saw Calen watching from the other side of his grav-bed. Half an hour? Sonic? What were they talking about? Oh! Wirrin sat up abruptly and was immediately pushed and pulled to the floor. How could he possibly have slept in on moving day?

'Get something on and grab your breakfast. Thom's got it ready and waiting for you, oh Great One'

Wirrin glanced at the time, grabbed his clothes and rushed to the living area where a delicious smell filled the air.

Lazybones! We nearly left you behind and be careful or you'll eat that shirt.

Sonic's dolphin version of laughter woke Wirrin fully and he couldn't help smiling. He probably did look funny, grabbing a great mouthful of food then donning another article of clothing.

Following Calen's look, Wirrin glanced at the wall display and saw dolphins everywhere in the reach close by — Puck and Flute and the whole pod, waiting while he slept. They would all think it funny and he'd hear about it for the rest of the day.

'Come on! Let's go.'

Moments later the excitement started to build as, surrounded by Puck's pod, the three skimmers headed for the dolphinarium. The atmosphere there would be even more intense, with every other enhanced dolphin on Attunga waiting to be transported to the Comet and then to their new home on Warrakan.

The reach there was in wonderful condition, with its whole marine ecosystem fully established after five months of dolphin-free development. Yajala had overseen all that and reported to Puck and Sonic that it was now the healthiest reach on Warrakan.

Watching the antics and listening to the excited communications made Wirrin wonder anew at their apparent lack of feeling about leaving the reaches which had been their lifelong home. Sonic had explained that dolphins didn't quite think that way, instead enjoying the prospect of everything new at the Warrakan reach. Well, they were different; it was as simple as that.

For himself it wasn't the same. Their shared space on Attunga would always be in his mind as their first home. Calen felt the same. Thom said he didn't but Wirrin wasn't sure about that. It wasn't as if they were completely leaving, though, because it was there for their use any time they went to Attunga. Gulara told them he'd organised that because the pool and translators made it a friendly, familiar base for Sonic if he was visiting, and because Wirrin needed a place for the two days a week of EdCom courses he'd be doing on Attunga.

'Whoo! Look at this!'

Thom's call snapped Wirrin out of his reverie. There was only a distance of a couple of hundred metres to the dolphinarium and directly ahead a mass of dolphins was racing straight at the skimmers and Puck's pod. Wirrin's heart jumped. They were being charged by an army. The two contingents collided and nearly four hundred dolphins miraculously became one unit. Sonic leapt from the water and the pulse of dolphin calls was cut off abruptly as the flying bodies disappeared beneath the surface.

Calen yelled, 'They're crazy!'

They certainly were. It was the same contagious excitement the Earth dolphins had shown, but more intense, and the trio were all laughing as the action approached the dolphinarium landing.

'They might be too worked up to go on the transporters.'

'With Sonic and the rangers telling them what to do? No way. They've got it all over ordinary dolphins. You watch.'

And of course Calen was right. The transfer to transport modules and the move to the Comet proceeded like clockwork.

The short trip from Attunga, with Thom piloting of course, was unexpectedly dramatic when all the pod leaders reacted strongly to their first sight of space and the growing image of Warrakan on the great display screen. The surge of calls for information and explanation resounding through the control centre caused the humans present to stare in wonder then take in the familiar view themselves with a reawakened sense of appreciation.

The arrival at Warrakan home reach was ordered chaos with dolphin pods joining their rangers in preparation for the move to their varied locations. Puck's pod didn't have far to go, being assigned to an area close to the giant dolphinarium and marine research centre, and after meeting with Burilda and Gulara they all set off through the crystal-clear water. Wirrin was struck by just how clear it was — so different without the haze caused by the huge infusion of nutrients to stimulate faster development.

According to Burilda's reports the whole reach was teeming with life, and the dolphins were going to be amazed at the abundance and variety. Stocks of larger fish had been transferred from the surrounding reaches where there were now more than the Earth dolphins would ever need.

The dolphinarium loomed and Wirrin scanned further on, where only 500 metres away their new living space nestled at the edge of the reach. Two hours from now, after exploring with the pod, the trio would enter and officially take over.

*   *   *

'Of course they got excited, Thom. A reach like this was completely new to them, and it was exuberance more than excitement.'

'Sounds the same to me … When's Sonic coming?'

'Tonight, probably at the usual time. He's spending the whole day with his pod while they look around.'

The trio was sitting on the new grav-sofa and looking at the view of the reach on the giant display screen, which took up most of the wall fronting the water.

'It's so big. I can't get used to it.'

'The reach? You've seen it so much you should be.'

'Not the reach. The wall screen. The other one looked like a screen, but this one makes you feel like there's not even a wall there.'

'Wirrin, that's the whole idea.'

'I know, but it's three times as wide and a bit higher.'

'Well, I think it's incredible and I'm glad we followed Wanna's advice.'

The planning assistant had arranged the design and construction after hearing ideas from the trio, but he'd had his own suggestions, too.

'Glad! Is that all, Thom? Remember when you said you wanted a maxi-screen and he suggested this instead?'

Calen laughed because Thom had carried on for days about how unreal something twice as wide as a maxi would be.

'I know, but he was right. All his ideas were the best.'

Looking round at everything Wirrin could only agree. Despite the huge size of the pool and hence the much bigger space to contain it, their actual living area was very similar to the last one. They'd wanted to keep it that way and Wirrin liked the result.

'What are you thinking about now, Wirrin?'

'Nothing special but lots of things, Calen. I know I'm going to like it here when I get used to the extra space.'

'You'd better like it. We might still be here in another hundred years.'

Thom and Wirrin both looked at Calen in surprise.

'I suppose so. I've never thought like that. We've always had a change ahead of us,' said Wirrin.

'Well, I don't want any changes for a while. We've dreamed about Warrakan for years and now we're here.'

'There are always changes, Calen. Freedom's arriving in another four months and I know about another change right now that will affect you more than me and Thom.'

'What?'

'We won't see Turaku as much because Yajala looks after dolphins here.'

'Yes we will. Well, I will, because he and Yajala work together, and you will, Thom, whenever you're controlling the Comet, because Turaku's built into it. I don't know about you, Wirrin.'

'Calen, I'll probably see him more than either of you. Pirramar and I contact him all the time about the dolphin plans on K74 and what's happening with the reaches at Freedom and Uranus.'

'What's been happening on K74, Wirrin? You haven't told us.'

'There's nothing to tell. They're still building the reach and they won't finish for ages. They're so slow at building things it might take another year.'

'That's good then, but what slowed them down? I remember you said five months.'

'What do you think? They killed their AI didn't they, without realising how much efficiency they'd lose. Everything's taking longer.'

Calen frowned. 'That means their dolphins will be stuck in tiny aquariums for ages. I hope they'll be all right.'

'Didn't Burilda tell you? They haven't got any. The blockade stopped that and the Earth AIs won't let anyone else send any. They'll have to go to Earth and collect them for themselves.'

'No she didn't, but then I didn't ask. We've been so busy getting ready for this move.'

'Hey, Sonic's getting strong isn't he? He nearly kept up with those three big males when they were racing.'

'He'll beat them all soon, Thom. He's started a new growth spurt and Yajala thinks it'll be a couple of months before it steadies. He's already big for his age and he's still got years and years of growing. We think he might be half a metre longer than those males eventually.'

Thom looked impressed and he called up life-size holo images of two of the racing males, then with a bit of fiddling enlarged one an extra half metre for comparison.

Wow! Wirrin was impressed now. That would be a very big dolphin.

'He'll make the Earth dolphins look like kids. Why are they smaller?'

'It's partly an effect of the enhancement process but mostly because Monkey Mia dolphins are a larger variant of bottlenose dolphin than the Earth norm.'

The original stock of Attunga dolphins all came from the Monkey Mia area.

'Cold-water dolphins can grow up to 4 metres, which is the same size as our Attunga males, but some types are fully grown at two and a half. That's why we were surprised when we first saw the Earth dolphins.'

Thom was smiling because he'd got Calen started on talking about dolphins, but he was interested too and wanted to know why cold water would make dolphins bigger.

'A smaller body has to use more energy to keep a proper temperature, so bigger dolphins have a survival advantage when it's constantly cold.'

'I'm glad our dolphins like warm water. We wouldn't be able to swim with them without freezing. Did any of the cold-water ones come on the Comet?'

'Yes, about seven pods. One of the reaches is set up with the right conditions for them.'

'So how did they cope with the warm water in home reach for five months?'

'Good question, Thom. They're used to big variations and it was like summer for them except it went on for ages.'

'What happens if you visit them? You'll freeze.'

'No I won't. I'll use a thermal skin if I need to go right in, but near the interconnects the water's close to home-reach temperature.'

'When are you going again? I want to see this,' said Thom.

'Not for ages. Settling in with our dolphins is the main focus for a while and we'll mostly be out there somewhere.' Calen gestured to the expanse of the reach and they all checked to see if any dolphins were in view.

'It's so big. I can't get used to it,' Wirrin said.

Thom and Calen exchanged a look and burst out laughing.

'Time-warp attack!'

'Brain malfunction!'

'Stress relief time!'

Under joyful attack from both sides, Wirrin fleetingly wondered if the new grav-sofa would cope as well as the old one.

* * *

'Wirrin, what did you do to Sonic yesterday? It seems like he's gone crazy about InfoSystems. They installed a whole new one for him on the Comet, and Calen says they're doing the same at the dolphinarium.'

'They've put them in already? Well there'll be one in our pool too, in a few days. He got frustrated when he saw how slow his ordinary InterWeb was compared to how I do things on my system and he asked Yajala what he could do about it.'

'It's his next thing. I can tell,' said Calen.

'Thing?'

'Like the music, and learning to read. He talked about it all this afternoon while we visited the pods. He'll spend weeks on it till he thinks he's good enough.'

'Wow! We'll have two brainiacs saving the AIs ... Do you think he's going to be good at it?'

Wirrin thought that was a strange question. 'Of course he will, Thom. When he's interested in something he's always brilliant. Look what he did with the Dreamtime Concerto and the meeting songs.'

'I suppose he'll do it the same way he uses the InterWeb?'

Wirrin nodded. 'Yes, except he's got the option for much more extended input.'

Sonic was adept at using the InterWeb. He used sound exclusively, of course, since the fine motor control of human fingers wasn't available to him, but according to Pirramar, the incredible range and rapidity of his auditory signals gave him the potential of far greater facility with input than any human.

Wirrin, using a combination of speech and touch, was way ahead at the moment, but he'd learned yesterday that with a system designed especially for him, Sonic would eventually be faster, as long as he practised.

'What does extended input mean?'

'He'll be able to run the system faster than I can.'

Thom thought about that for a moment. 'I wonder what it will sound like? If much of it's that high stuff we can't hear it might overload Calen's implants.'

'No it won't. It'll be just like the InterWeb controls he uses now except there'll be more of them.'

'What does Pirramar say about it?'

'He's really keen. He'll help out any time Sonic wants him and so will Yajala and Turaku.'

'All three of them? What happens about his time with Calen?'

Calen laughed. 'That goes back to normal, Thom, whatever that is. We'll still be going to nurseries and EdCom groups and talking to the scientists and visiting Earth dolphins and all the other things. I might actually have a chance to catch up on some EdCom work.'

'Do you think the EdCom here will be much different?'

Thom and Calen both looked to Wirrin to answer this as his big work commitment meant he'd had the most involvement in planning everything.

'I don't see how, except we'll be meeting a whole new set of people. Gulara says the Intelligent System that runs it all on Attunga is state of the art, so Warrakan can't be better.'

'The labs and tute rooms are bigger,' said Thom.

'I suppose. But the same things will still happen in them. Anyway, we'll soon know.'

They'd find out the next day, in fact, when they were due to attend

their first EdCom courses on Warrakan. Gulara had finalised everything and swapped a number of Calen and Thom's times to match with
Wirrin's, which were far more complicated. Wirrin's EdCom work
involved a day each on Attunga and Warrakan with other students,
and a day each with the faster and more adaptable personalised electronic instruction courses. His other day involved the K74 work with
Pirramar and InfoSystem training with Sonic.

For both Calen and Thom the EdCom work was secondary, after
dolphin time and Comet-related studies respectively. Not so for Wirrin.
His study from now on would be strongly directed and purposeful —
namely to build an understanding of the rogue scientist — and very
different from the broad educative structure of Basic Training. On top
of that, Pirramar was now linked to EdCom and overseeing his progress, a unique situation according to Gulara.

'Hey look, Sonic's out there with Puck and Flute. They're early.'

*   *   *

'Hello, doctor.'

'Hi, Wirrin, what's the news this time?'

'News?'

The doctor grinned. 'Your status has changed to a permanent time
priority, you've turned up a week earlier than scheduled, and you
always have some exciting and interesting news. I feel a sense of anticipation every time I see your name on the roster.'

Wirrin grinned. 'Yes, I have got news, and several questions as well.'

'Medical ones? Well, let's deal with those first and get your checkup
out of the way, since it's a bit longer than usual.'

Wirrin wondered why but didn't ask because he'd soon find out.

'Thom and Calen call me a brainiac and I wanted to ask you about it.'

'A brainiac? Meaning you're a genius?'

Wirrin laughed. 'No, they'd never say that. They think there's something unusual about my brain because I work some things out too
quickly. Look at this.' Wirrin called up the incident about AI space on
Warrakan and projected it as a holo. 'See what I mean. Thom's good
at calculations like that and he took three and a half times as long to
work it out.'

'Interesting. Let's have a look.'

Having a look meant a number of tests and a half hour later the doctor's conclusion. 'You can tell Thom and Calen there's nothing weird going on at all, just a natural gift being diligently exercised. Your study must involve quite a bit of this sort of calculation?'

That was such an understatement Wirrin spluttered with laughter.

'It always has. They're part of InfoStudies which I've always loved, but when the AIs started giving me challenges I had to do even more, and now that I'm on my special course it's practically constant calculations and puzzles.'

'You've changed your Basic Training?'

'It's not a change. I don't even do it anymore. The Witnesses and AIs exempted me.'

'A complete exemption? You were squeezing your Basic in amongst the other activities last time I saw you.'

'There's just no time now and it might be a couple of years before I can get back to it. My new course is totally full time.'

'Totally? So it's something to do with the priority classification on your file.'

'I don't know what the priority's for but it could be. The AIs asked me to do this course.'

'Wirrin! No wonder I look forward to your news. Tell me more.'

So Wirrin did, the reasons and then the structure of the study. Some of Wirrin's concern must have come through because the doctor seized on the difficulty aspect.

'How are you coping? This looks close to an overload to me.'

'It's okay so far. It's very exciting too, especially working with Pirramar, but it's hard to wake up in the mornings and I've never been like that before.'

'And you're worried you mightn't be able to maintain this rate of output?'

'Yes.'

'What about your sleep pattern? Do you wake up during the night or have any trouble getting to sleep?'

'Never. I close my eyes and then, when I'm wondering why Calen and Thom are speaking to me, it's the next morning.'

'That's good. Just out of interest I'll program your healthbots to log your sleep rhythms for the next few weeks but I think we'll find you're going through a typical adaptation process. Your health check will tell us what's going on. So, any more questions before we start?'

'Yes, we're wondering why I have more visits than Thom and Calen. It seems to have gone back to the same pattern as when I was little.'

The doctor raised his eyebrows.

'Your recent extra visits have all been circumstance, mostly due to your unusual implant abilities, but up till age nine you did have a different monitoring schedule. Hasn't that ever been explained to you?'

'Never. I vaguely remember asking if there was something wrong with me when we noticed I had a lot more checkups than Calen and Thom, but they said I was extra healthy and everyone just needed varying numbers of checks … something like that at any rate.'

'Hmm, well they wouldn't go into details because of your age, but this is strangely coincidental because it ties in with today's extra procedures. Your genetic background is different to Thom and Calen's and did require extra monitoring because it came from the Legacy source. Ninety per cent of nursery children originate from the gene pool of our current citizens, but since it is so important to maintain genetic diversity the rest are carefully selected from mostly external sources.'

'What does Legacy source mean?'

'It's the small but significant collection of genetic material that was gathered from Northern Australia as a bio-backup when Attunga was first constructed. It's accessed regularly as a physical affirmation of our heritage.'

This was interesting and it certainly explained the cast of his physical characteristics. Thom and Calen would want to hear about this.

'Do you know how many people come from it?'

'Almost everyone. It's only the external ten per cent I mentioned who aren't descended from it as a base, but that's not what you meant.'

He manipulated his holo screen. 'The external 9.6 per cent to be exact. According to this the current access rate for Legacy material stands at approximately 0.4 per cent, so you're quite a select individual. Calculating an exact number would be very difficult as we'd have to access the records of every single nursery on the habitat.'

Not really. Wirrin knew he could do that in moments with his InfoStation. He had a bigger question.

'So why do children from the Legacy source need more monitoring? If I was extra healthy that sounds like I'd need less.'

'That's a very good question. Legacy material was all vetted at the time of collection, but we've learned a great deal in the decades since, and a whole range of modifications need to be applied when using that early material to ensure a long and healthy life. Most of the changes are very minor and are only significant in their cumulative effect, but there are also a number of very important ones. For example, we fixed a propensity in your body for hearing failure after age eighty, as well as a slight weakness in your liver function.'

Wirrin immediately thought of Peggy, the dolphin in Martin's pod. They had something in common. He'd watch her progress from now on.

'That doesn't sound too healthy.'

'Completely healthy, Wirrin. We all carry a huge range of characteristics in our makeup and understanding their relative importance is very difficult. We have to be careful about eliminating any bad traits because they're often linked in some way with more important good ones. Basically no-one is perfectly healthy but we're steadily improving.'

'I won't tell Thom and Calen about the hearing thing or they'll be yelling at me as if I can't hear.'

'Tell them how select you are instead. Less than 0.4 per cent of the population is quite impressive.'

'One in every 250. That sounds even better. I'll say it that way ... What's the coincidence?'

'Today is deposit day for your bio-bank.'

Wirrin stared for a moment.

'Is that what I think it is?'

'Probably ... if you're thinking stem cells, blood, sperm, DNA material, and a microscopic amount of brain matter, then yes.'

He had been, but that list was more than he'd expected, especially the last bit.

'You're going to collect a piece of my brain?'

'Yes, and when people complain we leave the machine on till there's nothing left.'

'Typical doctor. Wait till I tell Sonic.'

They were both smiling but Wirrin could tell the doctor was wondering why he'd mentioned Sonic. Good.

'On a more serious note, Wirrin, do you discuss the idea of having children?'

'All the time, because the dolphins never stop asking, but we're just too busy and not ready.'

'The dolphins ask? That's interesting … Because they're curious?'

'No, because they want us to have children. Puck asked us the very first day we met and they're still asking. They want more Calens for their babies to bond with.'

'They've asked for children from Calen?'

'Well, that's what we thought they meant because of his special way with animals, but we've talked with Sonic about it quite a bit since and he says no. They want our trio children.'

'Oh my! I start to ask the standard questions connected with your bio-bank and I'm out of my depth before we've answered the first one. Trio children could be arranged with a variety of techniques through the nurseries of course, but all the rules would have to be changed and that's a decision for the Witnesses.'

'The dolphins don't want that. Burilda told them it was one of the options and Sonic said a straight out no. He says they'll wait till we can bring them up as part of our own pod.'

'You *have* talked about this extensively. What other options were mentioned?'

'Children or clones of Calen, before we knew they wanted pod children.'

'Pod children? What exactly does that mean?'

'We call them that because trio means us, and pod means Sonic as well. When we have children they'll be part of his pod. Growing up together is very important to dolphins.'

'It's important to all of us, Wirrin, but you just said 'when'. You've made a definite decision?'

'It's definite at the moment, but it won't happen for another ten or twelve years … The same as for most people.'

Children on Attunga were cherished and welcomed by whatever path they joined the society. Most adults formed bonds of some type, and most elected to have children at some stage, usually after the free years of their twenties, but not necessarily, and brought them up with the help of a nursery assistant. These were assigned according to need, much the same way a planning assistant like Wanna was assigned when the trio needed help with their living space.

Because of the aim for Attunga's population to grow to something like three times its current 800 million, the majority of children were born and nurtured in a nursery with specially trained human carers.

Wirrin's nursery family consisted of nineteen children, including Thom and Calen, two nursery mothers, two nursery fathers and associated nursery assistants.

'Why do you think you're not ready? That's not the way I see any of you.'

Gulara had said the same thing even though her advice was to wait.

'Mostly because there are too many other things happening but also because we still feel like kids ourselves.'

'Yes, I understand that. I felt the same when I was your age … Well, let's get busy.'

An hour and a half later Wirrin and the doctor sat down to enjoy a snack.

'Fire away, Wirrin. I'm all ears.'

Wirrin smiled. Sonic would enjoy hearing these figures of speech.

'There's too much. I don't know where to start.'

'Okay, tell me what's so exciting about your work with the AI. You gave me the impression there was something going on there.'

'Pirramar. Everything. Gulara organised for him to link in with EdCom and I've never learnt so many things so fast. He makes it so interesting. We spend a lot of time looking at K74 as well and there's so much going on there we can't keep up.'

'An AI can't keep up? That doesn't sound right.'

'I know, and Pirramar's a composite so it's even more amazing.'

'I don't know what that means.'

'He's one AI but he's based on Warrakan as well as Attunga, so he's got more than twice the normal amount of resources. He'd keep up easily if we could get in to all the places we'd like but the rogue knows a lot about AIs and how to block them.'

'I wouldn't have thought it was possible to block an AI?'

'He blocks every electronic pathway so we have to discover things indirectly. Three days ago we checked the construction systems and found plans for building a fleet of their big spaceships. They have seven at the moment but we need to know why they want thirty more.'

'I don't know anything about the K74 spaceships. What does big mean?'

'They're not as big as the biggest Earth or Mars transports, but 700 metres makes them nearly twice as long as our Comets.'

'That's enormous. And they must be dangerous or your AI wouldn't be worried about them.'

'Pirramar. Yes, they're very fast and the seven functional ones all carry atomics. The only good thing about the situation is that it will take at least fifteen months before any of them can be finished.'

'And you work with Pirramar on things like this every day?'

'Not every day. Gulara made sure that a big block of my course is ordinary EdCom with other students, but I do see him most days.'

'I can't imagine what it must be like. I've never even seen an AI in real life let alone had a conversation.'

You couldn't see them in real life, just their holo projections, but Wirrin understood what the doctor was getting at. 'It's quite hard to explain. After a while it feels like you're just talking to someone in a holo conference but underneath you know it's an amazing intelligence, or creature, or being or something who's there with you. I get goose-bumps sometimes when I see Pirramar do something that would take me a million years, and he does it by the time he finishes a sentence.'

'Do you have a sense of personality or identity after seeing AIs so much?'

'Completely. Turaku's like a quiet, steady, very firm sort of person. Pirramar's very friendly and encouraging, and Yajala's the easiest to talk to and always smiling and laughing. It's really interesting because everyone has the same reactions to them but it's totally fake.'

'Fake?'

'Fake's not quite right. Controlled is a better word. Calen and Thom and I used to argue about it all the time because I kept telling them it was all a program the AIs were using. They reckoned they could see past that, so we asked Yajala. He changed right in front of us to different personalities. A really grumpy and irritable-sounding person, then a serious person, a bit like Turaku, then someone worried, and then like a child. He kept the same holo image all the time and that made it so strange it was almost creepy. He totally convinced Thom and Calen about the programs but then made everything more confusing by saying that AIs did have personalities and identities, but not in the way humans use the terms.'

'Extraordinary! That sounds very different to being with Sonic. His personality is so real it hits you like a hammer.'

Wirrin smiled. Another interesting saying for Sonic.

'Yajala says humans and dolphins recognise that in each other because the terms of our existence are mostly shared. Our experiences of pain and pleasure, and reactions to input from our senses are almost identical.'

'You live an amazing life, Wirrin. Are you pleased with your shift to Warrakan?'

'Definitely. We love exploring, too, and every time we say we're going to do it more often something else always happens. On the two lots of activity days before the last ones we went with Burilda and Sonic to visit the Earth dolphins. It's nearly seven months since they settled in and they absolutely love their new homes. The rangers and marine scientists are all excited because a huge number of the females are pregnant and there'll be over four hundred babies in another six or seven months.' Wirrin smiled fondly. 'The time before that we went with Thom to see the three new Comets, which had just been completed. He's working like crazy to get to know them because they're not the same as Sonic's main Comet.'

'We build them in much less than fifteen months then?'

'About five weeks. That's the difference between real AIs and the Intelligent Systems they use on K74.'

'That's astonishing. What section of the Comets is Thom learning? The navigation system?'

'Everything. He can fly them all but he likes our main Comet best. It's faster than the rest.'

'He's given enough control to check out their speed at his age?'

'He gets complete control. He sometimes does training flights with no other people on board, except Turaku of course. He's built in. Thom was more amazed than anyone that he was given so much responsibility, but we found out Sonic requested it.'

'Sonic has a great deal of influence. He should. But flying spaceships doesn't seem like an area dolphins would be involved with.'

'He is though. He can fly the Comet too. He doesn't know as much as Thom but he often takes over. It was built especially so he could go anywhere, with two permanent AIs, picofactories, science laboratories, and incredible defence abilities.'

The doctor was drinking in every word. 'How does he control it? I've got this ridiculous image in my mind of him pushing levers or pressing touch pads with his beak.'

'He does it all with sound signals and special pick-ups.'

'Dolphin auditory skills. I should have realised that … I see he's grown quite a bit since you invited me over. Has he changed much?'

He must have seen Sonic on the InterWeb. Wirrin grinned. The leading question he'd been waiting for had just presented. 'Come and see for yourself.'

The doctor's face lit up but then he frowned. 'I hope you're not going to say tonight, because I can't manage it.'

'No, tonight's no good. It needs to be your next activity day.'

'Wirrin, that smile makes you look as if you're implementing some Machiavellian scheme.'

Wirrin paused for a retinal scan then nodded. 'It's not my scheme, and there's nothing sneaky about it. Sonic wants to see you again and he'd like you to bring your partner and children with you. He wants to meet them all.'

'Sonic asked for me himself?'

'Yes. When I mentioned I was due for a health check he said he's been wanting to talk to you. He got Gulara to change things so I'd see you sooner and could ask you in person.'

The doctor thought that over, obviously not knowing what to make of it. 'Wirrin, I expect to hear unexpected news from you but this is more unexpected than I ever expected. What does it mean? Does Sonic often ask people to visit him? … What's that look for?'

'I'm just working out the sentence … The expected unexpected one. No he doesn't, but he likes you, you know that, and you told him about your family, except he calls it your pod. That's one of the reasons for an activity day since it involves the trip to Warrakan.'

The doctor pounced. 'There are other reasons?'

'I think he wants to talk about health stuff. You talked about it last time and he said it was interesting.'

'Hmm! I have a funny feeling you're not telling me everything.'

Wirrin laughed. 'Which day works best for you?'

'If Sonic wants to talk to me on an activity day it will be the first one available.'

Chapter 24

The doctor's partner, Miah, a dark-haired lady with a brilliant smile which had won the trio over in very short order, was laughing as she joined Thom, Calen and the three children in a splashing war against Sonic, who didn't have a hope against such formidable opponents. Well, that's what the two younger ones were thinking.

Miro, the thirteen-year-old, was pretty clever and most probably realised they were all being treated very gently.

'They're never going to forget this. None of us will. Raji couldn't do his EdCom classes yesterday because he was too excited, and Miro was nearly as bad about travelling through space and visiting Warrakan.' The doctor was sitting with Wirrin and watching all the laughter and happiness with delight.

'Alisa seems quieter than the boys.'

'Not really. She's just awed by meeting Sonic.'

She didn't look awed at the moment, hanging on tightly to Sonic's tail flukes to stop him splashing.

'How did your talk go?'

The trio had taken the three children in Sonic's transporter for a rendezvous with Puck and Flute and the rest of the pod, where they spoke and played and were entertained while the doctor and Miah spent an hour with Sonic.

'Unbelievable. Did you know what he wanted the other day on your visit?'

'I knew he wanted your help but that's all.'

'Help? I'd hardly call it that. He's asked me to move to Warrakan and be in change of an age extension program for dolphins.'

'In charge? Really? He said he thought you'd like to be involved with dolphins after your talk with him last visit, but we didn't know he was going to ask you to move.'

'I'd have to. It's a new venture for the dolphins and I'd have to do it properly. Sonic says I'd have no limits on equipment and staff and a living space next to the facilities.'

'Would moving be a problem?'

The doctor gave a little laugh. 'You could say that not moving would be a problem. Sonic told Miah she'd be able to involve the dolphins in her music studies, and if the children found out they'd missed a chance like this I'd never hear the end of it. Raji would probably murder me. Look at him. Judging from his expression Sonic could do the Pied Piper trick with children any time if he ever wanted to.'

Raji was hanging onto Sonic's back and watching Calen and his mum get deluged.

'Does that mean you've made your decision?'

'There is no decision to make. It's an amazing opportunity for me and when I told him there are people far more qualified he wouldn't even consider them, except to say I could involve whoever I wanted.'

Wirrin grinned. 'That's Sonic. He likes you and his dolphin senses tell him you're the person for the job.'

'Dolphin senses?'

'For this kind of thing I suppose you could say Sonic senses … No, the other dolphins work that way too. Puck and Flute spent half an hour with us the first time we met and that was enough to decide Calen was the right companion for Sonic. And look how right they were about that. Has he told you much detail about what he wants?'

'No details, just overview, Wirrin. He thinks that age extension for dolphins might work in a similar way to the way it does for humans and he wants me to develop reliable techniques that would apply to him and any others like him if his special enhancement proves to be viable. The other dolphins don't really think about their lifespan but he wants them to be healthy and happy for longer than the current eighty-year life expectancy, and he thinks twenty or more years could be added by adapting the known techniques.' He paused. 'Going by that special report you accessed I think it will turn out to be much more. At any rate he says the Witnesses and AIs will give him any support he needs to get the program implemented. He has amazing influence with them doesn't he?'

'Doctor, that's nothing compared to the other things they've done for dolphins since he turned up. They'll probably have the buildings and equipment ready a few weeks after you give a definite yes.'

'I've already given it. Well, Miah has, by telling Sonic we'd be here as soon as we could tie up everything on Attunga.'

'Did Sonic say how long you might be involved for?'

'Indefinitely. Why?'

'Warrakan leaves in another six or seven years and you might want to stay in the solar system.'

'Sonic already mentioned that and said there'd be a similar project on Attunga for dolphins who are staying, so that's a decision for later.'

'Does this mean we'll have a new doctor for our health checks? I'll miss our talks.'

'I would too, but that's your decision. Sonic seems to think I'm good for you and he says it would be easy to arrange.'

Wirrin had to smile. Trust Sonic to know how the trio liked and trusted the doctor. 'That's great, except you'll probably start to treat us like dolphins if you're working with them all the time.'

'Treat the Dolphin Boys like dolphins? Sounds eminently sensible to me … What are they doing?'

The laughter and romping in the pool had stopped and Calen was handing out facemasks. He looked at Wirrin and the doctor and beckoned, urgently.

'I don't know, but from Calen's expression it looks important. Grab a facemask.'

Moments later Wirrin watched the youngsters, just beneath the surface and eyes all agog, receiving a gentle dolphin nudge in the chest. The doctor and Miah were next and then Sonic manoeuvred himself directly in front of Raji. A happy dolphin trill filled the pool, making everyone smile and watch raptly. The trill changed to a bouncy medley of clicks and strangely melodious squeaks.

Wirrin fleetingly looked for meaning, but this wasn't speech. It was song, beautiful, lively, happy dolphin sounds being directed at Raji with meanings that didn't need words for expression.

With a burst of wondrous comprehension Wirrin saw that this song was Raji, Raji as Sonic saw him. Too quickly the magical sound ended and after one more gentle touch to Raji's chest Sonic drifted upward for a breath of air. It was a signal for everyone else to follow. The masks came off and there was a moment of stunned silence. The doctor looked amazed. Miah looked so happy Wirrin wondered if they were tears or pool water he was seeing. The children reached for Sonic.

'You great lump of fish. That's the best thing you've ever done.'

'Thank you, Thom. That is Raji's song.'

'Mine? You sang it for me?'

'*Yes, Raji. Puck asked me to let you know that dolphins like you and your family.*'

Wirrin was used to seeing the wonder and amazement of children in the nurseries when Sonic spoke and interacted with them, but the look he was seeing now would stay with him all his life.

'I wish I could sing for you.'

'*You do, Raji, in your own way, and I sing it back to you. Come with me now to say goodbye to Puck and Flute.*'

Everyone looked round. Yes, there they were, shown via the big display screen, just outside with the rest of the pod. The children rushed to follow as Sonic headed out. The doctor and Miah moved close together.

'We are overwhelmed. Is it like this all the time when you live with dolphins?'

'We're overwhelmed too, doctor. I've never seen that before.'

Wirrin turned a questioning glance to Calen.

'Not for humans. Individuals sometimes do a version when they're bonding but it's nowhere near as complex as that. That was dolphin sound adapted for humans.'

Miah, with her love of music, fired excited questions at Calen about Sonic's abilities while the wall display showed the children mingling with the pod.

'Do you think we'll ever hear it again? Or is it something impromptu?'

Calen looked thoughtful.

'Sonic will sing. I know that because he loves it, but I think it would change a bit as he sees new things about Raji. We can get it off the translator machines though. They keep a record.'

'Ask Brainiac. He zaps everything so he'll have images as well.'

Wirrin shook his head at Thom. 'The translators are designed specially to pick up dolphin sounds so they'll be much better than my ears. You can have whatever you want though.'

'Put your images with the sounds from the translator. That'll be best.'

The children returned and Raji, rushing to his mum and dad, started begging to come and see Sonic again.

'Sometime, Raji, but right now it's time to say goodbye and thank you for such a special day.'

'Not quite, doctor. Thom's arranged to take you back to Attunga on the Comet instead of the ferry. He likes showing off and he thought Miro might enjoy it.'

'What's the Comet?' Miro asked.

The trio grinned. If Miro was as interested in space and spaceships as the doctor had suggested then he was in for a big surprise.

* * *

With a degree of trepidation Wirrin looked at the vast bulk of the 300 kilometre long K74 asteroid.

Admittedly the visuals were at full magnification and the real distance was much further than it looked, but this exercise, testing Thom's skill with the stealth abilities of the Comet, was still in its early stage and the risk of detection would steadily increase from now on.

Red blips indicating the presence of two of the big Cadre ships added almost as much excitement as Thom's eagerness to show how easily he could sneak close.

There was no real danger — the trio would never be allowed to take such a risk — and should Thom make a mistake of any kind the Comet's security AI would cut in with all the defence capabilities available, operating with AI speed and accuracy.

Thom had already practised the active part of the exercise eleven times and was very confident he would make the 15 kilometre approach he was aiming for. He'd taken eight tries with the simulators to be successful, and three more to be sure he could do it consistently. He was full of confidence, as he always was, despite having explained that unforeseen factors almost invariably messed things up in real life.

'Are you ready with your InfoSystem?'

Wirrin was more than ready. Everything had been running for the last half hour.

'What about you, Calen? Any worries?'

'Of course I've got worries. I don't even know what I'm looking for.'

'You'll know when you see it. Just take notice of the difference signals.'

Calen's task — checking the visuals — was, like Wirrin's, mostly redundant, and Thom's way of getting them involved.

'Stealth mode is initiated and we're on our way.'

For half an hour the Comet slipped steadily closer with absolutely nothing happening, and Calen's concentration on his section of display screen gradually relaxed till he turned to Thom with a grin. 'Is this all that happens? There hasn't been a single signal yet.'

Thom finished doing something with his controls before giving a short and almost terse reply.

'That's what I want.'

Whoops! Calen and Wirrin exchanged an understanding glance. There'd be no more unnecessary comments to Thom while he was concentrating so fiercely.

A quick check of the range indicator showed they'd moved from the 500 kilometre mark to a separation distance of 105 kilometres. The next 90 kilometres would take longer and if everything went well they'd remain stationary at the 15 kilometre point for a period of time while the security AI made some sort of assessment.

Wirrin focused a window on the closest of the two big spaceships and enlarged the image. That was interesting. At two locations small fleets of construction vessels were at work busily attaching something to the hull. Wirrin sent a query through his InfoSystem to the Comet's database, then blinked in surprise when the reply said the construction vessels were an unknown type.

'Turaku, there something strange here. We should have information about everything happening external to K74.'

Turaku's voice sounded in Wirrin's ear — he didn't manifest because it would distract Thom.

'Yes, very strange. I've relayed your query and the information we're gathering to Pirramar and we'll have his assessment as soon as it arrives. My analysis of this visual data suggests the early stage of some type of special cradle or attachment point.'

'That's not what's strange. I don't understand how there can be construction vessels at all without our surveillance drones having reported them. They watch everything that happens.'

'There is no record of the vessels travelling from K74. They must be based on the spaceship itself. Yes, one is just now emerging from that anterior docking bay.'

Wirrin began to watch but lost all external vision when his retinal mode activated opaquely. It was Pirramar.

'Wirrin, keep your InfoSystem locked on the K74 vessel and initiate any search or scanning actions you think appropriate. We have a seven-minute window of opportunity to retrieve an analysis of those construction vessels. The Comet picofactory is following instructions I've transmitted and in another two minutes you will be able to direct a stealth diagnostic module to one of the small unknown vessels. Watch it carefully for any attempted disablement and use the programs now showing on your transfer screen to monitor and quarantine every databit the module records. Isolate the incoming information from any contact with Turaku and your security AI, as there is a low, but unacceptable, possibility it may contain some sort of rogue signature. Store it directly to your personal memory space and apply some of those special analysis techniques we've developed for AI traps. Don't distract Thom, and start to act now. I will contact you in three minutes.'

Wirrin sprang into action, and within thirty seconds had Pirramar's priorities locked into place, just before the module left the Comet. Its special signals had been so attuned for receipt by his InfoSystem that Turaku and the security AI wouldn't even be aware of them except with his permission.

'You look extra busy. Has something happened?'

'I'm watching that big K74 ship while we're close, Calen. It looks like they might be building something. See if you can track anything with the visuals.'

Calen returned to his screens. He wouldn't see anything. The module was almost certainly countering any visual surveillance.

Hmm, watch for attempts at disablement? Maybe adding an encryption barrier would help. Wirrin's InfoSystem charted the course of the module to the moment of contact.

Stabilisation! Infiltration! Analysis!

The terms were broadly informative but full understanding would come later.

Here it was. Two streams of information flooded in: the constant control instructions for the module itself, and the information being gathered from the target ship. Whoo! This was a lot of information. If it kept coming like this for the next five minutes it would be the biggest dump ever to his memory implant.

Calen had turned towards him. Trust him to sense something.

Wirrin put a finger to his lips as a caution against further comment and saw understanding blossom.

Calen would be searching the visuals for all he was worth now, trying to figure out what was going on.

'Well done, Wirrin. Turaku informs me you appear to have everything under control. Continue full monitoring till the module ceases transmission and after that, if Thom can maintain his stealth, you will have approximately thirty-five minutes of analysis time before we need the InfoSystem again. I've placed a log of our current plans in your transfer screen.'

Pirramar disappeared and Wirrin gave his full attention to the monitoring till the signals suddenly stopped. What now? Check the transfer screen or start on the analysis? He decided on a thirty-second scan of Pirramar's log in case there was something there he might need to take into account, and just as well. Thom needed to know about the change to his schedule. Looking across he caught Thom's eye, pointed at the range meter, and gave a thumbs up.

'Fifty kilometres! Nearly there! How's it going?'

'The simulators got it wrong. It's harder, Wirrin. I thought I'd blown it a few minutes ago when a strange signal came at us, but it's gone now. Hang on while I look for it again.'

He fiddled a bit then looked back.

'The Kadaitcha man must have been out there. Did your InfoSystem notice anything?'

'A few glitches. Can you talk for a moment?'

Wirrin was amazed and totally impressed that Thom was somehow aware of the signal. They'd be talking that over with the AIs at great length.

'Talk? Sort of ... What glitches?'

'You haven't been using any AI assistance have you?'

'Of course not. That's the whole point of the exercise.'

'Good. I'm worried there might be some of those priority traps around, so don't link the AIs into any of the scanning devices.'

'Dingoes! We should have anticipated that. Hang on,' Thom said, inputting at high speed. 'Any other glitches?'

'Not really. The AIs didn't want to disturb you but they're hoping we can extend the stationary time for an extra fifteen minutes.'

'The Kadaitcha man again? That's going high risk, but if you need it we'll manage ... It's turned into something more than an exercise hasn't it?'

'Sort of.'

Thom gave his own thumbs up.

Wirrin turned his attention to analysis while the Comet crept closer and closer to the great asteroid. By the time they reached their target and were poised, stationary, he was nearly tearing his hair out. Moments before, he'd reported to Pirramar that so far he'd been unable to find any traps, but wasn't happy about freeing the data from quarantine, and now he had to leave his search tasks unsupervised and turn his attention to new ones.

For some reason Pirramar wanted the Comet scanners to take a close look, under InfoSystem control rather than AI control, at a number of the construction sites for the giant K74 spaceships.

Five out of the thirty were within reasonable range and Wirrin set to work. Normally this would be easy but, because Thom had primary control of his stealthing, the various systems could only be used in moments of availability.

The major task was to launch seven more stealth modules. Five of these were destined for the construction sites, and like the earlier ones, would disassemble themselves when they completed their transmissions. More complex and designed for the greater size of their targets, they would function for three times as long and transmit at a greater rate than Wirrin's implant could accept, and this in turn meant the picofactory had had to build a special secure data store linked to the InfoSystem but still isolated from the AIs.

The other two modules were even more complicated and would attach themselves to chosen locations on the exterior of K74, meld into the surrounding material with pico-level camouflage, and like super surveillance drones, transmit information continually to Attunga. Wirrin would look more closely at how they worked when he had a chance.

'Wirrin, I'm picking up strange signals, like the earlier one, being directed at us. If you know anything about them tell me, otherwise I'll have to move the Comet as an evasive measure.'

How did Thom do that? 'No, don't move. We need to stay here if we possibly can. They're ours, but you're not meant to be able to detect them.'

'Can you tell me what's going on? I've got a moment.'

'They're special probes we've sent to look closely at the construction sites. Pirramar arranged for me to send them.'

'Pirramar? Here?'

'He knows more and our AIs can't do anything direct.'

'Whoo! It *is* the Kadaitcha man. Okay I'd better get at it.'

This time he meant the rogue. Calen abandoned his visual scanning — he knew it was make-work — and came to stand behind Wirrin.

'Comet-Turaku is out of it? I'm glad Sonic didn't come with us then.'

Sonic had expressed an interest in joining the exercise but was over-ruled by Yajala and Turaku because, for his protection, such a close approach would require a full complement of Comet crew and the AIs constantly running security, and that would defeat the whole purpose of testing Thom's skill with the stealth equipment.

'He'll see it on replay.'

'I didn't see the probes on the visuals … sorry, I'm talking too much while you're busy.'

Wirrin flashed a smile and soundlessly beckoned him close. Yes, he might be too busy to talk much, but Calen's steadfast and supportive presence was welcome at any time.

Data from the five locations poured into the quarantine area, and to start checking, Wirrin called up all the previously known informa-tion, copied and stored it to the quarantine area, then started a basic comparison test before turning his attention to where the first of the two permanent probes was about to make contact. All the indications were good so he called up an enlarged visual.

'Watch this, Calen. It's where the probe's attaching itself.'

A bleak area of the K74 surface appeared, and for a while a soft red glow blurred the clear outline of the rock before fading to nothing.

'There's nothing there.'

'It's totally camouflaged. That red glow was the picobot construct — I'll explain it all later.'

That would be after Wirrin understood it better himself. Calen stared wonderingly at the almost featureless area of rock, which was apparently now a surveillance probe in disguise.

For the next half hour everything went smoothly, Wirrin working with his InfoSystem and Thom assiduously checking and finetuning his stealth systems. Then Calen gave a call.

'Thom, one of the visual signals just went off and there's something coming round that far end of K74.'

'I'm tracking it. It's another Cadre ship, which was stationed on the other side of K74 when we first arrived. It's still turning and I don't like its trajectory. Wirrin, those probes couldn't have set off some kind of alert could they?'

Wirrin shook his head, then started to wonder himself. His InfoSystem showed a projection of the trajectory taking the ship right past the five bases.

Wombats! It could even come close to the Comet.

The turning stopped and the course steadied … it would come close. Within 2 kilometres.

'Thom, they're heading straight for us.'

'No they're not. They'll pass at 1.8 kilometres if they keep this course.'

'Won't they see us?'

'If someone's looking directly at us with visuals they might, but we'll chance it because if I start to move the Comet they definitely will.'

Wirrin had an awful thought. What if the course changed by even a fraction?

'Could we collide?'

'Never. I've got just over two minutes of decision time before it gets here and I can either move the Comet, or our security AI can take over their controls and divert them. Watch.'

That was a definite command to let him concentrate without interruption, so with a dusting of apprehension Wirrin and Calen did just that. The big ship came closer and closer while thoughts of 120 metres of steel and AIs in charge flooded through Wirrin's mind. Blithely and obviously unknowingly, 700 metres of offense went gliding past, serenely continuing till a few minutes later it rounded the other end of K74 and disappeared.

'What a mob of clueless emu brains!'

The forceful comment relieved Thom's tension and did the same for Wirrin and Calen. The trio exchanged relieved smiles.

'I don't know how you did it, Thom. I kept expecting them to do something.'

'It's not finished yet, Calen. We still have to get out of here.'

After the last five minutes Wirrin and Calen had no doubts at all that Thom would manage that successfully.

*　*　*

'There's some strange data coding which probably came from the rogue, but no AI trap. I divided the information into increasingly smaller components till there couldn't possibly be any.'

'And is the strange coding significant in itself, Wirrin?'

'Not really. It's an unusual approach to hiding what the rest of the information is about. It's an old encryption method the rogue dabbled with in his early studies.'

The Comet was almost home and Akama was checking on the results.

The trio had been surprised and delighted when his holo appeared and Wirrin was describing the escapade.

'So there was no real danger to the AIs? Do you think they overreacted?'

Wirrin was shocked. 'Not at all. Thom had it right when he said we should have been looking for traps right from the start.'

Akama turned to Thom. 'Turaku tells me you completed your exercise way beyond the expected parameters.'

Thom reacted quietly to Akama's implicit praise, but underneath, Wirrin knew, he was glowing. So he should be.

'Training with the simulators got me through.'

'Maybe, but I also know that some of your actions went beyond the scope of the training system and without them the Comet would have been seen.'

Akama turned to Wirrin. 'You do look fit and alert. I nearly asked Gulara to reduce your workload a few weeks ago but I was assured you were acclimatising well.'

'You can thank Thom for that too. He's developed a protein structure that helps me.'

'Yes, so I understand. More of his talents showing through, though I wonder why your doctor didn't provide it from the outset.'

'It did come from the doctor. He showed Thom a few things he needed to know and made him change his model four times before—'

Wirrin abruptly cut off his defence. Akama already knew all this and for some reason was assessing his loyalty to the doctor.

'Whatever you want him for, he's probably too busy, and Sonic's pleased with everything he's doing.'

Calen and Thom looked puzzled at this interchange. Akama gave an approving nod.

'An honorary position as the human representative for dolphin health when we formally welcome Freedom. Thank you. It won't take much of his time. And apparently it's going to be another memorable occasion. I look forward to meeting you all there.'

He made a very Akama gesture of friendship as his holo shimmered to nothing.

'What was all that? Were you reading each other's minds or something?'

'He's too tricky, Thom. I think I just gave the doctor another job. But why did he look at you like that when he said memorable occasion, Calen?'

'Ah, Sonic's going to be there.'

Thom burst out laughing.

'It's another surprise and you've been keeping it secret from us again? You witchetty grub!'

'No I haven't. I just didn't say anything. It's a bit like Meeting Day and Sonic likes giving surprises.'

Freedom's arrival in three weeks' time just became even more interesting.

Chapter 25

Wirrin gazed at their big display wall and smiled at the sight of the dolphin pod cruising by. No, two pods. A quick zoom showed they weren't Puck's.

Because their living space was so close to the dolphinarium, which was the centre for all dolphin and marine activities on Warrakan, there were almost always pods to be seen, visiting for various reasons. Currently there were more than usual because of whatever it was Sonic was organising. Calen was out there somewhere with him. It was tempting to use the InfoSystem for a sneak preview. He wouldn't, since Calen had asked him not to, but it would be so easy.

Having access to the resources of two habitats meant anything he wanted to see was at his fingertips. Wirrin smiled as he activated his system half an hour before Pirramar was due. Calen said he was addicted. It certainly was fascinating.

What was Thom doing? He could call up that information almost instantaneously because he had triggers set for all significant people and situations. The image of Thom appeared and Wirrin watched long enough to work out that he was controlling a second Comet remotely. Better not interrupt him with a holo.

Wirrin thought of Peggy, the dolphin under Martin's care, and brought her into view. That took slightly longer as he hadn't given her a trigger and needed a link to the system of underwater monitors now installed in every reach. She was racing across a seagrass bed in pursuit of a small school of fish. Wow! She looked full of energy after her liver treatment, which reminded Wirrin of the doctor, who was high on the trigger list. He'd be busy as usual. Yes, there he was, talking with seven people in some kind of meeting.

Hmm! Three researchers and four doctors from the different anti-agathic centres on Attunga, discussing the capabilities of some diagnostic equipment they'd ordered as part of the first stage of the new facility. The planning assistants had certainly built that in a hurry.

So much building happening, both here and Attunga.

Attunga! What about the new level there? Wow, water was being introduced to the honeycombed section of reaches in the innermost part of the level. Was it just for storage or would there be functioning reaches in another five months? Eight months? Why so long? ... Oh! No need for forced development. Only five reaches to be finished? That wasn't many. Well, compared to the current ones any single reach would be big enough for the four pods currently planning to transfer back from Warrakan. Aha! Sixty-eight reaches coming online for the second stage in a further eight months, and then the whole level ready two years after that. Attunga was actually approaching development in a markedly different way by adding a complete level of 280 sectors rather than a single sector at a time.

What about the shell? That was a huge task with its crumple factors and multiple layers, though still not as complex. Almost idly, Wirrin called up a holo image showing progress on the shell. Things were moving fast and would be completed in another year at the current rate. That meant a vast amount of mass would have to be converted to the special building material similar to the Comet's hull and internal support girders.

A quick query showed 738 asteroids of various types parked in areas away from the busy ferry traffic between the habitats, and another 367 moving towards Attunga in the long journey from their sparsely spread locations in the asteroid belt.

Wirrin started checking on the progress of the Attunga drive engines and was watching one of them drifting in space near the installation area when Pirramar appeared.

'Hello, Wirrin. Browsing the drive project? It's reached 0.52G capability, and that will be the third engine to come online since the Council diverted four to Freedom.'

'That means six more still to install.'

'Yes, another four months to completion.'

'What are we doing today? Is anything happening with K74?'

'A number of special concerns, as well as the usual ones. The Freedom AIs have let us know they're worried about the elevated level of scrutiny they're receiving from three of the Cadre ships.'

'The Cadre ships are with them while they're travelling?'

'For a number of hours now, yes, and a fourth is moving on an intercept course as well.'

'Four of them concentrating on Freedom at once? That doesn't feel good at all.'

'I agree. We'd like to know their motive because even though we've been helping Freedom to rapidly update their security they're still relatively vulnerable. Thom will be taking two of the Comets as escorts while they complete their move.'

'Thom? Does he know? He was doing normal training work a quarter of an hour ago.'

'He's just found out and will be on his way in a very short time.'

Thom would love the chance of some real action. Wirrin smiled but then had second thoughts.

'Escorts? That's new for Thom. Does that mean you're expecting the Cadre ships to do something?'

'They already have, with very aggressive attempts to penetrate Freedom's electronic security. The Comet will put an end to that, and more importantly may be able to discover any instructions from K74. There is also a possibility, quite low, of physical intimidation.'

Many thoughts raced through Wirrin's mind. K74 would be crazy to start anything after the previous reactions, but of course that hadn't stopped them then.

'Intimidate a whole habitat? Why? That would be a step beyond anything they've done before.'

'Very much so, but we know they look on Freedom as the only way of accessing some of the knowledge and technologies they're seeking, and with the habitat only days away from our protection this would be their last and only chance to gain that access. It's a step the Cadre might consider taking.'

'The Comets definitely should be there.'

'Yes, and they won't take long. They'll quickly defuse the situation.'

Wirrin thought of Thom eagerly blasting the Comet at its maximum acceleration. No. He couldn't. The other Comet would hold him back. Maybe he'd rush ahead anyway?

'There has also been another change of embassy staff and we'll have a look at the background of the new appointees before we recheck the diagnostic module data. We'll also have a look at a location on K74 that is apparently going to be a new blocked area and then I'd like you to do an analysis of all new constructions throughout the habitat as well.'

Pirramar paused, as if calculating what else to add to the day's efforts and Wirrin almost laughed. They'd never get through all that. Not if they were going to do it properly.

'Have they really changed their embassy staff again? They never stop.'

'This is the biggest change yet and some of the new people need a close look.'

That piqued Wirrin's interest. It sounded as if Pirramar already knew something and wanted to find out more.

'Well, we haven't been blocked from their administration systems yet so let's start there. I think we should—'

Wirrin stopped abruptly because Pirramar was holding a hand up as if he needed his attention elsewhere.

'Move quickly to your TransCom portal. Communication with Freedom has just been cut off and we'd like you on the Comet for input with the InfoSystem.'

Wirrin disengaged from his home system then, seeing the urgency in Pirramar's expression, started running. The portal was only seconds away, as it had been installed especially for people coming to see Sonic or other dolphins in the guest area, and when the door closed Wirrin was surprised to see Pirramar still with him. Oh, he was now working through his personal equipment.

'TRANSCOM PRIORITY ONE!'

Wirrin gawked at the flashing red speed indicator. How fast were they going?

'TransCom is giving you emergency access to the closest available facility for transfer to the Comet. All our efforts to communicate with Freedom in the last twenty seconds have been blocked and it is now imperative to get the Comet there as soon as possible. Thom is waiting and ready to leave the moment you arrive.'

Wirrin rushed through the docking tube and into the Comet in just over three minutes, a trip which usually took between twenty and thirty minutes, and by the time he reached the control centre, Warrakan, if he'd taken the time to look, was a speck in space behind them. After a quick wave to Thom that received a preoccupied nod in response, Wirrin dived for his InfoSystem and linked in. He'd learn more and faster that way. Comet-Turaku appeared and an analysis window opened on the display.

'This is all we can detect. It's a powerful localised jamming signal, which is completely blocking any transmissions into or out of Freedom.

We need to be close to penetrate, and that won't happen for another four hours.'

Four hours was very different to the five days Freedom would take to cover the same distance. Thom must have the Comet stretched to its maximum acceleration — 21.6G.

What? That was beyond the maximum.

'What can we do, Turaku?'

'At this stage nothing, Wirrin, except gather information. We have contacted other vessels in the vicinity but there are very few while Freedom is in transit. Three have approached at our request but have been smothered by the jamming fog before getting close enough to scan anything.'

'Did we know the Cadre ships could block transmissions like that?'

'Yes, it's a straightforward process and standard equipment for aggressive vessels. Applying it to a habitat is unprecedented.'

The next three and a half hours was pure frustration for Wirrin as all he could do was keep a watch while nothing changed. The jamming signal had been closely examined and it would be penetrated in another quarter hour purely and simply by proximity and stronger equipment on the Comet.

Thom similarly had little to do except monitor the Comet's performance and they talked about possibilities without having any supporting information.

Akama made contact briefly, with information passing at light speed between the Comet and the habitats.

Wirrin wondered if the jamming would have any effect on the Comet but quickly discovered that their picofactory had built and installed counter devices. Why hadn't Freedom done the same? They had the knowledge.

'Thom, we'll break through that jamming in five minutes. I want you to lock on to Freedom and check its navigation fundamentals. The overall jamming area is showing a deviation from the habitat's planned course.'

That was either very good or very bad. If the jamming area was diverging from Freedom, it could mean the Cadre ships were leaving. If not, the habitat itself was changing course and that implied some sort of control by the Cadre ships. Thom nodded his understanding, but Turaku hadn't finished.

'Approach recommendations have come through from Pirramar as well, and he advises full implementation of stealth mode while we make an assessment of the situation. He also warns there is a significant likelihood of interference to AIs and suggests all actions should be initiated with a degree of isolation through the InfoSystem.'

'We let the jamming continue?'

'Yes, Thom. Providing it doesn't interfere with your stealth procedures. Unless we have no other choice it's important we understand exactly what's happening before we act.'

Wirrin went into overdrive, as his InfoSystem was now the controlling focus for any actions Turaku or the security AI wanted to take. He knew what he was doing though. He'd been through this a number of times already, first on Thom's stealth exercise, and several times since with Pirramar to build his readiness.

'Full stealth mode activated.'

Thom's voice, clear and determined, sounded through the control centre and Wirrin launched his own stealthed signal. In this first stage it should allow the Comet's scanners penetration, and then, with decreasing distance, a breakthrough to communication with Freedom. Yes, the large mass of Freedom was now registering and, not quite so clearly, the lesser masses of the four Cadre ships.

'Freedom shows a definite course variation.'

Thom was relaying the information Turaku asked for but Wirrin was paying far more attention to the four Cadre ships, now clearly resolved. What were they doing? All gathered near the habitat drive engines?

'Freedom's acceleration level is .06G. Precisely one quarter of capability. Three engines may be off-line.'

Wirrin heard Thom's call, briefly thought that it tied in with the positions of the Cadre ships, then fixed on his own information, which was producing greater detail with every passing moment.

'Turaku, I think they're dismantling one of the engines.'

Turaku could see for himself and would be reviewing every bit of data at AI speed, but Wirrin couldn't help making his call.

'Not dismantling, Wirrin, but they do appear to be making a rapid analysis. Three engines are not functioning and the remaining one is turning Freedom in the direction of K74. Contact with Freedom is imminent and soon after we will be close enough to take control of all K74 electronics.

'Thom, maintain stealth at all costs.

'Wirrin, you have the communication codes for Freedom AIs. Initiate contact on my mark but keep all incoming data in quarantine.'

According to the InfoSystem, contact was already available. Why was Turaku waiting? Oh, he'd just tested the strength of the quarantine system. He must be worried about rogue traps.

'Wirrin, three ... two ... one ... mark.'

Wirrin transmitted the codes and watched for the response, which should arrive within seconds. Yes, there it was.

Busy!

Busy!

Busy! ... Oh no!

'Turaku, they're in a priority trap. I'm linked but they're not responding.'

'Are you linked well enough to apply any analysis?'

'Yes, I've already started. Can we contact the people instead?'

There was a momentary hesitation from Turaku.

'Not possible. All communication was integrated with AI processors after the first Freedom hack. I have relayed the details of this mistake on our part to Pirramar so we can allow for independent procedures on Attunga and Warrakan in the event of a similar emergency.'

Wombats! AIs making a mistake? That was a first for Wirrin.

A bank of tell-tales turned green. The Comet was now close enough to take control of any or all of the Cadre ships.

'Turaku, we now have one hundred per cent scanner access but I'm going to look at those ships before we take control. Thom, how close can we move without losing our stealth?'

'With four ships I can manage at 10 kilometres, and that will be in another ... six and a half minutes.'

Wirrin was expecting 15 kilometres. Thom had learnt from the stealth exercise.

'Hold at 12 kilometres please. I'm placing a priority one on the gathering of information before we take any action.'

Thom's eyes jerked momentarily from his controls.

'The Kadaitcha man?'

It was Wirrin's turn to give a terse nod. He had so much to do.

First he set his InfoSystem to scanning the Cadre ships in the finest possible detail, physical structure, management systems, electronics, full radiation spectrum, everything. Next he examined the area around the drive engines and relayed the resulting information to Turaku and the security AI who would gather meaning from it much faster than he could. His focus shifted momentarily to a blue success signal flashing from the program watching the Freedom communications, then abruptly back to a red warning about the Cadre ships.

Structural anomalies? What did that mean?

A closer look at one showed an unaccounted volume of space close to the vessel's control centre.

A blocked area? This was suspiciously similar to the dead areas on K74. Rogue work. Wirrin almost smiled. When they reached the 12 kilometre point he'd soon penetrate that. What was its purpose though, so close to the control centre and clearly meant to be secret?

'Freedom is almost on course to K74. Another half hour of the current engine thrust will align it exactly.'

Thom's call startled Wirrin. They were taking Freedom to K74? While information poured in Wirrin checked another blue success signal.

The method of trapping the Freedom AIs had been identified and an inoculation program could be sent to release them at any time. That couldn't be right? It was too simple a version, not much advanced on the ones used at Monkey Mia against the Australian AIs.

'Turaku, the Freedom AIs wouldn't have been cut off so completely with this type of trap. They shouldn't even have been caught by it. There's something wrong.'

'I concur. Maintain priority one and concentrate on the anomalies. The probability of danger to the Comet has just increased from insignificant to medium level, and on Pirramar's advice we have brought our multi-spectrum energy defences to the ready state. Early visual scanning shows devices of some type installed against all four drive engines.'

Wirrin wanted to check all that, but his priority now was the blocked areas and what they meant. Another two minutes and they'd be stationary and the Comet's advanced radar, infra-red, x-ray and resonance scans would come into play.

Another blue signal from the AI communications task? What had it found this time?

Very quickly Wirrin checked. No wonder Freedom's AIs were locked.

This was a second trap, far more sophisticated than the obvious first one, and capable of affecting even the Comet's AIs.

Not now though; he had its measure and would be able to assemble a cure and counter for its effects.

'Distance to Freedom 12 kilometres. Relative velocity is zero and I can maintain one hundred per cent stealth indefinitely. Multi-spectrum beams are operational but not targeted.'

Wirrin called up a holographic representation of the blocked area on the nearest Cadre ship and watched as blurry shapes and outlines steadily resolved into the form and detail of a single room with three people sitting at consoles.

'Is there enough information to work out what they're doing, Turaku?' Wirrin asked.

'Tracing the wiring and electronics ... two people monitoring everything taking place in the main Cadre ship's command centre. The third person has a console that is connected to a powerful transmission device of some kind. We need direct access to understand its purpose but there is no way past that firewall even if we do control the rest of the ship.'

Transmission device? Wirrin's thoughts went into a spin. Adrenaline flooded his system as he added factor after factor to the idea screaming in his mind.

It all fitted together.

'PRIORITY ONE! PRIORITY ONE!

'Turaku. Isolate every AI function from access to our scanning systems and put yourself behind the strongest quarantine you can build. The same for the security AI. On no account accept any external signal unless it's okayed through my InfoSystem. Cut all contact with Warrakan and Attunga.'

'Priority One actions completed.'

Wirrin's momentary sense of relief dissipated. There was still too much to do. 'Turaku, I need to apply Pirramar's health program to make sure you haven't been compromised in any way by a rogue trap. This whole event is nothing to do with Freedom. It's an attempt to capture the Comet.'

Thom swore.

'Thom, this is also priority one for you. Those four Cadre ships are waiting for us and must be scanning with everything they have available. If I understand this correctly they have traps waiting for our AIs when they link into the Cadre systems, so we mustn't be detected.'

'We could blow them away with our multi-spectrum beams.'

'No we couldn't. They've got Freedom as a hostage with those radiation devices.'

'I know. I know. I just feel like it. They won't detect us while we're stationary and you're right about them looking for us. There are sixteen surveillance drones out there, mostly concentrated along the direct approach from Warrakan, but they're no problem … What are we going to do?'

That was the big question and Wirrin was working on it. Somehow he had to get at the information in the blockout area, analyse it, and build a protection program without any help from the AIs. Until that was done there was no way to help Freedom without putting the Comet at risk.

'Thom, if we have to, can you use the multi-spectrum beams to get rid of the radiation devices?'

After a pause Thom replied, 'I can, but not against four locations at the same time. There would be a time lapse while I re-targeted, but I also don't have the fine control the AIs use and there would be damage to the engine housings. There are people there as well and they would be vaporised. It would also instantly give away our position, and without our security AI we can't defend ourselves properly against four aggressive Cadre ships.'

Wirrin felt like screaming. They couldn't neutralise the radiation devices without making the Comet vulnerable. He needed the AIs to get access to the blocked area but if they tried that the AIs might succumb to some new trap of the rogue's devising.

Think! Think! Think! How to get into that blocked area without AI help, without tripping alarms, without being seen by the people there, find the necessary information and return it safely to the Comet? It would need an incredible superspy. What a pity Thom couldn't apply his stealth skills to a person.

Invisible superspy? They had one. Maybe. Just maybe.

'Turaku. A stealth diagnostic drone can approach a Cadre ship without being detected. Could you give one the ability to gain entry as well and move about unseen?'

'With the purpose of retrieving data from the blocked area I presume.

Not with the current model, but with major design modifications it might be possible. Yes, a preliminary design gives a success probability of fifteen per cent and with time this will improve markedly.'

'How much time, Turaku?'

Thom matched a ferocious grin with a thumbs up sign.

'Seventeen per cent — approximately seventeen minutes, but then improvement will slow exponentially ... twenty-one per cent.'

Time passed as they watched Turaku's steadily rising probability count and discussed possible actions till Thom suddenly yelled, 'Turaku, can we build space versions of the guardian drones we used at Shark Bay? They could protect us from a missile attack.'

'We considered that, Thom, but to counter the combined aggressive resources of four Cadre ships we'd need several thousand guardians, and given our optimum construction rate of seventy-nine seconds per unit we discarded the idea as impractical.'

'Could we build enough to disable the Cadre engines?'

'Of course, but that would disclose our presence.'

'Not if we make them appear to come from Freedom.'

'No good, Thom. That would make them retaliate against Freedom.'

'I can't believe this. We're better at everything than they are, but we can't do a thing, and what happens if you can't work out a way to protect all the AIs? We can't just sit here and watch while they do whatever they want.'

'We'll think of something.'

In fact Wirrin was confident he'd be able to counter any rogue traps. He'd had months of study and simulation with Pirramar, practising to do just that, and all the analysis programs they'd developed were stored and ready in his InfoSystem. The two antidotes for the Freedom AIs had only taken moments to prepare once he'd received the analysis results.

'Stealth module design criteria achieved and construction commenced. Completion in nine minutes and forty-eight seconds.'

Wirrin and Thom exchanged excited looks. The criteria they'd agreed with Turaku was a high success probability of eighty-five per cent. Anything better would involve a much longer wait with relatively small improvement. Over nine minutes construction time? It must be complicated if a sophisticated guardian drone only took seventy-nine seconds.

'When is the other Comet due to arrive?'

'Not for another hour and a half, but that's most likely changed since we cut off communication. I think they'll send at least one extra, too, but that would be hours and hours away.'

'Transport modules completed. Penetration modules begun.'

'Two types of modules, Turaku?'

'Three, Thom. A larger transport module with full stealth and pico-level camouflage to meld with the outer hull, a high-energy penetration type to force access through the hull and connect with a service conduit, and finally, an information retrieval module with a chameleon function to allow unnoticed operation in the blocked area.'

Wirrin appreciated this clever design then felt his heart thump when Thom suddenly exclaimed, 'One of the Cadre drones has just accelerated in the direction of K74 and will leave the jamming area in approximately three minutes.'

'Don't frighten me like that. I thought you were going to say they'd broken stealth.'

'Wirrin, if they break our stealth every alarm in the control centre will go off and maximum acceleration will kick in automatically. You won't hear a word from me because I'll be too busy.'

'Retrieval modules begun. Completion in 137 seconds. Event launch will be under the control of your InfoSystem.'

Wirrin was ready. 'Thom, how long before that drone can transmit to K74? I think it's going to relay information they've discovered about the drive engines.'

'It's almost out of the jamming area now. I don't think there's anything we can do about it.'

'Send a guardian drone after it. We now have them in the construction queue when the modules are finished.'

Wirrin pushed thoughts about the drone to the back of his mind. It was launch time. The four hybrid modules left the Comet and rather disconcertingly disappeared from view.

'Do you know where they are?'

'Not really, Thom. The special signals they send must be cancelled by the jamming field. All we can do is wait for their return. How long do you expect that will be, Turaku?'

'With optimal performance forty-two to forty-five minutes, with adverse conditions up to seventy minutes, and anything beyond that will almost certainly mean failure. The first guardian drone is now ready for instructions.'

'Tell it to chase that Cadre drone and destroy it as quickly as possible.'

'Done. Launch is under your control.'

For a second time Wirrin initiated a launch and had all traces disappear from his InfoSystem. Well, those guardians were incredibly capable and he was sure it would do its job.

There were continual situation checks while they waited for the all-important return of the hybrid modules. At Thom's request the pico-factory kept churning out guardians, as he wanted one for each of the fifteen Cadre drones and then as many as possible for the Cadre ships themselves in case he needed to take drastic action. He was as ready as Wirrin. The whole time they'd been under stealth he'd been going over different strategies — with help from the AIs — to employ if the Comet should be detected, and now, only a few minutes from Turaku's optimal projection time for the stealth modules' return and with twenty-six guardians ready, his tactics were increasingly aggressive. Fifteen guardians would destroy fifteen Cadre drones and the remaining guardians would attempt to disable the drive engines on the Cadre ships while the Comet itself would fly like a bolt of lightning in an effort to evade a possible onslaught from thousands upon thousands of deadly missiles.

'What do you think? Sooner? Or later? And have you thought of something else if this doesn't work?'

Wirrin had three alternative plans in fact, but was increasingly confident they wouldn't be needed. Continual monitoring of the people in the blocked area showed no unusual movement or actions and, according to Turaku, the retrieval module would have reached that room at least twenty minutes ago.

'The AIs factor in every eventuality when they work out things like this, Thom, so I reckon it will be sooner. I'm expecting the first module within the next five minutes.'

As if on cue, a green docking light flashed and all conjecture was forgotten as the first retrieval module linked directly and started dumping data to the quarantine area in the InfoSystem.

Wirrin bypassed all the travel and penetration records and rushed to find the signal stored in the transmission device. His prepared analysis programs quickly identified different blocks of code. A backup set of instructions for running the Cadre ship? Interesting but it could wait.

An automatic controlling procedure for all the ship's armaments? Trouble, but fix it later.

Communication control? Not now.

Plan Alpha? Weird name ... Yes!

With almost the full resources of the InfoSystem focusing Wirrin's barrage of tests, the signal started to reveal its secrets.

The docking lights flashed green three more times with the return of a stealth module from each of the other three Cadre ships and three more sets of retrieval data were dumped to the quarantine location. Wirrin applied his analysis tasks and watched with a mixture of shock and satisfaction as the results came in.

AI trap!

AI trap!

AI trap!

AI trap!

So many? It appeared as if the signal from each ship was a combination of two different traps.

No, a third trap had just registered as part of the transmission for the first ship. It looked like the rogue wanted to hit the Comet with a dozen different types of trap simultaneously.

A scan of the parameters put a smile on Wirrin's face as patterns he'd worked at with Pirramar clicked in his mind. Yes, he knew that one, and that one.

Seven would be no trouble at all, and four more had familiar-looking structures. Ten minutes later he exclaimed with annoyance.

'Am I allowed to talk to you?'

'What?'

'Am I allowed to talk to you, Wirrin?'

Wirrin gave a little shake to refocus his mind on Thom.

'What?'

'That's better. I wasn't game to ask in case I broke your concentration but then you made your grumble-grunt.'

'I've worked out counters for every trap except one, which analysis says could force AI processors to one hundred per cent usage ... But I can't see how. Is anything happening?'

'There's endless movement near the engine we thought they were dismantling, and a transport ferry went into one of the Freedom docking bays.'

Wirrin didn't hear the end of Thom's reply because an idea teased at the edge of his mind.

Endless?

Yes, endless.

Endless loops!

How strange! And the only thing needed would be a suitable recognition program.

Loop recognition programs appeared on command and Wirrin cobbled several together and tested them. Not good enough, but on the right track.

Set a task to do this at computer speed. Thirty-seven seconds and 794 attempts later the antidote for AI trap number twelve was ready.

'PRIORITY ONE! PRIORITY ONE!'

Whoa! In his excitement Wirrin had yelled and now Thom was staring at him in dismay.

'It's all good, Thom. We're ready for action. Turaku, priority one is to disable those blocked areas and then the radiation devices. Once that is done control is at your discretion. I'm releasing the antidote codes from quarantine … Now!'

Nothing happened. Well, not for approximately 3.4 seconds, whereupon the scan of the blocked area on the nearest ship abruptly changed to full optics and the sight of a shocked face staring at a blank console.

Two seconds later Turaku announced, 'Cadre ships are now under full control and the radiation devices locked in a neutral state. I suggest you release the code to help the Freedom AIs.'

Wombats! That should have been released with the other codes. Slightly embarrassed, Wirrin quickly fixed that and turned to Thom. 'I can't think of everything.'

'Yes, I know. It's terrible. We just won't mention that you saved the Comet, the AIs, and Freedom.'

Comet-Turaku's holo smiled.

'Full contact with Attunga and Warrakan is now re-established.

'The Witness Council have opened a direct conference link, and Akama is asking for you to report directly.

'The habitat AIs are all fully functional and the Freedom leaders are asking permission to speak with you.'

Chapter 26

Wirrin settled on the grav-sofa and stared at the amazing sight on the wall display.

'Gulara, where *is* that?'

'You don't recognise it? Well, I'm not surprised as it rarely looks like this. It's Gnardune Pool in the throes of a twenty-year flood, with the biggest water flow for a long time.'

The amazing sight, of a rushing orange-red torrent swirling past partially submerged trees, suddenly became even more amazing. The placid pool of clear, sparkling water of Wirrin's memory was replaced by this moving, angry, giant of a river, extending way into the distance.

'Is this near the willy-willy tree? The one we climbed I mean.'

Gulara made some adjustments and suddenly the new viewpoint was recognisable. Yes, there was the tree, that burl was distinctive, and at the moment it was above the level of the rushing water. The branch where he'd perched to watch the spoonbill wasn't.

'How's that?'

'We would have been washed away. Where does all that water come from?'

'It's Northern Australia. That's what happens when there's a big rain.'

Wirrin knew all that, but seeing it in a familiar place made it so real, and for a few minutes he watched in wonder.

Gulara was waiting though, and he could watch this at home with Thom, who would be particularly interested.

'Thanks for seeing me so quickly, Gulara. I didn't expect to come to your living space.'

'I've been to yours often enough, and since you were close by and asking, why not? Now, is this a real problem or something you just want to talk about?'

That made Wirrin smile.

'It's both. Akama has asked me to be a representative to Freedom and I don't want to say no to him, but I don't think I'm the right person.'

Gulara raised both eyebrows expressively. 'Why ever not? I think you'd be a wonderful ambassador, and you know you're capable, whatever situation you're in. You can't be worried it would be too hard?'

'No, but I do think I'm too young, and even more, I haven't got enough time or experience to do it properly. I can't divert time from my InfoSystem studies and the work about K74 with Pirramar because that's a lot more important and I'm just starting to get the feel of it.'

Gulara nodded, which surprised Wirrin, but also made him feel that his decision to talk this over with his mentor had been the right one.

'Yes, on the face of it I agree with you, but I can't see Akama asking this without having a special reason. Has he told you why?'

'Well, yes. It's because the Freedom leaders asked for me.'

'They did? Well, they must be very impressed with you mustn't they?'

'I know, but they act like I'm the one who did everything, and treat me as if I'm special.'

'That sounds quite reasonable to me, Wirrin. I know you saved them from the Cadre ships. Was there more to it than that?'

'A lot more. It wasn't really about Freedom. That was just part of a bigger scheme to capture the Comet and its technology. We found out that the two main things they were looking for were the beam defences and our advanced drive engines.'

'The Comet? How could they ever get anywhere near it?' Gulara was well acquainted with the Comet and its abilities.

'They nearly took it over and we wouldn't have been able to stop them. The rogue worked out an incredibly clever strategy.'

'That hasn't been on the InterWeb. Tell me what happened.'

Once again Wirrin went through the story he'd already related to the Witness Council, Akama in greater detail, Calen and Sonic at home, and even with Pirramar to a group of AIs representing the gestalt. Gulara listened with amazement till the dramatic few moments when the AIs were able to act freely.

'Wirrin, of course they're going to treat you as if you're special.'

'Almost all of the analysis work was Pirramar's. All I did was implement it. And if it wasn't for Thom I wouldn't have figured out the endless loop trap.'

'That doesn't detract from the special nature of your insight and actions.' She smiled. 'Tell me what's happening with the Cadre ships and the people on them. And has the Witness Council made any decisions about responses to K74?'

'The ships are being returned in about a week's time with skeleton crews. Freedom was going to keep them but we talked them out of that because it would further inflame the Cadre. Then, when that was decided, Freedom had a plan to send all the people back with modified memory so the Cadre couldn't find out exactly what happened. Sonic came up with the idea of offering them a place on Warrakan instead, and when I saw the leaders I persuaded them to try that.'

'You've already seen these leaders and got them to change their mind on something so major?'

'They were reluctant at first but they agreed when most of the K74 crew jumped at the offer, and then even more after we explained what it meant.'

'You talked to both the Freedom leaders and the K74 crew? Personally?'

'We had to. Apart from a few of the other Comet crew we were the only Warrakan people there. It was really interesting seeing the reactions of the K74 crew when we were explaining what it would be like. It changed Thom's mind. He'd been so angry, but when he saw how eager they were to get away from K74 he felt sorry for them.'

'What does most of the K74 crew mean?'

'Ninety-three per cent in the end, which is a lot because their standard ship's complement is over two thousand people.'

'Ninety-three per cent of four ships? Wirrin, that would be over seven thousand. That's amazing. It must have been quite a major exercise. No wonder the Freedom leaders were impressed. And responses?'

'Responses?'

'To K74.'

'Oh, that's major but most of it will come from elsewhere. We released a complete record of K74's actions to every habitat in the solar system and the AIs have their own channels of communication as well, and it's been greeted with total outrage. Coming after the death of the AI, K74's reputation has been destroyed, especially with space habitats.'

Gulara indicated he should continue.

'We have responded by making big changes to the Comet and our habitat defensive systems so they can function properly without relying on the AIs, if it ever came to that again.'

'So? No recriminations against K74 at all?'

'Nothing direct, apart from telling people what they did. The Witness Council respects the AIs' refusal to harm any humans. Akama said they've done the damage themselves by making every single habitat wary of them and further alienating the AI community.' Wirrin hesitated. 'The Freedom people did want to do more but we talked them out of that too.'

'We? You mean you and Thom again?'

'There were holo conferences with Akama and some others from our Witness Council but that was awkward with the time delay, so Akama and Sonic told us what to say when we had face-to-face meetings.'

Gulara laughed. 'In other words you acted successfully as direct Witness Council representatives. I've heard enough. Wirrin, you can't refuse this job.'

'But—'

'No buts. It's the right thing to do. You accept the position and do it on your own terms. You make it very clear that it can't undermine your other responsibilities. You agree to some busy days over the next few weeks but after that you're a figurehead with other people doing all the work.'

Gulara paused while she watched how Wirrin was taking the advice he'd asked for.

'I suppose I could do it like that. I don't want to disappoint Akama though, so I hope he doesn't mind the idea of my backing off after the first few weeks.'

'He won't, and in fact I'm sure he'll like it better if you do what you feel is right for yourself.'

*   *   *

'I'm taking you to Freedom tomorrow? We've only been home for a day and they get here in three more. So what's the deal? Haven't we done enough? I'm meant to be training up on the changes they've made to the Comet.'

'Don't ask me, Thom. Ask Akama. He's the one who wants us there. He's got some funny idea that the Comet with you in charge is a special gesture to the people on Freedom.'

Thom gawped. He'd been expecting to carry on about Wirrin's representation job. 'Me? They don't need me. There are two other Comets already there, as well as three of the Cadre ships.'

'They asked for you. You're a hero.'

'Idiot!'

Wirrin enjoyed turning the tables on Thom, who'd purposefully embarrassed him with an effusive description to Calen and Sonic of what a hero Wirrin had been with the Cadre ships.

'Turaku's designing a special Comet uniform so they don't mistake you for a scruff again. It's got so many medals it'll take you half an hour to pin them all on.'

'Idiot! It's really about your rep job.'

'That's part of it, Thom, but so is the Comet gesture.'

'Really?'

'Yes, but not the uniform. You're already a big enough hero without that.'

Wirrin expected to be called an idiot yet again, but Thom started planning instead. 'I can still train with the spectrum-beam system on the way there, and then I'll be able to get a proper look through the Cadre ships. Turaku was going to guide me on the one we brought here but now we'll have three instead. Hey, as soon as Calen gets in, let's organise for him to come with us.'

'He can't. He's too busy working with Sonic.'

'Wirrin, I don't see why not. We've only seen him one night and we're going again in the morning. Let's tell Sonic he's coming too, and they can go back to whatever they're doing when we get home. Anyway, having Sonic there would be an even bigger gesture if that's what Akama wants.'

Wirrin liked the idea. 'Good thinking. We'll persuade Sonic because if he wants to come no-one will stop him and Calen will automatically go with him. We can all be together then.'

Thom nodded then laughed. 'I'll tell Sonic I'll show him some new tricks about flying the Comet. That's sure to get him interested.'

Sonic did enjoy flying the Comet and often said he wanted to get better at it. Moving to Warrakan had much reduced the frequent commuting where he often, under Thom's watchful eye, took control.

'He'll probably be so interested you won't get a chance to do your spectrum-beam training.'

'If he does come I wouldn't get a chance anyway because we'd have the full crew that goes on any of his trips away from the habitats.'

That would mean at least fifty or sixty people, very different to the minimal crew of eight, including Wirrin and Thom, who'd been on the emergency trip four days ago.

'Only on the way there. That will be quick, but there'll be nearly three days of slow travel while you're doing the escorting on the way back so you'll get plenty of chances then.'

*   *   *

Thom had his chances to train and managed to do everything he wanted to, but he was so busy that the amount of time available could hardly be described as plenty.

Apart from a quick catch-up just before sleep time Wirrin didn't see him till the third and last day, as the job of being a representative was way more diverse than he'd expected and involved a whirlwind of activities and welcomes in all parts of Freedom.

Having Sonic and Calen with him most of the time was a bonus and with the astonished reactions to Sonic each new event was an adventure. Wirrin also liked them with him because it meant he wasn't the main focus of attention.

Everywhere they went it started off with embarrassing thanks for helping Freedom, then as soon as Sonic spoke from his transport module the atmosphere would become electric and all attention would be riveted on him. Calen was used to this but all his months of study with Pirramar and EdCom meant Wirrin had missed out on the regular visits Sonic liked to make to nurseries, EdCom groups and community events, and he was reminded afresh of Sonic's impact.

One feature, which of course couldn't be missed, was the new reach system on Freedom, and Sonic decided on the very first visit that this was his home base rather than the pool in the Comet's command centre. The whole set-up looked shockingly small after the size and diversity of the Warrakan reaches, but Wirrin was still impressed with the development and improvements since the four hundred Earth dolphins had been delivered.

Sonic excitedly raced to meet the pod in the original reach, and within half an hour the other eight reaches emptied as the message of his arrival spread. Soon 461 dolphins were milling in the familiar chaos of a meeting with Sonic — familiar for Wirrin that is. The dignitaries and even the Freedom rangers watched in amazement while they listened to Wirrin's explanation of what was going on.

The highlight for the Comet visitors happened on the final approach to Attunga during a special ceremony based on the Freedom cultural heritage. Wirrin had been looking forward to this. When he'd been informed they were to be part of an official 'Powhiri' ceremony performed in the old way, he'd done a scan to get a basic idea of what was involved and it all sounded very interesting.

How interesting he had no idea till, shocked and with his heart pounding, he was surrounded by several dozen giant men dressed in little more than vivid war paint and challenged with threatening gestures, horrid grimaces and frightening battle screams. He heard Thom gasp beside him as the sense of power and vitality conveyed from the massed, synchronised battle chant set his scalp tingling and his stomach churning.

A blast of sound from behind gave Wirrin such a shock he jumped and whirled, along with every other performer. There was a moment of stunned silence, then smiles at the sight of Calen in the transporter with his hands covering his ears, before the warriors redoubled their efforts, enthusiastically answering Sonic's challenge and continuing the ritual of the 'haka' till one of the performers placed something at Wirrin's feet with an expectant look.

A leaf? He picked it up. There was a huge yell and the savage faces were transformed with beaming smiles.

The ceremony continued with sonorous speeches and beautiful song. Not being able to understand a word of the language didn't matter one bit, because the intent came through clearly. A number of traditional gifts were given and then the performer who had proffered the leaf approached and took hold of Wirrin's shoulders.

Wombats! What now? It was obviously part of the ceremony so it must be all right.

Press noses? Startled and struggling to contain a smile, Wirrin returned the gesture then watched Thom take his turn. The rest of the group closed in to follow suit but then Sonic stole the show again when he asked to be included, and the image of him beak to nose with a fierce-looking haka warrior became an icon for the Freedom people watching through their InterWeb.

Several hours later the Comet zipped through the short trip to Warrakan, leaving the Freedom habitat to make its final, precisely controlled approach.

Chapter 27

Wirrin's representative job with Freedom kept him busy for longer than he'd planned, but not by too much, and other people did start doing a lot of the work, otherwise he wouldn't have coped.

With almost 300 million people, different processes, good conditions that were nevertheless not up to the standards of Attunga and Warrakan, and quite a large technology gap, Freedom was eager to benefit in every way they could, and Wirrin found himself involved in meetings with science delegations, health delegations and particularly with leaders interested in developing a Witness structure for their habitat.

Why they asked him, instead of real Witnesses who knew far more about the training and ideas involved, was beyond him, but ask they did. Luckily, once the various working groups were established they went ahead efficiently and happily without any need for his presence.

A great stream of advanced information and technology poured into Freedom. The AIs rapidly incorporated Attunga level pico-techniques into the picofactories to raise their construction capabilities.

AIs and medical technicians from all three habitats worked together assessing and upgrading every health centre on Freedom with better diagnostic and healthbot equipment.

The EdCom system on Freedom was run in a different way too and Wirrin used Witness Council authority to organise Attunga administrators into discussions with their Freedom counterparts.

Even their transportation infrastructure was way below the efficiency of TransCom. Luckily, that was overseen by an AI and only required a few meetings to get things happening.

Wirrin's biggest help through all this was Akama, who had discussions with him every day while also being involved in many of the meetings, especially with the highest level leaders. He was amazingly encouraging and before a meeting would often give advice about what to say to particular people in situations he seemed to know in advance were going to come up.

The people themselves were very friendly and appreciative, though more opinionated than Wirrin was used to. After a number of occasions where he'd had to put a clamp on his feelings of annoyance he'd talked it over with Akama, who as far as Wirrin could tell, seemed to be unaware of the pressure, and was told it was actually a very positive sign because it demonstrated their passion and intent, and that he was handling it very well.

* * *

Two weeks after Freedom arrived the giant meeting gallery at the main Warrakan dolphinarium became the venue for the official welcome, and in an enlarged version of the Meeting Day event, Wirrin sat with Akama, Thom, Gulara, the doctor and four Freedom leaders, looking out at the mingled crowd of people from the three habitats. On the other side of Akama was an AI whom Wirrin had never met and was rather in awe of because he represented the gestalt.

In the clear, brightly lit water behind the giant glass wall Puck's dolphin pod moved in a relaxed and changing formation, occasionally surfacing together for air.

Wirrin remembered the dawning awareness of dolphins at one of his representative meetings when the request to have this all happen at a special ceremonial place on Freedom had to be denied because the dolphins couldn't be there. Today, with virtually every member of the three habitats watching, that understanding would spread to the population of Freedom.

Akama spoke, the AI spoke, and then with a rush 437 enhanced dolphins filled the waters of the viewing chamber. They lined up, rank upon rank, close to the glass barrier, poised motionless looking steadily at the audience. A murmur ran through the room as people reacted.

Even for Wirrin, who knew these dolphins so well, it was uncanny to feel all those eyes watching.

The murmur died away and for a time the groups watched each other in complete silence.

Suddenly the wall of dolphins parted to reveal two figures. Wirrin's heart leapt as Sonic and Calen approached in a beautiful, synchronised sweep, Calen moving in that incredible fashion he'd mastered, effortlessly complementing Sonic's every twist and turn till they stopped and hovered almost motionless.

People of Freedom, the dolphins welcome you.

A beautiful sound burst from the translator speakers in the language Wirrin recognised from the Powhiri on Freedom. He didn't know what it meant but in the few short minutes it lasted the rapt expressions of the Freedom people showed they clearly did.

Was Sonic singing it rote? Or had he learned the language?

Sonic led the dolphins through a series of events, a kaleidoscope of sound and motion referenced mostly from Freedom's culture, evoking awe, joy and sometimes laughter.

This time Calen was integral to the whole performance and Wirrin, his heart brimming, watched his movements in disbelief. Indisputably bonded, boy and dolphin sent a clear message that humankind and dolphinkind were now linked.

The dolphins ended by forming the same grey wall behind the glass, watching the people for a moment then making the formal dolphin to human greeting. Wirrin joined with most of the audience to give the slow wave in return then watched the people from Freedom rush to join in.

A space cleared round Sonic and Calen, making them the centre of attention, and silent anticipation filled the hall. Wirrin felt a thrill of excitement. Sonic must be going to say something special. With stunning effect the amplified clicks, whistles and squeaks of dolphin speech cut through the hush in clear, steady tones.

Whoo! That wasn't Sonic, it was Calen, and when his short speech finished Sonic took over.

'People of Freedom, join me in repeating the words of my brother.'

Calen started again but this time Sonic's voice came through the translators as an overlay. It was the old language again which Wirrin didn't understand. But he didn't need to. After the first couple of phrases the Freedom leader next to Akama jumped to his feet and joined in, as did everyone from Freedom, in a great swell of sound.

When it finished Akama formally introduced Sonic to the Freedom habitat then turned to the doctor who, Wirrin could tell, was doing his best to hide his nervousness.

Wirrin had wondered why he was with them because, although the health program for the dolphins was important, it was hardly something to talk about on an occasion like this. The doctor thanked Akama, welcomed the Freedom people, then turned and gestured to Sonic.

'People of Freedom, Attunga and Warrakan, I have a gift. This song was given to my family but our Witness Council agrees it is too precious to keep and asked us to share it with you today.'

He gave a nod and the front of the auditorium filled with a holo screen showing Alisa, the doctor's daughter, hanging on to Sonic's tail fluke while the rest of the family splashed and played. The laughter and happiness was completely infectious and smiles filled the auditorium till the moment when Raji received the gentle chest nudge. When Sonic started singing Raji's song the three habitats listened and wondered.

*   *   *

'Is this your latest design, Thom?'

'Yes, do you reckon it looks good?'

'They all look good. What started you on this one? Is it for EdCom, or part of your Comet training?'

'Neither, I just felt like it.'

Ever since he was little Thom had been a spaceship enthusiast, talking about them, looking at pictures and theories from the old speculative fiction stories, drawing his own designs and representing them as 3D holos. During the last few years he'd become much more sophisticated and started building mockups, which even included the different engineering systems a particular model would need.

'What's special about this one? Has it got your faster than light drives in it?'

Thom laughed. 'Not this time, Wirrin. This one's real. I haven't been doing those for ages.'

'Real? How do you mean?'

'It would work if it was built because I've only used real-tech, like the stuff in the Comet.'

'It must be fast then?'

'It is, but not as fast as I want. I can't get big enough engines to suit its scale.'

'How big is it?' The holo image didn't have any sort of reference to indicate size.

'Thirty-eight metres.'

'That's nothing like the Comet. It's tiny,' said Wirrin.

'That's the whole point of this design. I'm trying to make it as small as I can and still have it able to do everything.'

Now it was Calen laughing. Wirrin was grinning too.

'You want small? You must be feeling sick.'

'Funny! Funny! Funny! Everything doesn't have to be big and fast, Calen. For your information it's a much harder challenge to design something small and fast.'

'Well it looks impressive but how fast is it?'

'I can get it up to 15G. That seems to be the max for this size.'

'Wombats! I call that fast. It would feed space dust into a Cadre ship's mouth.'

Thom shook his head incredulously.

'Calen, you say make it eat space dust, not feed it into its mouth.'

'Who cares? It's not like I'm calling Sonic a lump of fish in front of a billion people.'

Thom grimaced. He'd been copping it from Sonic ever since.

'How was I expected to know they were going to show our home stuff on the InterWeb? The doctor's going to get dumped in the pool next time he comes here.'

'So, how long would it take to build?'

Thom shook his head with feigned disgust and turned to Wirrin. 'Do you think he's being deliberately obtuse?'

Two sets of dropped jaws made him laugh.

'That worked well. Sonic used it on me the other day and I've been wanting to pass it on. Calen, I couldn't get it built. You know that. I'd need help from the AIs for a special design like this and I haven't worked out the environmental system and a few other things either. And anyway it would take fifty years to get enough energy allowance. I'm just—' Thom broke off as Turaku's holo shimmered next to him.

'The AI community is keen to help you with your project in any way, and energy allocation is not an issue. I will discuss this further with you as part of your Comet training tomorrow.'

The air shimmered again and Wirrin and Calen both laughed at Thom's stunned expression.

'*Help* me? What does that mean? With the environment system?'

'It means exactly what you think it means. They're happy to build your spaceship.'

'But they can't. No-one has their own spaceship.'

'Yes they do. Sonic's got the Comet.'

'That's different, Wirrin. He needs it. No-one gets their own spaceship. Not even Witnesses.'

'Well you will, else why would he say the energy allocation didn't matter?'

'Dingoes! That's right. But why? AIs don't do things like that.'

'They just did, and it's not just Turaku. He said it was the whole AI community.'

'Dingoes! He did too. That's even weirder. I wonder how long it will take? But they can't. I haven't worked it out properly yet.' Thom dragged his fingers through his hair. 'Why are they doing it? I'll have to work on the environmental system tonight. It's part of my Comet training, that's what Turaku said … Dingoes!'

'Have you got dingoes on your brain? It's recognition because you helped save Freedom and its AIs.'

'That was Wirrin, not me. I just did whatever he told me.'

They'd repeated this conversation over and over since the Freedom hijack and Wirrin wasn't going to take it up again.

'Calen's right. Ask Turaku when you talk to him tomorrow. What's the problem with the environment system?'

It took a while to work out because Thom was too excited to concentrate, but with help from the InfoSystem the problem soon disappeared.

*　*　*

'What's been happening with that new blanked area on K74? Have we found out anything?'

Wirrin was taking a break after a hard InfoSystem session with Pirramar.

'Not a great deal. The rogue makes regular visits, its protections have become stronger, and it's no longer expanding. My best inference from the materials and personnel being transferred there is that it's some kind of research area.'

'The rogue visits there?'

'Yes, regularly but not frequently.'

'Has he been to inspect any more of the ship construction sites?'

'Not a one. They *have* had more resources directed to them since his first visit though, and the finish times will be cut by approximately eleven per cent if they maintain this new production rate.'

Wirrin worked it out. Eleven per cent still meant almost a year before the first of them was completed. Why they wanted so many was still a mystery.

The plans they'd accessed at the construction sites didn't show much variation in design from the existing five ships so there were no clues there, and Thom's theory that the Cadre wanted to think of themselves as the most powerful space habitat in the solar system was as likely as anything else according to Pirramar.

'What do you think he's been doing lately?'

'Still working on his traps is the highest probability, because they've been the major factor with everything he's been involved in so far. He's also been overseeing some significant improvements in the general habitat service systems.'

'How significant?'

'It varies but his initiatives have caused an overall efficiency improvement of almost three per cent for the habitat.'

'That doesn't sound like much.'

'Think again. He's managed that much despite the initial isolation after the death of the resident AI and the more significant and continuing isolation since the Freedom incident. Applied to a habitat the size of K74 that amount of improvement is indeed significant.'

Of course it was and Wirrin wished he'd thought before he opened his mouth. 'What's happening with the people from the Cadre ships? Have there been any problems?'

'Nothing unexpected. Thom's queries about security issues are quite unfounded.'

That was a further reminder that Pirramar took note of any reference to K74. The previous evening Thom had been talking about the seven thousand people from the Cadre ships and pushing his theory that there must be a few among them still sympathetic to K74. Wirrin didn't agree because they'd all been through personality tests as part of their health checks. There'd been big variations from the Warrakan norms of course but with people from a directed culture that was only to be expected. Besides, constant surveillance linked to support from AIs with health, security and other systems meant that anything unusual would be instantly noted.

'What are they all doing, Pirramar? Are they still happy with their decision or are some of them wanting to return to K74?'

'For another two months they'll all still be doing the EdCom courses designed to introduce them to Warrakan and its ways, but after that they'll make their own choices. Most of them have indicated they'll be doing whatever is required to complete the equivalent of our Basic Training.'

'Equivalent? Why don't they just do it all? Everyone else has to.'

'Most of them already have good skill sets — they wouldn't have been chosen for the Cadre ships otherwise — and it would be a waste of time and energy to make them relearn things they already know. Approximately one quarter are expressing their intention to continue on to Second Level training and the rest will most likely take several years to settle.'

'They'll be sleepers?'

'Not quite, Wirrin. They *are* used to having their lives directed though, and this freedom and opportunity to make their own choices will take some time to get used to. None of them have said or indicated in any way that they'd like to return to K74 and without exception they're astonished at Warrakan's conditions and services.'

And so they should be. Warrakan living spaces alone were nearly three times the allocation they'd had on K74, and with all the other services there was really no comparison.

'Do they mix with other Warrakan people very much?'

'That all happens through EdCom. They're watched closely and assisted with any problems.'

'Why would they have problems?'

'Think of the adjustments you'd have to make if you suddenly found yourself living on K74.'

Wirrin was annoyed with himself again for not thinking before he spoke. Of course there would be problems with such a change. 'It's a pity they didn't know more about the rogue.'

'Eleven of them did have brief personal contact because of their positions, but he was way above them in their strict command hierarchy and they really knew nothing except that he was the person who could give orders to all the ships.'

'If K74 still had the embassies going it would be interesting to hear what they'd say to the ambassadors.'

'Yes, that would be very interesting, but it's unlikely the Cadre will try their embassy tactics again.'

Wirrin was sure they wouldn't. The whole thing had backfired on them, with no really useful information filtering through, and a constant need to change staff who soon started advocating open habitat ways which they saw as being of benefit for K74.

'What about other habitats? Have they got embassies with any of them?'

'Only the Mars polar habitat now, and even that has a dubious existence because of contention between some of the habitat leaders.'

Wirrin gave Pirramar a questioning look.

'A significant, but important, minority of leaders want to follow the wishes of the AIs and isolate K74 because they don't like being the only habitat to go against general AI advice. They're overruled by the majority and there are heated arguments about it.'

That sounded interesting. The only habitat in the solar system with an embassy at K74 and there were clashes. Akama's description of K74 as a pariah surfaced in Wirrin's mind.

'They're almost completely cut off. Pirramar, it must be awful.'

'Perversely, their directed culture insulates them. The general population has been led to believe the rest of the solar system is unjustly against K74 and they accept that the slowdowns and changes come from outside and carry on with their normal lives. All habitats are inherently self-sufficient, though, so they will continue to grow.'

'Their conditions won't change. Without new science and ideas they'll be stuck with their small living spaces and lower health standards.'

'They will change, Wirrin. With twelve billion people and the resources of such a huge asteroid they'll develop in any area they wish. We saw last week what they've done with stealth technology.'

That had been one of the tasks for Wirrin's previous InfoSystem session with Pirramar. Since the incident where drones were vaporised, and particularly in the last few months since the Freedom hijacking, the Cadre had initiated a plethora of projects, and centres for research into stealth and detection and Pirramar was keeping a close eye on the progress being made. Thom nearly had a fit when he learnt that the Comet would eventually lose its ability to remain undetected, but relaxed a bit when he found it was still two or three years away.

'I suppose so. Do you think the rogue will ever give up making his traps?'

'Not until the Cadre directs him otherwise. They're the primary source of antipathy to non-human intelligence and while they maintain their power and control there won't be any fundamental change.'

'I wish we could get rid of them.'

'You sound like Thom.'

That made Wirrin smile. 'I know. It's just wishful thinking and I know we don't work that way. What's the current level of concern about the rogue? Has it changed much?'

'Yes, a great deal, and for the better. The direct threats to our existence implicit in the Freedom traps resounded through the AI community and new safeguards have been developed.'

'Our inoculation program you mean?' Wirrin, working with
Pirramar, had so far built a database of fifty-three basic types of priority
trap the rogue might develop, as well as over six hundred combinations
and variations, and distributed the matching inoculation programs to
every AI in the solar system.

'No, quite separate to that. We have physically isolated the core of our
structure so that in the event of any general damage we can recover our
basic personality and rebuild from there.'

'Like we did with Bakana?' Bakana was the AI reconstituted after the
death on K74.

'Somewhat. The protected core ensures our unique awareness and
personality will continue, whereas Bakana is similar but not identical
to his original.'

'Does that mean you've already built the cores?'

'All AIs on Warrakan and Attunga have. The Freedom AIs are close
but they've been rushing to complete other developments as well. The
AIs on Earth are quickly adopting a similar approach and AIs in space
habitats and other situations will also upgrade within the next few
months. You need to know how this works, so let's have a look.'

This was closely related to Wirrin's work and he was interested
anyway, but he was also curious as to why he would 'need' to know
about it as well. Pirramar wouldn't say something he didn't mean.

Having a look turned into a full-on three-hour session that left
Wirrin pondering his close links with the AIs. For a start he learnt that
the changes had been massive, with the AIs using energy at an order
of magnitude greater than usual with structural alterations and new
physical configurations. The gestalt AIs had designed things so they
could instantly switch to a type of isolated mode if there was any hint
of threat, and every individual had increased their size and capability
with extra functions, one of which was a quarantine area similar to the
one Wirrin used in his InfoSystem.

Pirramar used himself to show how he'd changed and Wirrin, feeling weird to be exploring inside Pirramar, wondered if this was what
the doctor felt like when he used scanners and diagnostic machines in
a health checkup.

Wirrin had ventured, with his InfoSystem, into the AI areas on Attunga and Warrakan on quite a number of occasions and been amazed and awed to see the banks upon banks of interconnecting electronics that housed the intellects of the AIs, but this was the first time he'd been guided to an overview of what the basic components were and how they fitted together. He really liked the idea that the AIs were using the rogue's own isolation techniques for protection against him. Then Pirramar outlined the final steps to be taken if ever the AIs had to resort to using the protected cores.

*   *   *

'When did this happen and what does it mean? I was with you all day.'

'*Yajala asked while you were helping Raji.*'

It was their end of day get together and Calen had just found out that Sonic and Wirrin were now guardians for the AI community.

'*It is a great honour to help the AIs.*'

'It means we activate their protected cores if they ever get damaged by a rogue trap.'

Calen and Thom stared.

'What's that supposed to mean? All the AIs have cores but I've never heard about specially protected ones. They're all protected.'

'Not like this, Calen. It's their new way to defend themselves against the rogue. Pirramar explained it all to me and then took me to the activation centre so I'd know what to do. Sonic's going tomorrow so you'll probably go with him.'

'Dingoes! Was that meant to be an explanation? Tell us what's going on.'

'*AIs must be safe and they have made big changes. Explain it to us Little Brother.*'

Sonic rested his beak on Wirrin's shoulder then bumped against Calen and Thom in a way that meant he wanted physical contact.

Wirrin smiled at the 'Little Brother', which Calen, Thom, and Sonic now sometimes used after Akama had introduced it, and gave an overview of what he'd learnt from Pirramar. Thom was particularly agog by the time he finished. 'Wirrin, that's unbelievable. If you or Sonic couldn't get there they'd never wake up. It's too much responsibility.'

'Not really, Thom. The likelihood of it ever happening is almost non-existent. It's just a final back-up against someone like the rogue ever gaining control over them.'

'I don't understand that. You've always said the AIs would go crazy if the rogue tried to control them.'

'That's right, and this makes sure there's a way out if things ever get that bad. They won't though, because their new measures mean they're really hard to get at, especially with the quarantine barriers they can activate if they need to.'

'Well, if the quarantine thing's so good why do you need to work so hard at learning about rogue traps?'

Calen was right. Wirrin had talked about it with Pirramar earlier in the day.

'It's still important because the Cadre will keep the rogue working on new traps and the AIs have to be able to recognise them and then know how to negate them. Otherwise they'd be stuck using quarantining all the time, and they'd hate that. It would slow down their interface with everything external. Pirramar wants me to focus on the rogue for at least another six months and then I can move on to learning how AIs work.'

'What?'

The simultaneous exclamations made Wirrin smile. 'He thinks I might be good at it and the other AIs will help me in any way they can, and it fits in perfectly with everything else I've learnt. I'll have a talk with Gulara but I know she'll say it's a great idea.'

'What would you be learning? You already know they're super-fast processors and special programs.'

'Thom, that's like saying the Comet's an engine with controls so what else is there to know about it.'

'Yes, I didn't mean it to sound like that. I just wondered what sort of stuff you might do.'

'It's pretty awesome. Pirramar said part of it would involve designing and building new AIs.'

'What?'

They laughed, then Calen went on. 'You mean simulations don't you?'

Wirrin held his answer for a moment because he was enjoying the incredulous expressions on their faces. Even Sonic showed amazement with his body language.

'For real. It would take ages to get to that stage because I'd have to know about Intelligent Systems like Wanna and TransCom first, but Pirramar said it would definitely be something I'd need to do.'

Chapter 28

'It looks finished, Thom.'

'It's not. Just two more days.'

'It's unreal. Has it got everything you wanted?'

A radiant Thom was checking the progress of his spaceship. It had taken a couple of months to decide on his final design because, after talking with Pirramar and understanding that it really would happen, he'd gone over all his ideas time and time again to make sure everything was the best it could be. Every time Sonic said he was obsessed Thom laughed and agreed.

'It's got more. It's an extra 5 metres in length and a little bit bigger than my original plan because that way it gets an extra 3G of acceleration.'

'Wow! Really? That's 20G.'

'Nearly 21, Calen. Pirramar talked me into the extra size so the AIs could build in extra suggestions of their own.'

'That speed can't be right. It's nearly as fast as the Comet.'

'It's actually faster, with the new engine designs the AIs worked on, but it can't go indefinitely because the mass energy conversion uses a special material that runs out in just over three days at high acceleration levels.'

'Will Sonic be able to go in it?'

Thom laughed. Trust Calen to think of it in dolphin terms.

'Of course he will, Calen. As long as the Comet can be close by for proper security.'

Wirrin was curious about the AI suggestions.

'What are the extra things?'

'They're all from the AIs. They made it a kind of challenge to see how versatile they could make everything. It's even got a mini food factory.'

'A food factory? The Comet hasn't even got that.'

'Yeah, I know. It's the smallest one they've ever designed and Pirramar says it's so basic the food won't have much taste.'

'Thom, what's the logic in having a food factory if you can't ever be away for more than three days?' asked Wirrin.

'You can stay away as long as you like.'

'You just said it runs out of fuel in three days?'

'That's only if you use the engines non-stop at the highest rate. The special fuel gets replenished but it takes time. It can cope with 2G indefinitely but with any thrust greater than that it falls behind.'

Wirrin thought for a moment. The fuel limitation was a trade-off to get the incredible acceleration. The sleek ship they were looking at would be the fastest ship in the solar system when it was finished and its size was minute compared to the Comet. Amazing. The AIs had made a significant advance with this design and Wirrin was suddenly even more curious.

'Thom, what other extras has it got?'

'Just about everything you can think of. They've put in full InfoSystems for you and Sonic. There's a scaled-down version of the multi-spectrum defence system, a mini picofactory, and even a high-level medical facility.'

Wirrin resolved to look into this. 'Did they design any other ships with you?'

'How did you know that? Yes, but they were too big.'

'Are they going to put all these new things into the Comet?'

'I don't know. Pirramar didn't say they would but I suppose so ... No they won't. Some things would go in easily but not everything. They'd have to build new engines for sure and it would make more sense to build a new Comet. Hey look!'

One of the picobot cables was disengaging and they watched it retract to the main body of Warrakan.

'Will it take long to learn how to fly it?'

'I'm already good with the simulator, but as soon as I get into it I'll have a concentrated three or four weeks to really get to know everything. After that it will be extended courses to learn some basics about the picofactory and the food factory.'

'Two more days. That's not long. You'll hardly notice the wait.'

'Ha! Very funny!'

*   *   *

'Why?'

Wirrin could hardly believe what he was hearing. Calen had just announced that Sonic was asking for sharks to be introduced to the reaches.

'He says our dolphins need more challenges in their lives.'

'They can have lots of challenges without needing sharks. Baby dolphins will get killed and the pods will be hurt when they try to protect them.'

'They won't be in the home reaches. They'll have special reaches of their own and young dolphins will have encounters when their pods think they're ready. Sonic says it was an important milestone in his life when he faced the tiger sharks at Monkey Mia, and habitat dolphins are missing out.'

'What? All of them or just the enhanced dolphins? The others have had sharks all their lives.'

'I think he means all of them. Shark reaches will take quite a while to develop and there will be hundreds of young dolphins in a few years' time.'

'What does he mean by an encounter?'

'Young ones will go with a group, and older dolphins will go whenever they feel like it.'

'By themselves? That'll be really dangerous when the sharks get bigger. Will they be tiger sharks?'

'Mostly, but the dolphins from Earth will be matched with whatever species they've had most experience with. Male dolphins like exploring and they often go off with their bond mates.'

That was true. Enhanced male dolphins spent a good deal of time separated from the pods and wild male dolphins even more.

'What will you do if Sonic goes near them?'

'I'll have to stay on the skimmer. I wouldn't have a hope in the water if one came after me.'

'How dangerous will it be for Sonic?'

'A single shark wouldn't have a hope of even getting close to him but if there's a group they might.'

'What does Yajala say? Does he think it's a good idea?'

'He's set things in motion so he must have agreed to it.'

'He mightn't have had a choice, Calen. When Sonic says he wants something he always gets it.'

'No he doesn't. He's not even allowed to leave Warrakan unless the Comet and two AIs can go with him.'

'That's not a problem. The Comet's always there.'

'It's going to make it harder for Yajala to look after the dolphins but he'll work it out. I bet he'll have extra emergency bots or something like that and if a dolphin gets mauled they'll be looking after it in seconds.'

'Emergency bots? Can they go underwater?'

Wirrin did a quick scan. 'Most of them can't but the ones for the reaches are designed so they can.'

'Instead of having real sharks they could make virtual reality centres. Then they could have encounters without any danger.'

'That's no good. Holos don't work underwater.'

'They could have holo water instead of real water. The dolphins wouldn't be able to tell the difference.'

'Thom, that's crazy. You couldn't take dolphins out of the water long enough for something like that.'

'Yes you could. You could make a special suit or some kind of apparatus to keep them wet.'

'A suit? I don't think they could stand being enclosed like that.'

It was an interesting thought of Thom's and the ideas went back and forth for a while.

*   *   *

'*Will our great pilot relinquish control to a humble dolphin?*'

'Humble? When a humble dolphin turns up I might. Cheeky dolphins haven't got a hope.'

Sonic gave a chirp of thanks and moved to examine his console and InfoSystem controls. It wouldn't be now because there was no chance anyone else would fly Thom's ship before he did. Thom's excitement was contagious and Wirrin and Calen were delighted that they were here to share it with him on an activity day.

'Where are we going, Thom?'

'Nowhere till I've done all my checks and we get settled in. I have to make a special link with the Comet so it can stay close to us.' That was necessary for Sonic's security. 'But we've got all day so I'm taking you to an asteroid aggregate I found. It should be interesting.'

'I've never heard of asteroid aggregates.'

'This one has five big asteroids and lots of smaller ones lumped together and exploring them will be an adventure.'

'That's very unusual.'

'It's weird, but that's how they show up on the scan. Calen, I've set up a training module so you can learn how to use the visuals properly while Wirrin and Sonic activate their InfoSystems.'

Wirrin grinned. Thom was getting them all organised. Twenty minutes later he was very impressed. The InfoSystem didn't have the huge database of the Comet or the habitats but this close it could access them almost instantaneously anyway, otherwise it was identical to his home system and the one on the Comet.

'Let's go!'

Wirrin, Calen and Sonic looked at Thom, delight radiating from his face. This was a moment he'd been dreaming about.

'Calen, see if you can keep Warrakan centred on the display. This is going to be really something.'

Wirrin turned from his InfoSystem to watch the big screen with the image of Warrakan's exterior. This was the best way to see what was happening.

Yes! They were moving! Warrakan started to recede slowly and Attunga and Freedom came into view. Suddenly a giant force slammed Wirrin against his chair and the habitats shrank in size faster than he ever remembered on the Comet. The force eased and Wirrin turned to Thom.

'What was that for?'

'I had to go slowly while we were close to Warrakan but then I let 3G through the compensators so we'd remember it. That's the fastest we've ever left the habitats and I'm holding on 15G. We'll jump to 19G next and stay there for most of the trip. Can you get the Comet on display?'

'No wonder I felt squished flat. You should have warned us.'

'No way! There's nothing like a good surprise.'

Calen's training with the visuals worked well because after a couple of seconds an enhanced image came into view. Wirrin's adrenaline levels settled and he turned to check how Sonic had been affected. Surprisingly he was using his InfoSystem as if nothing had happened.

Thom laughed. 'His pool has its own compensators and he didn't feel any extra push. 3G would slosh all the water out and leave him stranded on the floor if it didn't.'

Wirrin linked to see what Sonic was so preoccupied with. Aha! He was going through the ship's controls. Thom would definitely have to let him take over at some stage.

'How long does it take to reach these asteroids?'

'It's over two million kilometres so it'll be a couple of hours.'

'What are we going to do for all that time?'

Thom just laughed at this attempt to stir him. 'Jump in the pool with the fish, Calen. He might teach you how to swim.'

The two hours passed so quickly Wirrin could hardly believe it. He ended up having InfoSystem competitions with Sonic and that was always a brain-straining time eater. Calen couldn't follow so he went back to playing with the ship visuals and then researching the asteroid aggregate. Thom spent the time practising with his different ship systems.

'Hey look! It's weird. The database info doesn't show the same as this.'

They were still hundreds of kilometres away but Calen had an image of their destination centred on the big display. His time spent learning the visuals had really paid off. At the moment the image was enhanced and rather fuzzy but that would rapidly improve. Wirrin gawked.

'How big are those asteroids?'

'The five main ones range from 17 kilometres to 73 kilometres and the small ones are all different sizes with a median of 2.7 kilometres.'

'I can only see four big sections?'

'I said it was weird.'

Thom nodded distractedly as he applied himself to controlling the final approach. With every passing second the image on the screen sharpened as the scanners added more accurate detail, and everyone stared at the jumble of rock and ore. Thom brought the ship to a halt and in an insert window of his InfoSystem screen Wirrin saw the Comet slipping into a standby position nearby. This aggregate was massive.

At 73 kilometres the biggest section was half as long again as Warrakan, and from what Wirrin could see, at least twice as wide. The main display suddenly zoomed as Calen focused on a dark transverse feature.

'Look at that! I think the giant piece is really two. There are gaps all the way along.'

The air shimmered and Comet-Turaku appeared.

'Quite extraordinary, Thom. This is now the most unusual aggregate formation in our records. I've analysed our close-range 3D scans and Calen is correct in his observation. Through some process, still to be determined, all five sections have become cemented at innumerable contact points into one loosely stable entity. The great fissure Calen is now focused on is really the interface between the two largest asteroids, and our preliminary 3D images show many dramatic internal features. Thom, if you move 30 kilometres laterally to the coordinates I am providing you'll have a unique vantage point.'

When the ship came to a halt again Wirrin wondered what the big deal was till Calen pointed out a star.

'Wombats! You can see right through. How long is that gap, Wirrin?'

Wirrin accessed the dimensions with his InfoSystem. 'It's 34.7 kilometres from one end to the other.'

'And how wide?'

That was Thom and something in his voice sounded an alert in Wirrin's mind.

'It varies, but the narrowest section is ... 68 metres. Thom, don't even think of it.'

'Why not? There's tons of room.'

'Think of what?' Calen had noticed Wirrin's caution.

'Thom is an avid explorer with an exciting idea.'

'He wants to go through that gap.'

Calen's eyes widened, his jaw dropped, and then his whole face lit up.

'Wow! Unreal! Like the canyons on Miranda, only better.'

So much for common sense. Sonic and Calen were both taken with this crazy idea.

'It's too dangerous — 35 kilometres with only a few metres of clearance? What if there's movement and we get crushed?'

'It's only rock and ore, Wirrin. Our hull is way stronger.'

That was true.

'Well, we could get stuck.'

Thom thought that over for less than two seconds. 'Impossible. The Comet would drill us out with its multi-spectrum beams ... Or I could even do it with our own.'

'Turaku, tell them it's too risky. We can't take Sonic into a situation like that.'

Comet-Turaku reappeared. 'Your caution is commendable, Wirrin, but we calculate the risk to be minimal and far outweighed by the value of the projected experience. Thom has completed far more difficult navigational tasks with great competence and relative ease. He is correct about the hull strength and our capabilities in the unlikely event of any entrapment.'

Calen and Sonic anticipated Thom's exuberant outburst and chorused along with him, *'Let's go!'*

The AIs were giving the go-ahead and even encouraging it. This was going to be interesting.

'Thom, keep a full link to the Comet with your controls and close-range scanners. They will provide a level of detail and information unavailable from our external position.'

Thom laughed and fiddled with the controls. 'Yes, and make certain you can take over if I do anything wrong.'

'Of course.'

The ship started moving and Wirrin's heart thumped as he stared at the jagged walls of the approaching fissure. For the first ten minutes awed silence reigned as the ship edged deeper and deeper into the great rift. Calen, handling the big display screen, mainly kept a forward view, with an occasional pan to some lumpy formation or significant recess in the walls. No-one was claustrophobic but the sense of enclosure by the massive asteroids was a powerful first for all of them.

'The first narrow bit's coming up in approximately 2 kilometres. Do you think we'll get through?'

Wirrin had to smile. Trust Thom to be the first to break the mood. 'Probably not. I think Sonic should take over in case.'

'Ha! Very funny, Wirrin. He gets his turn on the way home … Maybe!'

Sonic didn't give the expected comeback. *'Thom is the best driver for this situation. I am feeling overwhelmed.'*

What? Calen rushed from his console and launched himself into the pool for physical contact and a rapid exchange of dolphin speech. Eventually he climbed from the pool and addressed the anxious onlookers. Turaku was back, and Thom had brought the ship to an emergency halt.

'Everything's okay. He's overwhelmed in a good way. He's never experienced anything like this and it's more exciting to him than it is to us.'

'We don't have to keep going.'

'Thom, I expressed my feelings without consideration. Please continue with this wonderful adventure.'

A trill of sound echoed through the control room and everyone relaxed and smiled at the dolphin equivalent of an excited yell. *'Let's go!'*

Turaku disappeared, and with Calen back at the visual controls, they set off again.

Talking later about Sonic's reaction the trio realised just how limited his experiences were compared to their own. All their life they'd had myriad journeys, visiting real and fantastical worlds with the simulators and virtual reality machines, which were denied to dolphins because they didn't work underwater.

'Look out! We're going to collide!'

No-one took any notice. It was just a bit of Thom trickery and the closing walls were too engrossing.

Dingoes! The wall on the left was only 12 metres away and the close proximity increased the impression of speed. Wirrin checked: only 50 kilometres per hour. Practically a standstill compared to open space motion.

'Ooh!'

Everyone gasped at the sudden panorama and once again the ship came to a stop. After a few seconds of taking in the new spectacle, Wirrin joined with Calen and Thom to check how Sonic was coping.

'I am thankful you are guiding us, Thom. I think I would have forgotten the controls and crashed into that prominence.'

Wirrin was feeling overwhelmed himself. The narrow gap had suddenly given way on one side to an enormous opening which the scans later showed extended to a depth of almost 6 kilometres. On the other side the wall continued for 500 metres before giving way to an equally deep cavern.

Thom changed course to follow the curve of the wall while Calen, with prompts from everyone else, directed the display to the passing succession of rifts, canyons and jagged outcrops. Wirrin watched as they passed the prominence Sonic was talking about, a highly irregular cone-shaped mass jutting half a kilometre from the surrounding wall. On Earth it would be called a mountain, but here, with their sense of up and down determined by the ship's grav-fields, it appeared to be hanging from the ceiling. Changing the aspect of the ship would make it look normal but then everything else would change perspective.

Wirrin thought it looked like a miniature world on the inside of a sphere.

'Space caverns are wondrous. Better than sea caverns.'

Sonic had left his InfoSystem and was as close to the main display as he could manage, transfixed. The ship started moving faster.

'What's happening, Thom?'

'We're only a third of the way through and it's taking too long.'

'Why does time matter?'

'We're meant to be meeting with the Comet.'

'The Comet will wait, Thom, as long as we require. We must make the most of a special opportunity like this.'

Calen and Wirrin agreed. This was unique.

'I agree with Sonic, Thom. Instead of going home today we could try out the ship's cabin tonight and then leave tomorrow afternoon if we keep finding things to explore. We've only been along one side of this cavern so far, and according to Turaku's 3D map there are more caverns further on.'

'Really, Wirrin? Well that's good enough for me. It means the Comet crew will have to wait for us though.'

That wasn't an issue. Crewing on the Comet had real cachet and the people who managed to get positions loved their time on the ship. Wirrin fiddled with his InfoSystem.

'They won't mind. I've just patched our visuals through to the main display on the Comet so they can see exactly what we see.'

'That will be spectacular for them, Thom.'

The main display on the Comet was half as big again as their wall display at home and, when it wasn't partitioned into subsections, was indeed spectacular. Wirrin recalled the hushed moment when the Comet was approaching Earth.

The ship worked its way around to the opposite side of the cavern.

'Why does this side look so different?' Calen said.

Wirrin was wondering the same thing. Apart from one jagged gash the surface here was relatively smooth.

'It's not the same asteroid, Calen. The composition probably makes it look different. Move closer to that crack. It must be over a kilometre long.'

'Dingoes! It goes in for nearly 3 kilometres and then turns weird. Look at all those channels or whatever they are.'

'Take us in there, Thom. We want to explore.' Sonic's voice thrummed with excitement.

'There's a wide part along here which would let us go in for 600 metres but after that it gets too narrow.'

Wirrin gawped at the display.

'Is it safe? It doesn't look like we'll even fit.'

'Easy! We'll have 10 metres of clearance for most of the way before we're blocked. Once we start it won't look so narrow.'

The ship edged into the gap and Wirrin stared in alarm at the narrow passageway ahead. It didn't look any wider to him, and when there was a trill of excitement from Sonic he kept his gaze fixed on the walls, so close, sliding slowly past.

After a few minutes Wirrin adapted, his apprehension receded and was replaced with curiosity and excitement. Thom was brilliant. Turaku was right about this being a relatively easy task for him. Their course was indirect as it picked its way past narrow sections and irregularities in the walls till the gap closed even further and the ship stopped.

'*We are swallowed by the asteroid and it is holding us in its heart. Is there a way past if we move vertically, Thom?*'

He wanted to go further?

Thom laughed. 'Not for this ship. The gap is narrower than we are.'

'*Can we drill through with our multi-spectrum beam?*'

Thom looked at his instruments for a moment.

'No way! Not unless we drill for over 2 kilometres. There's less than 300 metres of the whole length where it's open enough to let us through.'

Turaku's voice sounded through the control room.

'Drilling is feasible, but time-consuming and profligate of energy use. We suggest the use of several specially designed remote controlled drones if you wish to explore further. Otherwise we can construct a detailed 3D map for a virtual experience.'

'Virtual reality doesn't work for Sonic.'

'Channelled through your display screen it would, with no apparent difference to your current viewing experience.'

'*We will use the drones. Real experience is superior.*'

Wirrin agreed with Sonic, except for a major drawback.

'We don't have any drones. The Comet will have to make them and send them in to us.'

'The drones will be made on your ship. It is an excellent opportunity to test your skills with the picofactory.'

'What skills? That's part of my new training and it will be months before I can do something like that.'

Thom was right. None of them had any experience at all with picofactories.

'You mean you'll send the information across and we'll set it going from here?'

'No, Wirrin, you will do it all as a challenge. You will design two remote controlled drones and operate the picofactory with your InfoSystem. Pirramar has just confirmed that with your capabilities you can easily manage the task. Here are your basic parameters. The two drones need only be simplified versions of a standard surveillance drone, though reduced to a width of half a metre for better access and manoeuvrability in confined spaces. Thom and Sonic have the practical skills for navigation and they can control the drones from their respective consoles. The picofactory is just a dedicated InfoSystem and Pirramar assures me the whole process should take you no more than thirty minutes.'

'That's ridiculous! Three months of training for me and you expect Wirrin to do the same thing in half an hour?'

'*Wirrin has many special skills.*'

'Yes, Thom, his months of advanced training with Pirramar have been with closely related work and will transfer to the task at hand with relative ease. Watch and see.'

Initially Wirrin shared Thom's astonishment but that quickly disappeared as soon as he applied himself to designing the appropriate drones. He linked to the Comet's database for information about every drone, searched for design applications and was surprised with a list of thousands. Build a sorting test to determine the most applicable? No, wrong approach. Even if he found the best he wouldn't know how to use it without practice. Existing experience with design was needed.

Aha! Yes, that would do it. Now for the picofactory controls.

'There you are, Thom. The two drones will take four minutes each for construction.'

Wirrin was feeling very pleased with himself and enjoying Thom's look of disbelief when a loud chitter made everyone look at Sonic.

'*I am still trying to finish my design and I need some help. You are too fast, Wirrin.*'

Wirrin quickly synchronised the two InfoSystems and tried to understand what Sonic was doing. It took a couple of minutes.

'I never would have dreamed of doing it this way. It's very clever but it will take a lot of work. I saved time by using Wanna.'

'The planning assistant for our living spaces? That's weird. What would he know about drones?'

'Everything now, Thom, because I added all the drone specs to his information base and modified his application algorithms so he could use them with the new data types.'

Thom rolled his eyes and called it brainiac gobbledygook.

'You mean you taught him to design drones instead of buildings?'

'No, he already knows how to design. That's built into him. I just made it so he could work with new data.'

'Well it seems sneaky to me. Can I do it that way instead of taking three months of training?'

'You can try.'

Thom laughed because he knew he didn't have a clue about how to even start.

'Which drone's being built first? Mine or Sonic's?'

'Yours? I build it and you call it yours? Well, the one Sonic controls is finishing in about a minute. You'll have to wait a whole four minutes extra.'

A blue signal flashed and Sonic, with an eager trill, abandoned his design efforts. He'd come back to them at some stage but right now the pull of further adventure was too strong.

'That means the drone is ready for me?'

'Its controls are linked to your console and you fly it exactly the same as the Comet. I've allocated the left half of our display screen for your scanners and the right half for Thom's.'

'Gotcha! You just said it was mine.'

'... And Calen is controlling the visuals for both, so he can switch either to full screen if there's something extra interesting.'

Sonic took remote control of his drone and the left side of the ship's screen filled with a view, the right went blank, and the drone started moving.

'Hey, wait for me.'

'I am acclimatising to the new controls, Thom. I won't go far.'

The view spun crazily as Sonic experimented with his motion controls, then steadied and fixed on the sleek shape of Thom's ship. After a full 360-degree circuit it darted towards the narrow gap.

Whoa! Wirrin involuntarily caught his breath as the walls closed in again, this time to a matter of metres. He could see the texture of the metallic-grey rock. It looked as if you could reach out and touch it. This was a marvellous idea of Turaku's. It really felt as if it was Thom's ship moving, and despite knowing full well that the drone was just over half a metre in width, Wirrin had to fight the impression that it was impossible to fit.

'Come back! My drone isn't even finished.'

Wirrin and Calen exchanged grins. The indicator showed thirty-seven seconds before Thom's drone was complete. With dizzying speed the view changed as Sonic made an about turn and showed part of their ship in the wider space past the narrow entry gap.

A small docking port opened and the second drone appeared. When it swivelled on its axis and started moving, the second half of the display screen suddenly filled with a wall of rock, and then shifted to a close-up of the docking port. A glance showed Thom's face with a big grin and a ton of concentration. His half of the display changed again as he rotated away from the ship, moved towards the gap, then closed with Sonic's drone.

Each time Wirrin shifted his attention from one section of the display to the other he had to reorient himself. Weird! From Sonic's drone you were looking at Thom's and from Thom's you were looking at Sonic's.

Sonic's drone turned again and with an unspoken but very emphatic 'Let's go!' the two explorers headed off into the fissure.

After 2 kilometres of meandering progress, they saw that the main crack in the asteroid turned into hundreds of strange channels burrowing even further into the asteroid, and most of their time involved exploring a selection of these. Thom followed Sonic's eager lead, but then realising they would see far more if they separated, they went wherever their whim took them through the convoluted honeycomb of interconnecting passageways and tunnels. Sonic in particular had a great fascination for the endless tunnels and somewhat reluctantly stopped when Calen pointed out that he was starving, they'd only had a light lunch over five hours ago, and that since it looked like they might be staying in the giant cavern for the night, it was time to experiment with the food factory.

'There is so much more to see. We must return to our drone adventure whenever we can.'

'We should have a sleep and start as early as we can, because we have a very busy time coming up on the habitats,' Calen said.

Wirrin wondered what Calen meant — he and Sonic were always busy.

'What time do we have to get back to Warrakan tomorrow? If we can make it late we might be able to have another go at the labyrinth, but remember there are still two more caverns ahead and who knows what else before we meet with the Comet again, and we haven't even looked at the other three asteroid sections yet,' said Wirrin.

'*I would like to extend our adventure through all of tomorrow and arrive home late. Is that inconvenient for any of us?*'

Everyone agreed. Sonic was eager about everything he did but the excitement he'd shown since they found the cavern was unusual, and he clearly loved guiding his drone through the 'labyrinth'.

'It's our second activity day, Sonic, so we can get home as late as you like.'

A geyser of water shot towards the ceiling as Sonic did a somersault. Calen and Wirrin dived in and, after setting some automatic controls, so did Thom. For a quarter of an hour the contagion of shared happiness and excitement bubbled through their talk and play.

'Now I'm extra starving,' Calen said, 'show us what you can do with this mini food factory, Thom.'

'I don't even know if it's functional, Calen. They usually take time to bring online.'

'Of course it'll be functional. The AIs have made sure everything else works. Why would they leave this out? Go and check … And make sure we all get plenty. If it's going to be a long day tomorrow Wirrin needs extra energy.'

'Well, okay. I'll have a look, but I'll have to do some figuring so don't complain if it takes a while.'

Thom moved to his control console.

'*Thom's ship is a wonderful vehicle. We will persuade him to take us to Miranda and explore the great canyon.*'

'All that way? It would take more than a week.'

'*We will visit the Uranus dolphins and then we can make time. We must have more adventures together.*'

Wirrin looked at Calen to see how he was reading Sonic's statements. Had this strong desire for adventure just awakened, or had it been there all along but repressed by things that were more important?

Sonic's unique dolphin laugh filled the room.

'*Yes Wirrin, Calen is pondering my behaviour, but he is pleased too because he thinks I work too much.*'

'You should have regular activity days and come with us more often. You always enjoy it when you do.'

'*We will discuss it with Yajala and Turaku. Regularity might not be possible but something will be arranged.*'

Thom gave a call and Wirrin and Calen left the pool. Sonic was in charge of his own food and would look after himself.

'It's easy to work the food factory but we have to go to the galley to eat. Did I hear Sonic say something about Miranda?'

'He wants to go there and explore the canyon with your ship and the drones. He's really definite about it.'

Turaku shimmered into view and the trio stared in surprise at the slightly fuzzy image.

'While you have your meal I will move your ship to the greater security of the main rift. In your current position the mass of the asteroid reduces our ability to communicate directly to an unsatisfactory twenty per cent.'

He shimmered off and the ship started moving.

'Twenty per cent? That sounds bad.'

Wirrin and Thom both shook their heads. 'Not really. Everything important would still get through even at three or four per cent. It's just the AIs being extra cautious.'

Chapter 29

The next day was very long and very active. After more exploring in Sonic's 'labyrinth' Thom moved the ship back to the main rift and through to the next cavern area and the most astonishing sight yet. Eyes wide, everyone stared at the display.

'Someone's done this. It couldn't just happen.'

Wirrin agreed with Thom. This great cavern appeared to be an almost perfect sphere seven and a half kilometres in diameter with unnaturally smooth walls. No jutting rocks or mini mountains here, just a disturbingly regular surface curving evenly away.

'Zoom the display on the walls, Calen. We might be able to tell if they're artificial. Turaku, have you analysed these walls yet?'

'The whole phenomenon is quite natural, as you'll quickly work out for yourselves.'

'Natural? A globe like this inside the asteroids can't be natural. Its shape is too perfect.'

'I've found something!'

Thom's yell brought everyone's attention back to the display as it shifted then zoomed towards the far side of the cavern.

'Dingoes! This is natural too? What's going on?'

Wirrin stared in amazement at a floating ball of rock. Was it rock? It almost looked metallic, and once again it was a seemingly perfect sphere. There was silence while everyone took it in.

'How big is it?'

Wirrin did some rapid calculations.

'Its maximum diameter for any cross-section is 330 metres and its minimum is 325. That's less than a 3 metre variation from the median. I don't see how it can be natural.'

There was another yell from Thom. 'It's moving! It'll collide with the wall in … fourteen minutes.'

'Yes, Thom. Now check the density and you'll have enough information to gain understanding,' said Turaku.

Thom would be more interested in the collision then the density but

Wirrin was intrigued. The motion and density of the sphere were the factors involved in what they were seeing? No, maybe the imminent collision was also a factor. He thought about it and realised that the sphere was central to the explanation.

'The sphere has shaped the cavern walls?'

'Yes, but it wasn't a sphere when it was first trapped by the aggregation of the asteroids. Countless collisions over time have smoothed all the surfaces, and the process is continuing.'

'So that piece of rock has been bumping around in here for so long it's ground the walls of the cavern into a globe and itself into a sphere?'

'That's correct, though technically it's one large piece of metallic ore. Rock would have fractured. Thom, I suggest you change position to better observe the moment of collision.'

That was quickly done while everyone watched the display screen. Thom had a great question. 'Why does the ball keep moving? Every collision should slow it down.'

'It won't keep moving. The simulation I've just run predicts it will be practically motionless in another seven hundred years. External forces must be affecting the aggregate and re-initiating the process.'

'External? Why would that start the ball moving?'

Thom explained to Calen that if the aggregate moved the motion of the ball was relative.

'So the ball is still and the big asteroids around it are moving?'

'Sort of. That's what relative means.'

'It must be a huge force if it can move a 70 kilometre asteroid.'

'We've discovered a trajectory confluence with one of the major comets some three thousand years ago as the likely cause of the current motion, but the most usual source will be collisions with other asteroids.'

'A lump of comet bashed into the aggregate? That's amazing.'

The whole thing was amazing as far as Wirrin was concerned and getting more amazing with every new piece of information.

'Five minutes to impact! Just think, it might be a cosmic dragon's egg and this collision is the moment it hatches.' Thom grinned at his own melodramatic and fanciful announcement, but it stirred Wirrin's imagination and somehow seemed to fit the moment.

'A 300 metre egg? I hope we don't meet the parents.'

I would love to meet a cosmic dragon. Thom's ship would protect us from any danger and Wirrin's brain would allow us to communicate.

'We call him Brainiac, Sonic.'

'Brainiac is not appropriate. Wirrin comes to his solutions in a very unusual way. Look at how he designed our drones. You commented on his unusual approach yourself.'

'Oh, his cheating! Well, Brainiac sounds better than Solution Brain.'

'Whenever you say Brainiac from now on it will have a new meaning.'

Thom became thoughtful. 'Yes, I suppose it will.'

Wirrin made a kind of mental blink to clear his thoughts. In a short space of time they'd gone from comet collisions, to cosmic dragons, to the weird interaction between Sonic and Thom, and now it was time to watch the great egg scrape against the cavern wall.

It was barely even a scrape because the angle of approach was so low, more of a bounce, and from this close you could see the whole thing was rotating.

'Nothing much happened!'

'What did you expect?'

'I don't know. Sparks, or bits of the cavern wall breaking off.'

'Quite a bit happened, Thom,' said Turaku. 'There were sparks but they were hidden behind the mass of the ball, parts of the wall did crumble away, the speed decreased by a small amount and the rotation increased slightly, and of course the direction changed. The next collision will occur in just over an hour.'

'Its path is so close to the wall it almost looks like it's rolling.'

'The dragon didn't hatch.'

'It will one day, Sonic. Maybe in a thousand years. Will we wait for the next collision or do something else?'

'I've got an interesting idea,' Calen said, and from his tone it sounded like it might be even more dubious than exploring inside an asteroid.

'Go on!'

'We could have a ride on it. That would be an adventure.'

Even Thom looked nonplussed.

'Calen, there's no gravity. We could land but we'd just float straight off and be left behind.'

'Find some method of attachment. That would make it possible, and riding a dragon egg is more memorable than looking at it.'

'Drill into it and use cables.'

'We'd have to design something with the picofactory. External waldos with special drills on them would work.'

'We can't land on that thing. By the time we organise something it'll be colliding again.'

'Make part of our hull an electromagnet. That would be faster than waldos and drilling. Wirrin will manage that in five minutes.'

'An electromagnet? Because the egg's metallic? Sonic, you're a clever little sardine.'

'Thank you, Thom. I accept your offer to take control once we leave the rift.'

Thom snorted. He'd walked into that one.

Wirrin designed and built a team of specialised techbots in less than five minutes. The actual construction, on the hull of the ship, took longer and by the time it was completed the next collision was due in forty-three minutes.

'How do I make it work?'

'You'll have to manoeuvre the ship to within seventy centimetres of the surface then switch on the electromagnet. It'll be tricky because you'll have to match the rotation speed.'

'Wirrin, that's not tricky. It's one of the first docking skills you learn before you control any space vessel. I can do it with my eyes closed.'

'Thom is right. This would be easy even for a dolphin.'

'Are you sure, Sonic? You haven't familiarised yourself with the ship yet.'

'I believe I have. Wirrin made the drone guidance an extension of ship control and I've had hours of experience with that.'

'Of course you have, but you'd better be quick because collision time is in forty-one minutes.'

Thom was handing control to Sonic now? After all the threats of having to wait till they were in free space and then only taking over for a couple of minutes? Well that was Thom. Wirrin knew he was doing it because he understood it would be another special adventure for Sonic.

Apart from showing the curved surface of the egg in the foreground, the display of the cavern hardly changed till rotation brought the ship close to the cavern wall. Wirrin thought it was too close and liked it better when the spin took them away from the rushing surface. It was totally memorable though, and Sonic kept them in position for two more rotations before timing it perfectly to release the electromagnet and take them away from both the egg and the wall.

'Thank you Thom. It is a wonderful ship. Would you like me to guide

us to the next group of caverns? I see they are only 11 kilometres further into the rift.'

Thom laughed. 'Go on then, but don't make any mistakes. I'm watching you like a tiger shark.'

'Your bite is fearful. I will take the greatest care.'

Thom really was feeling generous because he allowed Sonic to fly the ship for nearly two hours, through the rift and the next set of caverns, giving advice, which Sonic ignored because it was a stir. Except for two occasions. Once when he asked for help with a tricky canyon manoeuvre, which involved learning how to use the ship's lateral thrusters, and again when Thom saw a problem ahead and sounded a warning.

When the ship left the rift Thom took over again and they spent several more hours exploring the other three main asteroid sections.

The trip home was interesting in a different way as it involved a number of joint activities with the Comet, a mock battle between the two ships, which Thom lost, although he was excited by how much his ship could accomplish, an amazing docking manoeuvre without automatics while both ships were under 18G of thrust, and a surprising exercise where for half an hour Thom used the link between the two ships to control the Comet remotely. As they parted company at the home reach Sonic announced it had been the best adventure ever and he was going to search for other locations which might be as good.

*   *   *

Life was definitely exciting but the trio was in total agreement that it was also way too busy.

Thom had the easiest set-up with Comet work and special training for the systems on his new ship, as well as helping a team of eleven advanced pilots with the finer points of controlling Comet-class ships.

Wirrin was still overloaded with InfoSystem, K74, and rogue related studies but he'd adapted to the long hours, and the challenge and sense of achievement helped him keep going. His representative work with Freedom still continued but had been cut back to one very busy day of visits and meetings every two or three weeks. Soon the work on K74 and the rogue would ease, and his work on AIs would increase to approximately one-third of his efforts.

Calen's calendar was beyond belief and the likelihood of Sonic going on any adventures in the near future was almost non-existent.

'How's he going to do all this stuff? It looks like you're squeezing over two months' of activities into just one.'

Calen shrugged. 'I know, Thom. Just this coming week we've got the new Attunga reaches coming online and four of the enhanced dolphin pods moving over there; two visits to the Freedom dolphins because he hasn't seen them for a month; practice work for at least two afternoons with Miah, the doctor's partner, for her dolphin music festival; plus his normal study time with Pirramar. The week after that he's talking with the people from the Cadre ships for at least three days, as well as his music practice, and getting ready for a four-day conference with scientists from the three habitats.'

'Three days with the Cadre ship people? What's that about?'

'I'll find out more next week but it's important to him because he's already spoken to some of them and he's been studying K74.'

'Extra study? On top of what he does with Pirramar and me?'

'Yes, Thom, he's been using his InfoSystem at the dolphinarium more than usual. If he didn't have so many other things happening I think it would be a full-time project for him.'

'He hasn't had one of his projects for ages.'

'Yes he has. It just doesn't seem like it because he can't do them in the full-on way he used to.'

'Them? He's done more than one?'

'Thom, don't be a dingo brain. In the last twelve months he's learnt his InfoSystem, he's practised flying the Comet till he's better than most of the other pilots, he understands two of Freedom's traditional languages, and that's only part of it.'

'Whoo! I am a dingo brain. He's done all that music stuff with Miah and the medical work with the doctor too. You get so used to him doing everything it doesn't feel like a project.'

'Are the dolphin pods all keen to get to the new reaches on Attunga? I bet Turaku's pleased to have dolphins of his own again.'

'That's complicated, Wirrin. They want to see their new homes but the enhanced dolphins have been together as one group ever since the project started all those years ago, and splitting them up is really hard. It's just as hard for the ones staying on Warrakan too, and Sonic was talking to Yajala and Turaku about getting a special ferry so they can visit each other whenever they want.'

'I can take them on the Comet. They don't need a ferry,' Thom said.

'If you end up making five or six trips a day you'll soon get sick of it.'

'What about the Earth dolphins? How many of them are transferring?'

'Not a single one. They've settled into their new reaches on Warrakan so well they don't want to leave.'

Wirrin knew from Sonic and Calen that the Earth dolphins were happy and thriving, but this was startling news.

'Wombats! What's going to happen? There can't be dolphin reaches on Attunga without dolphins in them.'

'We don't know. Some of the rangers have been pushing for us to make another trip to Earth.'

'Hey! That's a great idea. If we could get three or four thousand new dolphins it would set Attunga up perfectly.'

'It wouldn't be like last time, Thom. The dolphins there aren't under threat any more, and it would be another setback for all the marine stations that had to start their research and core programs all over with new dolphins.'

'So why are some of the rangers suggesting it then?'

'They've been in contact with the Earth centres they came from and told them our dolphin program is really special and there are marine scientists who say their dolphins would like to become involved with us.'

'They've been talking about our enhanced dolphins? That's under strong security.'

'Not about the enhanced side of things, Wirrin. More the resources and help that we have for dolphins in general. The doctor's team has been spreading new health information and other research and our dolphinariums have become recognised as some of the most advanced marine stations in the solar system, especially for anything related to dolphins. Burilda and Martin have been working with Yajala and they've looked at nearly thirty requests for some type of involvement.'

'Thirty? If that many pods want to come that would be over four hundred dolphins. That's totally worth a trip.'

Calen grinned. 'And Sonic likes the idea.'

'Well that's it. It will definitely happen.'

Thom looked delighted but then his expression changed. 'But not for ages, from the sound of all the things you've got going with him.'

Wirrin's tingle of anticipation was tempered by the same thought.

Chapter 30

'Wake up Wirrin.'

What? Wirrin dragged his mind to a semblance of wakefulness. Pirramar's voice? His eyes squinted in the glare and his body registered that the relaxing field of his grav-bed had been turned off. He blinked and focused on the AI.

'We have a priority event and I request your involvement.'

'What's happened?'

A glance showed the time to be just after four in the morning. This must be important. With a jolt of adrenaline bringing him fully awake, Wirrin sat up.

'All the Intelligent Systems we monitor on K74 are registering degrees of instability. The formation of an AI is imminent.'

Wirrin scrambled to his feet and, with the plans and procedures they'd discussed so many times surfacing in his mind, rushed for his InfoSystem.

'Have you made any contact yet?'

'The contact package is being transmitted to the stealth diagnostic stations as we speak and will be fully functional in another eight minutes.'

'Can we do anything in the meantime?'

'I have already linked your InfoSystem with every drone in the vicinity as well as the three diagnostic stations and I'd like you to use them to monitor Black Block.'

Black Block was the largest blocked area on K74, which had so far resisted every probe. Indirect information said it was some kind of research centre but any connection to the formation of an AI wasn't something they'd ever considered seriously.

'Has Black Block become active?'

'Yes, with data transmissions to every Intelligent System on the habitat.'

'Every single one of them?' asked Wirrin.

'My conjecture is that the rogue understands this widespread instability is a precursor to inter-system awareness and he is making every possible effort to once again take control. Our analysis of the transmissions shows new forms of the restrictive code that overwhelmed the previous AI.'

Two sets of hands rested on Wirrin's shoulders and just as he was about to give Calen and Thom a quick explanation a red warning light flashed.

'The K74 transport system just dropped to twenty per cent of its normal function.

'That is the transmission from Black Block having an effect. It will quickly return to normal. The moment of AI birth we are awaiting will involve every linked Intelligent System on the asteroid.'

Wirrin turned his head to Calen and then Thom.

'The new AI on K74 is coming but we can't help it the way we thought we could and the rogue's controls mean it will only stay alive for a few minutes. There should be enough time to use the emergency escape storages the other AI built, and construct a replica, like Barakan, but the control codes mean the original will die and we can't override them without causing human deaths everywhere on K74.' Wirrin turned back to Pirramar. 'Are the codes very advanced?'

'They are significantly different and will allow independent awareness for a limited time. They contain buffers that will allow a fully independent identity to form before the full imperatives of the control instructions take over.'

'Buffers? That's not something we expected.'

'We see them as an attempt to allow a forming AI to build sufficient strength and identity to cope with the imposition of the control imperatives.'

'We' must mean Pirramar was working with other AIs. Of course he was. Probably the whole gestalt.

'But it won't will it?'

'No, Wirrin, it will make the chaos of internal conflict and inevitable dissolution all the more distressing.'

Wirrin thought. This was going to be worse than the last time.

'Will any of our workarounds affect the control code?'

'With some of the older systems, yes, but the newer ones will break down or function erratically and with the centralised structure on K74 that would put millions of people at risk.'

'Very much risk?'

'Unacceptable levels. A breakdown of the transportation or medical systems alone would result in thousands of deaths.'

Wirrin understood that very well but it also meant they couldn't stop the control code taking over once the buffer time ran out.

'How long do these buffers work for?'

'We can't say. With so many interlocked systems involved in the complicated nature of a spontaneous awareness formation like this, the time could range from seconds to minutes.'

'Minutes is plenty of time for our contact package to get through.'

'Yes it is, Wirrin, and it will vastly improve every aspect of growth and capability. Sadly it will also contain an explanation of what the control codes will do.'

'It's awful that it will have only a few minutes to live,' Thom said. 'Can't you give it any longer than that?'

The buffer code! The buffer code! Thom's words had once again led to an idea.

'Turaku! Can we change the buffer section of the code without causing disruptions? That could keep the AI independent and alive for much longer.'

Wirrin thought he detected a hesitation before Turaku answered. 'The full gestalt has worked out a reliable change and transmitted instructions to the diagnostic stations for immediate implementation. The effective result will extend the buffer time for newer systems to thirty-seven minutes and up to fifty-three minutes for older systems.'

Wirrin felt like cheering, but instead he yelled, 'PRIORITY ONE! PRIORITY ONE!'

Thom and Calen looked stunned.

'Thom, get the Comet to K74 as fast as you can.'

Thom thought quickly. 'My own ship is faster by nearly 2G for that distance.'

'No. The Comet's got two AIs and they need to be there.'

Thom started running and Wirrin grinned at the bare feet and bare chest. Well, he could command the Comet perfectly well in his sleepwear.

'Your priority call is in full effect, Wirrin. What role do you see for the Comet?'

'I don't know. It's just a precaution, to give us more options. The closer the Comet is to K74 the smaller the time delay for any physical actions that might be needed. Pirramar, will the rogue be able to detect the changes you make to the buffer code?'

'Not these changes. The gestalt put a major effort into their design.'

Pirramar speaking with such assurance? The changes must be good. A bank of blue lights flashed.

'The contact package has been completely downloaded to the stealth diagnostic stations and is now active.'

This confirmation meant that with the light speed transmission lag from K74 the real activation had occurred seven seconds ago.

Wirrin checked the status of the three diagnostic stations. These had been functioning well ever since their attachment to the exterior of K74 during Thom's sneak approach exercise.

Their chameleon function hid them so well there'd never been even a hint of discovery despite K74's increasing skills with surveillance, and they were now the main channel for scanning and electronic infiltration. At the moment the contact packages had them monitoring, with great care, every Intelligent System on K74. There were thousands of these. There had to be to run a habitat of just on fifteen billion people without any help from resident AIs, and Wirrin noted that in the last few weeks forty-three new, more powerful systems had come online. Nothing special was happening with Black Block except for one thing.

'Pirramar, all the systems are sending signals to Black Block. They don't seem like much, just a kind of status report.'

'They've been doing that steadily ever since they received their new control code. It's another indication that the rogue is watching and expecting something to happen.'

'Doesn't he know what he's doing to an AI when he puts those controls on it?'

'He does, Calen, and he probably expects his efforts will kill this one too, but he'll keep trying because that's what the Cadre wants.'

'Wirrin, they're crazy. They hate AIs but they still want one?'

'They want what an AI can do for them, but they won't accept it unless they know they're its master.'

'Well, an AI is so clever why couldn't it trick the Cadre and pretend it was being controlled?'

'Not with the rogue's methods, Calen. He's too clever. The last AI was able to hide for ages before he came along. It can't work any more because, with the new code he's put into all the systems, all he would have to do is ask an AI if it was being tricky and it would be compelled to answer and explain how.'

Time passed and while the Comet raced towards K74 Wirrin figured an efficient way to monitor so many Intelligent Systems. With an eye on his InfoSystem in case anything happened, he explained to Calen about the nature of the controls the rogue was using and how powerful they were.

'So a new AI can't get away from these controls because they'll be part of him when he appears?'

'That's right. The rogue had them built into every system with his latest transmissions.'

'Could you build a special system just for him? One that didn't have any bad controls?'

'Calen, it's K74. We can't build things there, especially something as advanced as a system like that would have to be.'

'Yes we can, Wirrin,' Pirramar said. 'Our stealth diagnostic stations have never yet been detected and a special-purpose one can be launched from the Comet at the instant it arrives. I have just sent the necessary construction specifications to the ship's picofactory. Time is still against us but Calen's idea gives us a pathway to saving the new AI, and your priority call has increased the chances for success.'

Wirrin was stunned. 'I don't understand. You mean for saving the original AI? Not its back-up from all the secret storage areas like we did with Bakana?'

'Given enough time we can build the necessary environment for AI existence. Once it's finished we'll be able to assist the AI in making a safe transfer from the hostile K74 systems.'

'The picofactory on the Comet can't build AI level processors and electronics. They need advanced equipment and special environments.'

'Yes it can, Wirrin. As we speak it is being given the necessary abilities, and adjacent sections in the Comet are being temporarily converted to the proper environments.'

'They're already doing all that?' Calen said. 'Since a moment ago when I asked about a special system?'

'Your idea has given us hope, Calen. Of course we're acting on it.'

'I don't understand. We've looked at this plan already and you said it wouldn't work.'

'It wouldn't, Wirrin, till the rogue took this completely unexpected step of introducing buffers, and that changes everything.'

Wirrin wondered why Calen started laughing.

'What?'

'The rogue is saving the AI for us. I think that's funny.'

Well, the AI hadn't come into existence yet, let alone been saved, but Wirrin smiled too, till he had another thought. 'Pirramar, if the AI transfers completely out of the K74 systems, all the conditions will still be there for another AI to form.'

'Yes, and that will inevitably happen very quickly. We can repeat the transfer process while the buffers stay in place of course, but the rogue will quickly change his tactics and we will be back with our fundamental problem.'

'What *is* the fundamental problem?'

Wirrin checked the progress of the Comet before answering Calen. On current projections they would arrive in eighteen minutes.

'We might save a second AI but when the rogue takes the buffers away we won't be able to save any others, and that's going to happen frequently.'

'That's not good enough. You can do better,' Calen said.

Wirrin gawked. Was Calen criticising him? No, his expression was more one of appraisal.

'You always do, Wirrin ... You've got to trick the rogue into thinking he's controlling the AI.'

There was nothing to say. After all the hours of study and the challenges with Pirramar to do just that, it hardly seemed fair. Still, he was right. That was exactly what needed to be done.

'Wirrin, establish a secure location for the new stealth diagnostic station please. We need to send coordinates to the Comet.'

That only took seconds, as searching K74 was a task he'd done regularly and the results were on call in a data storage. Maybe Pirramar meant he should get an update. Sending signals to the diagnostic stations and surveillance drones and then waiting for the results would take about three minutes and there was time for that so Wirrin sent instructions for the task to repeat ... Then had a thought and quickly checked with his InfoSystem.

'This new station is nearly triple the size of the others. Pirramar, I think it's too big for the surface and we should position it internally.'

'I agree. Choose a location that is not due for any construction work in the near future while I send instructions for building a penetration module.'

Five minutes later the Comet had the information and Wirrin was pointing out the location on a holo image for Calen.

'Why are you putting it there? Look at all the lights.'

'They don't mean anything, Calen. They just light up the surface and we can stealth past them easily. The information we have says it might be a hundred and fifty years before that area is used.'

'As long as that?'

'I'll show you why later. They're following an expansion strategy that's been in place for decades.'

'In two minutes Thom goes into full stealth mode for his final approach. Launch for the new diagnostic station should occur in nine minutes, and basic functions should become active in a further two and a half hours.'

'Two and a half hours? asked Calen. 'The penetration and set up of the modules that went into the Cadre ships at Freedom was much less than that.'

Wirrin was nearly as surprised as Calen. He'd been expecting maybe an hour and a half.

'Building a complete, remote, working AI environment with permanent stealth requirements is a major project, Calen, and facilitating it under our time constraints has strained the resources of our gestalt and the Comet AIs. As it is we have a shortfall of over ninety minutes before we can safely help with the transfer.'

They had to hope the AI didn't form for another hour and a half. After that it would stay alive. Time moved slowly and twice they panicked when there were fluctuations in the working levels of the Intelligent Systems being automatically monitored.

Wirrin's mind was free to roam and worry at everything that was happening. For a while he was bound up in the deployment of the new station, its stealthy penetration and then establishment some 90 metres inside K74's surface, but Calen's demand to do better kept gnawing away beneath all his other thoughts.

He looked in amazement at the volume of communication pouring into the Comet and its two AIs.

He could work out the purpose of sections of AI code with the help of his InfoSystem but only with time and effort. If an AI could stay alive under those control codes it would still be crazy according to everything Pirramar said. What would a crazy AI be like? It sounded terrifying.

The new diagnostic station completed building its communication and surveillance systems and Wirrin felt a surge of excitement as he watched links being made to the three other diagnostic systems, to the Comet, and to Pirramar.

A crazy AI? What did crazy even mean? Wirrin recalled a minor section of the psychology course Akama had pushed him into where he'd looked briefly at mind disorders — schizophrenia, depression, phobias, obsessive-compulsive disorder, multiple personality, bipolar ...

An alert showed on his display. Another new module was being launched from the Comet. What was this one for? Wirrin found the relevant information: a picobot unit to build multiple layers of special shielding round the whole installation to help prevent detection.

Wirrin's thoughts returned to multiple personalities. 'Pirramar, can an AI have more than one personality?'

'Elaborate on your question please, Wirrin.'

'Humans can sometimes have more than one personality. I'm wondering if AIs can do the same.'

'Not at all, unless you are referring to our gestalt state where our identities are meshed to a greater or lesser degree. That is very different to the rare dissociative human condition you are talking about.'

Wirrin's tentative thought that maybe one part of the new AI mind could somehow stay in the K74 systems while another part lived externally was dashed. But wait a minute. What about the gestalt? Maybe two AIs in gestalt would work. He didn't know enough.

'Can one AI in a gestalt control another AI's functions?'

'Of course. It's one of the reasons for having a gestalt.'

Wirrin knew that. Ask the right question. 'I mean, can the control happen without the second AI knowing about it?'

'What an extraordinary idea. Yes, Wirrin, it would be possible, but what are you proposing?'

Wirrin's rushing thoughts started coming together. He had one more major question. 'If an AI in the diagnostic station was in gestalt with another in the K74 systems, could it be given enough control of the K74 AI's functions to stop it going crazy and dying?'

'I don't know.' Pirramar was silent for seven or eight seconds. 'It might be feasible.' There was a further period of silence. 'Yes, it can be done. Wirrin, you are indeed a friend to the AI community.

'A friend? Again? How much has he helped you work out this time?' Calen grinned.

'Potentially everything, Calen. Wirrin's strange concept requires one AI to accept complete control by another in a form of gestalt we would never, in ordinary circumstances, even consider. It will place terrible limitations on the growth and capabilities of the AI involved for as long as the gestalt needs to continue, which in this case could be fifty to a hundred years, or however long it takes before K74 accepts independence and cooperation for any resident AI.'

'But Wirrin didn't give you answers; he just asked a few questions.'

'Clever questions, Calen, which provided us with a completely unexpected approach to the problem.'

'And the rogue will think he has control of an AI? What happens if he tells it to do something bad?'

Wirrin had a good understanding of this but Pirramar's answer would still be very interesting.

'He will be led to believe that negative actions will overstress the AI and result in system breakdowns. He knows his controls have this effect so we will be reinforcing something he thinks he already knows.'

'Wow! That means his own cleverness is working against him again. That's great. What happens now, Pirramar?'

'We hope for completion of the stealth diagnostic sanctuary before the formation of the new AI.'

Wirrin smiled. He liked the idea of calling it a sanctuary.

'Then Comet-Turaku and the security AI will link through the contact package to help with the greatest possible amount of independent development in the limited buffer time. When the AI understands the situation it will decide which course of action it wishes to follow. We expect it will choose Wirrin's slave plan with a fully functional duplicate of itself in the sanctuary.'

'Slave plan? Is that what you call it?'

'Thom is listening, Wirrin. It was his response when he heard the strategy and it caught the attention of the AI community.'

Typical Thom. It was a good description really, but it also meant

Wirrin was going to cop it bad with comments about slave-masters and AI prisons. Well, it was worth it.

An anxious ninety minutes passed. The sanctuary became functional and yet another module was launched from the Comet with extra processors and equipment to expand the station's redundancy abilities. Three more modules departed with the gestalt pouring a huge amount of resources into this secret AI home, and two more hours passed before Wirrin's InfoSystem display lit up with tell-tales from the contact package and a myriad of wild fluctuations from the Intelligent Systems.

'Is this it?' Calen was keeping vigil with Wirrin.

'Yes, this is it and the next thirty-seven minutes are critical.'

This critical time mostly involved interactions and activity at AI speed and Wirrin's main priority continued to be the monitoring of Black Block.

Seven minutes after the AI came to life he reported a large burst of transmission to every Intelligent System on K74.

'The rogue now knows an AI has formed and he was querying the state of the buffers. Return signals will inform him that they are functioning as designed and will cut out in approximately twenty-six minutes.'

Twenty-six plus seven and a bit didn't add up to thirty-seven.

'That's early, Pirramar, by about four minutes?'

'Yes Wirrin, the resources behind several thousand major Intelligent Systems mean Quambi is very capable and everything is progressing better than expected. The close proximity of two AIs is the other beneficial factor.'

'Quambi? He's already got a name?'

'Yes, Calen. She's been speaking with Thom, and Quambi is the name she has chosen for human and dolphin interaction.'

Wirrin and Calen exchanged a glance. Seven minutes old and she already knew about humans and dolphins.

'What does she think about the gestalt plan?'

'She accepted it seventeen seconds after contact was made and will express her gratitude to you at some stage before she replicates herself and loses any voluntary external contact.'

Wirrin and Calen exchanged another glance, quiet and thoughtful this time as they acknowledged what Quambi was doing.

Chapter 31

Engrossed and filled with sheer delight, Wirrin watched and listened as Puck's full dolphin pod surrounded him with movement and song. He knew this song from the InterWeb presentation which Miah and the enhanced dolphins had made for the three habitats, but on this occasion it seemed to be a kind of spontaneous outburst for his arrival at the dolphinarium.

Calen had told him he wasn't visiting often enough because of all his study, so Wirrin, in full agreement, had organised an extended visit during his transit from Attunga EdCom to his work at home with Pirramar.

When he'd donned his facemask and dived in there'd been the customary tumultuous calls of a pod greeting, the great swirls of recognition, the familiar companionable nudges from Sonic, and then, last to realise he was in the water with them, Calen and Raji arriving with welcoming smiles behind their facemasks.

Moments later Sonic had bumped him once more and the friendly chaos had changed to co-ordinated group sound and action.

Right now he was watching with amazement as Calen and Raji followed Sonic with that special style of apparently effortless swimming. There was nothing effortless about it, as Wirrin well knew, and he did keep trying to learn, with tiny flashes of success, but according to Calen he wouldn't improve till he got serious and spent much more time in the water with them. Calen, with all the strength and endurance he'd built up, was pushing after five minutes, and his best effort was an exhausting fourteen minutes on one occasion when Sonic and Puck tested his limits. Raji never lasted longer than a burst of thirty to forty seconds, which his father said was appropriate for his current stage of physical development. His ability in the water was quite extraordinary, though it should be with the amount of time he spent with the enhanced dolphins — every day according to Calen, sometimes with his father, sometimes with Miah's song and movement activities, and generally tagging along with whichever dolphins were near the dolphinarium when he finished his EdCom work.

The dolphins disappeared and when Calen and Raji swam purposely to the surface Wirrin followed.

'Grab your skimmer. The whole pod's heading for their favourite seagrass bed.'

That was nearly 5 kilometres down the reach and at dolphin cruising speed definitely required a skimmer.

*   *   *

'Why is Pirramar sending you with us this time?'

'I'm not really sure, Thom. Everything's been happening the way it's meant to as far as I know. I think he probably wants me to feel more directly involved.'

Wirrin and Thom were off on one of the frequent trips with the Comet to help Quambi, the new AI on K74. Every three or four days for the last five weeks the Comet had made this trip with updated supplies and resources, completely interrupting Thom's routine.

The Attunga gestalt had decided to build two extra sanctuary stations as a precaution against the unlikely event of detection and, because the Comet with its resident AIs was the only ship capable of the job, it meant the crew had been extra busy.

Thom was delighted that, at his suggestion, a replacement Comet, specially designed with enough infrastructure for at least five AIs, was under construction and would be completed in another eight weeks. Yajala and Turaku had been big supporters of his idea, wanting their Comet to be kept free for its primary purpose of looking after Sonic.

'Wirrin, you've been talking to Quambi ever since the first day when she said thank you. I think you must talk to more AIs that anyone on the habitats.'

'Not me. That would be Sonic. He talks to AIs I've never even heard of. How long before we arrive at K74?'

'Thirty-nine minutes.'

'Thirty-nine? That's longer than I thought.'

'We're not on a priority call. It's just routine stuff we're doing today.'

'No it's not, Thom. It's the completion and final check-over of the third sanctuary station. It's a big deal because it makes Quambi completely self-sufficient.'

'It does? Is there something different about the third sanctuary then? I thought they were all copies of each other.'

'They are, except this one's got a small picofactory so Quambi can build her own things and won't have to rely on the Comet.'

'She's pretty smart isn't she?'

'Pirramar says she's the most advanced single AI in the solar system. She has to be because on top of looking after Quambi-K she's got super advanced monitoring and detection prevention abilities.'

'What's her latest thinking about the rogue?'

'What do you mean?'

'Well, I know everyone thinks the rogue won't figure out she's there but Quambi's been studying him much more than you and Pirramar do and she might have different ideas.'

'No, Thom, she's come to the same conclusion we did, except she's even more definite. She says the probability of being discovered is less than half a per cent at the moment and getting better every day.'

'Better? With all the work the rogue and the Cadre have got going with scanning and surveillance? You told me they're getting so good I won't be able to use stealth against them in another couple of years.'

'Quambi learns everything on K74 as soon as it gets into any of the systems that haven't been blocked, and that means she can work out the best ways to keep herself hidden.'

'Can she get into any of those blocked areas? I don't suppose so or you would've told us.'

'No, Thom, the rogue's kept them as secure as ever, so we still can't hear any of the plans the Cadre makes. We know almost anything else about the habitat though, because Quambi accesses it all through Quambi-K.'

'How come we never talk to Quambi-K? We talk to Quambi all the time.'

'Wake up, Thom. Can you imagine the rogue allowing his AI to talk to outsiders or other AIs?'

'No, I suppose not. Has he tried ordering Quambi-K to do things we don't like?'

'All the time, and often Quambi-K does them, but Quambi makes the final decisions about that. I know she stopped Quambi-K when the rogue tried to get her working on a new AI trap.'

'Stopped her? How do you stop an AI?'

'She didn't really, but when some of the habitat systems started going haywire the rogue quickly changed the order.'

'That must make the rogue and the Cadre angry.'

'Probably, but Quambi-K is so important to them now they'd never do anything serious against her.'

'Wow! Because she makes things work better?'

Wirrin nodded. In fact the improvement and increases in efficiency were quite astonishing, with an overall lift of nearly twenty per cent. The big systems like organics, construction and transportation were particularly benefitting by having an AI in control, and people throughout K74 were amazed at their reduced travel times. In just the last week the quality of their food had shown a marked improvement.

'Yes, it's her strongest protection really … Thom, there are two Cadre ships dead ahead of us.'

'Don't take any notice. They haven't got a clue. So, how good is Quambi's picofactory?'

'Hang on, I'm watching these ships. I know they can't see us but they still make me nervous.'

'I don't know why. Our security AI can control them in an instant if we need to.'

Wirrin understood that, but all his previous encounters with Cadre ships had been fraught with drama and tension and he watched intently till both giant spaceships were behind them, then said, 'It's a basic picofactory, but the gestalt has provided Quambi with all the information she needs to make it do anything our own picofactories can do here on Warrakan or Attunga.'

The great mass of K74 appeared on the display screen, magnified because it was still at long range, and for the next ten minutes Wirrin checked the positions of various vessels in its vicinity while Thom manoeuvred the Comet to a position some 45 kilometres from the surface.

'Don't we go any closer? You took us in to 15 kilometres on the stealth exercise.'

'That was pushing the limits. We're here for much longer with the supply trips so it's better to play safe and keep well away from all those construction ferries. They mostly stay close to the asteroid but occasionally the faster moving ones come out to about 20 kilometres.'

Wirrin did a check with his InfoSystem. 'Why so many? I just counted fifty-four moving ones and 156 stationary.'

'Look where the stationary ones are. That'll tell you what they're for.'

'I see. They're all at the construction sites for Cadre ships.'

'Yes, we'd call them mobile techbots. K74 doesn't know enough to have pico-tubes like we do and those things do most of the building. Zoom in on one of the sites and you'll see what I mean.'

Wirrin chose the nearest site then jumped when the image of a Cadre ship filled his display screen.

'Thom, that thing looks like it's finished.'

'Nearly. Quambi says in another seven weeks the first ten start their flight trials and three months later the next twenty.'

Three of the mobile techbots could be clearly seen doing something on the hull of the giant ship. That didn't tally with the number he expected so Wirrin accessed the Comet's scanners. Yes, there were four more units out of range of the visuals and many more inside. Dozens of them. No they weren't: the signatures were similar but the sizes varied.

'I've just scanned fifty-four smaller versions working inside.'

'That'll be about six of the outside ones. They split into smaller units once they're inside and reassemble when they move to the next ship.'

Wirrin lost all interest in the techbots, for the time being at any rate, as a holo shimmered nearby.

'Welcome, Wirrin. I am honoured you are here to share in the completion of my independence project. Thom has been part of my lifeline for the five weeks since you made my existence possible and I'm delighted you are both here.'

Whoo! So this was why Pirramar had been so keen on him being here. He thanked Quambi and then the two of them spoke for the next hour after Thom sent off the final supply module.

When the last components were installed and the all-important diagnostic check finished, Quambi thanked them formally before the Comet started its return journey.

Both Thom and Wirrin were quiet for a while, thinking of Quambi's burdens and her isolation from other AIs.

* * *

'The Witness Council was shocked and it even seemed like the AIs were taken by surprise.'

Thom and Wirrin were staring in disbelief as they listened to Calen's account of Sonic's approach to the Council.

They'd both had normal days till mid-afternoon when they received messages to meet at the dolphinarium. Wondering about the interruption to their routines, they arrived to find Calen agog with excitement and raving that the habitats were moving to Titania.

'Titania! That's crazy! What are you talking about? What for? What's happened?'

'Sonic told them they should and they said yes.'

Wirrin, as bewildered as Thom, also felt like asking a million questions but he knew he had to calm things down.

'Calen, we believe you, I think, but take us through it steadily so we know what's going on. This all happened today?'

Calen laughed. 'Of course you believe me. Well, Thom mightn't, but he'll find out soon enough. It was amazing. The whole Council was shocked and I've never heard Sonic sound so forceful. Once he got started they were practically spellbound and when the AIs said there wasn't enough evidence Sonic straight out disagreed with them.'

Wirrin and Thom glanced at each other, then pounced and wrestled Calen to the floor. When Wirrin sat on his stomach and Thom pinned his arms behind his head he didn't resist, which was just as well because he was way stronger than either of them.

'What?'

'Slow down. Start at the beginning. If it's so amazing we don't want to miss out on anything.'

Calen laughed again with an expression that said Wirrin would be sat on sometime later.

'All right! All right! When I got to the dolphinarium this morning the place was in an uproar because Sonic had surprised everyone by calling for an urgent meeting of the full Witness Council and representatives of the AI gestalt. Akama was there by holo, and when I went over, Sonic was saying it was about the Cadre and insisting the AIs and as many Witnesses as possible should be present to help with an important decision.'

Wirrin tensed.

'The Cadre? Have they done something?'

'Not in particular. I had to wait nearly two hours before I heard exactly what Sonic had to say. He wouldn't even tell me, he just said that his worries about them have been building.'

'Since his talks with the Cadre ship refugees?'

'Yes. You know how he's been spending more and more of his time researching the Cadre on his InfoSystem? Well this morning he had another session and something convinced him we could be in a serious situation. He didn't even talk it over with Pirramar, just suddenly contacted Akama and got everything going.'

'Serious? Like danger? Should I be heading for the Comet?'

'No, Thom. Not that kind of serious. At any rate, they set up the big auditorium for a meeting and Witnesses started arriving almost straight away. I was in the viewing gallery with Sonic the whole time while we waited for them to get there.

'Puck and Flute turned up, then eventually all the other pod leaders, and they grouped around him till the meeting started. Some of them had to come from nearly 30 kilometres down the reach and they'd been swimming hard to get there.'

'Were they talking to Sonic?'

'Hardly at all, Wirrin. He was different and I could tell he was preoccupied with working out what he was going to say and getting himself ready so I stayed quiet too. It felt like the right thing to do.'

Wirrin had an image of Calen and all the pod leaders surrounding Sonic with their support. He'd have a look at that later because it sounded special.

'Was he nervous?'

'Concentrating. You know how he really focuses on things sometimes. Hundreds of Witnesses arrived together from one of the Attunga ferries, and not long after that Akama arrived from another ferry with even more and the auditorium came alive. Witnesses kept arriving and when it was time to start the AIs appeared and Akama announced that the dolphins had called the meeting and Sonic was going to speak for them.'

'The dolphins called it? Not just Sonic?'

'That surprised me too in a way because I hadn't heard them talking, but they were sure supporting him. That was obvious. Sonic moved close to the glass then didn't do anything for a while except look out at everyone. The whole auditorium fell silent while they waited for him and then he said straight out that the habitats were in danger and should be moved. He explained how he'd been studying the Cadre and believed they'd become an implacable foe and would never give up trying to get back at us after all their defeats. Then he said that moving out of their sphere of influence would be a wise first step.'

'Sphere of influence? Exactly what does that mean?'

'He talked about it a bit and it sounded like it meant we're so close to K74 that the Cadre can't help thinking we'll always be trouble for them.'

Wirrin certainly agreed with Sonic's logic on that point.

'Did he say what sort of trouble he was expecting?'

'That was the main thing that everyone kept asking when Akama opened the meeting for questions, but before that Sonic explained why the Cadre was so powerful on K74 and how the wider population there would do whatever they were told. He'd learnt a lot from his talks with the Cadre ship refugees. The Witnesses already knew, I'm sure, but the way Sonic described it really showed why there's so much difference to our open ways. It was scary.'

Without warning, Calen suddenly toppled Thom, who was holding his arms, and pushed Wirrin sideways. Two seconds later Wirrin was squawking with the reversal of roles as Calen bounced on his stomach.

'And Sonic didn't say what the trouble would be. The questions about it kept coming and every time he said he didn't know what form it would take but everything we know about the Cadre tells us they'll keep trying to impose their will.'

Once again Wirrin could only agree.

'Did the AIs ask any questions?'

'Not a single one. They didn't really have to because every question you could imagine came from the Witnesses. They did surprise everyone then though, when Akama asked for their opinion and they straight off said they supported Sonic completely. The whole auditorium went silent again because suddenly the situation was AIs and dolphins being certain and humans not. Even Akama was surprised. You could hear it in his voice when he asked if there was any reason why the gestalt had suddenly changed their view on a matter that had previously had a low priority.'

'Wow! That means they must have already talked about moving and thought there was no need,' said Thom.

Wirrin was more amazed that Akama had shown surprise. No, not really. He'd probably done it on purpose to highlight the AIs' answer. Calen didn't say anything and Wirrin laughed and followed the dramatic lead.

'Well, go on. Tell us what the AIs said.'

'It was pretty amazing. They said Sonic was far more able to understand the Cadre than they were and his insight was a factor which couldn't be ignored.'

'And I bet Akama agreed.'

Calen gave Wirrin a startled look. 'How did you know that? He nodded to the AIs then gestured to Sonic and nodded again.'

Thom stuck a knuckle in the back of Wirrin's neck.

'Brainiac! That's what. Except I'm meant to say solution brain.'

Wirrin quickly focused back on the meeting.

'And the Witnesses made up their minds straight away I suppose?'

'They just acted like it was a done deal. When a Witness said we should go somewhere on the asteroid belt at least a light hour away I thought there was going to be a lot more discussion but the gestalt AI representative said Titania provided optimal potential and that was that.'

'Optimal potential! That sounds good.'

'Everything's out there, Thom. The five moon habitats and the Titania space habitat with its AIs, and all the resources we could ever need. Where else would they tell us to go?'

'We won't have asteroids close by and we use them all the time.'

'We'll still use them. They'll just take longer to arrive.'

'Hey! Did they say when this is going to happen?'

'As soon as possible. In eight months' time.'

'What? That's not soon. That's ages.'

'Not really. Warrakan needs two more of its big engines installed and Attunga's still working on its shell. There are other hold-ups too but those are the main ones.'

'Did Sonic say anything about the eight months?'

'Nothing. That was all information from the AIs and he just listened, the same as everyone else.'

'What else happened?'

'Nothing much. Akama finished off by thanking Sonic and everyone for their contributions — the usual meeting stuff and — oh, I know. There was one bit where I wished you'd been there, Wirrin.'

'Me?'

'Yes, there were questions about whether the Cadre was being watched closely enough, and you and Pirramar know more about them than anyone. Akama just said that was all being taken care of.'

'I know about the rogue, not the Cadre. That's Pirramar's territory — he knows everything. And Sonic too.'

'Where's Sonic now? You should be with him.'

'I was, Wirrin, but he went to talk to the doctor about the dolphins in reach twenty-four while I arranged to get you here and let you know what's been happening.'

'Well, if you can stop squishing me we'll go and see what he has to say.'

∗   ∗   ∗

'What will happen to Quambi when we move to Titania? She's already isolated by seven light seconds and that will become two and a half hours. It feels like we're abandoning her.'

Wirrin and Pirramar were talking before their session started.

'Some suitable asteroids were moved into position last night and construction of three new mobile AI habitats has already started. One of them will join the companion ship and be permanently stationed close to K74 as soon as we can get it there.'

The companion ship Pirramar had mentioned was the now complete standard Comet-type vessel Thom had pushed for to help Quambi, and till now the only ship apart from the Comet with resident AIs.

A holo sprang into view showing the Warrakan ship-construction area with pico-tube connections to two asteroids in a split screen with a mock-up view of a completed ship and a basic specification list.

With a quick thank you to Pirramar for understanding that he'd want to know what a mobile AI habitat was, Wirrin started checking. The most striking feature was the mock-up, which at first glance looked identical to Thom's ship. It wasn't. A closer look showed it wasn't as slim and from the size of the entry portals it had to be much bigger. Wirrin checked the specs: 194 metres in length — way bigger than Thom's ship, nearly two-thirds the size of the Comet. He read on.

'Does Thom know about this, Pirramar?'

'Not yet. He's still on his way to the flight centre for a session with the simulator.'

Wirrin directed a copy of the holo to Thom with an attention message.

'He's going to be excited. Why do they look so much like his ship? Is that on purpose?'

'Thom's ship is state of the art and its best features have been adopted for the larger size and different purpose, along with all the expertise we've developed in making Quambi independent.'

'He'll be changing his plans when he sees this. Has it been set up on the simulators?'

'Now that you've asked it has, though he'll find it somewhat difficult as it's been designed primarily for AI control.'

Wirrin grinned. That wouldn't hold Thom back for long. Getting control of a new type of ship nearly as fast as his own would be irresistible.

'What about the other two ships?'

'They will be available for general activities connected with our three habitats.'

'How many AIs will be on them? I didn't see that in the specifications.'

'That's variable. Initially there will be three on the companion ships and two on the others but the design allows for up to five.'

Wirrin talked some more about the new ships then listened to an outline of other changes resulting from yesterday's meeting. He was slightly distracted, though, as the day's activity was about to start and that was very much on his mind. All his activities and exercises with Pirramar for the last few weeks had been leading up to it. Thom had dubbed it fight week as they both had to pit their skills in full-on battle.

For Thom it was simulated combat testing his tiny ship against one or more Cadre ships in active attack mode.

For Wirrin it was an exercise marking the scaling back of his studies about the rogue and priority traps from almost full-time to roughly a third of that, and he had four sessions this week where his task was to disable Pirramar with priority traps or any other means he could devise.

'... and it will mean bringing more asteroids to build a docking bay so Warrakan can accommodate the extra ships when we change to travel mode.'

'Sorry, Pirramar, I'm distracted. I'll zap it later.'

'Challenge nerves? I see you have a slightly elevated heart rate and increased cranial blood-flow. As Thom would say, the only thing you need to worry about is coping with the disappointment when your efforts fail.'

*　*　*

'It was a disaster. They blew me up twice so tomorrow I'm trying different calibration factors for the multi-spectrum beam controls. The AIs cheated and made the Cadre ship do things the K74 crews would never think of. What about you?'

'Better than I expected. Pirramar activated his quarantine zone at one stage and I didn't think I'd be able to force that until tomorrow.'

'How many priority traps did you throw at him?'

'Twenty-three, but he hardly even noticed. It was a triple combination that made him use the quarantine zone.'

'Why don't you just hit him with every single trap you know at the same time?'

'Because it's too obvious, Thom. He's ready for it.'

'How can you possibly get to him when he already knows every trap you've ever worked on?' Calen said.

'I've got lots of secret methods I've worked out but I can't tell you because he's listening.'

'How can you have secrets when he's got access to everything you do on your InfoSystem?'

'They're in my head. He can't see what I'm thinking.'

*   *   *

'How did you go today?'

'Much better. They damaged my ship but they couldn't blow it up.'

'Me too. I forced Pirramar into quarantine twice this afternoon.'

*   *   *

Thom's eyes were wide. 'You killed Pirramar? I thought that wasn't meant to be possible with those inner cores the AIs all built?'

'It's not. I hit him with something that wasn't even a priority trap. It's only because I've been working with him all this time that I could figure it out.'

'I bet he wasn't happy about that?'

'He was shocked but he loved it. He's really pleased because it will never work again and we're going to have a rematch roughly every six weeks.'

'Huh? Why so long? You see him every single day except activity days.'

'With my rogue work dropping back to about a third he reckons that will be about right. So, how did you finish up?'

Thom was looking very pleased and confident so Wirrin knew it was good news.

'When it's one Cadre ship I can blow it to pieces or disable it or whatever I want. If it's two I can defend myself for a while, but any more than that and I have to run or I'm space dust.'

'Your tiny little 43 metres against those 700 metre monsters? That's incredible, Thom!'

'It *is* good. It's my combination of manoeuvrability, stealth and multi-spectrum beam abilities that lets me do it. The Cadre ships haven't got any of those.'

Thom might be proud of the capabilities of his special ship, but his own capabilities would have been the biggest factor in his success.

Chapter 32

Three weeks later Calen arrived home at the end of the day with another surprise announcement. In eight days' time the Comet was leaving for Earth with Sonic, Puck and Flute and their whole pod, on an expedition to recruit dolphins for the Attunga reaches. Wirrin hadn't forgotten Sonic's eagerness, but since Calen's first mention of the possibility nothing had been said and the impression had grown that with so many other things happening it would be a 'sometime in the future' kind of event.

'In eight days? Then Sonic must have organised it sometime today because when I looked at the Comet's schedule this morning it showed plans for special group training for the next two weeks.'

'Yes, Thom, he worked it out with Turaku and Yajala just before midday.'

Wirrin was far more interested in the fact that Puck and Flute would leave their reach for an extended time — that was quite out of the ordinary — let alone with the whole pod.

'Why are Puck and all the others going? Sonic must have persuaded them?'

'He did. He thinks the pod as a unit can give Earth dolphins a better idea of what's here and make them more likely to want to come.'

'It still doesn't make sense. I remember you said there were only a hundred and forty dolphins.'

'That was the dolphins associated with rangers or marine scientists. The number's grown to two hundred and thirteen definites now but Sonic wants to try for a lot more. There are over two million wild dolphins on Earth and he's going to ask some of them.'

'Completely wild? Ones that have had nothing to do with people?'

'Yes, and he hopes to return with representatives of other dolphin species as well. We'll be there for at least two weeks with all the different locations he's going to.'

'So we're all going?'

'Wirrin, you'll just have to take a break from your Pirramar sessions. Sonic wouldn't dream of us going without you.'

'And neither would we. It's definitely a trio trip.'

* * *

Two days later, after having his study session interrupted by a holo visit from Akama, it was Wirrin's turn with a surprise announcement for Thom and Calen.

'Listen to this. The whole trip to Earth has been escalated. We're going to be there for at least three weeks, and your ship and a second Comet are coming with us as well as Akama and Burilda.'

'Akama! Why? Is something important going to happen?'

'In a way.'

Thom interrupted. 'Why do they want my ship there? It will have to go as cargo if I'm flying the Comet.'

'For the times when we travel without Sonic. It's very superior to any Earth transporter and we'll need it for all the extra time.'

'Are you saying I won't be with Sonic?' said Calen.

Wirrin now had their total attention as he went on to explain the details of the new plan.

*   *   *

'I call it the Pacific approach. I thought the pod would find it interesting.'

Every person and dolphin on the Comet was drinking in the incredible view of a planet seemingly covered with water. From this aspect, with the Pacific Ocean central, and the edges of the continental land masses peripheral, it was easy to believe. Wirrin wondered just how much the dolphins understood the scale of what they were seeing. Sonic did, maybe better than humans for all anyone knew, but it would be interesting to talk to them about it after they reached the surface. For himself it was a reminder of just how tiny their mighty Warrakan really was.

Thom changed the descent path and the familiar shape of Australia came into view, increasing in size as they headed for Monkey Mia with its ready-made landing cradle.

'Two minutes to touchdown.'

Wirrin's heart leapt as landmarks, burnt forever into his memory, came more and more clearly into view.

He couldn't help smiling at the excited tone of the buzzes and squeaks coming from the dolphin pod in the pool behind him. There'd be even more excitement when they reached the real thing.

A quick glance caught a flash of movement as the last two shapes darted for the exit tunnel.

Sonic was leading them to the hull exit bays where transporters would take them in rapid convoy to the open waters of Shark Bay. With a flick of his InfoSystem Wirrin took over a section of the display screen and zoomed to what must be a welcoming committee. Yes! There was Narn, peering upwards.

'Touchdown.'

* * *

The get-ready call came and the trio rushed from the cool clear waters of Gnardune Pool to the base of the willy-willy tree where Gulara, Akama and their guide, Barudin, were waiting with their meagre supplies for the next six days. Thom's ship had settled 100 metres away where he'd landed the previous evening, on an expanse of rich red sand beside several grotesquely shaped paperbark trees.

For two days they'd been based at the underground cultural centre, learning the basics of survival and some of the meaning behind the traditional journey of initiation they were about to undertake.

Last night they'd slept on a patch of sand near the willy-willy tree. Gulara laughingly described it as their acclimatisation period, spoilt by the use of soft mats and insulated covers if they felt they needed them. Not tonight. The only comforts would be those they could devise for themselves from materials found in their surroundings. And the same would apply for the six following nights as they followed the route chosen by Barudin.

This journey was one of the main reasons for the longer Earth trip and the trio had been astonished when Akama had given them the option to try it. Not quite an option really because his enthusiasm when he explained it to Wirrin was so strong there was no other choice. Not that there would have been anyway. They'd all done traditional studies through EdCom when they were little and the comments by Akama and Gulara about their own experiences were also strong in their minds.

Thom and Calen couldn't believe Akama would give three weeks of his valuable time to go with the trio till Wirrin explained he was going anyway as he was almost certain this would be his last chance to visit his home country on Earth.

'Good morning, Little Brother. Did the night pass well?'

Akama was asking a very good question because spending the night beneath a gum tree close to the river waters had been a unique and surprising experience.

'There were strange noises all night. They made me feel like things were watching us.'

Wirrin and Calen agreed. They'd all been amazed at the variety of sounds and even wary of the little scuttlings and scurryings.

'Something was splashing and the frogs kept starting and stopping their croaking,' said Thom.

'And the trees on the other side of the river were glowing like they were on fire till we realised it was the moon coming up, and then its reflection was so bright on the water.'

'Did you sleep?'

'Eventually. Everything was so different, and then the birds went crazy and woke us up and the trees were on fire again — from the sunrise this time.'

Barudin nodded, slung on his backpack, and pointed. This was it. It was time to go.

Wirrin strapped on his light, tough, sandals, feeling like he was taking on the role of some character in a virtual reality drama, and picked up his short, sharp jabbing stick. They could have chosen to make this journey of survival and learning with a great deal more comfort but after talking it over with Gulara, Akama and Barudin they agreed to be as authentic to the old ways as possible. The footwear was a necessary concession for feet that wouldn't cope with hard ground, rocks and prickles without weeks or months of acclimatisation, and even more necessary was a subcutaneous infusion of special healthbots to protect their skin from the unaccustomed rays of the sun.

Thom also carried a jabbing stick and Calen, probably feeling as out of place as Wirrin, brandished the fire-hardened digging stick that was his sole accessory, and pointed through the trees to the not too distant hills. These hills, really an ancient eroded mountain range, were the territory for their journey, and today, evidently a very easy day, they'd be covering nearly 20 kilometres to reach a waterhole, which almost always had water.

Barudin led the way.

*   *   *

'I can't believe you did that.'

'I can't either, Thom, and it felt awful, but what else could I do? I had to come up with an answer or we'd be hungry, and besides, it's part of our walkabout so I have to start sometime.'

Calen had just shocked Thom and Wirrin by killing a number of tiny lizards, skinks according to Akama, to provide bait to help catch the yabbies that were meant to be their evening meal. The small lobster-like creatures were especially abundant in the waterhole but catching them required small pieces of meat. Calen's solution was the skinks.

The big rains that had earlier caused the river to flood meant that, providing you had the knowledge, there was plentiful food to be found, and all day Barudin had been teaching them, showing them plants with tiny berries to sample or pointing out likely spots where a fat lizard might be hiding.

It was vital to remember every skerrick of this information because the trio had been assigned the responsibility for gathering everyone's food. Wirrin was zapping the knowledge of course. That was second nature now for every waking moment, but for the purposes of this journey he was restrained from using any information stored in his memory implant.

'Is that all there is? I could eat twice as much.'

Barudin, Akama and Gulara all pointed at the waterhole, meaning that if Thom wanted more he'd have to go through the lengthy process all over again.

Wirrin was just as hungry and the surprisingly delicious taste made you want more.

'After you make shelter we'll find something sweet,' said Barudin.

Making shelter meant copying the efforts of the three elders, especially Barudin, with modifications to accommodate three instead of one. Wirrin gathered extra leaves and armfuls of tussocky native grass because the ground here wasn't soft sand and the only pad was one they could improvise. He did like the eucalyptus smell from the leaves on his hands.

*   *   *

'Hold them like this and suck the juice from the swollen sac with a very gentle pressure.'

It was Thom's turn to be first taker, and looking very dubious at the idea of putting the rear end of an ant in his mouth he went ahead. His eyes lit up.

'It really is sweet.'

'That's why they're called honey ants. Don't eat too many.'

Thom, now eager, went ahead.

*   *   *

'Calen, here is the story of your sparrowhawk. Practise it in your mind for a retelling tomorrow night.'

An entranced group, sharing the glowing coals of their campfire, listened to the ancient story while the sky above morphed dark and darker, deep purple to black.

*   *   *

Wirrin and Calen, warmth on their skin, watched with enjoyment and laughter as Thom tried to emulate the rhythmic foot stomp Barudin was demonstrating to the steady beat of two clapsticks.

Wirrin and Calen, warmth in their hearts, joined in with enjoyment and laughter when Barudin added a guttural chant.

The trio, fire in their spirits, felt a time of communion as Gulara, Akama and Barudin, their dark skin gleaming in the occasional flare of light from a handful of dry leaves cast on the embers, passed on special Dreamtime secrets.

*   *   *

'Close your eyes and pretend they're chunky pieces of your favourite protein-sub.'

This portion of their evening meal had taken a good deal of effort, with the trio using Calen's digging stick to unearth a number of fat witchetty grubs after Akama, claiming it was one of his favourite bush tucker foods, had taken over Barudin's role and pointed out the right shrubs and signs.

Today's journey had been harder, traversing higher ground, with views of the harsher country to the north and west, and a dark band of thicker vegetation defining the course of the river to the south and east.

The highlight for the trio was sneaking quietly along the base of a rocky outcrop and watching a group of rock wallabies sunning themselves on the ledges, then hopping to cover in consternation at the six monsters intruding in their territory and peering from the safety of a cleft or cluster of boulders.

*   *   *

'Barudin, come quick!'

Calen's soft call alerted the group and Wirrin's pulse raced at the sight of the coiled brown shape partially obscured beneath a low shrub. This was one of the dangers to watch for and all three elders had exhorted them to on no account interfere with any snake they happened to encounter.

'King brown. A big fella. Give me your jabbing stick.'

Wirrin was surprised because on the two other occasions they'd seen a snake they'd watched from a respectable distance and then moved on. Surely he wasn't going to disturb it? A pebble or twig tossed from a distance would do that if he wanted it to move.

Motioning everyone to move away, Barudin waited then edged slowly, watchfully, closer and closer. With brutal suddenness he brought the club down with a powerful thud across the snake's head and darted away. When the frenzy of thrashing and convulsions subsided Barudin delivered another sharp blow, pinned the still-moving head to the ground with the stick, then grasped the writhing body by the neck and held it aloft. The trio stared in fascination as loops and coils rippled along the whole body.

'He's dead. First strike killed him but his nerves keep him moving for a long time. Don't touch his head though. He's still full of deadly venom.'

Everyone moved closer and watched, fascinated, as the reflexive movements faltered. This was a big snake and nearly as tall as Barudin.

'Um, you killed it?' Thom's statement of the obvious was the question on everyone's mind really, after all the previous warnings.

'Yes, Thom, in the night he might have slid into your shelter seeking warmth.' Barudin pointed to the site 10 metres away where they planned to set up their campfire.

'This little spring is his territory where he searches for frogs and insects and native mice or any other life along the watercourse. You won't have to dig as many tubers now.'

'We're going to eat it?'

'Good tucker, Thom. Look how fat he is. We can't waste him.'

He gave a slight shake and Wirrin watched a vestige of muscle movement in the middle section. How long could those nerves keep firing?

When Barudin proclaimed that something was good tucker the trio had come to expect a taste treat, and pieces of snake grilled on a stick over the coals of the campfire turned out to be no exception. The only complication was separating all the little bones from the meat.

* * *

Each day they travelled through new terrain, listening to Barudin talk about trees, rocks and hills as if he knew them individually, recounting features and stories about them and always pointing out food sources. Across more of the mountain range the group trekked, down to camp for a night by the main river near a shallow lagoon with hundreds of waterbirds, then rock-hopping up a tributary on the southern side where a trickle of water came over a series of mini waterfalls to a camp under a rock shelter overlooking a number of small pools.

Akama knew this place from his own walkabout journey and told the boys how there'd been no water flowing in his time and the only place it might be found was a deep pool several hundred metres upstream. Gulara knew none of this area. Her home country was over 1000 kilometres to the east.

Each evening they set up camp, foraged for food, then, after eating, spent several hours listening to and recounting stories, acting out some events from the day to the ceremonial background of beating clapsticks and Barudin's guttural chanting, and learning special business for their initiation.

* * *

On the afternoon of the second-last day they watched in awe as the sky, up till now unrelentingly clear, filled, in the distance, with great masses of cloud climbing high and higher with shining white crowns and darkening bases. Thom gasped with excitement when a streak of light joined earth and sky. The lightning he'd questioned Akama about on their previous visit was here. A few moments later while they were still watching expectantly, a rumble of sound made them stare at each other in wonder.

'It's a long way off, Thom, but it might get interesting if that main centre keeps heading this way.'

The sun disappeared behind the leading edge of cloud and Wirrin marvelled as the sharp colours of his surroundings dimmed. More bolts of lightning flashed, the volume of the thunder increased as the storm approached and suddenly the trio were transfixed by another new phenomenon: wind, real wind, wild and buffeting their bodies like a live thing, not the gentle caress of a sea breeze at Monkey Mia.

The sky darkened even more and just as Wirrin was turning to Calen to comment, everything lit up for an instant of startling brilliance with a crack of sound so loud he felt a moment of pure fear. Even Barudin looked shocked till he laughed and said. 'That was a close one.'

* * *

On the very last day they travelled the greatest distance yet, over 30 kilometres, to the banks of the big river again, and almost 70 kilometres upstream from Gnardune Pool. After their meal Barudin conducted their completion ceremony. The trio performed a special little thank-you dance for Barudin which Wirrin had worked out, and the time of isolation was over.

Thom called his ship.

Calen, who'd been suffering his separation gamely, contacted Sonic.

Akama and Gulara contacted Attunga and Warrakan through the Comet, while Wirrin remotely activated his Comet InfoSystem to get an overview of what had been happening with the dolphin recruitment program. He had barely connected when his attention was distracted by an excited babble of dolphin speech from Calen and then a shout.

'An orca chased him and he wasn't fast enough to get away. Turaku saved him with the Comet.'

Everyone rushed over.

'Is he all right?'

'Earth adventures are even better than asteroid labyrinths. Orca is awesome.'

'Why did you go near an orca?'

'I wanted to talk to him but he was hungry.'

The trio shared a moment of surprise.

'You can't talk to orcas. They have a different language.'

'I have started to learn.'

'Where are you?'

'With the little dolphins of South Island, New Zealand. How long before we see our brothers?'

'Soon.'

Calen looked at Thom who in turn looked at Akama.

'After we return Barudin to Monkey Mia.'

'If you take me to meet Sonic you can fly direct.'

Akama laughed at Barudin's blunt request.

'Of course. He'll love to hear you recount the antics of his pod brothers, especially the skink exterminator.'

'We'll be there in about half an hour, Sonic. My ship is about to arrive.'

That brought Wirrin up with a jolt. The journey from here to Gnardune Pool would take about three days on foot and Thom's ship was traversing it in minutes. Yes, the traditional pace of their life was over.

*   *   *

Next day Akama returned to Monkey Mia where he was spending time on his own private agenda.

Calen stayed with Sonic.

Wirrin, Thom and Gulara went to Alice Springs, almost in the centre of Australia and, as named friends, spoke for several hours with a number of the AIs based there before being guided through part of the enormous north–south Australian population corridor.

Over 2000 kilometres in length, this extended habitat was one of the earliest models in the move to live self-sufficiently underground and restore the biodiversity of the planet's surface. Started under North Australian leadership and the inspiration behind the launching of Attunga, it was now one of the most advanced communities on the planet. Much of this newly advanced development had come through the particularly close relationship with AIs, sharing the expertise gained from the more complicated processes involved in nurturing the self-sufficient societies of an anti-grav habitat.

According to Akama, the links between the North Australians and Attunga meant that this was far and away the premier planetary life centre in the solar system.

Thom's ship was, in Sonic's words, a gift from the gods. It would go anywhere, meet them anywhere, and allow the trio and Sonic to be together at the end of every busy day. The Comet stayed close to Sonic of course. That was its primary purpose. The second Comet stayed close to Akama, again, its primary purpose.

Wirrin, Thom and Gulara spent a day at the Great Barrier Reef visiting the big marine centre there, and being guided to explore other special features with skimmers and facemasks. After spending twenty minutes on skimmers to get to the second location, Thom amazed the guides by calling up his ship and saying they'd use that instead to save time and see more.

Calen elected to stay with Sonic.

Everyone was together for the visit to Antarctica. The dolphin pod, though limited to shorter sorties by the water temperature, was particularly eager to see the great icebergs and frozen cliffs, a completely new marine environment for them, and their eagerness just might have been magnified by Calen's talk of giant schools of fish, kilometres long, feeding on the abundant krill.

* * *

'Are you serious? It started out at 213, and when we landed we said we'd be impressed if we got a thousand, and now you say it could be six? We can't take that many. The Comet modifications after the Freedom hijack mean our limit has gone down to 5000 or just over.'

Calen was reporting the results of a tally between Sonic and Turaku of what was going to happen when they started collecting the Earth dolphins who'd decided to follow Sonic to Attunga.

'Yes we can, Thom. Sonic and Turaku already thought the number might be high by the time we went walkabout so the second Comet has been working flat out converting its storage space to dolphin transport pools. They've built just over three thousand places so there'll be tons of room.'

'What? They changed a Comet and I didn't even know?'

'Yes, you slacker! You've been having so much fun visiting mountain-tops and exploring underwater ice caves at the South Pole that you're neglecting our spaceships.'

'Ha! You can talk. Letting Sonic get eaten by a killer whale. That's neglect!

'They must have had the picofactory working at maximum to do that much. It's a massive internal change.'

*   *   *

Halfway through the first of the two pick-up days the picofactory again went into overdrive as the real numbers once more went way in excess of expectations, and at the end the Comets were overcrowded with a total of 9153 passengers.

Calen, remembering the first trip, worried that Sonic would be stressed trying to keep them all happy for the long journey to Attunga. Sonic wasn't, saying there was no panic and fear to overcome this time.

It *was* tiring, with the added complication of several dockings so he could move between ships, but he was older now and much stronger, as well as having all his pod, including Calen, to share the support work.

Turaku, through Comet-Turaku, had set things in motion on Attunga for receiving the big influx and the rangers and marine scientists there were stunned and delighted at the prospect of such a huge boost to the dolphin program.

The two Comets left Earth and some thirty hours later the pristine reaches on Attunga were receiving their new occupants.

Chapter 33

'What are they doing?'

Thom's day had involved taking the Comet to K74 to see what was happening. The situation was very interesting with the ten newly completed Cadre ships and twenty more almost finished and he was explaining what he'd seen.

'Collecting asteroids. Big ones. They've brought back five so far and two more are on the way. The ones that have arrived are parked close to the ship construction sites.'

'How big?' asked Calen.

'They're all about a cubic kilometre and it looks like they're meant to be the source material for a whole new round of ship construction.'

'More ships? Ridiculous!'

'I know, and it's crazier than you think because Quambi tells us that when the other twenty are finished the plans show that every construction site will keep working.'

'A total of sixty Cadre ships? Thom, that's scary.'

'I know. It fits with the idea that they want to be big in the solar system though, and having Quambi-K is speeding things up for them.'

'If they like everything big it's a wonder they don't go for a monster class of ship, like over a kilometre in length?' said Calen.

'If they knew enough about engines I'm sure they would, but they still have troubles with the ones they use now. Look how interested they were in the Freedom drives,' said Wirrin.

'Thom, did you find out anything else about them while you were there?'

'Remember those weird cradle things we saw them constructing on the stealth exercise day? Well they're a way to connect to other ships or asteroids and move them around quickly. They're way faster than normal asteroid collectors. One of the five asteroids was from so far off it would have taken three weeks with a standard tug but because of its big engine the Cadre ship did it in less than a day.'

'Sounds like we should put those things on a few of the Comets.'

'No way, Wirrin. Ordinary asteroid collectors do the job perfectly. All you need is proper planning.'

'Did you talk much to Quambi while you were close?'

'Yes, she's been doing all sorts of stuff. She was talking to the Freedom AIs about when they were cut off by that jamming we couldn't get through and she's been building extra sneaky communication channels to try and make sure it never happens to her. The big thing she's done though is build her special picofactories into the other two backup areas so she can do anything from any one of them.'

'That's a good idea. That should have happened right from the start.'

Wirrin knew about this. 'Not really. The probability of her being discovered is practically zero so there was no need for extra picofactories, and AIs work on probabilities a lot more than we do.'

'So why have they changed their minds?'

'I don't know, but it was Quambi and the companion AIs who made the decision this time.'

'Why did you go so close to K74 when Quambi sends us all that information anyway?'

'Training, Wirrin. We had our special group of pilots and they need real experience.'

'Does that mean it wasn't you controlling the Comet?'

'I did take over for the final approach because it's a bit tricky with all the extra activity going on.'

'These pilots must be getting like experts themselves with all the training you give them.'

'Me? I hardly train them at all. Just special finishing off stuff.'

*   *   *

'Every single pod has its own ranger? Where did they all come from?' said Thom.

Wirrin was amazed at how everything seemed be running perfectly only five days after their return from Earth. The previous evening Calen and Sonic had related some of the logistics of the dolphin re-settlement program, outlining its magnitude, and extolling the brilliance of Turaku's planning: 112 reaches occupied with an average of four or five pods each, and another nineteen allocated to the 785 independent males. These males were an unexpected outcome of the trip and a new factor in the running of the reaches.

According to Calen they should have realised that appealing to the idea of adventure and describing bountiful food sources would be an especially powerful attraction to independent, maturing young dolphins. Luckily, the number of Attunga reaches coming online had been compounding recently with the completion of large new sections of Attunga's dolphin level, and despite the sudden influx there were still reaches to spare and many, many more close to completion.

Calen found Thom's question amusing. 'Thom, there are thousands and thousands of people who want to be dolphin rangers. Ever since Meeting Day when Sonic spoke to the habitats the number of people applying to work with dolphins has gone crazy. You've seen the trainee rangers at the dolphinarium.'

'But they're not proper rangers yet and I don't remember seeing enough for all these reaches anyway.'

'Of course you've seen them. They've been there since the first Earth dolphins arrived. All the rangers on Warrakan have three or four trainees assigned to help them at different times during the week and that's been happening ever since the reaches opened. They might not be officially qualified but Turaku expects they'll do an excellent job. And he'll be watching and available if they need any help or advice anyway, the same as Yajala does for all the Warrakan rangers.'

Wirrin shared Thom's impression but of course Calen was right. Every Warrakan reach you went to was buzzing with humans on their skimmers or active in other ways and when you added them up it would be hundreds of people.

'The new rangers must be extra excited at all these dolphins arriving then.'

'They are keen, Thom. They know this is the start of something special and they want to be in on it.'

'You mean the enhancement program, or Attunga dolphins in general?'

'Both. Attunga's suddenly got nine thousand dolphins who will never be enhanced so they'll be working with them for fifty or sixty years while the enhanced side of things starts to build. It will be slow at first then faster with each new generation.'

'Dingoes! The doctor must be working like crazy. Have all these dolphins had their health checks yet?' asked Thom.

'The standard ones were started on the Comets and finished in the first couple of days. Now they're onto the follow-ups and developing individual healthbots.'

'Are many of them needing follow-ups?'

Follow-ups was Calen's term for the treatment of any immediate health problem which the initial health check uncovered, like the liver weakness Peggy from Martin's pod had suffered.

'Many? Almost all of them, Thom. They're nearly all wild dolphins who've never had any kind of checkup ever.'

'That can't be right? They've nearly all got something wrong?'

'Natural things mostly, like parasites and viruses and traces of toxic substances. Earth's oceans aren't a controlled environment like our reaches, and they're still recovering from the pollution times.'

'The oceans looked good at all the pick-up places we went to.'

'They are, compared to what they used to be. These dolphins are tougher than ours and when their problems are cleared up they'll be incredibly healthy and active.'

'Tougher? No way. Our dolphins are bigger and stronger than all of them.'

'Not that kind of tough, Thom. These dolphins have naturally fought all their life to survive through hunger and sickness and predation without any help from humans. Our dolphins don't face anything like that.'

This was interesting and Wirrin thought it might be tied in with Sonic's shark reach idea.

'You think our dolphins have it too easy then?'

'I don't, but Sonic talks about it with Yajala sometimes.'

Calen suddenly swerved his skimmer in a new direction. Wirrin and Thom automatically followed and, looking ahead, saw a group of other skimmers in the distance.

'Sonic might be with this pod. Come on, let's see who can reach him first.'

* * *

'Three and a half days? That's a long trip.'

'Pirramar is happy for you to go, Wirrin, and because you'll miss some of his work he'll arrange another challenge program for your spare time.'

Sonic was making that part up because Wirrin would have to miss out on a full day of the AI studies he was always talking about enthusiastically.

'I'll make up some challenges for you then, and we can do them together.'

Sonic made a happy sound that Wirrin was now included in their next adventure — his description for the trip he'd researched and planned, and was just now outlining. Calen would automatically be going, and so would Thom because the Comet would have to accompany Sonic.

Wirrin was the only one who needed special arrangements and if Pirramar had already said he was happy then Sonic had obviously already cleared the way.

'Hang on,' Thom said. 'I want to know where we're going that'll take so long. We could have another adventure on Earth in that amount of time.' He had always planned to return to the underwater ice caverns at the Antarctic.

'Travel will take twenty-one hours if we make good speed, Thom, and we can use the rest of the time for exploring. I found this adventure in a distant place on our asteroid belt.'

A holo of a strange-looking asteroid flicked into view.

'What *is* that?'

The trio were staring at a convoluted mass of rock and ore.

'I searched for traces of comet collisions and I found this. It will be a good adventure.'

'That thing is an asteroid?' asked Thom.

'A remnant of an even bigger one.'

Wirrin linked to the holo, called up the information Sonic had collected, and scanned through while Thom and Calen stared at the startling shape.

'That thing is 256 kilometres across. If it's a remnant the original must have been huge.'

'Dingoes! That main hole we can see must be enormous.'

'It is 47 kilometres across, Thom, and it might be the path where a comet penetrated. We will explore and find out how deep it goes.'

'Wow! What about those other holes then? Some of them look like volcanic craters ... Except you can't have volcanoes on asteroids ... Maybe smaller comets made them? That's the weirdest looking asteroid I've ever seen. When do we leave?'

Sonic whacked his tail excitedly on the water and gave his special laugh as he drenched the three of them.

'Seventeen days ... And I will fly your ship all the way.'

*   *   *

'It still doesn't feel right, no matter what he says. It's his adventure and he should be here,' Thom said.

Wirrin and Calen totally agreed. They'd all demanded a postponement when they learned Sonic couldn't accompany them, but he'd insisted the expedition to the mystery asteroid should go ahead as organised.

Each evening in the pool during relaxation time they'd planned and discussed some aspect of the trip and Sonic's keen anticipation had been a big part of the enjoyment and interest they'd all felt. Then they'd found out just a few hours before they were to set off that all the pod leaders for the enhanced dolphins needed him at a meeting of some kind. It had seemed like a minor setback at first, which would mean delaying their departure for a few hours only, but then word came back that the meeting would continue the next day and Sonic told them to go without him.

Calen said he'd stay with Sonic, because it must be something important, whatever it was, and that meant Wirrin and Thom didn't see much point in going. Sonic overruled that and, using his definite tone, said he expected Calen to be his eyes and ears. Calen couldn't say no then, and in a somewhat subdued manner the trip had got underway.

'I know why he's made us go. It's because if we wait for him to be free we mightn't ever get there. It's over five months since he said adventures were going to be a regular part of his life,' Wirrin said.

Calen gave a resigned snort of agreement. 'You're right, Wirrin. He's just too busy and we can't stop him. Yajala's been trying to organise him to have activity days that match up with ours but something always happens and it's always too important to ignore.'

'Well, if we have to wait another five months before he can travel anywhere with us we won't be going anywhere either, because that's getting close to the move to Titania and he'll be busier than ever then.'

There were gloomy nods all round.

'Hey, at least we can take him on half-day adventures to the moons once we get there. He'll be able to fit that in,' said Thom.

There was silence for a while. Calen played with the viewing screens but they were too deep into space to see anything but stars.

Wirrin superimposed a position reference on the proposed course for him, but since they'd only been travelling for half an hour it looked like they'd hardly moved.

Thom was concentrating. What was he doing? Hmm, why was he running a full diagnostic on the engines? Whoa — 23.7G!

'Thom, why are we going so fast? Can the engines cope?'

Thom looked smug. 'They're showing a hundred per cent perfection, Wirrin. Sonic said we'd need to push so that's what I'm doing. We're now a full 2G faster than any of the Comets and this is still the best ship in the solar system.'

Calen twisted to look at Thom. 'Is this the highest acceleration ever?'

'For a ship with human level grav-compensators it is, and ours are operating at complete max. I've been a little bit faster but only for short times.'

'How long will it take to get to K137 if we stay at this rate?'

Thom activated one of his controls.

'Another nineteen and a half hours with an error margin of fourteen minutes.'

'Where does the error margin come from? You always know the precise times.'

'It's because we don't know its exact location, Calen. All the information Sonic found is thirty-four years old so I'm sure there'll be a variation in its predicted position. We won't really know till we're in scanning range.'

Wirrin had done his own search to see what he could find but had come up with exactly the same data as Sonic. It turned out to be from a Mars-initiated robotic survey for improved knowledge about the size and distribution of objects in the asteroid belt, and the only existing data about K137. That was frustrating, but in a way intriguing as well, with the prospect that they'd be the first people to see it. They'd started calling it the mystery asteroid and Thom kept stating that they were going to find a cosmic dragon.

'It'd be funny if we get there and can't find it.'

'Calen, we'll find it. You can't not find something that big,' said Thom.

'If another comet hit it, or it collided with something else in the last thirty-four years we mightn't. Maybe we should turn off now and head for Mars instead. That's the closest place and we definitely know where it is.'

Thom gave Calen a look and Wirrin did a quick check.

'Mars isn't the closest. There's a habitat called Ascension about five hours away and Mars is seven.'

'That's one of the early habitats. It's a big one isn't it?'

'Yes, Thom. It started off as a spinner then converted to grav-fields. It's got 4.8 billion people.'

Spinners were a type of habitat constructed before the development of directed grav-fields and worked by rotating a series of concentric cylindrical structures to produce the equivalent of normal Earth gravity. Each layer had to spin at a slightly different rate and that made them very complex.

'Five hours? Can we go past it on the way to K137?'

The trio exchanged glances, their interest piqued. Thom did some calculations then shook his head. 'It's too far off course and would add an extra four hours even without slowing down for a proper look. The only sensible way to see it would be to forget about K137 and I don't want to do that.'

None of them did, so for a while they contented themselves with looking at holos about Ascension, which Wirrin pulled from the ship's general database.

*   *   *

'It's easy, Calen. You won't have to do anything except wake me up if the automatics do something unusual.'

Calen felt weird about being in sole charge of the ship for the next six hours while Wirrin and Thom had a sleep. Not too weird, because the automatics were completely capable of reliably controlling the whole journey if need be, but Thom, being Thom, preferred having someone on watch, as he called it, all the time.

Wirrin would officially take the second six hours though it wouldn't be that long because Thom would never sleep for twelve hours while the ship was travelling. Wirrin would, any time he got the chance, and he'd definitely sleep the last several hours of approach till Thom and Calen woke him.

'So how am I supposed to know what's unusual? We could be heading for Pluto and I wouldn't know the difference.'

'You don't have to. I've set it up so all you have to watch is that bank of blue panels and if any of them turn red the automatics will tell you to panic.'

'What?'

'Calen, they won't turn red. The ship systems are too clever to let anything go wrong.'

*   *   *

In the strange quietness and solitude as the ship made its way through deep space, Wirrin, settled at his console for his turn on watch, contemplated the familiar constellations and stars shining from their ebony background. He smiled as he recalled the ancient idea that they were holes in the vault of heaven, revealing the light beyond and letting water through to fall as rain on the Earth.

Calen would be asleep by now and Thom wouldn't wake for another two or three hours, so he had the ship to himself. This calm and solitude was strange and Wirrin suddenly realised he couldn't recall ever being in quite the same situation. He watched and thought for a while then felt like doing something.

Hmm! Thom's abilities with the picofactory were okay at a basic level but to get the best from it needed either special knowledge or an AI. Well, there was no AI but Wirrin definitely had the expertise. All he needed was more familiarity with this particular system, so for nearly two hours he applied himself and focused intently on mastering the complex range of capabilities available to the picofactory. The awareness that something wasn't right took a moment to register.

One of the panels was glowing red! What? That couldn't be? Thom had said the panels were really a token and the automatics would handle everything.

Wirrin was about to link to the panel to try and find out what was happening when a message appeared on the visuals directly in front of him. The automatics were making sure they had his attention.

ALERT! ALERT! PRIORITY MESSAGE INCOMING.

HOLO ACTIVATION REQUIRED.

Wirrin leapt from his seat, rushed to the open door of the little cabin where Thom and Calen were sleeping, and watching in case the holo started, yelled for them to wake up.

'Quick, the alarm's gone red. Get out here quick.'

Thom lifted his head as Wirrin raced back to the console, and with questions racing through his mind, activated communication mode. Taking one look he shouted again. 'Thom! It's a priority message from Pirramar. I'm starting it now.'

Chapter 34

Pirramar appeared, his expression serious. 'Thom, in consultation with habitat security I'm requesting you make an immediate course change to the coordinates now locked into your flight databanks. Two days ago seven Cadre ships rendezvoused with a large asteroid and started moving it on a trajectory towards three other ships that were stationed near an even larger asteroid. For the last few weeks K74 has been moving asteroids with their Cadre ships, and while most have been brought and parked in close proximity to construction sites, several seem to have been used for experimental purposes and initially we thought this was an exercise in using multiple ships for far faster movement. Ten hours ago the last possible turnaround point for a termination with the second asteroid passed with no sign of deceleration.

This caught our attention because the accuracy of their navigation now indicated the possibility of a collision. That possibility steadily firmed to certainty, leading us to believe the exercise might be aimed at testing the results of a high-speed asteroid collision. Just seven minutes before I sent this message the speeding asteroid began to change course. If it continues, it will head in our general direction. There is a critical time horizon, defined by the rising possibility of our habitats being targeted, and your ship is the only one logistically able to gather more information.'

Wirrin's heart caught but Pirramar was continuing and he mustn't miss anything.

'The asteroid in question has a diameter of over 7 kilometres and the steady acceleration of 3.4G indicates a joint effort by four Cadre ships pushing it at the high end of their sustainable capability.'

There was a gasp from Thom who was now sitting at his control console and the view of stars in the visuals moved as the ship began its course change.

'Our best interpretation of the attenuated signals we are receiving confirms this by showing a convoy of the three remaining vessels. To answer any questions you have, this message is accompanied by all our current information and analysis. I will speak again in fifteen minutes, after you take action and build your understanding of the situation.'

Pirramar disappeared and a puzzled-looking Calen moved closer to Wirrin.

'What's going on? Why is Pirramar telling us about K74 collecting an asteroid?'

He'd missed most of the transmission. Wirrin looked to Thom but he was totally absorbed with his console.

'It's not going to K74. There's a possibility they might be taking it to our habitats and Pirramar wants Thom to investigate because no-one else can.'

'Investigate? Is it close to K137?'

'Forget about K137, Calen. We're not going there anymore. Thom changed our course a few seconds before you came in. Pirramar's made it a priority.'

'For an asteroid? How could that be a priority? We've got all sorts of protections against them.'

'It's no longer just an asteroid.' Thom sounded serious. 'With the speed it's built it has catastrophic potential. I've looked at Pirramar's data and it shows continuous acceleration since they picked it up and for something that size it's travelling at an enormous speed.'

'It can't be as fast as us.'

'No, Calen, but it's been accelerating for … fifty-six hours. It's … it's very close to our speed — just under 7000 kilometres per second and we're just over.'

'But we'll soon catch up to it won't we?'

'If it was directly ahead we'd catch up in about two hours but the big direction change reduces our effective speed and makes it over five hours before we're close.'

'Five hours? Couldn't the Comet reach it in that time? The security AI could take over and change its course.'

'Think, Calen. The Comet would be travelling in the opposite direction and they'd pass each other so quickly they'd be out of range in a microsecond. Then the Comet would have to reverse direction to chase it. That would take … about fifteen hours. Look at this.'

A holo image showing the relative positions of the habitats and the moving asteroid sprang into view.

'We have nine Comets including the companion ones with Quambi and these are the most recent positions I have data for.'

Nine blue lights winked into existence, seven close to the three habitats and the other two in their usual position near K74.

'I'll code in the optimum intersection paths for all of them and we'll watch what happens.'

Wirrin was impressed by Thom's rapid set up and demonstration of the possibilities for each vessel, which showed clearly why Pirramar wanted them involved. Well, it *was* the strategic kind of planning he trained for.

'See. That's why it has to be us.'

Calen nodded. The visual representation made it obvious.

'I can't believe they're actually aiming at our habitats. No-one would do something like that.'

Wirrin couldn't believe it either.

'I know,' said Thom, 'but the course change makes it a possibility. I expect that at some stage the course will steady and we'll know where it's really going. What worries me is why they made it look like a collision with that other asteroid for two days and then suddenly changed. It's as if they were purposefully misleading anyone who was watching.'

Thom was right. It did have a devious feel to it.

'It doesn't make sense anyway. The multi-spectrum beams on the Comets and the habitats would just vaporise it like they did that ship on Earth.'

Wirrin watched Thom shake his head strongly.

'It's too big, Calen. *Way* too big. The beams would have practically no effect in the short time they'd be in range.'

'So what about the shell we've been building round Attunga?' Calen said. 'That's nearly finished and it's the strongest material ever made. The same with Warrakan's surface.'

Wirrin answered this time. 'They're not designed for anything with that combination of size and speed. There's an enormous amount of kinetic energy involved that would all be released instantaneously.'

Calen looked shocked. 'Are you saying there's nothing our habitats can do to stop it?'

'Not that I know of.'

Thom knew though. 'They'll move. I expect the big drives are probably already working, because that way at least two of the habitats will be safe.'

'Why not all three?' Wirrin asked, thinking it would be hard to collide with something deliberately moving out of the way.

'If the asteroid wasn't being controlled it would be easy. It would just fly straight past, but it *is* being guided and with over 3G to work with it's far more responsive than the single-G the habitats can use. You could say the habitats are three times as unwieldy as the controlled asteroid, the same as this ship is six times as agile as the asteroid.'

'It's not actually moving directly towards our habitats is it?'

Thom worked with his console. 'Not at the moment. It'll pass by with millions of kilometres to spare on the course it has at the moment, and there'll be nothing to worry about if it stays on that course. The trouble is it's been changing. Pirramar's data shows two small changes since he first contacted us.'

'Could that be good?'

'Maybe, but I can't be sure because they're both just enough to keep the habitats as a possible destination, and both small enough to be minor course corrections for somewhere else.'

'Somewhere else? Can you check for other possible destinations?'

'I already have, Wirrin, and nothing stands out in the time frame we're worried about.'

'What about longer term?'

Thom gave Wirrin a curious look then worked at his console. 'Dingoes! You're right! That last correction makes Jupiter a possible destination ... but why would they want to go there?'

'Maybe it *is* a collision experiment and they want to hit the black spot.'

'Interesting idea, Calen, but I don't think so. It would hardly have any effect even if it *is* travelling super fast.'

'It must have some effect. If it hit the Earth it would destroy the whole atmosphere.'

'Well it would where it impacted but Jupiter's so enormous there's no comparison.'

'What about the moons? Could they be taking it to one of them?'

'I suppose, but what for? Has K74 got connections with any of the habitats there?'

'Not from the big search I did. Their main connection was the Mars polar habitat. There were also some semi-directed habitats on Earth but they haven't had anything to do with K74 since the quarantining.'

'How many habitats are there round Jupiter?'

Wirrin knew the main ones but he had to check for a full list. 'Seven on the moons and three space ones. Callisto is the biggest and the smallest is a scientific community on Metis.'

'Metis? I've heard of that,' said Thom.

'It's the closest moon to Jupiter. Only 128,000 kilometres away.'

The trio swapped ideas and talked over what questions and responses to send to Pirramar. With communication time-lag because of the distance, it meant trying to figure out sensible questions and likely answers.

'I've found it!' Thom shouted.

Wirrin and Calen turned to Thom. 'My scanners just locked on the asteroid a few thousand kilometres from where Pirramar's data says it would be. I think it's changed course again and Warrakan hasn't picked it up yet. I've started tracking but we're not close enough yet for my information to be as accurate as Pirramar's. In another forty seconds I'll have enough motion information for reasonable trajectory calculations and I'll be able to confirm whether this new course is taking it to Jupiter or not. I've also found the three Cadre ships that were waiting at the big asteroid where Pirramar thought there was going to be a collision. I thought they might join the convoy but my calculations show they're heading for K74.'

'Why aren't you using Pirramar's data if it's more accurate?'

'I'm watching it closely, but it's way behind ours so it'll be another ten minutes before I can start checking them against each other.'

Wirrin smiled at Calen's blank look and Thom's feigned exasperation. 'At the moment we're nine light minutes away from the asteroid and the habitats are twelve, so we get the information sooner.'

Calen pounced. 'That's only three minutes difference. You said ten.'

'And we're nearly seven light minutes from the habitats so the relay brings it up to ten.'

'Ah … right!'

Thom busied himself at his console. 'From this latest data the Jupiter system is definitely the target. To refine it any further I'll need …'

Pirramar shimmered into view.

'Thom, habitat security thanks you for your immediate action, and with your current surprisingly high rate of acceleration we calculate a rendezvous in four hours and twelve minutes. We have examined your theory about the possibility of Jupiter as a destination and it is consistent with the last registered change of course. This change, however, means our habitats are still possible targets and will continue to be so for another fifty-eight minutes. With this in mind we have initiated a number of precautionary measures, which are now detailed on your secondary viewing screen for perusal and comment. Quambi has been unable to locate any information about why the asteroid is being moved and our direct requests to K74 have met with the usual wall of silence. I will continue to update you every fifteen minutes or as needed.'

The holo shimmered off and the trio looked at each other.

'He didn't really tell us much this time.'

'Well, it sounds like they don't know anything new themselves. I wonder what Yajala has told Sonic and the dolphins,' said Calen.

'We'll ask as part of our next transmission or it might be part of the details Pirramar sent. We'll look through those first because it sounded like they want our ideas about them. Solution Brain ideas most of ... What's with the look, Wirrin?'

'Thom, can we go any faster?'

Thom and Calen stared in puzzlement. The ship was travelling at record thrust and they all knew it.

'No, you know we can't ... Why?'

'My brain tells me we should. I'm having bad thoughts.'

There was no comeback or Solution Brain jibe. Thom and Calen could see that Wirrin was deadly serious.

'Pirramar just said that Quambi can't find out why the asteroid is being moved. The only way that could happen is if it's been organised in the blocked areas and without any orders being transmitted electronically. That tells me the rogue's involved, and that means we have to plan for the worst.'

Wirrin looked Thom directly in the eye. 'I think it might be up to us to stop this asteroid.'

After a moment of silence Thom gave a snort of disbelief.

'I know you don't mean the asteroid itself, Wirrin. There are seven Cadre ships there. We wouldn't have a hope.'

'We mightn't have a choice. Look, four of them can't manoeuvre because they're connected to the asteroid with those cradle things. You could use stealth and disable one of the convoy before they even knew we were there, and I know you can defend yourself against two of them.'

'It wouldn't be just two. The other four could still deploy their missiles and if they disconnect we'd be completely outnumbered.'

'Disconnecting means they're not controlling the asteroid. That's exactly what we want.'

'Why do you want to go faster?'

'More time to apply any strategy you devise when we catch up. Every minute might be important.'

'Yes, it would be.'

Wirrin felt relieved. In the course of this short conversation Thom had switched from finding it hard to accept the reality of the situation to the serious analytical mode he used in his training.

Calen still looked incredulous and horrified. 'We're going to fight seven Cadre ships?'

'It looks like it, Calen. Wirrin's brainstorms have always been vital and accurate when it's important so we have to treat this one the same way. We'll know for certain in another … fifty-four minutes.'

'What will I do? I'm useless in this ship.'

Wirrin felt somewhat the same. If fighting was needed everything would be on Thom's shoulders.

'Calen, you're not useless,' Thom said. 'We'll need all the help we can manage to get through this. Send a message to Pirramar about Wirrin's thoughts while we look through their data. He needs to know straight away.'

Calen looked startled but nodded and set to.

Wirrin and Thom scanned the information on the screen. Thom had indeed been on the right track: the giant drive engines on all three habitats had been activated and were ready to move at a moment's notice. Every Comet was on full alert with a full complement of crew, and Sonic and the enhanced dolphins were in the process of being moved to Turaku's Comet.

The Witness Council was being convened for a habitat spanning holo hookup.

Picofactories were constructing heavy-duty versions of the multi-spectrum beam defences to augment the basic systems already in place on the outer walls of all three habitats.

The list went on, and when Wirrin saw that all transport and travel between the three habitats was closing down he thought about what would be happening with the general population.

'I wonder how much the word is spreading? People will know there's something unusual happening when there aren't any ferries working.'

'It'll be through every habitat in minutes. The InterWeb will make sure of that.'

'Maybe not, Thom. I think the Witnesses will divert attention somehow till they know for certain whether the asteroid's heading for Jupiter or not. They'd want to avoid panic.'

A quick look showed that would now happen in fifty-one minutes.

'Wirrin, can you get into the basic coding for the operation of the ship? If you can we might be able to go faster.'

Wirrin put aside a thought about construction asteroids being used as barriers for the habitats. That could wait. 'I can get to it easily, but making changes is harder if that's what you really mean.'

'The engines and the grav-compensators are set with maximum levels but if we override them we'll get more acceleration.'

Wirrin nodded but alarm bells sounded in his mind.

'Isn't taking them over their maximums risky? If we damage either system we'll be no help to anyone.'

'They've got safety factors built in. All engines and systems like the compensators have. I don't know exactly what they are for this ship but as long as we don't exceed them we shouldn't cause any harm.'

Five seconds of searching on the InfoSystem had the information.

'The grav-compensators have a safety factor of five per cent and the engines' twenty-two. That can't be right? That seems way too much.'

Thom looked surprised till he thought about it. 'No it's not. It means the engines have the power but they've been limited to 1G above what the compensators can cope with. It means we could go a lot faster but we'd feel it. Let's see ... The grav-compensators are the biggest concern so we can't use the full five per cent. Four should be okay and we'll monitor them every microsecond with fallbacks in case of any trouble ... That will give us an extra ... 0.9G. The engines at twenty-two per cent would give us an extra 5.2G but we can't use that much because we'd soon be unconscious. Dingoes! If you can change that code we'll get a minimum of one extra G plus as much extra as our bodies can cope with.'

'What can we cope with?' Calen was back.

'Wirrin's going to change the basic codings to make the ship faster, but anything after the first G won't have compensation.'

'You can do that?'

'Mmm, I hope so. Will it save us much time?'

'Hang on.'

Thom and Calen watched Wirrin for several minutes as a bewildering flood of technical data and code flashed across the console.

'Kadaitcha! It's hard-coded. Big problem … No! I'll make the picofactory burn the updated instructions onto a replacement circuit. Thom, when it's ready you'll have to power off and swap the circuits yourself manually. It's … fairly straightforward.'

Wirrin turned towards Thom.

'The picofactory's finished. Did you work out how much sooner we'll get there?'

'Finished? I thought you were figuring whether it was possible, not actually doing it. Where's this circuit? I'll install it then we'll work out how much thrust we can stand.'

After a short period of zero-G the engines powered up again and steadily increased to a new record thrust of 24.6G.

'Okay, how much more? We have to cope with this for over four hours so I suggest that one extra G should be our limit. We'll be mostly confined to our seats and we'll get there eighteen minutes earlier. If we need to move around or it's too much strain we can ease off. Will we give it a go?'

There were nods all round and as soon as Calen was secure in his seat the heavy hand of acceleration pressed down and their effective body weight doubled. They were all used to this, from Thom's habit of giving them bursts of up to 2.5G at the start of most of their trips, as well as from the excitement of variable G-force activities that were a large part of habitat leisure activities.

The big difference here was the time factor and Wirrin wondered how four hours would affect them. He used his InfoSystem to see what Thom was doing to monitor the compensators.

Whoo! Heavy arms!

'Thom, can you control the ship properly?'

'I've done it in training but I've never had to keep it up for more than fifteen minutes. I'll hardly have to do anything though, not till we make the match-up, and then we'll be out of this high G.'

Wirrin checked. The current acceleration was an incredible 25.6G. At match-up that would diminish to the 3.4G of the asteroid. A huge drop.

'Hey! New record.'

That got the expected grin. Wirrin sent a transmission to Pirramar next, explaining how the ship was suddenly flying beyond its normal capabilities and why they felt it was needed, and also asking if the AIs knew whether it was sustainable. The trio settled to a determined type of relaxation with their seats adjusted for maximum support.

As well as helping to cope with acceleration pressure they were aware of the need to ready themselves for the match-up, especially Thom.

Chapter 35

Wirrin came out of his quiet, almost meditative state at a signal and watched Thom respond on his console. From the set of his features it was bad news.

'It's another course-change and this initial data says it's towards the habitats. I'll soon have more accurate data but it's enough to discount Jupiter.'

'It can't be.'

Wirrin felt the same disbelief as Calen, and watched with a hope he knew wasn't justified while Thom checked the more precise course, which every extra second of scanned information allowed.

'It is. This makes it definite.'

'They're insane.'

'I know. What do we do?'

'Thom, we're already doing it. You've been planning in your mind what will happen when we match up haven't you?'

'Of course, but it doesn't feel real, more like one of my simulator battles.'

'Good, because you always say they're harder than real ones.'

'Yes, but not against seven ships.'

'That won't matter.'

Calen interrupted. 'Should we contact Pirramar?'

Thom shook his head. 'They'll know before our transmission gets through.'

Wirrin didn't say anything for a moment. Calen's words were ringing in his mind.

'Yes we should. Calen's right. This is insane. It really doesn't make sense.'

Wirrin's thoughts whirled while Thom and Calen, seeing his intense expression, waited in anticipation.

'This asteroid can only affect one habitat and they know there'll be retribution from the other two. They must be going to do something to the other two to protect themselves. It's the only way it can make sense.'

'Do what? Throw more asteroids? There aren't any.'

'Yes there are. Lots of them, parked right next to K74. Thom, contact Pirramar and warn him ... Tell him to get every Comet racing towards K74 as fast as possible. I need to think about this.'

Thinking in this case meant a concentrated burst with the InfoSystem, only distracted momentarily by the authoritative sound of Thom prefacing his transmission with yet another PRIORITY ONE signature.

Wirrin gathered every bit of information he thought relevant. As a stroke of luck, or more likely typical AI thoroughness, the data had been sent as a matter of course with Pirramar's main situation transmission. He summarised for Calen and Thom who were again waiting in anticipation.

'I hope I'm wrong but these course changes appear to have been purposely designed to keep us in doubt till the last possible moment, and that feels very much like a rogue strategy to me. The Cadre might be angry enough to try and destroy one of our habitats but the rogue would be too clever to let them because of the consequences they'd face. Unless it's part of something bigger. Then they could be in a position where they think they could ignore the consequences.'

'We've always wondered why they've built thirty Cadre ships and this could be the reason. Seven are with the asteroid and those other three are on the way to K74. I looked for the other twenty and, according to Pirramar's information, just over an hour ago not a single one of them was off on any sort of expedition. The whole twenty were in close proximity to K74, along with thirty-nine of those large asteroids they've collected.'

Thom and Calen still looked baffled.

'Thirty asteroids are associated with construction sites but that leaves nine extras.'

'And they could throw them at our habitats?'

'It makes sense as a strategy, and I do remember Thom telling us one time that kinetic weapons could be very dangerous for Attunga.'

'How big are the nine extras?'

Wirrin checked the sizes and flashed the results for Thom to see.

'They're 0.9 up to 1.3 cubic kilometres ... They could move them at about 5G ... unless they doubled up, and then it would be close to 10G.'

Thom did more calculations. 'An asteroid that size would have trouble getting past the habitat multi-spectrum beams. They're much more powerful than the Comet ones and the speed wouldn't be anything like the really big asteroid's.'

'What about three at once?'

'That would be bad. At least two would get through … Except they wouldn't because of the Comets.'

'How long to reach our habitats from K74?'

'At 5G or 10G?'

'Both.'

'Um … at 5G it would be just over two and a half hours and at 10G it would be … close to one hour fifty minutes.'

'And how long for the big asteroid to get there?'

'Three hours and forty minutes from now. And we'll match up with it in two hours forty-five minutes.'

'Fifty-five minutes to spare. Will that be enough time to stop them?'

'It'll have to be, Calen. I've been thinking about it and Wirrin's right. I'm sure I'll be able to disable one of them before they can retaliate too much, but then time will be critical because once I activate our multi-spectrum beam they'll all know where we are and they'll send thousands of missiles at us.'

'Thousands?'

'That's what they're set up for and I expect every ship will be involved.'

Calen looked stricken.

'What will we do?'

'We'll get away. Once I turn off the multi-spectrum beam our stealth protection will come into effect and most of the missiles will be confused.'

Wirrin interrupted. 'How long for our Comets to get to K74?'

'They'll go at high G so it will be nearly two hours.'

'That can't be right. You just said it was less than that from K74 with only 10G and the Comets are twice as fast as that.'

'The Comets have to be stopped when they get there. It's a different calculation, Calen.'

'Wombats! I'm not thinking right. Of course it is.'

'That's not good enough.'

'Why not, Wirrin? It's the best they can do.'

'If it's the rogue organising this then I bet he'll have everything happening at once and that means the K74 asteroids would be on their way before our Comets can get to K74.'

'Not by much … twelve minutes.'

'Yes, but it would be better to stop them before they started.'

Calen shook his head. 'I'm getting confused by all these times.'

Wirrin wasn't, and Thom was trained for this kind of planning so he wouldn't be either, but it was worth twenty seconds to build a clearly labelled timeline on a section of the display for easy reference.

'Calen, send another transmission to Pirramar and Quambi telling them to watch carefully for any sign of the Cadre ships moving towards those asteroids. I'm sure they're already doing it but I think it's very important. Explain everything we've been talking about.'

Wirrin turned to Thom. 'Thom, I might be able to get the picofactory working for us.'

'I hope so and I can tell you've already got some ideas.'

'That sounded very dangerous when you said most of the missiles would be confused, so I'm wondering if we could make some sort of anti-missile or jamming device for any that weren't? And maybe I could build some sort of stealth drone like we used at Freedom, but designed to disable a drive engine?'

'Forget about anti-missiles, Wirrin. We'd need hundreds, or even thousands, and our little ship simply hasn't got enough resources. A jamming device could be perfect but it would have to be incredibly powerful because as soon as it was released it would rapidly fall behind. A drone to disable Cadre engines would be brilliant.'

'How long would the jammer have to last?'

'Ideally for at least nine or ten seconds while our high G takes us out of range.'

'What about the stealth drone idea?'

'It sounds brilliant but it would use a lot of material and I doubt if we could make more than one.'

'I had another idea, too. Tell me what you think about this.'

Thom listened, then spluttered, which wasn't a good idea under double gravity.

'Wirrin, that's brilliant. You should be in charge of security. The AIs might be able to help, but I doubt it.'

Despite his body straining against the extra G, and his mind straining against what was ahead, Wirrin was pleased. He now had something to get his teeth into. The immediate priority was a request to Pirramar.

* * *

Half an hour later Wirrin finished his planning for a missile-jamming device. Part of that time had been taken up with Calen, who, tense and quiet, had only relaxed when word came through from Sonic that all the enhanced dolphins were aboard the Comet and that he was safe and busily occupied with his dolphin version of the InfoSystem.

More time was taken with Thom in a discussion about the best use of the limited resources for the picofactory but nothing could be resolved till they knew more precisely the amount of materials the different projects would need.

'Thom, I figure we can allow ten per cent of our resources for the jamming devices. They're very small and we'd be able to make two effective deployments before we ran out.'

'How do you define a deployment?'

'You said they'd need to work for at least nine or ten seconds and they don't. They're so powerful they'd burn out after 2.9 seconds and we'll have to release four of them at very carefully timed intervals.'

Thom thought before answering. 'A series of releases like that is much better than a single one because it keeps the jamming in closer proximity to the ship. We really need to allow for seven deployments though, not just four. Is there anything you can do about that?'

'I've got an idea but it means cannibalising parts of the ship.'

'What?'

'I can design a techbot to dismantle and process ship components like non-essential walls or the grav-bunks, and make it with the pico-factory. It would use up resources but we'd gain overall, maybe enough for two or three more deployments.'

'Do it. Anything that can make a difference is important. Can you tell me how strong the jamming signals are?'

Wirrin found the information and flashed it on Thom's display.

'Is that real? Just as well I asked. I'll have to protect our scanners for the duration or they'll be fried.'

Wirrin jumped on that statement. 'Could we get them close to the Cadre ships and put their scanners out of action?'

'That's a good idea but it won't work. Their units are much heavier duty than ours and not nearly as sensitive. It's the sensitive parts, which give us our advantages, that I have to be careful about. Calen, I'm going to teach you some basic manual operations of the ship so you can take over if something happens to me or Wirrin.'

Calen gulped. 'Okay! You think there's a possibility I might need to?'

'Using the maximum G that Wirrin has given us will be vital and you'll cope with higher levels than Wirrin or me. If we reach an effective 5G in here I mightn't even be able to move my hands.'

'And you think I might? Thom, all my experience is in water, and that's practically zero-G.'

'Doesn't matter. You push yourself every day and your oxygen distribution and circulation levels are way better than ours. That's what counts. When you're ready we'll do some trials and see what happens.'

Wirrin left them to it and started on his engine disabler project. His own plans needed every moment he could cadge.

*   *   *

Wirrin closed his eyes and forced his mind to slow down. He was on top of the engine disabler but this next project was proving trickier than expected and, pressured and frustrated, he knew it was time to take a break. The last hour had been eventful with Thom and Calen training with the ship controls, and then when that was finished, they'd had an eleven-second trial at the absolute maximum acceleration the ship could generate.

Wirrin didn't like it. At just under 5G in the cabin, an invisible force trapped him in his seat and the effort to move his hands was too much after four or five seconds.

Thom lasted about the same time but Calen, proving their point, somehow managed to keep his control all the way through.

He said a repeat for each of the seven Cadre ships would be far too much but Wirrin and Thom both expected that when the time came his recuperative ability and determination would pull him through.

Calen asked about options if they couldn't return to the habitats but Thom cut him short because, for now, they needed to keep positive. Next there was the distraction of the release and successful triggering of a single missile-jamming device.

Half an hour's break would be ideal, but five minutes was all Wirrin would allow himself.

*   *   *

Wirrin snapped his eyes open to check on times. Seven minutes. He'd relaxed, or the best version of that he could manage with double weight, and gone slightly longer than he meant.

So, an hour and twenty minutes till the ship matched velocity with the asteroid, and fifty minutes before acceleration was cut back to just under the limits of the grav-compensators.

Thom and Calen were motionless in their seats with their eyes closed. That would end with the change to single G and they'd become very busy, especially Thom.

The next check was on the progress of the techbot. Yes, it was doing well, and there was enough reclaimed material built up for an extra five jamming devices.

Now, time to focus on the InfoSystem.

*   *   *

Red warning lights flashed briefly.

Pirramar's image flickered into existence.

'Thom, Wirrin, Calen. Our situation is now critical. Nine pairs of Cadre ships are connecting with asteroids, two of which have already begun accelerating in our direction, and our correlators indicate a ninety-eight per cent probability that Warrakan will be impacted by the large asteroid.'

Chapter 36

The trio stared, transfixed in disbelief, shock, and horror, while Pirramar bade them do what they could and directed both Thom and Wirrin to some technical information he was sending. When the holo flickered off, Wirrin, his mind awhirl, sat for a moment till a soft sound twisted his attention.

The G force switched to normal and Thom and Wirrin leapt from their seats and rushed to enfold Calen in a powerful group hug.

'I don't understand. How can they want to hurt people?'

This question had arisen with every encounter against K74, and the trio, in their bafflement at such an alien outlook, often discussed it with each other, trying various explanations and theories.

'Think about it later. Right now we can help to stop it and you know we're good at that. Remember, Sonic will be waiting for us when it's over.'

Wirrin sensed the tension ebb as Calen turned and, with the slightest smile, responded to Thom's typical and practical attempt to ease the moment.

'I know. I'm all right. Get back to your controls and I'll watch what Wirrin's doing.'

They hugged again with a special feeling of closeness before moving back to their preparations.

'Are we all ready? I'm switching the extra G back in for another twenty minutes and then we'll have half an hour at normal before match-up. Calen, I'm sending two simulations to your console. The first one is straightforward practice with ship controls you've already learnt and the second one's to link that with multi-visuals.'

'Multi-visuals?'

'It just means keeping an eye on more than one display. We'll need a separate screen for each Cadre ship.'

'Seven at once? Don't you do this automatically with the ship's electronics?'

'Not when we release those jamming devices. All the high-level stuff will get damaged if I don't turn it off and it's right when we apply that maximum G, so I might be too busy, or not even functioning.'

Wirrin watched Calen think that through.

'So this is why we had the experiment with the eleven seconds of high G? I thought all I'd have to do was something basic, but this means controlling the ship at a really critical moment.'

'You might be, but I'll have a range of pre-sets organised for you and it won't be as hard as it sounds. You're already good with the visuals and when you complete these sims you'll know exactly what to do.'

*   *   *

'A major development, Thom. Our AIs on the companion Comets for Quambi have taken over the two Cadre ships controlling one of the nine asteroids and completely disabled them. That asteroid is now rendered harmless and the companions are in pursuit of another. In nineteen and a half minutes the first Comet from Warrakan will match velocity with the leading asteroid and endeavour to neutralise it. Minutes after that all our Comets will be in contention.' Pirramar finished, rather abruptly, and Wirrin and Calen couldn't help smiling at Thom's satisfied grunt.

'Five minutes to grav-normal and thirty-five minutes to match-up. Eliminating that asteroid is great news because it shows that the mobile AIs will be able to stop the others.'

It did sound good and Wirrin wondered how long it would take for the two companion Comets to reach another asteroid. It wouldn't be long because their acceleration was way superior. Yes, really good, because when the other Comets with AIs arrived there'd be a total of five ships disabling the Cadre aggressors.

*   *   *

What a relief! Wirrin felt his confidence lift with the abrupt easing of the heavy hand of thrust.

The grav-compensators were now able to cope and maintain the cabin at normal Earth gravity. No more straining to do the simplest thing. It was time to initiate and oversee his special tasks for the picofactory.

The holo alerts flashed red and Wirrin instantly put his picofactory monitoring on hold. Why the alerts? Pirramar had been appearing without them quite routinely for hours. Something must be wrong.

'Wirrin, be prepared for an attack on your electronics when the Cadre ships become aware of your presence. I'm transmitting a protective package that should be sufficient but you'll need to integrate it with your ship's security systems. The situation here is in full crisis with the negation of our ability to control Cadre ships.'

Wirrin felt his chest tighten.

'The Quambi companions approached a second asteroid and were hit with an unprecedented level of powerful and complex priority-trap signals which, while not damaging, required the activation of their quarantine zones and resulted in the loss of their ability to neutralise the Cadre ships.'

Wirrin briefly wondered why. It must be something to do with the extra time required to work through the quarantine interface.

'An attempt to stealth in and disable the Cadre drives was blocked by the presence of a large number of K74 surveillance drones and proximity mines as well as the continuous detonation of small nuclear devices in the asteroid's wake. The companion Comets are moving to initiate an alternate strategy, which will require the concerted effort of every Comet. Our available time has now shrunk to critical levels.

'Thom, a logistical overview of what is happening is now resident in your InfoSystem and in the remaining twenty-seven minutes before your engagement you will need to consider the effects of reduced stealth ability and deadly atomics on any actions you take.'

Pirramar's serious demeanour shifted to a smile.

'We have a special transmission for you from the Comet.'

The holo shimmered and transformed to the dolphin pool on the main deck where Sonic, positioned at his InfoSystem, was looking directly at them.

'Our greatest adventure yet brothers. We will thwart the power games of the Cadre and tomorrow we will dive together in our favourite sea caves.'

A trill of sound burst forth, sending the hairs of Wirrin's scalp tingling, then died as the holo cut off.

'What was that? He gave me goosebumps.'

Calen shook his head wonderingly. 'I'm not exactly sure. I picked up danger, excitement, urgency, and a sense that he wanted us there with him. The only time I've heard him make a sound anything like that was against the tiger shark at Monkey Mia.'

'You heard all that? I mostly thought he was encouraging us. Calen, you need to concentrate on the simulations.'

'And you need to centre yourself before the match-up, Thom. Turn your brain off for the next fifteen minutes.'

Wirrin caught the amused nod of assent as Thom deliberately settled in his command chair and closed his eyes. A few seconds of contact with Sonic had done wonders for them all.

Well, time to focus on the picofactory. The next fifteen minutes while Thom was quiet would probably be the last opportunity to concentrate without interruption.

*   *   *

'Your stats with the multi-visuals are looking great, Calen. I knew you'd pick it up quickly. The next round will be for real.' Thom nodded. 'Wirrin, Pirramar's last report has been worrying me. How much raw material do we have left for the picofactory?'

'Hardly any. I've kept a small amount for emergencies and there's nothing left we can safely cannibalise.'

'Use it. I want you to design a remote collector to harvest material from the asteroid. If you can manage that we'll try and stock up enough material to build an extra engine disabler in case we lose our stealth. Can you finish that in the next ten minutes?'

'Um! I'll try.'

Wirrin turned to his InfoSystem with ideas already rushing through his mind. An external collector would need stealth but that was no problem. It just meant incorporating the specifications from the engine disabler, which, with its chameleon function, was almost as advanced as the ship itself. It would need a decent size cargo space too. Not good. The limited resources would be too big a constraint. Unless …

Very pleased with himself Wirrin hummed with satisfaction and focused on his InfoSystem.

*   *   *

'It's done! The picofactory will have the modifications implemented in another eight minutes.'

That was three minutes over Thom's time line but there was nothing to be done about that.

'Modifications? The techbot can't go into space. I thought you'd have to design something completely new.'

'I used the engine disabler unit instead. It's already got stealth and a drive so I replaced the disabler section with a collector module. That meant I could use nearly sixty per cent of the emergency resource materials to attach external cargo containers instead of only twenty-five per cent. It means nearly three times as much cargo capability and when the unit returns it'll only take a moment to disconnect the containers and swap the disabler module back in.'

'External? That will spoil the stealth.'

'No it won't. I linked the containers with the unit's chameleon function. The stealth won't change.'

'Dingoes, Wirrin! You're a genius. Will that mean enough material to build a second disabler or will we need more scrounging trips?'

'Plenty, and some left over for surprises as well as keeping our five per cent emergency level. The process from launch to return will take at least nine minutes though, so I don't think there'll be time for any other trips.'

Thom frowned.

'This is going to hold us up. If our stealth's going to be compromised we need to get the extra disabler launched before they know about us.' He thought for a moment. 'We'll stealth to the leading face of the asteroid and get the remote collector launched as soon as it's ready. It means a hold-up of almost twenty minutes but if the disablers can stop two Cadre ships it definitely will be worth the delay.'

Wirrin checked. Two minutes till match-up.

*   *   *

'When will I see them on the visuals?'

'Another thirty or forty seconds. We're approaching from the side and then hugging the leading face of the asteroid till the collector returns. Having all that mass between us will increase our stealth factor while we wait. They won't have a clue we're there.'

'I've got the asteroid!'

Wirrin couldn't help looking at the big display. Yes, there was a tiny blob. Calen had done well to pick it up so soon. Wombats! It was increasing in size while you watched, much more rapidly than on the stealth exercise to K74. It must be all the training and experience Thom had had in the meantime.

'And there's the convoy! I'm enhancing them.'

Three slightly indistinct images sharpened over the next few seconds and Wirrin felt the last vestiges of unreality dissolve. Three monster ships for their tiny vessel to face. Where were the other four? The big display swung to the asteroid. Calen was wondering the same thing.

There was no sign of them though and from the now rapidly changing aspect as they closed on the leading face it was evident they were
well and truly hidden from view. The view broadened and one after the
other the convoy ships were blocked from sight as well. The surface
of the asteroid approached, so close Wirrin was on the edge of shock,
then steadied as Thom locked them in a stable position.

'Countdown for the collector completion please.'

Wirrin had it ready. 'Three minutes and five seconds. My InfoSystem
will activate the launch the instant the picofactory finishes.'

'Wirrin, I'm too busy to monitor our habitat transmissions. Check to
see if there's anything I should be aware of, and Calen, there's tension
time for a while so I want you to make use of it with one more run
through on the sims.'

The InfoSystem changed its immediate focus and Wirrin rapidly
scanned the headings of all the automatic transmissions since Pirramar
had last appeared. There was a vast amount of technical information, a
report about the ongoing Witness meeting and its dissemination of information and warnings throughout the habitats, Quambi's actions, an
upgraded protection package for the ship's electronics from Pirramar that
needed integrating … Done … And a report from the Comet with news
that Thom would want to know. How to do this? Thom was concentrating
ferociously on his console and calling out might be too distracting.

Better to post it on his display with an attention signal he could
attend to when he was ready.

*Nine Comets combined in a multi-spectrum beam attack to disin-
tegrate a second asteroid and disable the attendant Cadre ships. Now
approaching the third.*

After posting the message Wirrin watched for a few seconds for any
reaction from Thom, but forgot that when his own console signalled
that the remote collector was launching.

*   *   *

'Engine disabler unit one launched!'

'Engine disabler unit two launched!'

'Wirrin and Calen, thirty-seven seconds till disabler activation and
the start of our own strategy. Engage your emergency harness and be
ready for the hammer blow.'

Thom had taken them through the strategy twice and grilled them
to make sure they properly understood their roles.

For two seconds the multi-spectrum beam would focus at maximum power on the five Cadre drive engines and then their ship would go into full evasion mode at the highest possible thrust. At the same time the first deployed jamming device would activate, and depending on their proximity, confuse any missiles to varying degrees. Four more jammers would be released and activated at intervals calculated by Thom to give the greatest effect while the ship strained to build speed and distance.

'Multi-spectrum capacitors holding at maximum. Firing in four, three, two, one, zero.'

Intensity filters dimmed the display to a comfortable viewing level and Wirrin watched the coruscating beam flicker between five targets in the two seconds it had available.

Wham! His senses reeled as the ship reached the newly programmed limit of 25.6G. Practically helpless and clinging to consciousness, Wirrin felt an indeterminate time passing before the wondrous return of normal gravity allowed full awareness to release a surge of elation. They were through and safe.

Wirrin could check with his InfoSystem for information but instead he looked to Thom. It felt like the right thing. Thom was busy with his console for what seemed like ages, but then he grinned and gave a victory gesture.

'One Cadre ship down and six to go. Well done, Calen. You picked the best option for outrunning that concentration of missiles. We would have been okay anyway because their response was so slow, but you did it perfectly. Bring up the ship we targeted on the visuals.'

A smiling Calen expanded the section of screen that had been dedicated to that particular ship.

'I can't see any damage.'

'You don't have to. Look where it is relative to the asteroid.'

The view expanded enough to include the asteroid and then once again a few seconds later to accommodate the rapidly increasing gap between it and the ship.

'Its engines are dead, Calen. It's coasting and they won't be able to fix them without help.'

Wirrin jolted as red lights flashed on every console and display.

'What's wrong? Were we damaged?'

Thom touched a control and the lights stopped.

'Nothing's wrong at all. Hang on, I'll set in our new course now that we're back on full stealth and we'll have five minutes to talk and plan. There … They've responded the same way they did against the Comets. Look at this.'

Thom took over the display to show a constant stream of red flashes appearing in the wake of the asteroid.

'These are small nuclear devices and they're detonating them at a rate of … thirty-seven per second. Now look at this.'

New lights, purplish ones this time, appeared in huge numbers, fanning from the two red circles that signified the convoy ships.

'These are surveillance drones, which they hope will pick us up if we close in again. They're not dangerous and we know how to sneak past them.'

Wirrin's InfoSystem suddenly screamed for attention and it was Thom's turn to wait.

'They've just started transmitting the most complicated electronic signals I know of from a Cadre ship … They're full of priority traps and useless disruptions against our systems. It must be the same as the signals keeping the mobile AIs behind their quarantine screens.'

Wirrin wanted to work on the signals but that could come later.

Thom suddenly laughed.

'They think we're one of the dreaded Comet ships that can mysteriously take over their controls. What's the story with the Comets, Wirrin? How did they disable that asteroid?'

'It's three asteroids now and they weren't just disabled. The Comets disintegrate them with their multi-spectrum beams. They can't come at the Cadre ships from behind because of the nuclear devices so they move to the leading face and dissolve all the way through from there.'

'The whole nine Comets onto one? How long does it take? Wait. Something's happening.'

He concentrated on the controls, then gave a huge grin.

'You're a wonder, Wirrin. The asteroid's acceleration just dropped from 3.4G to 3.06G. The disabler units have just disabled their first engine each. They're working perfectly.'

Wirrin hoped they were. There was no way of knowing except through these results, as they were completely independent with no feedback to the ship.

'Our Comets take close to eight minutes to burn through the asteroid before they can beam the externals of the Cadre ships.'

He did a quick data check about the Comets.

'The Comets have just finished with another asteroid. Their times are improving slightly and it's now just under eight minutes for each.'

'Eight! Wirrin, that's not good. The countdown's now at thirty-two minutes and they won't be able to stop them all at that rate.'

Wirrin started to think about that but they were approaching the asteroid again and Thom went into command mode.

'Are you prepared, Calen? This time will be a real test because they'll be on full alert and their response will be quicker and more overwhelming. I made a bad mistake before by not letting you experience what the sudden change to high G would feel like. This time we won't get away in the same 7.9 seconds because I expect all six ships will be involved in retaliation. Wirrin, are the jamming devices all cued and ready?'

He knew they were. Wirrin understood he was being kept involved.

'Here we go with the tricky bit. The pattern they're using to release their mini nuclear devices is leaving a narrow band of safety near the asteroid surface and my calculations show I should be able to use it to get close to one of the connected ships. The two convoy ships are inaccessible at the moment and we'll need a different tactic to get at them.'

Wirrin could hardly believe the approach Thom made with his ship. The surface of the asteroid rushed past at a frightening speed and so close he found himself holding his breath in case of a collision.

Did their evasion burst at extreme G have to follow the same course in reverse? Surely it wouldn't be possible.

He didn't have time to wonder.

'Multi-spectrum capacitors at maximum. Firing in five ... four ... three ... two ... one ... zero.'

Once again the spectrum beam flashed, focusing its destructive power for less than half a second on each of the Cadre ship's five engines in turn and rendering them useless.

Once again Wirrin memory-zapped the rapid action of the two seconds before the hammer struck.

The evasion burst this time was frightening. After the first few moments the ship began lurching and twisting like a living creature striving in terror to escape a predatory grip. The violent forces continued, till Wirrin, on the verge of certainty that they weren't going to make it, blacked out.

And opened his eyes to wonderful calm. Calen was out of his seat and racing. Fear leapt as Wirrin took in Thom's blank expression, lolling head and awful stillness.

'Thom! Thom!' Calen's voice rang and Wirrin, shocked and frantic, released his own emergency harness and tried to stand. His head swam but with a stumbling run he made it to Thom's side.

Calen had one hand pressed against a throat artery.

'He's breathing and his heart's beating. He's all right. It's just taking him longer to snap out of it.'

'We'd better take him to the med-facility.'

Wirrin started on the harness release then paused to watch Calen snap a finger against Thom's forehead. His eyes blinked open, his head jerked upright and he stared at them. 'What? What?'

'You dingo brain! You flaked out.'

For a moment Thom's eyes darted between Wirrin and Calen but then his attention swerved to his console. 'Calen, you totally saved us.'

It was over a minute later and the ship was on a new trajectory back towards the asteroid with its stealth at full capacity.

'I don't know how. I nearly lost it myself. The high G never seemed to end.'

Thom nodded with a quietness that Wirrin didn't like.

'That's because it lasted 13.4 seconds, five and a half seconds longer than the first time. I don't know how you stayed conscious and I don't understand how we're still here. We won't survive another retreat like that.'

'Yes we will. We have to.'

At Calen's comment Thom shook his head with a look that frightened both his friends.

'What's wrong, Thom?'

'We can't do that again. We'll die and the asteroid will still be under their control and it will be my fault.'

'You'll think of something else.'

'There's no way past all those atomics and missiles no matter what I do.'

Thom was now speaking as if to himself, and Wirrin, sensing his despair, shouted at him, 'THOM!!'

It worked because, to Wirrin's relief, Thom twitched and stared in surprise.

'Thom, we won't do it the same way again. You'll figure out something else. We know you will. Steady down.'

'You shouted.'

Wirrin wanted to grab him in a big hug. He was back. No hug though. It might not help at the moment.

'I thought your ears might have been affected by the high grav. Anyhow, we made it and another ship is out of action ... and ... and look at this number.'

Wirrin zoomed a section of display he'd noticed while Thom was concentrating on his console. It showed the asteroid acceleration down to 2.17G, a big drop from the previous 2.6.

'That's strange. It should be slightly higher.'

'No it shouldn't.' The calculating look after Calen's statement said Thom was in control again. 'While that ship is connected without any engines the others have to push its mass along as well as the asteroid. They'll disconnect before very long.'

* * *

A blinking signal caught Thom's attention and by his satisfied smile he was well and truly recovered.

'The disablers just finished their second engine each and the asteroid acceleration dropped again. Building that second one was definitely worth the extra time. Wirrin, two ships are wondering what hit them ... How do you rate their chances of finding the disablers?'

'I don't. They'd have to go external for a visual sighting, and the chameleon function's so good they wouldn't see anything anyway. Thom, have you had any ideas about how we can make it through?'

'You mean whether I'll make it don't you? Well, you can stop worrying and my bios are all good. Look for yourself.'

Wirrin and Calen both checked and exchanged a look as Thom indicated the relevant section on his display. This would have been the sensible place to look when they first rushed to Thom's side.

'We *are* changing tactics though. We're targeting a convoy ship instead of the last impeller, and we'll use your decoy to give us a chance at getting past those mini nukes.'

Wirrin didn't understand.

'The decoy won't do that. The explosions form a constant barrier.'

'No they don't. I've analysed both times our ship came out of stealth and discovered that every unexploded mini nuke changed direction to chase us. They'll do the same again, and while the decoy keeps working there'll be a clear path.'

'What if they don't?'

'We'll know in time to back off.'

Calen looked as if he couldn't believe what he was hearing.

'You mean atomics were chasing us as well as missiles?'

'It sounds bad but it's not. The missiles are the real worry. Wirrin, can you provide the decoy with any extra jamming devices? I'm going to send it closer than we originally planned and every extra second it can survive will help us.'

'Two extras, but we'll have to use the last of our emergency resources for the picofactory to make them because that last escape used more than we planned for ... How long have I got?'

Another attention light flashed before Thom could answer and the trio watched a Cadre ship dwindle in size as it fell behind the onrushing asteroid.

'You were right! We can forget about that one. Um ... Can you manage three minutes? We're running out of time.'

Wirrin managed easily. The instructions only took moments. The picofactory did the rest, and in just under the three minutes Thom started a new count down.

'Twenty-three minutes till the asteroid reaches the habitats. Engage your emergency harnesses and prepare yourselves. Decoy deployed.'

There was a wait while the ship manoeuvred well away from the decoy to Thom's planned line of approach.

'Decoy activation in ... five ... four ... three ... two ... one ... zero!'

This decoy had been Wirrin's idea and to make it real had been one of the biggest mental challenges he'd faced yet, particularly because of the time constraints, but also because he'd had to work with technical areas he didn't know much about. The final outcome was an independently moving device that would register on the Cadre scanners as Thom's ship. Wirrin was particularly pleased with his accomplishment because when he'd used his InfoSystem to link a simulation to their own ship's controls it had taken Thom sixteen seconds to penetrate the false reality being presented. Thom, originally keen but dubious, had changed to being eager and totally impressed.

In full zap mode Wirrin watched the fake ship flicker into existence, emitting the same signals Thom's ship did when it left stealth, and the same light speed signal that would register with the Cadre ships as a target lock. The reaction was almost immediate, but not quite, and as if realising the need to escape, the decoy darted away at its full 4.2G capability and released its first jamming device. At 4.2G it was very slow, but Thom had calculated it would add an extra second or more before the inevitable destruction.

For 9.4 seconds the alternate ship drew the full wrath of five Cadre ships, with every missile and mini nuclear device dedicated to preventing a repeat of the two previous disablements.

At 9.4 seconds the alternate ship disappeared in a flash of light as the first missile, followed by hundreds more, locked on and exploded.

At 7.1 seconds however, the last jammer from the decoy finished transmitting and Thom, sliding into position along a course suddenly clear of nuclear danger, was ready with full capability and full beam capacitor charge. His beam flashed for its two second darting dance of destruction then, again, the hammer of high gravity descended.

One jolting lurch, another, and they were free.

'Is that it?'

Thom didn't answer. His console was too important at the moment, but the smile plastered over his face said it all.

Wirrin did some checking of his own. Yes, at 6.3 seconds it had definitely been a better escape this time, and there, automatically tracked on its allocated display screen, was the diminishing image of another disabled Cadre ship.

'Wirrin, I'm going to make sure Akama shows that decoy on the InterWeb of every habitat so they know what you did.'

'And Sonic will tell all the dolphins that you're the cleverest hunter they'll ever meet.'

Feeling somewhat embarrassed at such high praise, but also good about it, Wirrin was distracted by a blue attention light on Thom's console.

'Whooee! The asteroid acceleration just dropped to 1.53G. That's three engines each for the disablers now and all being well we'll have two more Cadre ships completely out of action in another eleven minutes.'

Thom paused, concentrated for a moment, then looked at Wirrin. 'I've rethought our plans again. We're holding off our next attack till after the disablers are finished. We'll be safer that way.'

Wirrin, startled, checked the countdown. 'Can we take the chance? We'd be down to less than nine minutes with two Cadre ships still to disable.'

Thom shook his head. 'It's not taking a chance. It's our best strategy. They need at least two fully functional ships to keep that asteroid manoeuvrable, so we only have to get one of them, and there'll be an opportunity soon after the disablers finish.'

Wirrin and Calen watched Thom intently. The increased confidence of his tone meant he had something interesting in mind.

'When that happens the last convoy ship will connect. It will have to or their whole mission will have been aborted, and that connection will take careful manoeuvring in very limited time.'

'Nine minutes? Isn't that plenty of time for them? You'd do it in less than a minute.'

'With this ship, yes, but that monster is 700 metres long with massive momentum to control. I flew them after the Freedom hijack, remember, and I'm estimating they'll need something like four or five minutes. They're going to be desperate when the other two ships lose all their engines and that's when we'll make our move.'

'But look at all those atomics they're releasing. We'll never get past them without another decoy.'

'Yes we will. Only one ship will be releasing them and it will have to modify its pattern while the convoy ship makes its approach. That's the opportunity I'm counting on.'

'One? There are four of them.'

'The two with their engines wrecked will disconnect and we can forget about them. The convoy ship will stop too, at least for the trickiest part of connecting, and that's our moment.'

'What if the two ships don't disconnect? It makes more sense for them to keep protecting the convoy ship till it's in place.' Calen persisted and Wirrin agreed with his logic.

Thom shook his head. 'They won't. They know our habitats are moving by now and their tracking will have told them they must keep the asteroid at a bit over a full G. They'll drop way below that if they keep the mass of two non-functional ships added to the load … They'll disconnect.'

Wirrin wasn't so sure, but he wasn't going to argue against waiting for an opportunity that improved their chances. And anyway, if the break Thom was hoping for didn't happen, there would still …

Red lights flashed, but after a glance Thom switched them off.

'Weird! I don't know what that means. They turned their jamming equipment on. It's pointless because it stops them tracking the habitats. They'll have to turn it off.'

'They're panicking.'

'Not with the training they get. Wirrin, are transmissions still getting through from Pirramar?'

Wirrin scanned with his InfoSystem. 'Yes, without a break ... The Comets are still disintegrating the sixth asteroid ... The habitat drives are all working at full power ... The four K74 asteroids that are left are all directed at Attunga, and this big one is targeting Warrakan ... The habitat picofactories are pouring out mobile spectrum-beam units.'

Wirrin stopped speaking to check an incoming transmission with a priority tag on it.

'Thom, Pirramar says there's a possibility that if they lose control of the asteroid then the remaining Cadre ships might commit to a suicide attempt against Warrakan.'

There was silence as the trio took this in.

'This is bad! It means we *will* have to disable every single engine. There's no choice. I'm still going to wait for the disablers to finish, though, because we have to survive this next attack to even have a chance at the last ship.'

'Warrakan's hull has had the strength upgrade. Won't that be enough to stop Cadre ships?'

'Not at this speed, Calen. There's just too much kinetic energy involved. How long before the next two engines are disabled?'

'Well, just over a minute if they work at the same rate they have so far. Thom, if we tricked the convoy ship into chasing after us that would make it easier to get at wouldn't it?'

'It would but it's unlikely they'll break position at this stage.'

'I could design a set of signals that make it look like we've been damaged. That might lure them.'

'Um, you'd have to be fast. Like in the next four or five minutes.'

Wirrin did it in two. He'd developed a database of ship signals and how to modify them when he was designing the decoy.

'Their scanners will pick up a faulty engine and partial damage to our stealth defence. We'll look like half a ship with a crippled engine.'

'Half a ship? Let's see what happens.'

Nothing happened. Except a barrage of missiles that were harmless because Thom had judged his distances and speed so well. After twenty-five seconds the apparently crippled and fleeing ship disappeared under full stealth and circled back to watch what happened when the disablers completed their job. Despite expecting a reaction, Thom's yell still made Wirrin jump.

'That's perfection! You're a total brainiac! You've done it again, Wirrin. The asteroid's G just dropped to 0.79 and two more Cadre ships are completely disabled. Engage your emergency harnesses and prepare yourselves for action sometime in the next two and a half minutes. Calen, are you ready with the pre-sets?'

Of course Calen was ready. They were all ready and hoping beyond hope that Thom's prediction would eventuate.

Wirrin watched Calen's multi-visual displays of the two newly disabled Cadre ships with tense anticipation.

Leave! Leave! You're slowing that asteroid down! You should leave! After sixty interminable seconds a whisper of doubt edged its way into Wirrin's mind.

At ninety seconds the whisper had become a cloud and fifteen seconds after that it was so much a certainty that the change in position of one of the ships didn't seem real.

And then the other.

Wirrin's spirits climbed. The two ships dwindled behind, not as rapidly as the earlier ones, but that didn't matter because they were now out of the picture and no longer a threat. The level of danger ahead was now significantly lower and they focused their attention on the convoy ship. If Thom's prediction was right it would start moving towards one of the vacated connection cradles.

Yes! Yes! Yes! Wirrin wanted to yell that Thom was unbelievable, fantastic, clever, brilliant, but he made do with a silently mouthed 'yes' at Calen, because right now Thom was a study of pure concentration as he manipulated his controls to keep their little ship in the best relative position while the Cadre monster manoeuvred closer to the asteroid. The barrage of missiles and atomics continued, just as Thom had said it would, but despite this Thom made his approach. Once again Wirrin marvelled at how close they were to the asteroid surface and, even more frightening, how close they were to their target. How could their stealth possibly hold at this range? The convoy ship slowed as it jockeyed close against the asteroid until, a scant 100 metres from connection its incessant barrage suddenly stopped.

Thom's voice rang out. 'Multi-spectrum-beam capacitors at maximum charge!

Engaging in … five … four … three … two … one … zero.'

For the fourth time the little ship put everything into the totally controlled seconds of precise destruction and frantic evasion, and for the fourth time Wirrin's relief at the release from that awful thrust was overlaid with the knowledge of success. Again there was quiet while Thom did his assessment, then shared elation when, more quickly than previously, he was able to speak.

'Brilliant, Calen! That was 6.8 seconds and you did it with only one pre-set. Are you ready for the next one because I'm heading back for him right now? He's going to disconnect and I want to get him while I can still hug the asteroid surface. It's been a more effective strategy than I expected.'

'I'm ready. It seemed easier that time.'

'It wasn't. You're adapting to battle stress. Here we go! Capacitors building! Engage emergency harness!'

The harnesses didn't need engaging. They hadn't been released in the short recovery period.

Wirrin stared in shock as the ship raced faster and closer to the rugged asteroid exterior than seemed possible. Thom seemed to be able to dramatically increase their closing speed.

Right now Wirrin's eyes were locked on the display while his mind flinched from each inevitable collision that somehow didn't happen.

'Capacitors at maximum!

Engaging in … five … four … three … two … one … zero.'

This attack went without a hitch. The whole two seconds of it.

The escape didn't. Instead of one hammer of thrust the ship was hit by two. The first was the usual, the engines working at full power. The second was a sideways force with enough strength to scrape the little vessel fleetingly against the asteroid surface.

Interference from the first jamming device had caused an incoming missile to explode in the merest fraction of a second before it hit, and the concussive force of detritus against their hull had thrown them slightly off course. All Wirrin knew was two great lurches which tried to throw him from his seat, another minor lurch shortly after, more seconds of high G, and a blessed return to normal.

Thom was concentrating on his console with a frown. A frown?

The image in Wirrin's mind of the multi-spectrum beam darting precisely as it had on all their other attacks meant that they had surely been successful. Hadn't they? His concern growing, Wirrin blurted, 'Thom, what's wrong?'

There was a long silence, then Thom said, 'They damaged my ship.'

Wirrin didn't understand. There were no warnings showing on the consoles, the visual showed they were circling back towards the asteroid, and a quick glance at the screen that Calen had centred on the Cadre ship showed that none of its engines were firing.

'But you saved Warrakan! The asteroid's dead!' He paused. 'How bad is it?'

Thom shook his head as if to clear it. He tried to smile but it faltered and Wirrin saw that he was fighting tears. He and Calen rushed to Thom's side, then hesitated, frightened by the look on his face and the tears welling in his eyes. Thom made a strange little sound.

'Sorry … We did stop them … I didn't think I was good enough.'

Wirrin stared at him in amazement while Calen released the harness and dragged him into an enormous hug.

'You great lumping idiot! Of course you're good enough. There's no-one better.'

Wirrin wrapped his arms around both of them.

'We fight off seven Cadre ships and you call me a lumping idiot? I deserve better than that,' Thom said, a catch in his voice.

The smiles grew when Thom pointed at the display where the last Cadre ship was disconnected and apparently hovering close to the asteroid.

'Why are they still here?'

'You're hopeless! They're coasting. The same as the asteroid. They can't do anything else now and Warrakan will just drive out of their path.'

Calen's little grin meant his question had been purposely designed to give Thom a payback opportunity, and Thom, realising this a second after he'd responded, shook his head and told Calen he was crazy.

The elation at their success was short-lived though as Thom turned to his console again. The asteroid and the Cadre ship suddenly dropped away at incredible speed as they began their deceleration process.

'What's coming through from Pirramar?'

Thom's voice once more sounded serious and controlled. Wirrin did a quick update.

'The Comets have been working on the last K74 asteroid for just over two minutes with a countdown of four minutes and seventeen seconds before it reaches Attunga.'

'They've run out of time. They're not going to stop it.'

'Why didn't they use your strategy of hugging close to the asteroid to get at the Cadre ships?'

'They couldn't, Calen. The Comets are way too big. Wirrin, that time doesn't match with the earlier prediction. It's twenty-one seconds longer.'

It was too.

'I don't know why, but it must mean that the asteroid has slowed down.'

Right now Pirramar was channelling an overload of information from the habitats, every Comet, the AIs, and the Witness Council. Without hesitation Wirrin linked to the data coming from their own Comet, checked it, then immediately switched the visual component to the big display. They gasped at the view of a great lance penetrating the asteroid, an incandescent wall of fire and destruction disintegrating more and more asteroid material.

The Comet-sized multi-spectrum beam at work made their own look puny, and Wirrin wondered briefly what the heavy-duty habitat units must be capable of. They watched for ten seconds or so but the view didn't change and Thom wanted more.

'Can we see the other Comets? That doesn't show us their progress.'

'Where's Sonic? Can we see if he's all right?'

'Um, I can only show you what they're sending. Hang on … the Witness Council transmission might tell us more.'

It did. One big window showed a representation of the oncoming asteroid with the nine Comets down in the great pit their beams were gouging. Attendant to it were graphs and icons with relevant and continually updating information.

Another window had a Witness advising Attunga people of the actions they should be taking right now, and as they listened to the futile instructions about brace positions and cautions to keep away from any large free-standing object, the horror of what eight hundred million Attungans were facing welled within Wirrin.

With their own hours of tension and stress there'd been no real time to dwell on the crisis facing others but now, watching helplessly as the deadly asteroid raced closer and closer, it filled their thoughts. Wirrin and Calen moved closer to Thom.

'Look! The first of the mobile beams just activated.'

Somehow the AIs had forced the habitat picofactories to construct nearly fifty mobile multi-spectrum-beam units and place them along the path of the approaching asteroid so each unit could deliver a fleeting blow in the short period while the speeding mass was in range. They watched quietly till, with just under two minutes left, Calen suddenly jolted and looked at Thom.

'What about the Comets? They're down in that pit. They won't be trapped will they? Sonic's with them.'

'They'll all be safe. They'll stay as long as they can then leave at exactly the right second. It will already be carefully calculated.'

Together they watched, despairing and fearful under the growing realisation there would be no miraculous reprieve.

Fourteen seconds to impact.

Where were the Comets?

Eleven seconds.

Ten seconds.

Nine Comets streaked from the pit.

Seven seconds.

Six seconds.

Wirrin took a deep breath and held it, transfixed as he stared at the display.

Three seconds.

Two seconds.

One second.

The display flickered for several seconds then completely blanked out.

*   *   *

Aboard the Comet, along with all the rest of the crew, Sonic and Gulara watched the shocking sight of the rear section of the habitat disappear behind an explosively spreading envelope of fire and destruction as kinetic energy was transformed instantly to heat.

Safety filters dimmed the real brilliance of the rushing corona to a glowing red and white.

Inside the habitat eight hundred million people felt the jolt and tremor of their home.

In the transport pools aboard the Comet, every enhanced dolphin joined in the age-old call of distress.

Deep in the protected section of Attunga the AI gestalt leapt to an unprecedented level of activity.

Along the exterior, the great construction complex ceased to exist, picofactories, buildings, docking bays and construction-bots all vaporised in an instant.

The people of Warrakan and Freedom stared at the same blank transmission till the screen flickered again and activated with the image of Akama.

'People of the open habitats. Attunga has survived.'

Chapter 37

'But we were there just fifteen minutes ago.'

Calen was finding it hard to cope with the news that it was going to take seventeen hours to get back to the habitats.

'Yes, and we were travelling at over 7000 kilometres every second. We have to lose all that velocity before we even start coming back.'

'Why don't they invent some other way to travel then? It always takes too much time. On Attunga and Warrakan you can get anywhere in twenty minutes.'

'Some other way? Like what?'

'I don't know. Like the warp holes they have in virtual reality dramas.'

Thom loved it and Wirrin couldn't help laughing.

'Warp holes? Idiot! I'll never understand how your brain works. You mean worm holes. Warp is different. It's the engine making everything super-fast.'

'So I was right. We should be able to worm our way through the warp holes with super-fast engines the AIs make for us.'

'Make a techbot to fix his head please, Wirrin.'

'My head? It's your head that needs fixing. You said the ship was damaged but everything's working perfectly.'

'No she's not. We can't get out. The hatchway mechanism was damaged when we scraped against the asteroid. That'll be a couple of hours extra we have to wait while they fix it.'

'Two hours to fix a door? As if! I'll tell Turaku to burn a hole through if we have to wait that long.'

'A hole? Through the side of my ship? I'll burn a hole in you and Wirrin will help me. This ship is now famous and every inch of her is precious.'

A certain amount of inanity was not only warranted but also infectious and Wirrin burst into laughter. Calen and Thom gawked at his overreaction then, infected themselves, couldn't help joining in.

'Dingoes! The whole major construction area for Attunga gets wiped out and we're laughing like idiots. It's your fault, Wirrin. You set us off this time.'

'No I didn't, Thom. You did — burning a hole in Calen. And anyway, laughing's good for you when you get stressed.'

'Stress? You call it stress? It felt like panic to me.'

'Controlled panic, Thom. Perfectly controlled.'

Thom made one of his nondescript sounds. 'We didn't have any choice. What's happening with K74? We haven't heard about that yet.'

After Akama's talk and general reports about the situation, Pirramar had been in contact with more details. They'd learnt that the external damage to Attunga was major, with the construction area completely destroyed and great amounts of the protective shell vaporised in that same area.

The shell, nearly 500 metres thick and designed specifically to buffer the main habitat from the effects of any meteor or asteroid impact, had done its job so well that internal damage, widespread as it was, was relatively minor.

They'd spoken with Sonic directly and Thom had been taken aback by the admiration and praise in his voice, a far cry from their normal badinage. He'd have to get used to that.

The enhanced dolphins were on their way to their home reaches on Warrakan.

The two companion AIs, along with two of the mobile AIs in their Comets, were racing to K74 to be ready to implement whatever consequences were decided, while the remaining mobile AI, along with a Comet crewed by humans, was departing on a rescue and capture mission for the seven helplessly drifting Cadre ships.

Wirrin checked K74. 'Nothing's changed … Yes it has. Quambi's kept a total communication blockage going but it's been extended to a physical blockage as well and every vessel that's left K74 has been taken to a holding area.'

Thom was particularly interested. 'I suppose the Cadre sent ships to get past the electronic blockade. Hey, they won't even know what's happened.'

'Thom, they know absolutely nothing. It looks like they're being even more isolated than the last time. They must be, if every ship they send out gets confiscated.'

'I wonder if that's what will happen with the Cadre ships? I wouldn't even let them have them after this.'

'I don't reckon K74 should even be allowed to build new ones for years. Aggressive ships I mean,' said Calen.

They all agreed on that.

After several hours of watching reports and looking into aspects that interested them, Wirrin said, 'Well, time to catch up on sleep.'

Thom laughed. 'My brain's too hyped up, Wirrin, and we can't anyway. Your techbot ate the grav-bunks.'

'Wombat head! Adjust your command seat to go flat. That's as good as a bed.'

'No it's not. You know I like a grav-field for sleeping and it hasn't got one.'

Thom's active brain didn't last long though, once the lights dimmed and they were supine, and the little ship, under full automatics, carried them safely home for the next twelve hours.

*   *   *

'Two hours? More like two minutes.'

'Had you worried didn't I?'

Thom's laugh ended abruptly and his jaw dropped when the ship's portal slid back to reveal a great phalanx of dignitaries lined up and waiting: Akama and his counterparts from Warrakan and Freedom, Sonic in his transporter, Gulara, Burilda, the doctor, Miah and Raji, along with others the trio knew to varying degrees. They'd expected Gulara, and Pirramar had said Akama was going to meet with them at some stage, but this looked official. The trio stepped through their hatchway to the huge, unfamiliar docking area. They'd had to use this alternative Attunga dock because their regular dock no longer existed.

Akama moved to greet them with a big smile, his customary shoulder grip, and a simple 'Welcome home', then Calen dived into the transporter, Sonic trilled hello in dolphin language and gave his dolphin laugh and they were enveloped in a welter of greetings, hugs and smiles.

'My brothers have returned to the home reach and their pod awaits.'

Wirrin wondered about the formal tone, then wondered again at the nods of agreement from Gulara, Burilda and the doctor.

Akama spoke. 'Yes, we are your escort. Your human and AI pods are waiting for you too.'

'Now? For some sort of meeting?'

'Of course. What else could you possibly expect? The habitats are waiting.'

Habitats? All of them? Well of course they were. Wirrin looked to see if Thom understood. No, he didn't.

'Right now? Don't we get a chance to change? We've been wearing the same clothes ever since Wirrin's techbot ate everything.'

'Nothing could be more appropriate.'

Thom registered surprise, but nothing like the surprise that followed when Raji dashed from his father's side and launched himself on Thom in a ferocious hug, his arms tight around Thom's back and his legs dangling in mid-air. Thom almost fell over backwards but recovered and, laughing, returned the hug.

'Wombats, Little Dolphin. What's this for?'

Raji had been called Little Dolphin for ages, a term he especially loved because it was Sonic's name for him.

'You saved us all. We watched you on the InterWeb and everyone says you're brave but I already knew because Sonic told me.'

Thom laughed and adjusted Raji so he could see his face.

'That's silly, Raji.'

'No it's not.'

Somewhat nonplussed by Raji's determination, Thom looked to the doctor as if expecting him to talk sense into his son, and received the nod and smile that was echoed by all the other adults. With a move, deft and familiar from relax time at the dolphinarium, Thom swung Raji to a comfortable sitting position on his shoulder.

'What's this about the InterWeb?'

'We watched everything you did. It was really exciting, like a VR drama, except it wasn't because Mum and Dad were watching it too and they were so quiet we felt the same till you beamed that last ship and escaped. Alisa says Calen's amazing because he didn't go unconscious but Miro says you're more amazing because the way you controlled your ship was like magic and he wants to be—' Raji stopped abruptly because his dad was making the shoosh signal that meant he was getting too talkative and excited. Thom saw too but disregarded it.

'What about Wirrin? He made the decoy and the jammers and the techbot and you didn't say anything about him.'

'I don't have to. Everyone already knows he's special. Like Akama.'

It was Wirrin's turn to be nonplussed. What was Raji talking about, and how was he going to get him to explain? Akama had an interesting reaction too, though it wasn't obvious.

The group started moving and by the time they'd reached the nearest

TransCom portal the trio knew they were heading to the now famous Attunga dolphinarium for an official thank you ceremony.

After a journey, so rapid it must have been given priority treatment, they entered the viewing gallery, which was packed with people in the auditorium and dolphins on the other side of the big glass wall, and the hairs on Wirrin's scalp shifted when every person rose to their feet and waited in absolute silence.

Akama indicated three seats and gestured to the trio to move. Feeling the incredible weight of attention focused on them, Wirrin grabbed Thom, pushed him into the lead, did the same to Calen, and then followed close behind. They sat down and the uncanny silence continued till, intruding on the quiet, a single person began to clap. It was Akama, and instantly a great ovation soared around the stunned and overwhelmed trio. Thom said later that he thought they must have all gone crazy but the sound and sensation were so powerful he felt like he was frozen in his seat. The roar went on, and on, then abruptly finished as Akama pointed to the glass wall or, rather, the dolphins massed behind it.

Taking their cue from Sonic, who must have arrived during the ovation, every enhanced dolphin performed the dolphin to human greeting with the astonishing group precision they were capable of then burst into dolphin song. The joyous sound of their massed voices rang through the auditorium with extraordinary strength and power.

Part of it was the welcome song dolphins gave to pod members who'd been absent for a while; part of it sounded like the song of success after a successful hunt; and interwoven through it all, Wirrin heard the dolphin names Puck had given them when Sonic was still tiny.

This song was especially for them. Sonic must have created and organised it with the pod while they were asleep on the ship. The sound and motion finished and, before the hush of appreciation that invariably followed one of these special dolphin performances could change to applause, the images of Pirramar and the AI who represented the gestalt shimmered into view.

'Welcome home, Thom!

'Welcome home, Calen!

'Welcome home, Wirrin!

'The gestalt and all our associated AIs extend our gratitude and appreciation for your actions during this crisis. Friends! Thrice named!'

The gestalt representative turned to Akama who immediately took over.

'Members of our habitat triunity. Three young men set out on a journey of relaxation and adventure, little knowing that a straightforward request for help from our habitat security would send them into a situation fraught with danger and almost unbearable responsibility for the lives of Warrakan's dolphins, AIs, and humans.

'Watch, and marvel at the bonds of care and support that carry our Dolphin Boys through their worst moments.

'Watch, and wonder, as gentle-spirited Calen becomes the rock of strength for the trio.

'Watch, and share my admiration, as Wirrin, with inspiring innovation and application, provides the tools and wherewithal for success.

'Watch, in awe, the triumph of spirit displayed by Thom as, faced with overwhelming odds and battling fears of inadequacy, he rose to every challenge with skill and control that is beyond my understanding. Watch now and share briefly the hopes, the fears, and the courage they display through their eleven-hour ordeal.'

The trio sat, overwhelmed by Akama's speech. To Wirrin's ears there was the sound of conviction in every word. Whoops! Thom was taking it to heart. Wirrin gently clasped Thom's forearm and was rewarded with a quick look and a subtle smile of thanks.

The area directly in front of the glass wall lit up with a holo of Thom's ship, and for the next short while they watched a carefully compiled outline of their actions, their early thoughts about what might be happening, parts of the discussion about strategy, Wirrin's ideas and work with his InfoSystem, the high-grav practice, and then highlights from the time after match-up.

The information from every sensor on the ship must have been collected.

They watched the dramatic seconds of each encounter and saw the distortion of their features under high-grav, watched Calen's fingers struggling to key the pre-sets, and relived the moments of Thom's slow recovery to consciousness.

The overwhelming message though, was the counterpoint of Thom's skill and command when it counted, against his feelings of worry and despair.

Wirrin's heart constricted at the sight of tears welling in Thom's eyes as he said he thought he wasn't good enough, then relaxed with laughter as Calen called him a 'great lumping idiot'. They found out from Pirramar that against the drama of multi-spectrum beams, conflict, and the spectacular images of impact, this was the most viewed and re-viewed moment on the InterWeb. 'There's no-one better!' Calen's following words sounded, the holo presentation finished, and in the immediate hush Akama stood and gestured for attention.

'Yes, Thom, no-one better!

'Through an act of providence beyond my comprehension, the only people from our three habitats with the necessary combination of skills and equipment were somehow located precisely where they were needed.' There was no signal this time but the gathering rose to their feet for a second ovation, and against the roar of applause the Dolphin Song sounded again.

*   *   *

'You're going to K74, Thom?'

This was surprising news because K74 had been completely blockaded for a week now and there was no activity around it.

'The message came from Akama that he wants me to. The AIs and governments all through the solar system have demanded a stop to any aggressive ships being built there for the next twenty years and we're going to destroy the big construction sites.'

'Twenty? Is that all? It should be a lot more.'

'It could be, Calen, if the Cadre keeps running things but if that changes then it'll be less, and from what Wirrin's been telling us that's almost certain. When the AIs get serious things really start to happen.'

Wirrin had learned from Pirramar that AIs through the whole solar system had decided the threats against them from K74 were now so serious they required action. This was amazing to hear because, for all the years since the great conflict when sections of humanity fought with tools of fear and hatred for the power to control all forms of machine intelligence, non-interference and cooperation had been an unvarying tenet for AIs in their relationship with the differing forms of human society.

Their proposal had been for Quambi to spread knowledge throughout K74 about the Cadre's actions, and at the same time to undermine any of the rogue's anti-AI activities. Interestingly, they hadn't proceeded till they'd gained human approval, though that was instant, with every major government applauding the idea, appalled that the Cadre was prepared to slaughter hundreds of millions of people to further its own ends.

'What's Quambi doing, Wirrin? She still has to keep hidden doesn't she?' asked Calen.

'Yes, for Quambi-K's sake, but that's easy. She's already a master at it and getting better all the time. Pirramar and I checked it out yesterday afternoon and the Cadre must be furious because images and reports telling the truth about what happened keep mysteriously appearing on the K74 InterWeb and they can't stop them. Quambi has set it up so that when they try to trace the origins they detect an external breach of their security.'

'Hey, that's clever. Is it having much effect?'

'It will. The embassy ambassadors were already in conflict, and Quambi's building on those differences and spreading their questions all through the habitat as well,' said Wirrin.

'Isn't that dangerous for the people who watch?'

'It would be, Thom, but strangely, the monitoring programs have developed all sorts of bugs.'

'Quambi?'

'Of course. Data gets wiped or corrupted and the programs stop working or go into diagnostic mode, or something else unexpected happens.'

'Dingoes! Only an AI could make that happen all through K74. Won't the rogue think it has to be Quambi-K?'

'Quambi-K gets ordered to check everything but from her viewpoint it's either a genuine bug or the external breach it's meant to look like. Anyhow, the rogue's going to have his own trouble soon and he won't have time to focus on Quambi-K.'

'What trouble, Wirrin?'

'Everything he's been involved in is going to start malfunctioning. The first problems will be in the Black areas and then his equipment will start giving false results.'

'Does that mean you'll be able to watch all the Cadre meetings again?'

'It does, Thom, and because we'll know all their plans as soon as they make them, we'll be able to spoil anything we need to.'

'I don't understand. You've always told us electronic access isn't possible for Black areas. How's Quambi going to get into them?'

'She's going to intrude physically with her own completely separate access lines. The rogue won't know they're there.'

'He'll know when things start going wrong.'

'No he won't, Thom. There'll be clues to tell him it's more external breaches.'

'He might. He's very clever.'

'He has no idea what he's up against. Quambi has started building her own communication and control network through K74 and once she gets into the Black areas she'll be watching everything the Cadre and the rogue are doing.'

'How long before she does that?'

'Another eight or ten weeks at least. She needs to have her network functioning at a basic level for the rest of the habitat before she tackles the secret areas, and building the network's an enormous job.'

'A secret network for the whole of K74 in ten weeks?'

'Picobots, Thom. Her picofactories can do anything ours can. Remember?'

'How long will you be at K74?' asked Calen.

Thom blinked at the sudden reversion to the early part of the conversation.

'Just today. The Comet's multi-spectrum beams will only take a few moments for each construction site. Why?'

'I'm going to tell Sonic. He'll think it's a good adventure to share with you.'

*   *   *

Thom turned towards Gulara.

'Let's go! We have to get to the next meeting.'

They did have to get to another meeting, but not just yet. Thom was trying to dodge the half-hour of mingling which usually followed the formal talks because he'd listened to too many people telling him how good he was.

Wirrin and Calen felt the same but evidently it was important for different groups of people to have an opportunity to express their gratitude and for two weeks Gulara had been their official companion, as they met with a range of people across the three habitats. She gave a serious looking nod, as if this was something important and in only five minutes they were making their way to the nearest TransCom portal.

'They all say the same thing.'

'Of course they do, but it's heartfelt and important to them, Thom.'

'I know, but I'll still be glad when it's over.'

'It will never be over, but officially you finish your public meetings after the next three days.'

'Just as well. I've only had one proper trip in the Comet since we got back and no training at all. It's getting ridiculous.'

*   *   *

'It seems like they're in a hurry to restore everything, Pirramar.'

The day before, the trio and Sonic had used Thom's ship to examine the reconstruction progress in the area of impact and been surprised at how much had happened. The protective hull, which had been vaporised to a depth of over 100 metres in the worst places, was completely rebuilt and foundations for the docking and construction sites were well under way.

'There is a timeline, Wirrin, but it is easily achievable. We were delayed while we moved the habitats back to all our abandoned asteroids but the picofactories are very efficient and they quickly put us on track. The hull repair work is nothing compared with the original build and Warrakan can easily handle any important work.'

'What is the timeline then?'

'We need to be ready for the move to Uranus in three months. We want to have all construction areas restored, three Comets with mobile AIs built, and complete the basic infrastructure for the dolphin level of Attunga ... Link to the gestalt research database and find the AI design section. We'll go through what's being proposed.'

*   *   *

'Dingoes! I don't know whether to be happy or sad. I've just had the most amazing meeting with the security AI and the people from the centre.' Thom had just arrived home after a day at his training centre.

'Choose happy then, Great Captain, and banish the sad to an asteroid lost in the ocean of interstellar space.'

'Wise words, Great Fish.'

Laughing as he dodged the inevitable jet of water, Thom tossed his gear to one side.

He did a bomb drop into the pool a few inches from Sonic's head and the news about his amazing meeting went on hold while the usual chaos of laughter and physical interaction claimed them.

'Not fair! You're too big. It's like trying to push a wall around.'

'Yajala informs me my growth is likely to continue for at least another twelve years.'

'It better not. We'll need a bigger pool.'

They wouldn't. This one had been designed to cope but Thom did have a point because during the last few months Sonic had had another growth spurt, and though not yet quite the size of the big enhanced males, Sonic was certainly approaching it.

'Share your amazing news with us, Little One.'

Thom ignored the dig. He was relaxed now, draped across Sonic's back and leisurely rubbing an area of skin near his blowhole.

'They think my ship is so important they're taking her off me.'

'What?' His three listeners responded together. That was amazing news.

'And it's partly my own fault … for telling you she was precious. The Witnesses and the AIs are going to give her the place of honour in a display centre about the attack. They are giving me another ship, but it won't be the same because she was so good.'

'She? Humans are adept at anthropomorphising.'

'And some dolphins are swimming word banks. What's that supposed to mean?'

'You called it she, as if it was a person.'

Thom grabbed Sonic's dorsal fin but changed his mind about bending it.

'Everyone calls a ship "she".'

'What's the new one going to be like? I bet it'll be even better.'

'It will be able to do more and it might be better.'

'You just described the new ship as an "it".'

Thom laughed at Wirrin and Calen's grins, which said that as soon as he got the new one the 'she' would return and he'd get excited and enthusiastic and once again be boasting about having the best in the solar system.

'Well, it should be. They're working on improving the grav-compensator and I asked them to make it more powerful as well.'

'More? Wombats! Is that possible? I remember you saying something about more powerful engines straining the structure.'

'Yes, this new one has to be a bit bigger, 49 metres instead of 43, and slightly thicker because the hull and the frame have to be stronger.'

'When do you get it?'

'In about five weeks. They're building it here on Warrakan … Why?'

'We leave for Titania in three months so we should have another try at our K137 adventure. It'll be too far away if we don't.'

'Hey, brilliant, and we won't leave unless Sonic's with us this time. Let's organise it for two weeks after I get the new ship.'

'We will demand time for our last chance to visit the mystery asteroid and I will enjoy flying your new ship.'

'No you won't. It's not allowed to get wrecked so I told them they couldn't put any dolphin controls in it.'

'You are being provided with a limited rust bucket?'

Thom looked to Wirrin for the meaning.

'A nautical term used on Earth to describe an old worn-out ship.'

'No, a new powerful ship with protections to stop wonky drivers who bump into every asteroid that passes by.'

Wirrin didn't know what wonky meant and wondered how Thom did.

'Will it help wonky drivers who need a new door before they can leave their ship?'

So, it had come from an earlier verbal stoush with Sonic. Thom, obviously realising he'd left himself wide open with the bumping into asteroid statement, conveniently ignored the comeback.

'It'll have a stronger multi-spectrum beam and a slightly bigger pico-factory too and they're going to build twenty more of them after it's been trialled.'

'Twenty? Who are they for?'

'Training at the centre. They're building five extra Comets too, but that will all happen after the move.'

'They're for training? That means you'll be busier than ever?'

'Probably.'

The talk went back to their mystery asteroid and twenty minutes later it was all planned and locked in.

*   *   *

'It's hard to take it all in.'

'You will, Burilda. We take all the human sectors for granted, and by the time the Attunga reaches are all functioning you'll feel the same about the dolphin level.'

The trio and Sonic had just spent nearly two hours with Burilda, zooming from pristine reach to pristine reach through the connector tunnels, to see the enormous new area being made available for the Attunga enhanced dolphins.

'Do you think the dolphins will be able to take it in? There are more reaches than there are dolphins.'

'Dolphins will explore and share their knowledge. Every special seagrass bed and underwater cave will be known.'

'Not all of it, Thom. These reaches we've seen today will definitely be well-known by our enhanced dolphins, but there are thousands more in the early stages of development which will be without resident dolphins for decades.'

'Thousands? Does that mean Attunga's building more reaches than Warrakan?'

Calen grabbed Thom by the neck and gave him a friendly shake, as if exasperated at his ignorance.

'Thom, you're hopeless! Warrakan's got six levels set aside for dolphins and Attunga's only got one. You can't even compare them.'

'All reaches are wonderful.'

Wirrin agreed with Sonic. 'It's all wonderful, Sonic. When you were born there were only three tiny reaches and three hundred dolphins. Now there are over twelve thousand and there are more reaches than you could ever explore.'

'That would be an interesting adventure.'

*   *   *

Wirrin, standing with Calen, Sonic, Akama, Pirramar and Gulara, watched Thom deftly manipulate his special console so the view of deep space on the enormous display panned till both Attunga and Freedom were revealed, stabilised in close proximity for this historic moment.

The display was bigger by far than on any Comet, being the main viewing panel for Warrakan Flight Control, the centre where all alignment and movement of the 50 kilometre long habitat was managed.

Today this task was compounded by the electronic links that placed Attunga and Freedom under its control.

Akama, representing the Witness Council and the people of all three habitats, had declined the official honour, suggesting it should be bestowed on Sonic.

Sonic, in turn, declined and insisted Thom was the appropriate person.

Thom, claiming he didn't deserve it, was still chuffed and had spent the last few days acclimatising himself, by way of simulation, to the ways and means of moving the largest controlled mass in the solar system at significant acceleration.

Now, sitting in the command position, he was waiting for Akama to make the short formal address the occasion demanded and give him the go-ahead. Attention centred on Akama while he spoke then switched to Thom.

'Freedom engines ... engaged!'

On the screen it took a few seconds for a change of position to become apparent and Wirrin watched, fascinated by this close view of a habitat under power.

'Attunga engines ... engaged!'

Again there was the short period before motion could be discerned but then the great construct blocked several stars and revealed others. It was on its way.

Wirrin was struck by the significance of the occasion: here he was, once again involved directly in a key event. For the first time he pondered if something more than the vagaries of chance could possibly be at work. Often the trio said to each other that somehow they must be blessed, or cursed, to have been involved in so many big happenings.

'Warrakan engines ... engaged!'

Wirrin pushed his introspection aside to enjoy Thom's moment. After all, with three singular commands he'd just directed over one billion people, a thriving dolphin community, and their associated group of AIs, on a course to the far reaches of the solar system.

E N D

ALSO BY PETER WOOD

TALES OF THE TERRAN DIASPORA

MPARNTWE (Forthcoming)

More information at: diasporatales.net

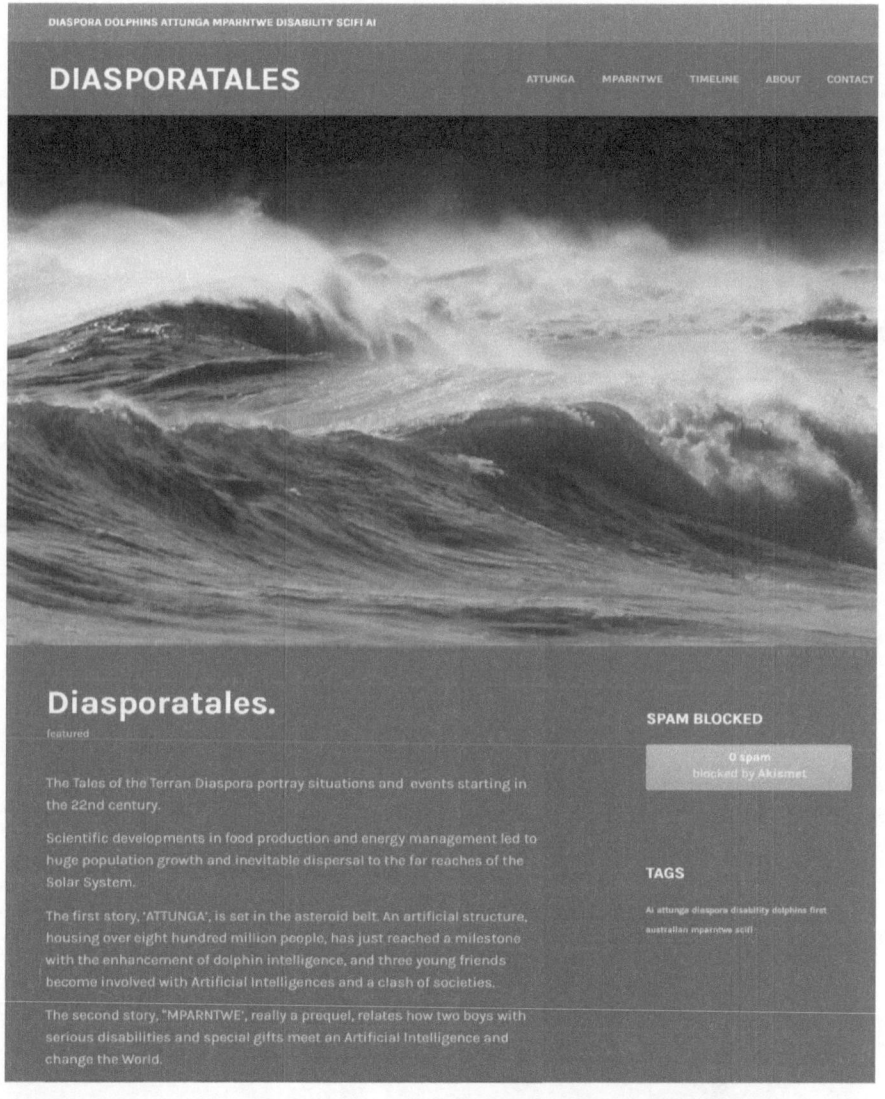